Alice K. Arenz

PORTRAIT OF JENNY

By

Alice K. Arenz

Copyright © 2016 by Alice K. Arenz

Take Me Away Books, a division of Winged Publications

All rights reserved as permitted under the U.S. Copyright Act of 1976. No part of the publication may be reproduced, distributed or transmitted in any form or by any means, or stored in a database or retrieval system, without prior permission of the publisher.

This book is a work of fiction. Names, characters, places, and incidents are the product of the author's imagination and are used fictitiously. Any resemblance to actual events, locales, or persons, living or dead, is coincidental, except for the instances where they were used in conjunction with a business on purpose.

All rights reserved.

ISBN-13:978-1-944203-33-7

DEDICATION

For Greg—without you, I'd still be typing!

ACKNOWLEDGMENTS

This book was a long time in coming. So, it is with a grateful heart I finally have the chance to thank my wonderful, supportive doctor, Dr. Jane, for all things medical. She was—*is* a good sport, even more so when I asked her a ton of questions back in the 90's for a book that might never see the light of day. Here it is, Doc. I hope I got everything you told me right. Any mistakes are on me!

As always, I want to thank my wonderful family, editors, and my publisher Cynthia Hickey and Winged Publications for bringing this book to fruition. You guys are the absolute best! May God Bless you all.

I prefer writing about the time before cell phones were in everyone's hand/pocket; I believe it makes the mystery and suspense a little different when you don't automatically have a phone at hand—no pun intended. I hope you'll like it, too! aka

May 1991

Chapter 1

They say everything begins with the closing of a door; when one is closed, a new vista opens. Perhaps that's what happened, though I doubt very much Tara would like to be considered a door.

This was it, the last fight, the final straw that broke both Tara's back and mine. I was tired of being accused of thinking with the lower part of my anatomy, and she was just plain tired of me. She never came right out and said it, of course; that wasn't Tara's way. No, the hints were far more subtle, the words more graphic than anyone would expect to come out of that sweet ribbon of mouth.

Maybe she was right; maybe it was the sex all along. As I trudged through the rain, I couldn't for the life of me come up with a reason for staying with a shrew like Tara Morgan otherwise. The "relationship" wasn't among my top most intelligent decisions in life, with this latest encounter irrefutable proof.

I shook rainwater from my eyes and pushed back a lock of unruly hair which I kept fairly long. It was a hangover from my younger days when I'd been determined to be a hippy and join an artsy commune. I'd never made it to either, hadn't even succeeded in getting to Greenwich Village in New York, a lifelong dream. I'd settled, instead, on a small

Midwest community with an excellent art school within its College of Humanities and become one of the Establishment—or whatever they called it now. I was a teacher, after a fashion, on staff at the local university and still hoping this would be the springboard to my future.

Three years ago, Tara had been one of my students. She'd taken Art History for a humanities credit, and it was obvious from the first day she had no interest in the subject. She'd come into class with her short skirt riding high on her thighs and, as she sat in the front row, made no effort to behave in the least lady-like fashion. I'd done my best to ignore her, succeeded, too—while she remained in my class. But after the semester was over, Tara continued to pursue me.

Though I avoided her for most of the following term, my determination to keep my distance hadn't lasted. I was flattered—what man wouldn't be? Here was this nineteen-year-old beauty who was after *me*, nearly eight years her senior. So, against my better judgment...

Once our relationship started, I was ridiculously monogamous even in the face of substantial knowledge Tara was not. In our case, she was out sowing her wild oats while I remained faithful and true. A little backward for this day and age, perhaps, especially when one recalls my desire to join a commune, but that's the way it was.

I had no delusions of marriage to the lovely Tara Morgan, though I did feel ridiculously responsible for her. So when she accused me of intruding into her personal life and lifestyle, I couldn't deny it; I knew she was right. I also knew it was over.

I kicked absently at a puddle, the water sinking into the soft leather of my expensive shoes. They'd been an extravagance like Tara, and like her, I wouldn't be sorry to see them go.

I remained in the puddle, surveying the scene before me. The afternoon was prematurely dark. Street lights had been fooled into thinking it was night and lit the dim afternoon with a phosphorescent glow. The park was to my right, Murphy's bar to my left, and ahead lay the entrance to the lane leading to the university.

I was finished with classes for the day—for the semester, actually, and wouldn't be teaching again for some time. My leave of absence had been granted, and for the next year I was off to try my hand as a true artist. A friend in Kansas City promised a showing in her gallery next February, lacing the invitation with hopes for the future and the lure of big name critics to view my work. Once I'd cleared a few things from my office, I was done—then it was time to find the inspiration I so badly needed.

The blast of a car horn from behind drew me from the puddle and back onto the sidewalk. Tara went by; her final dig was flipping me off as her car splashed through a large puddle, spraying me from head to foot. It didn't matter. I was already soaked through. At least I knew she'd meant it this time when she said "get lost you stupid, dreamy-eyed bastard!"

I laughed dryly, the only thing about me that was currently dry.

She'd once told me it was my eyes that had drawn her to me. Later, it became the thing she criticized most—that, and the fact I found her *too* incredibly sexy. It just didn't correlate. But then, I was only a man, one of the lower forms of life, not worth much consideration in the long run.

From everything I'd heard over the years, I'd thought it was the insensitive breed of my kind that were up for criticism. It never occurred to me that being too sensitive would also prove a failing in a woman's eyes. Perhaps that meant I wasn't supposed to have cared about the other men she saw, the dangerous chances she took to "experience life while she was young." I didn't know, didn't particularly care at the moment.

Now, where to go?

I couldn't very well show up at my office looking like a drowned rat. Mrs. Winston would have a heart attack at the sight of me, and she was far too efficient a secretary to lose like that. Murphy's drew me, but my head already ached, and no matter how good a beer, or several beers, sounded at the moment, I knew it wouldn't help matters.

I stared over at the park shrouded in rain and fog. No one was there, not even the inevitable pigeons. I could sit in the gazebo to keep from getting any wetter—if that were possible—and maybe I could think. Maybe I could figure out what went wrong, where I'd failed. There are always choices; we may not make the right ones, rarely even realize there *are* right ones. But somehow, somehow I knew that at this time, *at that moment*, the only possible choice was the park, the gazebo. And for some reason I may never understand, I needed to get there *now*.

I didn't bother looking as I crossed the street, a mistake in late afternoon when the college crowd is prowling the streets at the end of term. A carload of students went by, honking their horn and tossing obscenities out the window—wonder if they ran in the same circles as Tara?—and I jumped out of the way, skidding to an abrupt halt at the other curb, barely catching myself before I fell.

Without having a drink, I had that curious drugged, almost numb, feeling as I wended my way through the soggy bushes and over to the gazebo. The rain had ceased for the moment, but fog seemed to suddenly blanket the area with a peculiar thickness almost making me wish for a return of the torrential downpour.

I stumbled up the final step, and as I passed beneath the eaves, the gazebo's leaky gutter dripped onto my head sending a rivulet of water down my neck and back. A shiver passed along my spine following the wake of the water, and I rushed in under the roof and over to the far side of the building where benches overlooked the majority of the park. I threw myself onto the bench and shook the rain from my hair and jacket, reminiscent of a shaggy dog as the spray flew from side to side.

Linden wasn't wealthy, but the city council made certain that what they had was well-cared for. Hidden by the fog were beautiful, flowering bushes of lilac, azalea, and spirea, and apple trees in full bloom lined the outer walk on the far side. In a few weeks, roses and dozens of other flowers would fill the entire park with their heady scents. Everything had been laid out in an orderly fashion, nothing left to chance. Volunteer trees and bushes were quickly eliminated so the park maintained its decorative arrangement as prescribed by its designers. There was a place for everything, and in University Park, even nature was subject to strict rules of conformity.

I remembered the wild, untamed park I'd wandered and explored as a child when visiting Linden. While some images remained clear and strong, others were lost in a part of my brain that had been damaged long ago. What I did recall were acres of wooded areas with winding paths and wild flowers growing among the brambles and poison oak and ivy. There had been a tiny brook, now diverted past the new edge of the city, and a small pond that had been drained then later covered over with asphalt for one of the surrounding streets. Little remained of the parkland of my childhood—except in my imagination.

It had been more than twenty years since the city rezoned the vast acreage, building roads and offering up lots for business development. They'd left only the small, six square blocks in the center of the original park for the modern one of today, civilizing the area with businesses on two sides, the entrance to the university on one, and the start of a residential area on the other. It was beautiful and functional, a tribute to both the designers and city fathers, but minus the allure and attraction that once drew me as a small boy.

The one thing I approved of was the addition of the mammoth gazebo that stood in the middle of it all. An octagonal structure built of weather-proofed oak and set on a thick cement base, its lattice work and open-air sides with domed roof reminded me of something one would've seen at the turn of the century, the center of the town square and activities where bands played for the enjoyment of the community on hot summer nights. No bands had occupied the building in my recollection, but in its twenty odd years the gazebo had proven its worth many times in various other ways—its popularity making the park the hub of the town's festivities. As a result, it was rare for the area to be unoccupied, for the gazebo to be peopleless. Even rain failed to keep mobs from thronging to the park for their outdoor enjoyments. As this kind of thing was not for me, I usually avoided the area despite the draw it had for me. So, having the park and gazebo to myself on this rainy afternoon made it an especially nice and rare occasion. And I was determined to make the most of it.

The inside perimeter of the gazebo was lined with benches, and with picnic tables spaced evenly across the center, all provided wonderful views and the ability to house the maximum amount of picnickers. I looked out upon the empty gazebo, the solitude of the place granting me a strange kind of contentment.

As I settled back on the bench, my eyes strayed across the park, spotting the outline of the jungle gym and swing set. Cloaked by the fog, they looked like prehistoric monsters from a by-gone era: a fitting background for continuing my novel.

I pulled Crichton's *Jurassic Park* from an inside jacket pocket, relieved to find it had remained dry. I rubbed my temples and the back of my neck impatiently, then opened the book. Despite my headache, the relaxation I gained from reading made it a perfect stress-releaser, and I was soon lost in the novel and oblivious to my surroundings.

I've no idea how long I was there when the small voice first came to me and, for a moment, even wondered if I'd imagined it. I continued reading, caught up in the danger and suspense when I heard the sound again. Knowing how fog could distort sound, I looked behind me, attempting to penetrate the unusually thick mass to locate and identify the intruder. The soft giggle came once more—the direction now distinguishable.

I'd been so absorbed in the novel, I hadn't heard the arrival of the girl seated directly opposite me on the far side of the gazebo. She sat with her back partially to me, an arm and small hand extended out beneath the eaves, rainwater trickling between her fingers. She laughed again, a light, tinkling sound that reminded me of a child. I moved silently on the bench to better my view—totally entranced by what I saw.

Sudden beams of sunlight pierced the clouds and fog, casting an eerie glow over the girl and the area she was in. A halo seemed to surround her, giving her an otherworldly appearance. She was as caught up in her game with the water as I'd been in my novel and was completely unaware of my watching her.

She sat with her knees pulled up against her chest, a long, gauzy print skirt completely covering her legs and feet. She wore a white, peasant-type blouse which was nearly hidden by chestnut-colored hair falling past her tiny waist. Even sitting as she was, I could tell she was small, and my initial reaction was that she was only a child. The illusion was soon vanquished, however, when, with a tilt of her head, her eyes suddenly met mine.

My breath caught in my throat, and I'm sure the tentative smile I offered did little to cover the embarrassment of being caught spying on her. The realization did not cause me to avert my eyes, however, and I continued to stare and be stared at in return, unabashedly.

All my life I'd heard of Elizabeth Taylor's remarkable violet eyes, the exquisite color so unusual and alluring they captured and held one's attention. I'd never met anyone possessing such orbs—until now.

Large, gentle violet eyes were locked onto mine refusing to look away or even to blink. They were heavily fringed with dark lashes that despite the distance, I determined were naturally that way, devoid of make-up. The small, heart-shaped face had been delicately chiseled with high cheekbones, a trace of dimples in each soft cheek, and a perfect bow-shaped mouth. The girl's pert little nose tipped slightly in the air as she regarded me with obvious interest, and I felt this sudden, overwhelming sense of déjà vu that I couldn't shake off. Something about her was as familiar as it was alien.

I quietly cleared my throat in preparation of speech, but it was the call of a bird that finally broke the spell between us. She turned her head in the direction of the sound, sending a cloud of silky chestnut tresses across the side of her face.

"A signal the storm is over?" My voice echoed hollowly in the wooden structure, bouncing off the open sides and falling flatly in the stillness of the park.

Another quick turn of her head, and the fall of hair was pushed aside, the small head cocked to one side. A smile spread slowly across her full lips.

"I like the rain." It was as though she was testing her voice, the words spoken almost hesitantly. A hand went to her mouth, her fingers playing across her lips, then removed to reveal an even broader smile. "I like the way it feels as it runs between my fingers."

Again she held her hand out under the dripping gutter, and I watched as the water trickled between her outstretched digits.

There seemed a sensuality about the action that stirred me emotionally, and I felt the urge to go to her and draw her small body against my own. Not ordinarily compulsive by nature, this idea surprised me, and I forced back the impulse that had arisen out of nowhere.

For the first time since I'd noticed her, I realized her clothing was completely dry in contrast to my own rather bedraggled state. For an instant, I felt awkward and self-conscious, especially since I was still fighting that unusual urge—but it was only for an instant. The moment those violet eyes met mine once more, I was lost, completely caught up in the girl before me.

"You come here often?"

The question was inept, and I could have kicked myself for having asked it. I still wanted to move closer to her, examine her from every angle, my artist's eye preparing the figure before me to transfer her likeness onto canvas. Even this was odd. I'd always steered away from portraits, never feeling capable of giving the subject the proper three-dimensional look. But this girl...

"It's nice here." She withdrew her hand from beneath the gutter, pulling it in to watch the remainder of the water run between her fingers. "Do *you* come here often?" She gazed up at me, the smile still playing about her lips, the question innocent rather than mocking.

I shook my head. "It's usually too crowded for my taste. It's a beautiful spot, though."

She nodded. "I don't care for crowds, either."

She dried her hand on the hem of her skirt, then stood and stretched her arms over her head. The action set in motion a long chain with an ankh at its end, both swinging and bouncing lightly between her breasts. Even from where I sat, I could see the unusual design of silver and gold entwined, and wished again to have a better look at the girl.

My assumption that she was short was correct; she couldn't be more than five feet if that. There was a delicacy about her, an overwhelming presence of femininity that was so rare in girls today. She wore it casually, as one might an old, familiar piece of clothing, which added to her overall attractiveness. I guessed her at around twenty but knew immediately that her very smallness could add to the illusion of youth. But the vitality I sensed from her was no illusion. She seemed to radiate a kind of controlled sense of being, abundant energy that was held tightly in check. It floated about her like an aura, visible in even the minutest of movements.

I'd never been particularly shy, deliberately withdrawn was more like it. But now, for some reason I couldn't quite fathom, I found myself at a loss. I wanted nothing more than to approach her, could, in my mind's eye, see myself seducing her. But that was the make-believe. The reality was that I was so taken in by the vision of loveliness before me that I had absolutely no idea what to say, how to move. I think she sensed my confusion, and rather than frightening her or turning her off, she seemed intrigued.

I was held transfixed as she appeared to float across the gazebo with her eyes downcast, their long, sweeping lashes and her secret smile making it impossible to catch my breath. Coming to, I ran nervous fingers through my hair in an effort to make myself more presentable.

"You should use an umbrella next time." She stopped a short way in front of me near the edge of one of the picnic tables. Lowering herself gracefully onto the seat, she clutched absently at her pendant as she regarded me with obvious amusement.

I felt the heat rise from my neck into my face, and wondered idly about the last time I'd blushed. It wasn't a normal reaction for me, my response to the girl seeming to prove just how special she was.

"I didn't mean to embarrass you," she said softly, lowering her eyes from mine once more.

"You didn't, er, well." I laughed. "You're right. I should've used an umbrella. Actually, I had one when I started out. Guess I left it at my last stop."

I made a futile attempt to straighten my wet clothing, quickly realized the uselessness of the effort, then sat back to drink her in.

The blush came readily to her face, touching the high cheekbones and adding to her overall beauty. Her eyes seemed to take on a darker hue as the rosy glow spread across her face, and she looked at me frankly, completely aware I studied her every move.

"I'm being rude—"

"No, no. It's all right. Really. I," she smiled broadly. "I'm flattered. It's not often a girl sees such honest admiration in a man's eyes. I like it."

"Honest?"

She nodded. "Completely. No come-ons, no overt acts to seduce me. Why, you actually seem quite shy, even a little embarrassed to be so interested in me." She drew her legs onto the bench and hugged them to her as she'd been doing earlier. "Whether you know it or not, you're really quite sweet. And, I'd imagine, very nice looking when you're not soaking wet."

"Thank you. I think."

She laughed.

"My name's Richard Tanner." I held out my hand, but she made no move to take it. Seeing her hesitation, I withdrew it and made a show of tucking the book back inside my jacket pocket.

"I'm Jenny."

She'd spoken so softly, I'd barely heard her. I leaned forward, intent on continuing our conversation when the sound of my name called from somewhere in the park behind me caught my attention. I turned in the direction of the sound to find the fog had lifted considerably since my arrival. Chuck Stinnet, a friend and fellow instructor, was coming toward me, and I answered his wave with one of my own. I turned back to Jenny prepared with an apology for the interruption, and to my surprise, she was nowhere to be seen. A quick look around proved she had gone as she'd arrived: silently and without notice.

I couldn't help showing my disappointment, and as Chuck emerged into the gazebo, he knew instantly there was something wrong. Unfortunately, he misread what he saw and launched into a speech about lost love and the joys awaiting me in finding someone new—not a subject on which he was an expert.

I'd no desire to discuss the break-up between Tara and me, wanted desperately to brush him off and go in search of Jenny, but Chuck held me there with his concern. Out of respect for our friendship, I forced myself to sit still and listen.

"Tara's convinced you should be locked up, Richard. She came breezing into Lambert demanding to see the old man, and when he wasn't available, talked to anyone who would listen. She claims you really went off the deep end this time, and she wants nothing more to do with you." Chuck plopped down onto the bench a few feet from me and loosened his tie. "Personally, I think this is the best thing that could happen to you, my friend. If I were you, I'd quit moping and say good riddance to the lovely, but deadly Tara Morgan. She's got a great body, but beyond that, the girl's the bitch of the century and you're better off without her."

I'm not a prude—far from it—and consider myself a liberated male who easily accepted the equality of both sexes and the rights of all individuals to express themselves as they saw fit—myself included. When I'd become an instructor, I'd worked hard to throw over bad habits like cursing, concerned that if I wasn't careful I might one day offend someone in class and find myself in trouble. Stinnet was amused by this and constantly baited me. He knew how to get a rise from me, and recognizing what he was up to, I refused to react to his vulgarity, which only seemed to fuel his assumption that I was mooning over Tara's loss.

His dark eyes regarded me seriously as they took in my appearance. I knew in a glance what he was thinking and decided to quickly set his mind at ease.

"I haven't been sitting here pining for my lost love, Chuck, so wipe the smirk off your face. As a matter of fact, before your untimely arrival, I was having an interesting conversation with a very beautiful young woman."

He raised a bushy eyebrow. "Really? I didn't see anyone."

"And that means she wasn't here?" I laughed. "Give me a break, okay? As far as I know, she recognized your voice and, knowing your reputation as the campus Lothario, took off to save herself."

Stinnet laughed heartily. "You wound me deeply. Romeo, perhaps, but never Lothario."

His sheepish grin radiated a kind of pride. In his mid forties, Chuck Stinnet possessed a charm that I'd often compared to Paul McCartney. He had the same sad, puppy-dog eyes and impish grin as the famous singer, and while McCartney felt secure enough in himself to allow his graying hair, I knew Chuck's deep brown was maintained by an admiring beautician on the other side of town. He worked out four times a week at the university's fitness center and ran five miles the other three. The result was a body that was fit and trim, free of fat and the sag of encroaching middle age. But with his roving eye and fondness for the ladies, one could have expected nothing less.

His escapades were well-known among the majority of the faculty—he'd had more involvement with students outside the classroom than inside for years. Why it was tolerated was anyone's guess. Chuck insisted it was because he was careful. I figured there was a more underhanded reason—maybe he had something on his dean that made his dismissal impossible. Whatever it was, he maintained a certain discretion, except where his friends were concerned. With each passing year, the list of his conquests grew, causing me to wonder if he was going for the Wilt Chamberlain award among university professionals.

I fidgeted under his gaze, aware more than ever of my downtrodden appearance. The wetness that once seemed tolerable was now a source of irritation, my pruned skin chafing beneath the sodden clothing and shoes.

"I feel as if you've placed me under one of your blasted microscopes. Would you quit staring at me as though you were about to prepare me for dissection!" I stood and paced the width of the gazebo, the pounding in my head matching that of my steps. I went over to the area where I'd first spotted Jenny, and looked down at the bench in the hope of finding something she may have inadvertently left behind.

"So what was it this time, Rich? What *exactly* sent Tara off in a huff and led you to wandering in the rain?"

Without looking at him, I shrugged and continued my search. "What does it matter? She's gone—again, and this time, I'm determined not to be drawn back no matter how she plays it."

"Um. Strong words, my friend, and ones I've heard you declare before. Think you can stand by them?"

He was right. As much as I hated to admit it, I'd fallen into Tara Morgan's traps far too often.

"So what did she say?"

"That you pulled another Jekyll and Hyde on her over at the Snack

Shack. Of all places," he shook his head. "Couldn't you have found somewhere a little less public? I suppose you should count yourself lucky it wasn't at the height of the day's business or everyone in town would know what happened."

I closed my eyes tightly and lowered myself onto a nearby bench.

"I simply tried to convince her that it was unwise to fly off to Japan with someone she barely knows."

"Ah, Nagoochi. All that money and power would be a definite attraction to someone like Tara. Has she slept with him yet, or did she say?"

I threw him a look of distaste. "I think you're the only one on campus who hasn't experienced Miss Morgan's considerable charms."

"In this case, you might be right. But I'll never tell." He laughed, delighted by my expression. "Down boy, down. Tara's not my type, nor I hers. She's not your type either, Richard."

Once again, he was right, though I'd never admit it. I gazed out across the tranquil grounds of the park, hazy in the afternoon light, seeing it as I had as a child—wild, tangled undergrowth, thick stands of trees along the outer perimeter, a paradise for adventures.

"You sure airing your differences in the Snack Shack was a good idea? I mean, shouting that Tara is nothing but a whore is a little out of character for you."

His voice brought me out of my reverie, reverting my attention back to him.

"I did that? I don't remember." I sank back into the bench. "I remember losing my temper when she mentioned Nagoochi but little after that. I don't know. Perhaps I finally wised up and decided to allow pride of self to take over. I'm not sure what I said, but I recall her countering with some obscenities. I nearly walked out, but felt I had to give it another try, convince her she was making a mistake. It didn't work, of course. I left to a resounding "get lost you stupid"..." I shook my head. "I fully intended to at that moment. Get lost, I mean. I ended up here instead."

"Where you met an equally mysterious young woman who disappeared just when things started to get interesting." Stinnet grinned. "Unfortunate. Just as unfortunate as spilling Coke all over Miss Tara. I'm sure it was an accident, but with her railing at you like a banshee, I don't believe Tara will give you the benefit of the doubt. Especially with every eye in the place on the two of you. Humiliation is not something she would suffer in silence."

I remembered pushing at the table as I stood to leave, Tara's shrill voice directed at my back as I walked toward the door, but nothing of what was said. I'd been determined to get out of the restaurant as quickly as possible, going so far as to toss a twenty at the clerk behind the register as I went past. The idea of Tara's drink spilling on her sent an unusual thrill of pleasure through me, and I laughed—then was rewarded with thunderbolts of pain searing through my brain. I lowered my head into my hands, massaging my temples, and wishing I'd thought to bring Tylenol with me when I'd left my apartment that morning.

"Your head's hurting again." Chuck reached into the pocket of his coat and drew out a travel pack of aspirin. "Here." He tossed them to me, and I gratefully took out a couple and swallowed them dry. "It must be bad if you're willing to take those things without something to drink. Makes me sick to think about it."

I closed my eyes and slid across the bench until I was against one of the corner walls, then eased my head back for support.

"Thanks for the meds. I didn't get much sleep last night, and between grading finals and Tara, the migraine got a pretty tight hold on me."

"Yeah, right." Chuck stood. "Look, I'll be honest. After Tara came into Lambert spitting lead, I took it upon myself to search for you. I left just as she declared her intention to go to Drake's house to inform him of just how unstable you are. Not that the old man will believe a word she says," he added quickly. "But there could be problems if he fails to assuage her sufficiently. You get my drift?"

I knew exactly what he meant. Tara would not be averse to taking her complaints to the top. If she could be the cause of a formal reprimand or me losing my job, it would make her day—maybe even her millennium. Again I had to wonder how I'd managed to remain tied to someone that spiteful and vindictive.

"I'll call the professor or stop by on my way home. I've promised to talk with him before my leave becomes official, anyway. I appreciate the warning, though. I'm sure he's capable of calming her. It's whether or not it will be enough for her to drop it."

We stayed and talked a while longer, my thoughts continually straying to Jenny. As the afternoon wore on and the sky cleared, the park began to fill with people—a sign for my departure. We left the gazebo and walked amiably along the pathway in the direction of the university, parting when we got to the wye. I watched as Chuck headed back to the school, remaining at the junction until he was out of sight, then turned and started for Professor Drake's house.

Chapter 2

The clouds had completely disappeared leaving the sky a crystal blue in the glow of the late afternoon sun. Birds chirped in nearby trees while others busily gathered worms which had been driven from their underground homes during the storm. Everywhere there was a bustle of activity as all living creatures seemed to gain a renewed sense of hope and purpose with the cessation of the storm: squirrels chattered amiably at one another, rabbits dared to make an appearance in the open, dogs barked, and a cat skittered across the path in front of me.

The human animal was in evidence as well, their almost sudden appearance after the storm like some age-old custom inbred through centuries of discipline just as in the lower species of life. I watched in my off-handed manner, the secret observer more comfortable with putting the images on canvas rather than being an active participant. Jenny had been correct in her deduction that I was shy—it was something I'd been dealing with most of my life. I enjoyed being around people as long as I was able to maintain a certain distance—especially with those I didn't know.

As I made my way out of the park and along the sidewalk in the direction of the professor's house, I nodded to people I knew, aware of their stares and unspoken questions in regard to my appearance. I briefly considered going to my apartment to clean up and change my clothes but decided against it. Professor Drake and his wife had seen me in worse condition and were sure to take it in their stride.

The Drake's lived on Park Lane, a picturesque street lined with majestic trees, well-kept lawns, and impressive-looking residences. Although it was now several blocks from the edge of the park, it had once been the start of the residential section—an almost exclusive area for the university bigwigs and professors. It was still beautiful and well-appointed but hardly exclusive. As Linden had grown, progress moved university personnel beyond the old-fashioned cliques into other portions of town. Larger, more impressive homes took the place of the two and three story brick houses on Park Lane, stating the affluence of small town living on a university professor's salary. This may or may not have been the way they looked at it, but it was definitely the way the townspeople saw the situation.

The Drake's home was of red brick dyed pink from over a hundred years of the Midwest sun. Window casings and the long porch that spanned the front of the house were painted a creamy off-white, the intricate curlicues and gingerbread trim adding to the overall charm of the place. No matter how many years passed, or how old I got, I always saw their home through the eyes of a child—anxious for the door to open and my summer adventures to begin. Despite the fact that my last childhood summer had been spent here more than twenty years before, I could still taste the excitement and anticipation.

The Drake's and my family went way back. My father had been one of the professor's first advisees when he'd started teaching at Linden. They'd become fast friends, the seven years difference in their ages creating a kind of brotherly relationship. Edmund Drake had been my father's mentor, their bond of friendship strengthened by the introduction of my mother a short while later.

Throughout their school years, my parents maintained intimate contact with Edmund and Janet Drake, with the professor and his wife standing up with them at their wedding. When I came along, "Uncle" Edmund and "Aunt" Janet were always in the background, providing an added security for a child with busy parents and no other living relatives. From the time I was five, I spent summers alone with the Drakes who saw the importance of giving a child the time to ramble alone and create his own adventures. I'd treasured those summers, hating the return to the city in the fall, and the drudgery of school and afternoons alone as a latch-key kid. As much as I loved and adored my parents, the Drakes were able to offer me a time when my imagination could run as free as my being—something I yearned for the other nine months of the year. For five summers I'd had this special freedom of body and soul, and then, abruptly, it was taken away. Too much freedom and not enough discipline, my mother stated, led to my getting hurt in the park the summer I was ten, forcing my parents to leave their jobs and come to Linden. I'd lain comatose in the hospital for two agonizing weeks, a period my parents refused to discuss afterward. When I was well enough, I was taken home and given the discipline my mother believed I needed. Although we visited Linden as a family, I was never allowed to spend any time alone here again. It was a terrible blow to me, this denial of freedom the Drakes had offered. Through no fault of their own—or mine, for that matter, the traditional summers remained a thing of the past, my "accident" in the park rarely referred to. It had been my parents' way of dealing with something unpleasant, something for which no one had an answer. While they seemed capable of dismissing the subject by simply refusing to discuss it, my mind would not grant me such luxury.

I had no memory of that night, nor of the preceding day, no clues to what led me out into the park in the middle of a storm. Even my subtle questioning of the Drakes over the years failed to yield anything further about the incident. For years afterward, I would awaken from a nightmare I could not recall, drenched in sweat and shaking like a leaf, terrified of the unknown. I'd quickly learned not to mention the dreams to my parents, their tight-lipped expressions and watchful eyes almost as frightening as the dream itself. I'd never understood their attitude, felt hurt and somewhat rejected by it, and confused by their reaction to any mention of my accident. As time passed, so did the disturbing nights, leaving only the chronic migraines as a reminder of that long ago incident in University Park.

As I stood across the street from the Drake's, memories of the old days flooded my mind, arousing my curiosity, and questioning my parents' attitude concerning that time. For the first time, I realized they, too, had been afraid. But of what? Was it the fear of my not remembering, or of a memory that might be revived? Neither made much sense to me and, as in the past, I was forced to dismiss the thoughts.

A cool breeze rustled the leaves on trees and bushes sending trickles of water in its wake and rippling the puddles in the street. With a deep breath, I crossed the street and strode up the sidewalk to the Drake's door.

Janet must have been nearby when the bell rang, for the echo of the door chimes had not yet diminished when the door was flung open to reveal her standing there. Her arched eyebrows had always given her a perpetual look of surprise, never failing to cause me to stand taken aback for a moment. Today was no different.

Despite the warm smile and dark eyes that crinkled in pleasure at the sight of me, she retained that somewhat startled expression which I'd always regarded with restrained amusement. I grinned back at her and leaned down to place a kiss upon her flushed cheek.

Kindness was a word that epitomized Janet Drake. While she insisted she'd become a teacher to fulfill her maternal instincts, it wasn't the whole story. Janet opened her heart and her home to students and faculty alike, offering services and advice, pointing out where improvements might be made and offering encouraging words to buoy one's spirits and build self-confidence. It seemed nothing made her happier than to assist a student and help them understand the beauty to be seen in a poem, the world that could be opened within literature of all kinds. If she could be the key to unlock the door to their imagination, she was ecstatic, and watching them learn and grow in appreciation was the greatest reward she could ask for.

Her duties as wife of the head of the College of Arts and Humanities were often demanding, requiring dinners and entertainment of the upper-echelon of the university and visiting dignitaries. She managed all with an assurance and self-confidence my mother was in awe of and often envied. She was a woman I loved and admired—an individual with her own special charm and warmth, and I felt fortunate to call her my friend.

Janet regarded me with her dark, almost black eyes, and shook her head. While the smile remained on her lips, I discerned from the tightened expression that she was holding back, denying herself the words she wanted so badly to say.

I patted her on the arm. "It's all right. Don't worry."

"Oh, Richard!" She put her arms around me and squeezed, then released me to stand back and take in my appearance. Her upper lip curled slightly in a manner I recognized as dismay, but again she held her tongue. Instead, she reached up to her shining gray hair, absently patting the short locks that curled slightly at the nape of her neck. Withdrawing her hand, she released a heavy sigh.

"She was always a nasty little chit, not half as good as you deserve."

"So you've often told me."

"But you never seemed to listen, did you?" She closed the door, and taking me by the arm, led me down the darkly paneled hallway. "Trouble with you, my boy, is you've never given yourself enough credit. And, by the way, you look like hell."

"Thanks. Walking in the rain agrees with me. I might make it a habit."

"Really?" She wrinkled her nose slightly as she drew herself up to her full height. She was tall, appeared even taller because she was so slender, and with hands on her hips, head cocked to one side, looked quite formidable. "Should you decide to carry through, Richard, do yourself a favor and invest in some appropriate rain gear. On your salary, you can't afford too many ruined suits." She lifted a corner of my jacket and with another sigh, released it. Her face became serious, her dark eyes narrowing from whatever thoughts now occupied her mind. "I suppose you know she was here trying to cause trouble."

I nodded. "I'm sorry she bothered you—"

"Don't be. Edmund let her have her say to get it off her chest, then sent her packing. She'll be leaving Linden within the next forty-eight hours, and has agreed—but Edmund will tell you all that." She stopped before a door I knew to be the professor's office and tapped gently upon it. "I'm not sorry to see her go, and you shouldn't be either. I don't want you moping or pining away over that two-bit hussy. Good riddance is all I have to say."

Janet's gentleness and charity had never extended as far as Tara, but neither had I known the extent of her dislike for the girl. I was a little astounded by her vehemence, and equally amused. I gave her another smile of appreciation and assurance, and answered the professor's inquiry by opening the door and peering around it to reveal myself.

"Richard, my boy. Come in, come in. I was hoping that might be you." Edmund Drake looked out from beneath shaggy gray eyebrows, a smile creasing his well-worn cheeks. "I see you hovering there behind the boy, Jan. No need to fuss, dear. Everything's under control." He stood up from behind the vast mahogany desk, stretched his back and neck, and came to the door to greet me with an outstretched hand.

Although it had been no more than a day or two since our last meeting, he received me as though it had been years. After shaking my hand firmly, he gave me a half hug, clapped me on the back affectionately, then took my arm and led me over to one of the many chairs before his desk. Rather than returning to sit behind the desk, he seated himself in the mate to the one I occupied. Smoothing invisible wrinkles from the legs of his trousers, he beat a quiet tattoo upon one knee and regarded me solemnly.

"Suppose you tell me what happened. I've heard Tara's disjointed tale of woe and would like to hear what you have to say. Did you intentionally douse the young woman with her own soft drink?"

He looked so serious I couldn't help but chuckle. "I'm sorry. I realize the gravity of the situation, and under other circumstances—"

The smile returned to the professor's lips. "No offense taken, of course. But you do realize, Richard, that to make certain the girl carries her tales no further, I had to promise to treat this as I would any other complaint regarding my faculty. That this has nothing to do with your conduct on campus or your students is beside the point at this juncture. Tara Morgan is capable of causing the worst kind of trouble, as we both know."

"Yes, sir." I swallowed back another laugh recalling Tara's face as she'd driven by in the rain flashing me the bird. "As for her drink, I believe that was an accident. It's all a bit hazy."

He lifted an expressive eyebrow as he thoughtfully rubbed his chin. With as much detail as possible, I related the incident in the Snack Shack, combing my memory for things I'd as soon forget.

As near as I could recall, the lines of communication broke down at the mention of Nagoochi and went quickly downhill from there. At the onset of our meeting it was obvious our relationship was over. It shouldn't have bothered me that she was going off with the man; it wasn't the first time. But something about it set off a kind of protective instinct that was still intact despite the beating it had been given over the last three years. Whatever it was, Tara succeeded in breaking it, and me, and by the time I'd walked out of the restaurant, I hadn't cared what she did, or who she did it with.

Professor Drake listened to the story, a grave look upon his face. When I'd finished the tale, I sat back in the chair, feeling again the report of the pounding within my head. I tried to ignore the flare of pain, my eyes remaining upon the countenance of the man opposite me.

At sixty, Edmund Drake was still a striking man with wide, powerfully built shoulders and the physique of a man fifteen years younger. He was a little taller than me, perhaps six-three or four, with a lean, firm abdomen and a body that spoke of strength. He retained a full head of thick, gray hair still streaked with its original black. His bushy gray eyebrows gave his pale eyes a hooded expression, something I'd seen him use to his advantage when forced to discipline a student or gently reprimand a colleague. His face was kind, given to smiles and good nature, creased with years of sun and laughter. He was neither old, nor grandfatherly, his age simply adding to his overall dignity while not diminishing his vitality or zest for his profession. He was advisor, friend, and confidant—forever the Uncle Edmund who had nightly shared my adventures of warm summer days.

"Um." The professor cleared his throat, made a temple with his hands, steepling his index fingers, and tapping them together before his nose. He peered at me thoughtfully, the gleam in his pale eyes telling me I had nothing to worry about: the incident at the Snack Shack would not go beyond these doors.

"I suppose I don't have to tell you to watch your back, Richard. Though Tara has nothing with which to officially harm you, her tales could cause considerable damage nonetheless. If she decides to discredit you, well," he stood and walked to the other side of his desk. "She could make things so unpleasant you might be forced to resign your position. I'd hate to see that happen."

I nodded. "I understand, sir, and I give you my promise to steer clear of her."

"I think that would be wise. She's off to Japan within the next two days, and until that time, avoiding contact with her would be in everyone's best interests. Out of sight out of mind, as it were. Perhaps when she returns..."

"*If* she returns." The disgust in my voice caused the professor to shoot me a stern look. "Don't worry, sir, it's over between us, as I said. But it still bothers me the way she throws herself away. Somewhere beneath all that bluster is the frightened little girl that first drew me to her."

The eyebrows again raised in surprise. "Frightened little girl?" Shaking his head as if confused, he continued to regard me as he sat down. "And here I thought it was the animal magnetism, the raw sexuality of the girl that had thrown the two of you together. I'm afraid I never noticed anything frightened or little girlish about your Miss Morgan. Saw it with your artist's eye, did you?"

"Or imagined I did. Perhaps it was wishful thinking." I shrugged, the motion sending a new wave of pain from the back of my neck up through my brain. "Tara was, *is* an enigma. My attraction to her unexplainable."

"So you've stated before. Richard," Drake leaned forward on his desk, his elbows resting comfortably upon the polished surface. "Have you accepted the fact that despite what you saw, or thought you did, you cannot change the young woman and mold her into whatever it was you hoped she would be?"

"I, uh, yes. It was a long time in coming, but the message finally got through." I stood up to pace the room. How many times had I brought him my problems, not just concerning Tara, but so many other things over the years?

My eyes roamed around the familiar, comfortable room—the wall with floor to ceiling bookshelves, the various paintings depicting birds of all kinds, the window seat where I'd been allowed to sit as a boy and become lost in some book or other. I felt suddenly nostalgic. He had counseled and advised me in a way I'd never gotten from anyone else— not even my parents.

Another wave of pain nearly brought me to my knees, and I clutched at the back of a nearby chair.

Had what I'd seen in Tara been imagined, another facet of my personality like the "dreamy eyes" she'd quickly grown tired of? I wasn't sure of anything right now other than my need for an Ativan and bed. It didn't matter if it wasn't yet six o'clock; the migraine had such a firm grasp on me that the only way to quell the pain was a drug-induced sleep.

"Another flare-up of headaches?" The professor asked with sympathy. He knew the background and origin only too well, and like my parents, had always been reluctant to discuss the matter.

"Too much stress preparing for my leave of absence, I suppose. And with the exhibits coming up—"

"Of course. The Arts Festival is set to open the last weekend in June." He smiled. "Still concerned about not having enough to display?"

"It's not necessarily the quantity but the quality. I'm not entirely pleased with what I've got, would like to have a few more that I feel are *beyond* good. Remarkable is what I'm shooting for."

"Any ideas?"

I shook my head. "Before the dates were finalized, my mind was alive with more pictures than I'd have a lifetime to paint. Now, I sit before the canvas, brush in hand, unable to make realistic clouds, let alone an entire study."

Concern etched across his face. "You have to let go, son, put your father's death behind you, look to the future. He would be inordinately proud of you, your accomplishments. He *was* proud of you. It's only in your own mind that you failed to make your mark before his death. If you could begin to accept this, I believe you'd find your creative muse unblocked."

"Perhaps you're right. I don't know." I sat and leaned against the back of the chair. "If you think I'm messed up, you should see Mother."

"Janet spoke with her just the other day. She's pulled herself up from the doldrums and has decided to take a cruise. I can see from your expression she hasn't discussed this with you. My advice is for you to urge her to go, encourage her to get on with her life, so you can stop worrying about her and do the same. She's a strong woman, Richard. Far stronger than either you or your father ever gave her credit for."

We talked a while about my mother's plans, Professor Drake clearly trying to ease my mind. He knew how hard I'd taken my father's sudden death from a heart attack a few months earlier, knew how unsettled I'd felt because of the gulf that had come between us through the years.

It's not unusual for a father and son to drift apart. I knew that, accepted it. What had basically stood between us—my desire to be an artist—was not a big thing as they go and had seemed to disturb me far more than it ever had him. I'd been determined to prove myself to him, reveal my talent as a promising artist worthy of being taken seriously. The Kansas City gallery exhibition scheduled for February was to be the start—he'd died within weeks of finalizing the date, never to know I was to have my first big break.

My mother had fallen apart, leaned heavily on me for the first couple of weeks, and after I'd returned to Linden and work, called me nightly for long talks about the past. Throughout her reminiscing about the old days, she never mentioned my tenth summer or the accident, skipping that period of time as though it never existed. At first, I thought little of it, but as the days and weeks passed and I relived my life through her stories, I saw the beginning of a pattern develop, a pattern that seemed to set the tone for our relationships those many years before. There were those happy, seemingly carefree days and years before the accident when we were a tightly knit family; then there were all those years after when our family unit seemed held together precariously at times—unbalanced and teetering on the edge. On one side were the parents, lost in themselves and their work. On the other was the son, growing into adolescence and watched carefully for any signs of behavior that might signify trauma from a time he could not remember. No wonder we drew further and further apart! How could we retain even a semblance of closeness when discussions were restricted, carefully structured to eliminate any chance mention of upsetting topics? This may have seemed necessary to them in the days and weeks following my accident, but afterward? Why had the tone continued? What had they been afraid of?

My parents often confided in the professor and his wife, and I was again tempted to put the question to them. But only tempted. Knowing they would consider discussing the subject a breach of confidence, I remained silent.

I agreed to encourage my mother to take her trip, promising my support in convincing her to go. After a gentle refusal of their dinner invitation, I left the Drake's and headed for my apartment.

I had a loft above Weisher's Bakery eight blocks from the park along University Way—the main entrance to the school. It was a tall, narrow, three-story building over a hundred years old set in among others of its kind in a section of Linden which once served the university and surrounding area's needs. As Linden grew, most of the businesses moved on to newer and better locations, but a few remained in this quaint section of town retaining its hold on Americana—life at the turn of the century.

For the last twelve years, the building housed Weisher's, before that a deli, and further back, a restaurant and grocery store. In its early days, the owner and his family lived above their establishment on the second floor with the upper one used for storage. Sometime in the last twenty-five years or so, a previous owner had leased out the lower two floors for business purposes and retained the upper one for himself. According to my landlady, Florence Weisher, a Midwestern implant from Queens, the gentleman had either been an artist or known one, which was the reason for the transformation from attic storage room to the spacious apartment and studio I now occupied.

The skylights in the southwest corner of the great open space which included the kitchen, living room, and studio, had clearly been placed for optimum light as were the long, nearly floor to ceiling windows which ran the length of the western wall. Built-in shelves and cabinets with etched glass fronts were perfect for storing paints, brushes and other necessary paraphernalia of my trade, and a large, walk-in closet with special lights, sinks, and racks provided storage as well as a darkroom should I be in need of it. Cream-colored walls added to the overall effect of spaciousness as did the combination of polished wood floors, rich, chocolate-brown carpeting, and the dark green tiles in the kitchen area. The floors were graduated, a step down from living room to kitchen and from living room to studio, the straight lines of windows and walls from back to front offering no obstructions that would create unnecessary shadows or variances in the natural lighting. Even the electric lights in the ceiling and walls were placed for maximum effect, indirect where needed, direct where it would do the most good. Everything from floor to ceiling had been designed so as not to disturb the delicate balance of concentration and role of creation. I didn't know the architect but had to compliment his work and style. No one could have asked for a better studio—the Master's themselves would have been honored to have such accommodations.

I had little furniture to boast of: a couch, a couple of easy chairs, kitchen essentials, TV and stereo equipment, a desk, an old parson's table where I kept supplies near at hand, a makeshift easel my father designed and built years before that I found myself unable to replace, and a multi-position desk chair whose fabric was so covered with paint stains that it was difficult to distinguish its original color. Remarkably, the hodgepodge collection went together rather well in its present surroundings and looked completely at home.

As I climbed the outside stairs, the tantalizing smell of freshly baked bread and rolls assaulted my senses. I retraced my steps, making a detour through the kitchen of the bakery, waved at Mr. Weisher who was elbow deep in flour, and went into the front of the shop. Mrs. Weisher spotted me from the corner of her eye, winked, and continued speaking with her customer.

"Come on, Mrs. Hopper, what's the difference? One loaf, two. You know your man will eat 'em before they've a chance to grow stale. Live a little dangerously."

The other woman glanced longingly at the loaves set before her on the counter, then finally agreed to the sale, adding a dozen cinnamon crisp cookies in the bargain. Once she was out the door, Mrs. Weisher turned her full attention on me.

"I don't know the problem with that woman, but every week it's the same thing. Her old man must be a real fruitcake or something the way she acts, hemming and hawing over the purchase of an extra loaf of bread! Now," she wiped her hands on her apron and leaned over the counter toward me. "What'll you be having today, Richard? A loaf of wheat or rye?"

"I think I'll take your advice and live dangerously." I grinned. "Give me one of your crusty whites. It's been a long time since I've had any."

She reached into the display case and removed one of the loaves then turned to the back board to wrap it.

"Been out in the rain I see." It wasn't an accusation, simply a comment.

"Had some heavy duty thinking to do. Unfortunately it corresponded with the onset of the storm."

"It wouldn't have anything to do with that Miss Morgan who's always hanging around here, would it?" Mrs. Weisher turned back to face me, the wrapped loaf of bread in her hands. She regarded me skeptically as she laid it on the counter between us. "No need to answer, I can see it right there on your face." She took up her apron, studying its swirled pattern of flowers before wiping her hands on it. "She was here not more than fifteen minutes ago, mad as the dickens and demanding that I leave my customers and let her into your apartment."

"She *what*?" I couldn't help my astonishment, although from past experience with Tara, nothing at all should surprise me.

Mrs. Weisher nodded her head so vigorously that a strand of gray hair escaped the tightly wound bun on the nape of her neck. Chubby though dexterous fingers tucked the hair back into place, her eyes never leaving my face.

"She said she wasn't about to take no for an answer. Started to get real huffy, too, alarming my customers and embarrassing me to boot!"

"I apologize for the trouble. I—"

"It's not you needing to apologize. Uh-uh, no siree. That girl's the one who should be standing here saying she's sorry. But I'm sure that day will come as soon as there's a frost in Hades." Mrs. Weisher rang up the sale, and with hands on her ample hips, watched as I fished my wallet from still damp pants. "She's a piece of work, that one is, Richard Tanner, and if your thinking out in the pouring rain concerned her, I hope to the Almighty that you were asking Him for a way out."

Again, I found reaffirmation for a decision that had been too long in coming. Why had it taken me so much longer to see and accept Tara for what she was when others seemed to have recognized it all along?

I handed over the payment for the bread, picked it up from the counter, and thanked my landlady for having refused to give into Tara despite her persistence.

"Papa and I figured that if there was anything miss high and mighty was needing from your place, she could just wait until you were around to give it to her. Cheek is what it is, downright cheek. Someone ought to teach that girl a lesson or two in manners. How she ever got this far in life without them is beyond me."

She was still shaking her head over Tara's faults when I left her, picking up our conversation with an innocent customer who had just walked in the door of the bakery. I left the way I'd come in, through the kitchen, stopping long enough to apologize to Mr. Weisher for Tara's behavior and assure him it wouldn't happen again—my fervent hope.

Rather than using the outside entrance to my apartment, I used the Weisher's staircase that ran past their storeroom then on up to the third floor. This inside door opened up into the kitchen on the east side of the apartment. Directly opposite the door and a little to the right was the only inside wall which separated the multipurpose living area from the hall that led to the bathroom and single bedroom.

A piece of paper was stuck in the door jamb, the cryptic note reading "Look for message on front door." I recognized the handwriting instantly as Tara's, and an involuntary shiver raced along my spine. I had no desire for further communication with the girl, didn't even want the contact made through a letter. One could only take so much abuse, and I'd had my fill from her.

Still, curiosity urged me to the other door. I removed the Post-It from the small smoked glass panel, shut and locked the door after me. Switching on a nearby lamp, I read the message—"You've got some of my things and I want them before I leave. Don't try to keep me out, Richard, or you'll pay." I wadded the paper up and threw it toward an overflowing trash can filled with discarded sketches.

"Damn!" The word echoed through the quiet apartment, exploding inside my head like a bomb that suddenly detonated. I slammed the loaf of bread on the kitchen counter and reached for the phone. I didn't have to put up with this, not after everything—

Four numbers were dialed before I came to my senses and hung up the phone. This was what she wanted, another encounter, another chance to ream me for all her perceived hurts and injuries at my hands. She knew I was no match for her, and in my current state of mind with the migraine pressing for relief, I would again be at her mercy.

I went through the apartment like an automaton searching for items I recognized as Tara's and tossing them into a plastic garbage bag. Toiletries, a sweater and jeans stuck behind a closet door, a pair of canvas shoes, even the gourmet dinners she'd placed in the freezer sometime in the distant past, all of it was thrown haphazardly together. After cinching the sack closed, I removed a piece of paper from my sketch pad and wrote her name across it with the message for her to leave me the hell alone. I taped the note to the outside of the garbage bag, then threw the thing onto my front porch. I should have felt something, compassion of some kind or even regret over a relationship that had ended after so many years. Yet there was only a sense of relief mixed with a strangely intense kind of anger which was totally unlike me.

I looked out across the wide-open space of the living room, kitchen, and work area. The windows and skylight reflected back the muted colors of a sunset purified by the afternoon's storm. The color and hues from without mingled and accented the cream-colored walls, the subdued tones of carpet and furniture. It was a glorious sight, a painting in the making as the sun dipped gracefully behind the magnificent oak and maple trees lining University Way. In the distance, the Bell Tower struck the hour, cars rolled silently past in the streets below, and the final day of the spring semester came to an end.

My stomach gnawed at me, but the pounding in my head forced me to resist the urge to find something to eat. Instead, I went to the bathroom and dug the bottle of Ativan out from behind other prescription drugs, and downed one and a half of the small tablets. In the living room/workroom, I sank onto the sofa, pulled off my jacket, and rolled it into a pillow. As I lay upon it, I concluded that nothing else could damage the coat as much as the rain had, and I would worry about replacing it at a later date. Right now, all I wanted was sleep, to allow the medicine to carry me beyond the pain in my head into a new day.

In a matter of minutes, I was drifting pleasantly along, seeing the events of the day unfold before my eyes but thankfully removed from them to a place where no one could reach me. As I relived the incident in the Snack Shack, I saw Tara's flushed and angry face and reflected on our relationship, on how I had been initially drawn to her because of some perception I'd had of her as a "damsel in distress." This hadn't been the first time I'd tried unsuccessfully to play hero and attempted to save someone who neither needed, nor wanted to be saved. What was it about my make up, my personality, that cast me into such a role? And how was it that I continued to repeat the scenario when it failed so miserably before?

"Too soft." I muttered, my eyes opening and fastening on the wadded-up sketches that covered the floor near the recycling can. "It's my damned dreamy eyes. See what I want, not what's really there. Too romantic."

A peace descended over me as I closed my eyes, gratefully shutting out the unfinished work and the pain that had followed me most of the day.

Chapter 3

Darkness. Vast, impenetrable.

Unrecognizable blasts of noise assaulted me, sounds so alien I felt my only recourse was to run. My legs leaden, dead weights that made progress impossible, I struck out against the eerie blackness with outstretched arms.

Water streamed down the sides of my face into my eyes, soaking my skin and clothing. I turned, changed direction, prayed I would find an outlet from this horrifying world of darkness. My breathing ragged, arms and hands remaining thrust out in front of me, I encountered something cold and damp, its skin slick and smooth. Terror shot through me as I withdrew my hands and carefully backed away from the unseen entity.

Suddenly, the thing grabbed me, clutching me in a horrible embrace! I tried to scream, to fight the all-encompassing strength that held me, but felt so small and powerless against it.

Powerless, and utterly terrified...

I flew up from the couch like a shot from a cannon. Sweat ran in torrents down my face, along my sides, and down the back of my neck. The jacket I'd used as a pillow was gripped so tightly the knuckles of both hands were white, aching. It took a great deal of concentration to finally loosen my hold on the shredded jacket and let it fall limply to the floor by my feet.

I shivered, still shaking, the terror of the nightmare having followed me into reality. Threads of sweat trickled from my forehead into my eyes, touching the corners of my mouth. My parched lips tasted of salt and a sourness I associated with fear.

Warm air filled my lungs with a soothing caress, every breath bringing me closer to the calm I sought. Pushing damp hair off my forehead, the coolness of my hands offered relief to my burning face. I sat back on the couch, rubbed sleep from my eyes, and determined to relax, ashamed the dream affected me so much.

The glow of pale morning light filtered in through the windows and skylights chasing away the remaining shadows and fears from the nightmare. As the warmth and light grew, my head cleared, and my heart returned to its normal beat.

It had been a long time since I'd had a nightmare of such magnitude. A very long time. There was a simple explanation—too little food, too many disturbing events, and a killer migraine that sent me to bed early in the evening. It was daylight now, the migraine gone, and the main source of my problems would be leaving for Japan with her latest lover within the next twenty-four hours.

I stood and stretched, the sour odor of body and day-old clothing more than a little disgusting. Wrinkles and mud stains seemed permanently embedded in my trousers, and my toes peeked through holes in "new" dress socks. I hated to think what my shoes looked like. In the course of one walk in the rain, I'd succeeded in ruining a couple hundred dollars worth of clothing. Not good for someone who would be living on his savings for the next eighteen months.

Rather than brooding, I headed for the bathroom and a much needed shower. After regulating the water, I pulled the curtain to let it run while I retrieved clean clothing from the bedroom. Back in the bathroom, I wiped steam from the mirror in preparation for a shave, and noticed my eyes looked heavier than usual. Attributing it to the way I'd awakened, I dismissed it and continued my morning ritual.

The hot water was comforting, soothing to body and soul. By the time I'd dressed, I felt revived and ready for any challenge the new day had to offer. My fingers itched to get at paints and canvas, and I couldn't help smiling as I realized my creative muse appeared unblocked after such a long dry spell. As thrilled as this made me, first things first: if I didn't have some breakfast, I'd be asking for another migraine.

Delectable smells from the bakery below joined those of bacon, eggs, toast from the bread I'd gotten from the bakery the evening before, and freshly "brewed" *instant* coffee. The aroma had me eager to dive in, but after only a bite or two the doorbell rang, interrupting my feast.

Believing it was Tara, my first instinct was to ignore the bell, to sit it out quietly until she'd gone away. However, when the bell was followed a few minutes later by a loud, persistent rapping, I changed my mind.

The limited view through the peep-hole revealed someone I didn't recognize. A fairly tall man with rather nondescript dark hair graying at the temples tapped his fingers impatiently against the door frame. I watched as the distorted figure noticed the garbage sack containing Tara's things, then bent down to read my brief message. Other than the lift of an eyebrow, his expression didn't alter, nor did it change when I abruptly opened the door and asked what he wanted.

"Richard Tanner? I'm Detective Hargrave, Linden Police Department." He held out his shield for identification, and after my acknowledgment, whipped it back into his pocket. "I wonder if I could come in a moment to ask you a few questions."

Curious, I stepped out of his way and indicated for him to enter the apartment. As I closed the door and turned to follow him, I couldn't help wondering what Tara fabricated to get the cooperation of the police. Two days ago no one could have convinced me she was capable of such a thing. Now, I accepted it as easily as one does the rising of the sun in the morning. Did that mean I was fickle? I wondered.

Detective Hargrave was scanning the area before him, taking it all in, I was certain, with eyes of a trained professional. I saw those eyes light on the shreds of my jacket where it still lay on the floor, then quickly move on to my studio. He walked into the sun-drenched area appearing to study the many canvases on the walls and stacked upright on the floor.

"Nice place you've got here. Lots of light and space." The tone was friendly, conversational. "You're an art professor at the university, aren't you?"

"Instructor, yes." I folded my arms across my chest and continued to watch him guardedly.

"These are good. Ever sell any?" He leaned down to look at one of the canvases, a landscape which was an idealized version of University Park.

"Now and again." I answered his question simply, refusing to be drawn into the apparent camaraderie he was trying to exude. I'd seen enough movies to recognize the "good cop" routine: reel them in with kindness, then drop whatever axe you're about to grind. Hargrave was on the upswing, and my gut told me Tara was the force bringing it down. Since I had nothing to hide, it was easy to play it cool and wait for the detective to tell me what was on his mind—though I did want to finish my breakfast and answer the creative itch before it vanished.

While Detective Hargrave studied my paintings, I decided to relax and study him. He wore a suit that looked almost as bad as the one I'd just taken off, and his lightweight beige overcoat had definitely seen better days. He was about my height, rather squarely built with wide, meaty-looking shoulders and arms, and a craggy face with old acne scars dotting his cheek line. He had a deep, nearly monotone voice, and narrow gray eyes that I was certain could look quite menacing when he wanted them to. I guessed him to be in his late forties, early fifties, and from his demeanor and air of confidence, decided he was the epitome of the hard-nosed cop.

Hargrave finally stood and stretched his back before he faced me. As his coat swung round over his knees, I thought it should have been the traditional trench coat of gumshoes and detectives like TV's *Columbo*. He gave me a half-smile as he continued his examination of the apartment.

"Bet this was once used as a kind of warehouse. That the bedroom and bath down the hall? One or two bedrooms?"

"One. Detective—"

"Looks like I interrupted your breakfast, Mr. Tanner. I apologize for that. Smells good, too. The coffee alone s'about to send me into orbit."

I had to keep myself from rolling my eyes, the ruse was so obvious. I asked if he'd like a cup, warned that it was instant, and with his gracious thanks, went to put some water in the microwave. In the three minutes it took to prepare the coffee, he hadn't spoken a word, and I wondered if this was another tactic to shake my confidence. I refused to allow it to get to me, however, and prepared to play host to my rather unconventional guest. I set a tray with sugar, cream, the two cups of coffee, and some of the Weisher's excellent glazed donuts—if the old joke about cops and donuts was true, these could set me up with a friend for life!

As I carried in the tray, I noticed Hargrave had returned to my studio and was poking around in items on the old parson's table I used as a kind of desk/catch-all. He'd just picked up a sketch pad when the placement of the tray upon the coffee table caught his attention.

"Smells great." He gave me an appreciative look, then held up the pad. "Mind if I take a look at your works in progress?"

I doubted if my refusal would have made any difference—he'd already opened the book.

"Suit yourself." I took a seat on the sofa, and while he seemed lost in some sketch or other, nonchalantly reached over and tucked the ruined jacket under the couch.

"Wow! Wow!" The narrow gray eyes widened a fraction of a degree as he raised them to mine. "She's a knock-out. A real honest-to-God beauty. You gonna paint her?"

What was this, another trick of some kind? I regarded him with a little more impatience than was probably wise. He took up on it immediately, but it didn't keep him from continuing to leaf through the pages.

"I mean it, Tanner. This girl would knock all those landscapes out of the park. She's gorgeous. Who is she, girlfriend or student?"

I literally had no idea what he was talking about. The last time I'd used the pad, there had been one or two sketches of the gazebo, an outline of a park in a town south of here, and a scenic view from atop some bluffs near Omaha. He saw my confusion, seemed curious about it, but rather than commenting on it, brought the pad over and set it next to the serving tray on the coffee table. I felt him sit on the other end of the sofa, saw him grab a donut from the corner of my eye, but couldn't turn my head, couldn't take my eyes from the sketch before me.

It was one of the drawings I remembered—the scenic view of the bluff and beyond—but now it was different, vastly different. Where before the only living thing depicted had been a hawk high above the valley, now a girl sat on the edge of the bluff, her head thrown back to the sky, her long, flowing hair mingling with the grasses on the hillside. I recognized her at once—how could I not?—it was Jenny, her tiny, perfect features offering new life to the once dry and desolate landscape.

I flipped back a page to the sketch of the park in nearby St. Joseph. Krug Park, always so filled with people whenever I'd visited, had been drawn with no one save the inevitable ducks that resided there at the pond. Despite the fact there had been both children and adults bent over the railings feeding the birds the day I'd drawn it, none of them had been included: I had opted for the peace and tranquility of the bird population dotting the gray-green water as the trees lining the pond swayed in a gentle breeze. Now, however, a girl in a peasant blouse and long multi-colored skirt stood at the edge of the pond, her hand outstretched as she tossed morsels of bread toward some nearby ducks. The smile on her face revealed the trace of dimples in each cheek, her eyes danced with mischief, and her beautiful hair floated around her like a cloud.

I turned the pages to find sketch after sketch had been altered by adding Jenny's mysterious presence, not just as I'd seen her yesterday, but different somehow. It was as though, as though she'd been there all along, the something that had been missing. As strange as this was, even stranger was my not remembering having changed the drawings at all.

"So, who is she? She looks vaguely familiar, can't place why." He shook his head as he took a swig of the coffee. "She a professional model or something?"

"Uh, no. Actually, I only met her recently." Determined my hands would not shake, I picked up my coffee and washed down a bite of donut. Watching him warily, I leaned back against the couch.

"Must've been pretty taken with her. I've gotta admit, she makes a good subject. You should think about doing a portrait of her."

"Maybe I will." I eased myself into the corner of the sofa and drew up a leg as I turned to face the detective. "Don't you think it's about time you let me know what this visit's all about?"

Hargrave put the last of his donut in his mouth and washed it down with a swallow of coffee. Setting the cup back on the tray, he brushed his hands together, then regarded me solemnly.

"Don't usually get so caught up with my surroundings like I've done. Have to apologize for that, Tanner, but I got to hand it to you, you've been a good sport about it. Been on the job around sixteen straight hours now, and was truly about to drop when I got here. This little snack helped rejuvenate me and I want to thank you." He moved to the edge of the couch, unbuttoned his jacket, and removed a notepad and pen from an inside pocket. "Now, Mr. Tanner, Richard, do you know one Akiro Nagoochi?"

Here it came, whatever it was Tara put him up to—everything had changed, the thrust of his shoulders, the narrowing of the eyes, even the tone of his voice was crisper, less familiar.

"I don't actually know him, rather of him."

Hargrave recorded my answer in his notebook, placed the tip of his pen on his tongue for a moment, then looked down at the floor. Bending, his hand went beneath the edge of the sofa and he pulled out my ruined jacket.

"Mind telling me how this happened, Richard?"

Holding myself in check, I remained seated and answered him calmly. "Actually, I do. Look, Detective, I've been extremely patient and hospitable, but I really haven't got all day. I think you'd better stop beating about the bush and come out with whatever it is you have to say. I'm sure we've both better things to do than play whatever game Tara Morgan's put you up to."

He raised expressive eyebrows, and continuing to hold onto the jacket, said, "When Miss Morgan failed to show up at Nagoochi's last evening, the gentleman decided to go looking for her. He found her in University Park, beaten to a pulp and barely alive. Right now, she's in City Hospital, stabilized, but still unconscious." He paused for a moment to gauge my reaction, took in my disbelieving face and the sweat that was forming on my brow. "You wanna tell me about it?"

"Tell you—Good God, you don't think I—that I—" I jumped up from the couch and rubbed my face briskly with hands that had turned ice cold. I saw Tara's broken and bruised body lying helplessly near the foot of the gazebo, rain pelting her mercilessly—the vision so clear, the force of it striking me in the gut and throwing me off balance. I grabbed onto the couch for support, the food and coffee churning in my stomach, my mind reaching for anything that might erase the picture from my brain.

"Richard?"

I fought to regain my composure and looked steadily into the detective's eyes. "The last I saw Tara was in the Snack Shack yesterday afternoon around the beginning of the storm. We'd had a disagreement, and I walked out and left her there."

"From what Nagoochi told us, it was a little more than a disagreement. He said you were both shouting at one another and that as you were leaving, you deliberately dumped Miss Morgan's drink in her lap."

That was it, the boost I needed. "That was an accident. The glass must have been too close to the edge of the table, and when I got up, I bumped against the leg or something, and it fell. I'm sure in Tara's mind it was a deliberate act, but take my word for it, it was nothing more than an unfortunate accident."

"Do you deny that you were quite loud with your verbal abuses of one another?"

"The key words here are "of one another". I think if you'd ask around, and, unfortunately, there were plenty of witnesses, you'd find that it was Miss Morgan who was the most verbal. She didn't appreciate my concern for her plans to take off with someone she barely knows, and she told me in no uncertain terms what she felt about my opinion. We'd had discussions like this before, and I knew it was useless trying to make her see reason, so I started to get up to leave. She said a few more nasty things—I couldn't tell you exactly what—I lost my cool and retorted something equally abusive, then slammed out of the chair and left the restaurant. End of story."

"Not quite." Hargrave flung my jacket over his arm and appeared to consult his notes. "According to Nagoochi, she was coming here to pick up some items she'd left in the apartment—the ones I noted on your porch, I assume. Anyway, when an hour went by and she didn't show up, Nagoochi says he called here and got your machine. That started him worrying, which is when he went to look for her." His eyes narrowed to little gray slits. "Where were you, Richard?"

"Right here on this very couch, sound asleep." My voice was even, my eyes staring straight into his.

"You got anyone who could corroborate that?"

I held fast to a temper that was slowly boiling to the surface. "I got home sometime after six last evening. I came in through the kitchen of the bakery, spoke to Mr. Weisher, bought a loaf of bread and visited with his wife for a few minutes before going back through the kitchen and up the inside steps to the apartment. I'd had a migraine for most of the day, and by the time I got home, all I wanted was to sleep. So I took some medicine—"

"Over the counter or prescription?"

"Prescription. And then I crashed. I didn't hear the phone because when I'm working at the school or in my studio, I usually have the machine pick up immediately."

My explanation was answered by silence, the detective seemingly absorbed in recording what I'd said. While he was busy writing it all down, I walked over to the desk on the far side of the living room and sure enough, the light was blinking on the answering machine. Out of curiosity, I pushed the button for play-back and was soon assaulted by Tara's voice. Her message was short and simple:

"I know you're there, Richard, you jackass. Pick up the freaking phone!"

A few expletives later and the beep signaled the end of her message and the beginning of Nagoochi's. A soft, heavily accented Asian voice full of concern emitted from the machine: "If you have seen Tara, or if she is there, could you please to give me a call," was followed by his number.

Turning, I saw Hargrave studying me intently, and I felt a cold shiver steal along the length of my spine.

"She's got a mouth on her, I'll say that for her." He shook his head. "She always like that, man?"

"No, not always."

He waited to see if I would say more, and when I didn't volunteer further information, repositioned himself on the couch and prepared another approach.

"You said that when you got in last evening you took some medication to help you sleep. You do that right away, or did you wait awhile?"

"Almost immediately."

A nod. "Almost. What about that stuff on the porch, when did you do that?"

I knew I didn't have to answer his questions, was getting damned tired of them to be honest, but where was the choice? If I had nothing to hide, as I didn't, there wasn't any reason to skirt around the issue. If I acted offended, he'd be suspicious. All I wanted was for him to go so I could phone the hospital and see how Tara was doing. Besides, what could any of this have to do with what happened to her?

"Look, when I went into the bakery Mrs. Weisher told me that Tara had been there earlier and tried to get them to let her into my apartment. When they refused, she threw a fit. She came up here and left me a note—another of her scathing opinions of me. Knowing how she'd embarrassed the Weisher's and their customers, I was more than a little ticked off at her. I got the garbage sack and searched the apartment for her stuff. When I was pretty sure I'd found everything, I tied it shut, put the note on it, and threw it onto the porch."

"And as angry as you were, you were still able to go to sleep. Just like that."

"With the assistance of my medication, yes, just like that."

He shook his head. "Sorry, Richard. I just don't buy it." He removed my jacket from his arm. "This makes it even more difficult to believe." He eyed me speculatively. "What about the coat, Richard? You wanna tell me about it?"

I'm a patient man, God knows I've had to be to put up with Tara for the last three years, but now I'd taken all I could from the man.

"Am I under arrest, Detective Hargrave?"

"Arrest? Course not. Who said anything about an arrest? We're just sitting here having a nice, quiet conversation."

"If I'm not under arrest, Detective, then I'd like you to leave." I returned to the side of the couch where he was sitting and held out my hand. "And I'd like you to give me the jacket, please."

Hargrave looked hurt and made a show of staring at the jacket and then at me. "Ah, man, let's not do this. Things were going so well."

"I think I've been more than hospitable and cooperative. Now I'd like you to go."

The detective stood up slowly, replaced the notepad and pen in his coat pocket, then stretched his back before heading for the door.

"Guess I don't have to tell you to stick around Linden, Richard. We might have to ask you down to the station in the next day or two."

I ignored the condescending tone. "I'm not going anywhere."

"Good. That's good." Still holding the jacket, he opened the door. Once more I held out my hand for it and was greeted with a hard, steely gaze.

I didn't know the law well enough to know if he could leave with the coat, knew that my insistence on its return looked suspicious, but by now, it was the principle of the thing.

"Don't try to destroy this, Richard. It would make me extremely unhappy with you." He tossed the jacket over my arm and went out the door. "By the way," he stopped on the top step and regarded me with narrowed grey eyes. "Do you often do things you don't remember afterward?"

The question took me by surprise. "What do you mean?"

"I may be just a dumb cop, but I'm smart enough to recognize those sketches were altered, the girl a recent addition."

"So?" Remain calm, nonchalant.

"So, you had no idea what I was talking about when I asked who she was. And when you saw the drawings, you couldn't believe what you were seeing."

"I-I think you're misreading what you saw."

He shook his head. "Nah, I don't think so. It gave you quite a shock. Quite a shock." He reached into his pocket and pulled out a stick of gum. "Imagine, Richard, just imagine that if you could draw that well and not even remember doing it, think what you coulda done to the ex-girlfriend you were so pissed at. Kinda makes you think, doesn't it?" He gave me a malicious grin, then turned and walked down the stairs.

Chapter 4

I'd been stunned by news of the attack on Tara, and even now, alone in the apartment, found it difficult to believe or accept. Just as hard to believe was the suspicion of guilt Detective Hargrave harbored against me. It was unthinkable, totally ludicrous for him to suspect me of harming the girl. Yes, I'd been angry with her, tired of the way she'd used and abused me, but I would never hurt her physically. That wasn't me, wasn't in my make up.

I stared down at the shredded fabric of the jacket still in my hands. Seeing its condition, it was understandable the detective had his doubts. Adding fuel to his belief in my culpability was my reaction to the sketches and Jenny's addition to them.

What was it he said? Something to the effect that if I could have changed the drawings without realizing I'd done so, imagine what else I could do without being aware of it. The thought was far from comforting.

I couldn't explain the sketches, had no memory of having changed them. That was something I had to accept whether I liked it or not. Also, having just met the mysterious girl the previous afternoon, I'd no choice but to acknowledge that her addition to the drawings had been made sometime last night. Since I could account for the time until I laid down on the couch, it meant the work was done while I thought I was asleep. Definitely not a good sign.

Sleepwalking? Was it possible for someone to undertake such an intricate task while actually still asleep? And, if that were possible, could I have—

A thousand things ran through my brain at once, images plastered upon images, pictures, sketches, reality, and fantasy all crashing against one another, vying for dominance. Looking again at the torn jacket in my hands, a terrifying thought rose above all others.

What if I *had* done something to Tara? What if, God forbid, she'd come over here last evening and confronted me while I was in some sort of fugue state? Was it possible that in such a condition I'd snapped, followed her into the park and—and...

I rejected the scenario instantly, forcing logic to intercede and inject a sense of reality into the wild conjecture. I was not, could *never* be, the violent type no matter how far I was pushed. Perhaps it made me appear less manly, even a wimp, but I'd never seen the purpose or use of physical fighting. I could make a far better stand verbally, confront any enemy with a semblance of dignity. If it went beyond what could be discussed, rather than resort to my fists, I was the kind who'd turn and walk away. Tara knew this, had, at first, been attracted to it. Later, it became just another thorn in her side, a lever to use against me.

I recalled the many times her small hands pummeled me for some wrong she'd felt I'd committed, the scene's inevitable end of her being comforted in my arms while the true story unfolded. Those times, she would grow quiet and reflective, apologize for the abuse, and beg my forgiveness while she thanked me for being so kind and gentle. That had been in the beginning. Toward the end, I often found her picking at me mercilessly, doing her best to push me over the edge and follow her into whatever madness held her. There were no follow-up scenes of forgiveness, no tears, apologies, or seeking comfort within one another's arms; not on those occasions. Instead, I frequently found myself walking out on her in the middle of yet another tirade of insults; walking out and seeking a cool breeze to clear my head and relax my body, trying to find the answer, the way to finally and completely disentangle myself from this girl that gradually wore me down and started me questioning my own worth.

Weak? I'd never considered myself so. Looking at oneself objectively and without bias wasn't really difficult. I knew my faults, and I had many, but there were also strengths to my personality that I was proud of.

I'd always believed in myself, in my abilities, wasn't arrogant but, rather, self-assured, confident, and sometimes too stubborn for my own good. A sense of humor was important to me, and something I usually looked for in other people. I prided myself in truthfulness—insisted on it from others, and thought that patience, understanding, consideration, and the ability to forgive and forget were all attributes to strive for. I rarely lost my temper, exercised constraint when I did, and believed that one should "practice what they preach." To come right down to it, I tried my hardest to be the best person I could be, working to learn from my mistakes—even if their acknowledgment was a long time in coming. This often resulted in being told by friends and my parents that I was too soft-hearted and gentle, and definitely not cynical enough for the world as we knew it. To make matters worse, my belief in love—the heart-stopping, gut-wrenching, happily-ever-after scenario where a couple worked through their problems rather than calling it quits when things got tough, appeared to make me unrealistic in their eyes. Case in point, my failed relationships, especially this latest one with Tara Morgan.

While I'd not consciously considered marriage to Tara an option, I suppose that somewhere at the very core of my being the thought had been responsible for the continuation of our on-again off-again affair. I'd hate to think it was stupidity or weakness on my part—while I freely admitted to repeating dumb mistakes, I didn't believe I was actually stupid.

My ego had suffered at Tara's hands, especially within this last year, but the damage wasn't irreparable. I knew I'd bounce back, and after the pain subsided, be even better than before. Just because the relationship had been a failure didn't mean I was out for revenge or capable of hurting her physically. I refused to believe this possible, not only because my continued emotional involvement with her would have balked at the idea, but it just wasn't in me to hurt someone.

Still...

"Beaten to a pulp" was the way Hargrave put it.

I gazed down at my hands, finally dropping the jacket. As it fell unceremoniously to the floor, I turned my hands over to examine the knuckles. There were no bruises, no broken skin or signs of trauma. Even the nails retained their manicured appearance.

Weapons?

A wide, flat board and the sound it made as it came into contact with flesh was so vivid I fell backward against the door as though I'd actually been struck. I again saw the vision of Tara lying at the foot of the gazebo, her broken and bruised body being assaulted by the wind and rain as a dark form stood over her, the board rising again, ready to strike.

Sweat ran down my face, stinging my eyes, and my breath felt as though it was strangled deep within my chest.

Imagination. A wild and vivid imagination, the very thing that gave me my creative urges and inspiration to paint. That was all, nothing more. It was my stock in trade to be capable of seeing what wasn't there, to fantasize and create images from another's words. I'd been told about the attack, and my over-developed imagination took the information and drew upon it, presenting a picture in my mind so clear it seemed reality. There was no basis in fact, no proof of it being anything more than the bridge of words and images.

That self-same imagination now conjured up the feel of the cold, slick skin of the monster from my dream. The memory was as vivid as if it just happened, the sense of danger and fear as real and imminent as in the dream.

I pushed damp hair back from my forehead where it had fallen and rubbed viciously at my eyes.

What was happening to me? Spurred by the power of suggestion, I'd placed myself in the park with Tara, and from that point, entered a kind of *Twilight Zone* that thrust me with deadly force back into a nightmare! I felt sick, the few bites of my breakfast and coffee swirling within my stomach, threatening to come up.

It wasn't possible, deep within me that knowledge struggled for supremacy. And as I felt the inner turmoil as certainly as I would a pin prick, another thought arose, one that comforted and calmed, wiping away any self-doubts.

It hadn't been raining last night.

I recalled the beautiful, clear sky as I looked out across the tops of the trees last evening toward University Way. The crystal clarity of the softening blue, the streaks of red, violet, and gold as the sun began to set. There had been no clouds in the sky, nothing to signify there would be another storm. No, I was sure of it. It had not rained last night.

Breathing became easier in face of the conviction I couldn't have been involved in whatever happened to Tara the night before. As my mind cleared and took the visions for just that, I was even able to accept the reasons that led Hargrave to question my innocence. It was a logical conclusion, and after the scene in the Snack Shack, probably seemed an open and shut case. I didn't imagine he'd had the chance to check further into Tara's background, or I'd have been on the bottom of his list of suspects.

Out of my trancelike state, I grabbed up the closest phone—one located among the litter on the parson's table—and dialed the hospital. I was transferred to the intensive care nurse's station where I was firmly told that news about that particular patient could not be released over the phone. However, if I wished to come down to the hospital, there was the possibility I might get in to see her.

Could they have my name? Self-preservation intact, I declined to answer and hung up with a quick good-bye.

I had to see her. It wasn't just morbid curiosity but a need that welled from deep within me. She'd hurt me, infuriated me, and made me regret ever having known her, but there was still a part of me that cared. Chalk it up to three tumultuous years, or perhaps not wishing ill upon anyone, especially someone I'd known so intimately. However you looked at it, the fact remained that I desperately needed to see her.

At the kitchen sink, I splashed cold water over my face, the sting washing away the remaining cobwebs from my brain. The smell from my discarded breakfast caused my stomach to again churn uncomfortably, and as an afterthought, I tossed the cold and greasy mess into the trash can and put the dishes in the sink. Afterward, I retrieved a windbreaker from the closet, and left the apartment for the hospital.

The back side of the Weisher building faced an alley which opened on one end and halted abruptly just a half block down on the other side. I kept my car, a Citation that had seen better days, parked against the fence blocking the alley's dead end. I rarely drove the thing in Linden, kept it more for trips than anything else, and as I headed for it now, wondered if it would even start. The last I'd used the vehicle was four months ago at the time of my father's death. I'd come back late, and hadn't paid much attention to the level of the gas tank, or anything else for that matter. As unpredictable as the vehicle was, it was likely out of gas and the engine locked up from neglect.

Surprisingly, the Citation sputtered slowly to life with the tank sitting at a fourth; more than enough to drive across town to City Hospital.

Linden City Hospital was a modern structure not more than five years old. It sat on the edge of town in what had once been a corn field. Aside from the hospital itself, there was also a large building containing doctors' offices, a separate physical therapy unit, and the groundwork for what would be a fifty bed nursing/convalescent home. It was an impressive, albeit imposing complex, and one of the finest medical care facilities in this part of the state. While I was familiar with the physicians' office building, I'd never been in the hospital and had to ask several times for directions to ICU.

City Hospital's intensive care unit was set off in a wing by itself, the cluster of rooms forming a semicircle around the nurses' station. After my recent visit with Hargrave, it was difficult to guess what the staff's reaction might be to my request to see Tara—even possible I'd be given the boot by a muscle-bound orderly before the words were out of my mouth. Self-conscious, and more than a little reluctant to be recognized, I approached the area cautiously, eyes and ears open, with senses trained on my objective.

Perhaps it was naive, but I hadn't expected to find a police officer stationed outside her door. I knew she'd be watched by the nursing staff, that was a given, even believed that visitors, if she were allowed any, would be carefully monitored. So, it was a shock to see the officer there for her protection, and what his presence intimated made my desire to see her even greater than before.

There was a straight-backed chair shoved against the wall out of the main aisle way. The man sat stiff as a board, shoulders resting lightly against the observation window, head slightly bent in concentration on the magazine he held before him. As absorbed as he appeared in his reading material, I noticed that even the slightest sound caused him to raise his head in attention, his eyes quickly scanning the area for any signs of danger. Once, his eyes slid over me, taking in my presence, then dismissing me with a nod of the head. I didn't recognize him, or any of the on-duty staff, and encouraged by the officer's attitude, decided it was worth a chance to venture forward.

I'd fully intended on going directly to the desk and asking about Tara, and would have done so had I not seen Nagoochi standing in the doorway of her room. I side-stepped to the outside perimeter of the semicircle with what I hoped appeared a poised and confident gait, occasionally glancing into one of the open rooms as though searching for someone. I needn't have bothered; the nurses behind the desk were too preoccupied with their charts and monitoring equipment to notice me.

As I neared the apex, I heard Nagoochi speaking to the officer, their voices too low to distinguish what was being said. I was a room down from them when one of the nurses swung out from behind the desk and joined the two in the open doorway. I managed to duck, unnoticed, inside a nearby room—luckily vacant—just as she pulled up alongside the officer and Tara's latest beau.

My heart was like a trip-hammer in my chest. I didn't like playing this game of hide-and-seek, never wanted to be a spy or into covert activities. Nor did I care much for being made to feel guilty about something I hadn't done. But then, neither did the thought of being bodily escorted from the hospital appeal to me. It was better to play the game for the time being than face the possible alternative.

"Not the most riveting assignment you ever had, eh, Johnny?" The young woman asked with a laugh, a hand upon the policeman's shoulder.

"That's true. But it could be worse. You hanging in there, sir?"

If Nagoochi answered, I didn't hear him, and when I peered around the door he was nowhere in sight. The nurse and officer had their heads together whispering, their conversation punctuated by laughter. After a few moments, the woman pushed playfully at the officer's sleeve, and with a wave of her hand, disappeared through the open door into Tara's room. I waited to see if he would follow, but no such luck; he continued at his post outside the door, head bent once again to his magazine.

As I stepped back out into the main hallway, there was a flurry of activity around the desk. Medications, clipboards, stethoscopes and other paraphernalia were being gathered in preparation of rounds, and before I had the chance to make them aware of my presence, the remainder of personnel dispersed for visual checks on their patients.

I stood at the station desk a moment, nodded at the officer when he looked up, then shrugged my shoulders in what I hoped was an "oh well, it can wait" attitude. I continued on past the officer, stopping two rooms down from Tara's. With the station temporarily vacated, I had a clear view of her room through the glass window behind the officer's head.

She lay motionless in the bed, her head almost entirely swathed in bandages. Pale blond hair lay loosely about her shoulders, her face in repose—a state I'd rarely seen it in. There was a tube in her mouth, lines connecting her to heart and pressure monitors, and intravenous lines feeding into her veins. There was no denying it was Tara, even from this distance I recognized the curve of her now bruised cheek.

I was outraged that someone had done such a thing to her. She looked so small and helpless that my heart jerked, and I knew no matter what had transpired between us, an undeniable bond remained.

Beads of perspiration dotted my forehead, and my hands clenched angrily at my sides as I recalled Mrs. Weisher's statement that Tara needed a lesson in manners. Knowing her as I did, I couldn't help but wonder if she'd finally pushed someone too far. But, no matter what her actions, she hadn't deserved such treatment.

There was the taste of bile in my mouth, and I swallowed hard trying to force it down. I started forward but stopped when I saw Nagoochi go to stand next to the nurse. They conferred for a few minutes, then the man went to sit by Tara's bedside. He reached out and clasped one of her hands as the nurse hovered nearby methodically checking and rechecking the instruments and making notations on her clipboard.

There was nothing I could do. If I attempted to enter the room while Nagoochi was there he would call the officer to stop me—that was if I had made it past the policeman in the first place. As badly as I wanted to be near her, to ask how she was doing, it wasn't worth the scene or the disturbance it might cause Tara or the other patients to risk it.

I'd just determined to leave, when a hand on my shoulder startled me. Turning around with my heart caught in my throat, I had that strange sense of guilt one has when being caught doing something questionable. I fully expected to find Hargrave or, at the very least, another officer ready to interrogate me about my presence, and was relieved to see my own physician.

Dr. Joyce Noland regarded me through the thick lenses of her glasses. "I thought that was you. What are you doing hovering about in the halls?" Her eyes went from my blanched face to the police officer and back again.

"Of course." She placed her arm through mine, and drew me down the corridor to a supply room. There she urged me onto a stool, and the next thing I knew, was placing a paper cup of water into my hand.

"You're white as a ghost." Dr. Noland put one hand to my forehead while the other grabbed my wrist to check my pulse.

"A little fast, but otherwise normal. No fever, but you're sticky with perspiration. You having a migraine? No? Good." She leaned against one of the cabinets, legs crossed at the ankles. "Let me guess, as Miss Morgan's one time lover you've been fingered as the culprit."

I gave her a weak smile. "Something like that. A Detective Hargrave brought me the news bright and early this morning. He let me know I was supposed to remain available for further questioning."

Dr. Noland smirked. "Rather heavy-handed of the man, considering."

I raised an eyebrow in question. "Considering?"

Joyce Noland brushed at the pristine white coat and eyed me speculatively. "Tara Morgan's got a reputation in Linden, Richard. I'm sure you're aware of that. She's a natural born troublemaker, and as such, has made a lot of enemies." Her eyes narrowed. "You wouldn't happen to know anything about the attack, would you?"

"Of course not!" Indignant, I jumped up from the stool prepared to leave, but once again, her hand on my shoulder stopped me.

"Don't get all excited, man. I had to ask, didn't I?" She gave me a thin-lipped smile as she pushed me back toward the stool. "Now, let's take a look at you." Her hand went back to my forehead and she nodded, apparently satisfied. "You're getting your color back. Are you feeling steadier?"

"I was doing fine until you startled me."

"Oh? Then I apologize. Actually, I'd been watching you for several minutes before I decided to approach you. Didn't like the pallor of your skin." She shrugged. "A hazard in this business, I suppose. When you see someone who looks as though a breath could knock them over, it's instinctive to run to their rescue. When that person also happens to be a patient—well?" She raised her hands in a form of surrender, her pale eyes sliding over me in another quick examination.

"Look, I apologize if I've been rude. It's just..." I let the sentence dangle with a nod from the doctor.

Joyce Noland had been my neurologist for the last five years, and during that time we'd gotten to know one another fairly well. She admitted to being fascinated by my case, to the form of amnesia that hid the details of my long ago accident. As often happens between doctor and patient, we'd become friends as well, and while she didn't know everything about my relationship with Tara, she knew enough to guess how I was feeling.

She patted me sympathetically on the shoulder. "I'll go see what I can find out. You stay put."

There was an odor of cleanliness and disinfectant about the room that was overpowering to the point of being nauseating. Its pristine white on white decor and harsh lighting added to the starkness, the plain white, gold-flecked tiles and shining stainless steel fixtures as cold and impersonal as only a hospital can be.

Dr. Noland returned within a few minutes, her thin lips drawn into a grim expression.

"The patient was in a semi-conscious state when brought in last evening. Seems she went under shortly after the examination began and has been out since—which is not necessarily a bad sign. She's being given medication to avert possible complications from the head trauma, CAT scan looked good, though, so I'd say it's simply a matter of time. Aside from a couple of cracked ribs, most of the other wounds are superficial, no internal damage. She just looks bloody awful."

"You're not on the case?"

She shook her head. "No, one of my esteemed colleagues, Dr. Astin. He's very good, Richard, a neurosurgeon with the steadiest hands I've ever seen."

I raised my eyebrows in mock surprise. "Here I thought you were the best."

Dr. Noland grinned. "One of the best, yes. The best, well, that's debatable. However, back to your Miss Morgan. Astin believes she'll be coming around this afternoon. He doesn't expect her to be capable of giving interviews for a while, so you'll have to fight off the police for a bit longer. Think you can hang in there?"

"I'll give it a try."

I thanked her for the information and left the hospital considerably less shaken than when I'd arrived. While the visual confirmation had been far worse than anything my imagination conjured up, Dr. Noland helped set my mind at ease.

The Citation balked and died three times before I was able to get it out of the parking lot, and it choked and died a final time approximately half-way across town. I managed to get it to the side of the road and safely out of traffic before it refused to budge further. After verbally abusing the little car on its performance, I locked the doors and started out on foot.

I stopped at a garage I knew, tossed the manager the car keys and told him where he could pick the Citation up for repairs. He laughed when I mentioned it had stranded me, reminding me of the warning he'd issued some time ago that such a thing was possible. Water pump, fuel pump, whatever, I remembered the warning now it was too late. At the moment, the car was the least of my concerns.

Without wheels, however, I'd have to put off clearing out my office, and I made a mental note to phone the secretary about the delay. That gave me the rest of the day to try to recapture the mood I'd awakened with. I had a little more than six weeks until the exhibition in the Fine Arts gallery on campus. Time enough, if granted the inspiration, to try for those "remarkable" pieces I was aiming for.

The deep azure of the cloudless sky foretold of the beautiful afternoon and evening that could be expected, the kind of day when all you want to do is be outdoors. The sun had warmed considerably, drying the few remaining puddles from yesterday's rain, but there were still soggy patches of earth where the drainage wasn't as good, and I attempted to avoid these not wishing to ruin yet another pair of shoes. I walked quickly, used to this form of exercise, but aware of very little around me. It didn't seem to take long to reach the far side of University Park, and the sight of it seemed to bring everything back into perspective.

I considered going the long way around rather than taking the short cut through the park, but after a brief argument with myself, decided that would be foolish. There wasn't any reason to avoid the park because of what happened to Tara. If anything, it was as good a reason as any not to avoid it.

The west side of University Park still maintained some of its original wildness. There was a small grove of trees on the outer edge flanked by rhododendron and azalea shrubs with a horseshoe shaped verge and a couple of benches. The central sidewalk passed a few feet in front of the area with pebbled pathways jutting off in all directions. It was a popular area with couples, offering both the atmosphere and seclusion necessary for making out.

This morning, however, there were no young lovers lurking in the shadows. Instead, police tape had cordoned off the area, and it was teaming with officers. I recognized Hargrave instantly; he was kneeling next to a colleague and appeared to be examining the patch of ground in front of him. Thus occupied, I hoped to make it by the area unnoticed. But I'd never been very good at sneaking around—my visit to the hospital this morning perhaps the only exception—and I hadn't taken three steps before the detective was calling out for me to wait.

"Out for your morning constitutional?" Hargrave carefully picked his way across the lawn, cursing when his foot sank into a hollow just before reaching the sidewalk. Grimacing, he shook his foot, sending mud and water across the other pant leg.

"Damn. I should be home in bed instead of out here playing mud pies." He brushed the worst of the mud from his trousers, then turned to look at me.

"So, returning to the scene of the crime?"

I let the sarcasm go, swallowing back a retort. "You find anything?"

He shrugged. "We'll make a few casts, but the ground's so wet I'm afraid they won't be very accurate. Haven't had the chance to check back in with the hospital, so you wanna tell me how she's doing?"

"What makes you think—" I picked up my pace, leaving the detective temporarily behind. "She's expected to regain consciousness later today." I flung over my shoulder. "It may be a while before you can talk to her, though."

"Yeah, well, it'll wait. How 'bout you, Richard, think you can wait?"

I stopped then, rounding on the man, my fists clenched tightly by my sides.

"I don't appreciate your insinuations, Hargrave. As a matter of fact, I'd say you're dangerously close to getting a harassment charge thrown at you."

"Hey, now, wait a minute—"

"No, you wait. I've freely admitted to having an argument with Tara yesterday, told you everything you wanted to know—"

"Except about the jacket."

"And I refuse to be treated like the only suspect in this case. You'll have egg on your face when Tara confirms my innocence."

"That may be, and if it happens, I'll be happy to apologize. And you're right, I am dogging you. But I'm a man that goes on gut instinct, Tanner, and my gut tells me you've got something to hide. Take that jacket for instance. You still have it, don't you?"

The gazebo was in view, mid-point across the park. The sun picked up a hint of silver in the black shingles, setting the object off beneath in a kind of halo. There was a family at one of the picnic tables unpacking a hamper, two small children darting among the tables in a game of tag. The childish laughter rang out clear and strong, catching Hargrave's attention and pulling his eyes from my face.

"Looks like the park's department needs to get out here and patch up the foundation." He nodded toward the gazebo and I saw the cracks extending from the ground and halfway up the side facing us, with a smaller webbing of cracks splintering upward. "Can't say I've ever seen it that bad before. Damn hard winter, I suppose." He stopped on the sidewalk a little in front of me, his grey eyes narrowed against the sun. "Maybe you didn't do the crime itself, but a hunch tells me you know who did."

"If it's someone who knows Tara, there's a chance I may know them as well. But if you're thinking I'm involved in some sort of cover-up, you can forget it. Believe me, Detective, I wouldn't stand idly by and let anyone get away with this, let alone do it in the first place."

"Turn in your own mother, would you?" He remarked cynically. "Admirable."

Someone called out to Hargrave, and he waved an impatient hand in their direction.

"You just remain available, Richard, old man. You never know what kind of damaging testimony can turn up." And with an insolent grin, he walked past me, leaving me alone and wondering exactly what he was up to.

Chapter 5

One moment you're in a steamy love affair and the next, the middle of a heated argument that blows the whole thing apart. When you realize there's nothing left to save, the normal scenario is eventual acceptance and moving to the next stage of your life. I hadn't been in a "normal" relationship, so why should the break-up be any different? And with Detective Hargrave on my back, it didn't look as though things would change any time soon.

He said he relied on instinct. Gut instinct? Well, the man did have somewhat of an overhang, but I doubted it ever told him anything—especially when to leave the table.

I laughed to myself, pleased that in light of the situation, I hadn't totally lost my sense of humor. Granted, my facetiousness wouldn't get me anywhere with the irascible detective, but maybe it would help preserve my sanity between now and the time Tara proved my innocence.

I'd never been on anyone's "hit list" before, and while some might consider it a novelty, being on Hargrave's was quickly becoming a pain in the ass.

Not thinking about the detective or the unconscious girl in the hospital would be difficult, but I had to give it a try. Beyond prayer, there was nothing I could do for Tara.

Never deeply religious, when my father died I saw the comfort Mother seemed to gain from her pastor and congregation, and tried a tentative prayer or two on my own. They'd helped at the time, offering calm to a troubled mind and soul. After returning to Linden, I'd found a church and attended Sunday morning services for a while. It hadn't lasted long. I'd felt stiff and uncomfortable, too confined by the rules and rigors of organized religion. I decided my belief in God was intensely more private than what could be shared with an entire congregation.

Tara had laughed at me, stated that my "getting religion" for such a short duration only proved it was a waste of time. I'd protested, tried to explain my view of the subject, but knew it wouldn't do any good. If not an atheist, she was at least an agnostic, her only religion that of Tara Morgan. So now, as I rattled off a brief entreaty to God asking for His help in healing Tara, I was filled with a double uncertainty: coming from me on her behalf would doubtless do little good.

As for Detective Hargrave, I couldn't even guess what he saw, or thought he did, when he looked at me. The notion I knew Tara's attacker, that it had been a deliberate rather than a random act, was as disturbing as his belief I might be the guilty party. Of course, it was possible I knew the perpetrator. As I'd told him, if it was someone who knew Tara, I likely knew them as well. But knowing the individual and condoning such violence were totally separate things.

I stopped for a moment on the path, threw my head back into the sun, closed my eyes, and took a long, deep breath of the warm spring air. Sounds drifted to me on the gentle breeze, sounds I'd been too worked up to notice a few minutes before. There was the echo of childish laughter coming from the playground, the squeak of swings and merry-go-round, the occasional caution from a parent to be more careful. Birdsong filled the air; two blue jays squawked at one another in an elm at the east edge of the park, and a squirrel chattered amiably near the base of a tree.

Opening my eyes, I saw a dog dash past, trailing a broken leash behind him. A boy in his early teens ran after it, calling its name. I watched as the dog paused long enough for his young master to near him, only to dart away once more as the boy leapt toward the broken leash. This happened several times before the kid understood what was going on, then he loped over to a nearby bench and sat wearily upon it. Gradually, the dog realized the fun and games were over and slowly, cautiously, approached his master.

The boy remained still, watching from the corner of his eye. Finally, the recalcitrant pooch settled on the ground at the lad's feet, looked appealingly up at the boy, then lay its head upon its forepaws. Only then did the boy reach down and retrieve the leash, tying its broken end to the piece he still held in his hand. He glanced lovingly at the animal, patted its head a couple of times, and spoke to it quietly.

The very normalcy of the scene helped restore me, pushed back the disturbing morning and granted a much needed reprieve. I continued on my way, anxious to get home to the empty canvas waiting for my renewed inspiration.

A sleek black Porsche with a plush red interior was pulled at an odd angle beneath the stairs leading to my apartment. I recognized the car instantly, and looked into the nearly nonexistent rear seat to check if Lily remembered to bring the canvases I'd requested. The area was empty, and gazing up the steps to my door, knew she'd never carry them up to the apartment and risk a broken nail.

Lillian Reston, a most unlikely patron of the arts if ever there was one, was the manager of Art Magic, a gallery boutique on the Plaza in Kansas City. A former resident of Linden and one time instructor of home economics in the local high school, Lily always felt she was made for bigger and better things. She'd found her niche a little over six years ago while vacationing in Kansas City.

Matthew Marzetti, owner of Art Magic, had taken a shine to Lily one afternoon while she visited the gallery. It wasn't long before Lily quit her job and moved to KC to be close to her "benefactor." Over the years, their relationship continued despite Marzetti's marriage and Lily's penchant for younger men—a category under which I happened to fall.

She'd seen some of my work in the Fine Arts gallery in a campus exhibition five years ago. Something about the paintings spoke to her, and she'd looked me up with an offer to carry some pieces at the KC gallery. First, however, she had to persuade Marzetti that I was good enough to hang next to artists he'd hand-picked throughout the country. But true to her word, and despite his objections, Lily soon had my work displayed.

It had taken nearly a year for the first piece to sell, a year during which she'd often been forced to defend me to an uncooperative Marzetti. After that first sale, she declared herself my official patroness, and set her mind to convincing her lover to give me an exclusive exhibition. She'd been tenacious, and gradually managed to work more and more of my paintings into the gallery. The sales over the last two years finally convinced Marzetti to take the chance, and the exhibition date was set for next February.

During this time, I saw Lily with increasing frequency. In the beginning, she would stop by the apartment once or twice a year when she was in town visiting her family. Later, it was every two months. Now, it was once a month, and she made her reason for visiting blatantly obvious.

Lillian Reston, the shapely blonde mistress of a suspected KC mobster, was determined to seduce me.

In her early forties, Lily had used her relationship with Matthew Marzetti to lift, tuck, and modify an already attractive face and body to one of singular beauty. She was a stunning creature who used her feminine wiles to get what she wanted—at least, the majority of the time.

Flattered by her attention? I wouldn't deny it. But crazy, I'm not.

Chuck Stinnet, one time friend and late admirer of the beautiful Lily, had informed me of her lover's uncontrollable jealous rages, ones that left previous paramours in the hospital with various broken bones and disfigurement. An excellent reason to keep my mind trained on painting and not on the woman sponsoring me.

I groaned when the key turned too easily. In my haste to get to the hospital, I'd left the door unlocked, which meant Lily was inside. After the morning I'd had, fighting off her subtle advances was not something I looked forward to.

There was a heavy scent of cologne wafting out of the apartment as I opened the door. I didn't recognize the fragrance, but knew from its thickness in the air, she'd set the stage. Seduction rather than art was on her mind, and I braced myself against the inevitable.

Trying not to gag on the over-sprayed scent, I left the door open and raised the window on the screen door. Hoping to create a sufficient cross draft to clear the air more quickly, I rushed over to the bank of windows opposite and opened a couple of them as well.

The noise should have roused her from wherever she was hiding, but there was no sign of her. It was too good to believe she might have given up and gone down to the bakery to kill some time, but I crossed my fingers nonetheless. Shrugging, thankful for even a momentary respite, I yanked off my windbreaker and tossed it onto the couch.

Sunlight poured in through the skylight, bathing the entire studio in a dazzling, brilliant light. A prepared canvas sat on the easel directly beneath the skylight, its vast emptiness calling out to me. I already knew what I wanted to paint; I'd seen the preliminary sketch just that morning.

I grabbed up the drawing pad from where it still lay on the coffee table and took it with me into the studio. Slowly flipping through the pages, I again caught my breath at the sight of Jenny's small figure gracing the otherwise flat, lifeless sketches. I took time to study the detail of the drawings, the quick lines and shadings suggesting they'd been done hastily and not with as much care as the initial viewing suggested. Still, there was enough to show the thought—conscious or unconscious?—that had gone into the girl's placement in each drawing, positioning her to make the most of her presence, designed specifically to add more charm to each of the scenes.

The view from the bluffs near Omaha was my objective. I remembered the day clearly, the azure sky, the whisper of wind in trees and tall grasses covering the hillsides, the mournful lowing of cows far below in the valley, and the majestic grace of a hawk as it glided though the sky high above me. I'd been alone but for the hawk and sounds that echoed through the bluffs. Alone, but not lonely.

My company had been in the form of visions my senses created to go along with sights and sounds. I'd sat upon the crest, looking into the valley, sketch pad propped firmly on my knees as my hand wielded the drawing pencil, seemingly of its own accord. Little conscious thought attributed to what ended up on paper. I'd taken what was absorbed by my senses and transferred it to the sheet before me.

I gazed almost longingly at the sketch, at the small form of Jenny, my imagination attempting to place her next to me that day. Closing my eyes, I felt the childlike hand catch hold of mine, her head light on my shoulder, the chestnut hair blowing across both our faces.

In the vision, she turned to me, a knowing smile touching her lovely mouth as I bent my head toward hers. Her breath was warm upon my cheek, her tender young body yielding against mine, her arms pulling me down to her as we lay back upon the grass.

"Wherever you are, take me with you."

My eyes flew open, and I jumped nearly a foot at the sound of Lillian Reston's rather husky voice. I stared at her, dumbfounded, so lost in my vision it took a while to regain my composure. Lily took advantage of the moment, crossing the remaining space between us, and coming to stand next to me at the parson's table.

"What are you working on that could produce such a remarkable trance?"

I snapped the sketch pad closed, drew in a deep breath, and proceeded to cough uncontrollably from inhaling too much of Lily's overdone cologne. She patted me on the back and, after helping me into the desk chair, went to the kitchen to get a glass of water.

"You had the most rapturous expression on your face just now, darling, I just hated to interrupt."

Then why did you? I thought nastily. "A sudden inspiration." I gasped out to her.

"It must certainly be something wonderful. I can't wait to see it."

As she came back across the living room, water glass in hand, I noticed her general state of undress.

Dressed in a hot pink teddy, her large, enhanced breasts barely covered by the sheer fabric, Lily approached, moving her hips seductively as she neared me. Her blonde hair, straight from a bottle, was piled atop her head, small ringlets strategically placed on either side of the perfect oval face.

She'd opted for a deeper blue contact lens today, making her eyes appear almost black. Mauve eye shadow, a soft peach blush, and delicate rose lipstick added to the already pink and white perfection of her skin tones. Her long, shapely legs were bare, her feet encased in high-heeled slippers the same shade as the teddy. She was thin, but well-proportioned, her height and poise reminiscent of a model.

I took the glass from her hand, moving my head back slightly to avoid coming into contact with her breasts as she leaned toward me.

"Thanks." I croaked, moaning inwardly. Today she meant business.

Lily pushed the supplies from the edge of the table and seated herself upon it. She gracefully crossed her long legs, and tucking them slightly beneath the table for support, once again leaned toward me, her left breast nearly springing free from the narrow piece of material attempting to cover it.

"Want to share that inspiration, darling?"

No, I did not. What I wanted was to put a stop to this once and for all.

"You know we can't do this, Lily." I took one of her hands and pulled her up from the table and out of the studio, pushing her in the direction of the hallway.

"Can't or won't?" She pouted. Her dark eyes swept across my body as she licked her lips. "I believe you could, Richard. As a matter of fact-"

I grabbed her hands before they reached her objective and pushed at her angrily, wondering for the thousandth time why I'd continued putting up with her advances.

The answer was simple: no one else had believed in me enough to give me such opportunities. Was it worth her seduction attempts, or was this yet another example of selling myself short?

"Ah, Richard, why must you always spoil things? I thought with Tara out of the way you and I might—"

"What about Marzetti?" I drew away from her, my benefactress leering at me as I did so.

"Oh, posh! He'd never know." She sidled up to me, placing her arms about my neck. "You know you'd like to."

"That's where you're wrong." I removed her hands, backed away, and frowned. "You've gone too far, Lily. This has to stop."

Again she pouted. "I wish you'd stop insisting on being such a gentleman!" Her husky voice became even thicker as she came toward me. "Come on, Richard. Live a little."

I turned on my heel and was on the far side of the living room before she could make another move. None of her previous efforts in seduction had been this extreme. I never expected her to go this far and thanked God for the strength to resist her.

Cloaking myself in a mixture of anger and righteous indignation, I took a deep breath and turned to find she was slowly making her way across the room. I started to say something when both of us jumped at the sound of another voice.

Chuck Stinnet stood gazing through the open screen door, a look of amusement etched across his face as he regarded the scene before him.

"I didn't mean to interrupt anything, as I plainly see I have. Perhaps I should go—"

"Don't you dare!"

Lily flashed me a dangerous look, freezing me where I stood. She grabbed my windbreaker from the couch and tugged it over the sexy teddy. With her head thrown back haughtily and her back straight, she strode past the open door and down the hall toward the bedroom. The moment she was out of sight, I motioned for Chuck to come in.

"Was I in time, or did the lethal seductress have her way with you?" His lopsided grin made me burst into nervous laughter.

"You were in time, thank God. I think she was about to rape me."

He gave me a swift examination. "I'd say you were seconds away from earning a readjustment on your nose, arms, and, perhaps, more important equipment. If Marzetti ever catches wind of this—"

"And who's going to tell him, Chuckles? You?" Lily entered the kitchen quietly, buttoning the front of a pale pink silk blouse. "Ever hear the one about killing the messenger?"

"Messenger? Me you mean? Ah, Lily, darling, you wound me deeply. I'd never tell. I like Richard far too much to see him squashed into a pulpy mass of unidentifiable flesh." Stinnet laughed heartily. "And if you want to keep your little game here a secret, you shouldn't run around half naked in front of open doors."

Lily's face and neck turned an ugly shade of red. Instead of fastening the belt on her slacks, she yanked it off and dangled it like a whip in her hand. She snapped it back and forth across the floor, her blue eyes almost black as they bore into Chuck.

Chuck continued to regard her in amusement, and I could tell from the gleam in his eyes that he enjoyed baiting her. I also knew him well enough to know that without interference, he was bound to continue.

"Lily." I spoke her name softly, but with as much command as I could.

She took her eyes from Chuck, her flushed cheeks still fiery. She glared at me, then lowered her eyes in resignation and, perhaps, some embarrassment. Without a glance at Chuck, she spun on her heel and sauntered back down the hallway. When I heard the bathroom door close, I heaved a sigh of relief and collapsed upon a corner of the couch.

"That was close."

"Think she would've hit me?" Stinnet remained standing, looking in the direction she'd gone.

I shook my head. "She's not the violent type."

"A lot you know." He gave a small laugh as he sat in a chair opposite me. "When we were going together, many eons ago, she got so ticked off, I ended up with a black eye. Don't underestimate her, Richard. I wouldn't put it past her to tell Marzetti that *you* seduced *her*!"

I eyed him speculatively. I knew a little about their stormy relationship. Lily was a senior in high school when they met; Chuck was attending the university. He'd said there was something about Lily Reston that not only held his interest but held it long enough for them to become engaged. The engagement lasted nearly two years when something, or someone, came between them. Neither of them would talk about it, rarely even spoke to the other if it could be avoided. The only reason I knew this much about their past was because the day Chuck warned me about Lily, he'd been drinking to such excess, the story just slipped out.

Hoping to steer the conversation onto safer ground, I asked what brought him by.

Chuck raised a bushy eyebrow, the corner of his mouth forming something close to a sneer. "You name the source, they have the scoop of what happened to Tara last night. KRTV had an interview with Nagoochi first thing this morning. The little freak is accusing you."

"Damn!" I'd been right to avoid the man at the hospital. "That all?"

"All?" He raised an expressive brow. "So far the media hasn't much to say, just the report of an attack which is being investigated. I guess there's a crackdown by the city council, and the cops are cooperating. With the university, and summer tourism right around the corner, Linden doesn't want any bad publicity. I expect them to put this to bed as quickly as possible."

"You'd think by now the city would realize you can't just sweep something like this under the rug." Fully dressed, and completely composed, Lily joined us. She sat on the far end of the sofa, flinging a canvas tote on the floor at her feet. She regarded Chuck intently, the look they exchanged making me feel totally left out.

"They did it before, sweetie, they'll do it again." Chuck said. "This time, however, they can't shrink the park. I don't think the townies will go for that."

"After just one incident, no." Lily leaned back against the couch, crossing her long legs. "But what if this isn't an isolated incident? What happens," her voice lowered to a near whisper, the words containing a slight shudder. "What if *he's* back?"

"Excuse me." I cleared my throat to gain their attention. "But as the prime suspect in this case, I'd like to know what the devil you're talking about."

"Prime sus—yeah, even without Nagoochi's nasty insinuations on the air, I suppose you would be. And after that scene in the Snack Shack yesterday—Good God, Richard, you've got yourself some major trouble."

"Trouble? And what scene in the Snack Shack?" Lily glared at the two of us. "Talk about being in the dark! I think you've some explaining to do, Richard Tanner. If you've done something to jeopardize the exhibition, I need to know about it now."

Against my wishes, or better judgment, I gave a synopsized version of the disagreement between Tara and myself the day before. While Lily's full attention was on me, I saw Chuck giving her the once-over, an approving gleam in his eyes. As I finished up the story with Hargrave's visit that morning and the run-in we'd had later in the park, Chuck's interest returned to me, a brooding expression settling upon his countenance.

"Sounds like this guy's taken an instant dislike to you, old buddy. I wonder why?"

"That's obvious. He's a jerk." Lily summed it up nicely. Despite my agreement regarding the detective's character, there was little comfort in sharing the same opinion.

While Stinnet continued to stare off into space ignoring the two of us, Lily attempted to assure me everything would be fine once Tara regained consciousness. Something was taken from that reassurance, however, when she asked if I thought it possible Tara would accuse me of the attack out of spite. I tried to shake off the suspicion, not admitting the thought had crossed my mind once or twice throughout the morning.

Chuck suddenly jumped up and went to stand over Lily. She gazed up at him, annoyed.

"What?" She demanded.

"Hargrave. Doesn't that name ring a bell?" He stared down at her.

"Think, damn it, Lily!"

In a quite unsophisticated move, Lillian Reston stuck her tongue out at him. The demand he made of her, though, appeared to be working. Her dark eyes seemed to glaze over for a moment, her face becoming deadly serious. A light appeared to go on, and with a grimace, she met Stinnet's eyes.

"It's him, isn't it? The same as the last time." Something akin to a moan issued forth as she turned her ominous gaze on me. "You do have a good alibi for last evening, don't you, Richard? Something that can be substantiated in case, I mean, should anything happen and Tara doesn't come out of that coma?"

I looked from one to the other of them. "You're hiding something, and I'd like to know what it is."

"Fine, fine. But first, how about answering the lady's question?"

I shook my head in frustration. First Hargrave, now two of my friends. I didn't want to think what might happen next.

"You know how I felt when we left the park yesterday. After my visit with the Drakes, I thought I might collapse in the street. Luckily, I didn't. I made it home, picked up some bread at the bakery, discovered Tara had been by harassing the Weishers, and came up here to find she'd left me a note. She wanted her stuff, so I packed up the lot of it—"

"Ah, that explains the bag on the porch." Stinnet laughed. "Nice touch, Rich. Bet Hargrave liked it, too."

"He wasn't particularly amused, no." I swallowed hard as I recalled this morning's interview. "Anyway, after I finished gathering her junk, I took some medicine and crashed on the couch. Next thing I know, it's morning and all hell's broken loose. I've gone from a merely eccentric would-be artist to suspect number one in the beating of my ex-girlfriend. Not exactly a jump up the ladder of fame and success."

"And Hargrave knows all about the argument in the Snack Shack?" Lily leaned toward me, no thought of seduction on her mind now. She regarded me anxiously, as though she expected me to be grabbed suddenly by the detective and locked up.

"Nagoochi told him. But it wasn't the only reason he was on my trail."

"There's more?" Stinnet said, his voice dripping with sarcasm. "This just gets better and better."

I shot him a look that sent him quietly back to his chair.

"Seems Tara had decided that no matter what I thought about the idea, she was going to come retrieve her stuff. She told Nagoochi her intentions and said she'd be back in an hour. When she didn't show up, he called here looking for her."

"And you had your damned machine on, right?" Lily made a face. She hated leaving messages on answering machines, and invariably told me so before every message.

"Right. And by that time, I was out and didn't hear a thing." I rubbed at a spot on my jeans. "According to Hargrave, Nagoochi waited a while longer, then went out to look for Tara. He was the one who found her in the park."

Lily's eyes met mine then hastily turned away. "Where?" She asked softly.

"He didn't tell me at the time, but when I was passing through on my way home from the hospital I found out quickly enough. It's that small enclosed area there on the west side. The one they call the lover's quarter."

Stinnet nodded. "Nice secluded area. Probably the most private. Not too many lights over there, and far enough away from the gazebo and playground that no one would hear unless she'd let out a hell of a scream. My guess is she was bushwhacked and didn't even know what hit her."

Now it was Lily's turn to nod. "Sounds like the same M.O." Though she turned back to me, I noticed she avoided meeting my eyes. "Was she, er, was she r-raped?"

"I talked with Dr. Noland at the hospital, and that wasn't among the list of things she reported." I stared at them suspiciously. From the looks they kept exchanging, it became increasingly obvious they had something in mind, and I didn't like the thought of remaining in the dark.

"You think she would tell you? Just like that?"

"Cut it out, Lily! Joyce Noland's his doctor."

"Oh. Sorry. Well then, that's different."

"Unless," Chuck Stinnet steepled his fingers and regarded me over the tops of them. "Rich, I want you to be honest with us—whatever you say, it stays right here between the three of us." Lily nodded in agreement while I squirmed uncomfortably under their gazes.

"These migraines you've been having lately, they can get pretty severe sometimes. So severe, in fact, that the pain or whatever seems to shut things out. Makes you go blank at times."

"What the hell—" I jumped off the corner of the couch and began pacing restlessly.

"Now, Richard, give me a moment, all right? I'm not trying to do anything more than a little damage control." Stinnet came over to where I was pacing and stopped the action by placing a hand on either shoulder. "It hasn't happened often, and when it has, it's been of little consequence. Except, perhaps, yesterday afternoon in the Snack Shack."

"So I blocked some of it out. When I got thinking about it later, it all came back quite clearly. Too clearly." I said evenly. "What's your point?"

I'd spoken harshly because I already knew the answer. It was one I'd wrestled with earlier after Hargrave's departure.

"Is it possible that you blacked out, consciously at least, and—"

"How the hell can you even suggest that?" Lily was on her feet and pulling Chuck around to face her. "Richard's got to be the most gentle, considerate man I know. Completely and entirely incapable of doing something so horrible. Besides, I thought we'd already agreed that it was most likely the Stalker."

Chuck visibly winced at the last statement. Again I looked from one to the other of them, confused, and demanding to be told what they were talking about.

"First of all, I guarantee that I didn't beat Tara or anyone else last night. I can't believe you'd even think it of me. Now, before this little tête-à-tête goes any further, I want to know what all these secret looks, innuendo, and "Stalker" business is about."

They parted, each going to a different section of the room. For a time, neither spoke or looked at the other. Then, with a nod from Lily, Chuck took a deep breath and started speaking in his best lecturer's voice.

"You're not from around here. Oh, I know you used to visit with the Drakes for several summers when you were a kid—how old are you anyway?"

I told him, and he nodded.

"Thirty, and the last time you were in Linden you were what, nine, ten? Too young to know what was going on." He leaned back against the area of the parson's table Lily had cleared earlier and folded his arms across his chest. "About twenty-two, twenty-three years ago, there was some maniac attacking young women in and around University Park. At the time, it bordered the university separating it from the rest of the community. It was maybe fifteen, twenty acres of wild, untamed land right on the edge of town. It was a kind of nature park, lots of trees, a brook, a pond we used to take small rafts on to fish, and lots and lots of trails."

"I remember playing in the park. Professor Drake and I built a treehouse back in the woods one summer. It was a great place for a kid to ramble. But what has this got to do with—"

"Everything. The mayor's daughter was the first of the girls attacked. Raped, beaten, a horrible thing. They'd already started talking about rezoning, but there were a lot of hold-outs—until about six months later when Missy Gordon was found barely alive. She was a senior at the university, a bright, beautiful girl, and very popular." Chuck closed his eyes and sighed. "The guy did a real number on Missy. She never fully recovered, brain-damaged from the blow to her head. It wasn't long afterward when heavy machinery was brought in and they began clearing out the trees."

"We were terrified." Lily added. "They put all the kids on a curfew, and even the adults were told to avoid the park after dusk. It was like something out of a movie."

"University students, of which I was one, were forbidden to leave the campus after five in the evening without express permission. Linden was locked up tight. But it didn't make much difference. Neither did the lack of progress in the redesign of the park.

"Two assaults like that in six months might not seem bad by city standards, but in a place like Linden—it was as though Hell had opened up for business in this quiet community. When we'd go into town, the university students I mean, the people would glare at us. You could tell what they were thinking, that it had to be someone from the school, not one of their own. It gave me the willies."

Lily agreed. "And for people like me who were dating a uni, we were treated as if we'd betrayed the rest of the town. My parents always liked Chuck, but after Missy, they totally changed."

"You're right," I said, amazed by the story. "I'd no idea about any of this. How long did it last?"

"That's kind of hard to say. There was another assault over in Oxford a couple months after Missy. A few months later, one in some town near St. Joe. But between Missy Gordon and Hilary Brockton there were almost eight months." Chuck shuddered. "By this time, the maniac was being referred to as the Linden Stalker by the media. Not exactly the way the university or city council wanted people to think of the community." He smirked. "Things were rough, enrollment went down in the two years since the first assault, and as publicity grew, and more places in the hundred mile radius were reporting similar assaults, the fear increased. Since it all seemed to have started here in Linden, the name stuck." He paused for a moment, gazing out across the room but obviously not seeing it. "Everyone thought Missy was bad, but I understand he left Hilary considerably worse. They saved her life only for her to take it a few months later. That would have been twenty years ago."

"Twenty-one this month." Lily said softly. "Hilary was not only a friend, but a cousin. I think her attack and death was what spurred the council into action. That was the summer when the rezoning around the park was completed and the new businesses and houses started construction. They put up the gazebo, ordered in the playground equipment, thinned out the trees and shrubs, and put in the lamps. By fall, it was a completely different place."

"So your cousin was the last?"

Lily and Chuck exchanged a long look.

"In Linden, yes. I'm not sure about other places."

"There were rumors about one incident here," Lily ignored Chuck's warning glance. "But there was never any substantiation."

"That case was totally different." He argued, throwing her a stern look.

"Not totally. The victim was male, true, but he had been beaten, and it happened in the park. There was just never any, I mean, it never came out whether or not rape had been involved." Lily turned her back on us, her face suddenly a bright red.

I watched Chuck as he fidgeted at the parson's table, absently picking up items and setting them back down. As I looked from one to the other of them, a strange tingling started up the base of my spine till it gripped me hard at the nape of my neck.

"Just when did this last attack take place?" I croaked, my voice oddly restricted.

Lily turned slightly to exchange a brief glance with Chuck, then walked into the kitchen.

There was an unnatural stillness in the air, a thickening of ozone or an invisible fog. The silence was suddenly broken by the sound of water running in the sink and the soft crunch of the carpet beneath Chuck's loafers as he walked over to me.

Even before I saw his face, before a word was spoken, I knew the answer to my question. And with this knowledge, over twenty years of wondering, twenty years of my parents' concerned and frightened faces flashed before my eyes.

As another migraine began its ascent up the back of my neck to pry its way into my brain, I met Chuck Stinnet's eyes with assurance.

"July 1, 1970." My voice was almost a whisper.

We stared at one another without blinking, the silence of the apartment once again settling around us. Neither of us moved, not even a facial twinge.

Lily's voice at the edge of the kitchen broke the spell, and I grasped onto a nearby chair to keep myself from falling as she confirmed my statement.

"It was you, Richard. You were the last."

Chapter 6

It had been a morning of revelations, and as I listened to Chuck Stinnet's quick explanation, my mind raced ahead forming my own deductions and conclusions.

"At first, the papers simply reported that a juvenile had been found unconscious in University Park. There were no names, no details, nothing to actually connect this incident with the others."

Lily nodded her agreement. "Not even the sex of the child was revealed. It was as though someone had put a security blanket around the incident and zipped it up tight."

I eased myself into the chair I'd been holding onto. "What happened to cause the information to finally come out?"

"Hargrave." The two said in unison.

With a glance, Lily deferred to Stinnet, and he continued. "He decided there had to be a connection, which ultimately led the media to you. Even then the report went something like "ten year old Richie Tanner was found unconscious in University Park." The Drakes were mentioned, of course, but that was it. Reporters tried to interview them, the hospital staff, and your parents, but the lid was tightly sealed. You were a nine days' wonder, Rich." Chuck gave me a reassuring grin. "No gory details to come back to haunt you. But from what you've told me, they might have been a bit more comforting than the speculation and innuendo that you were one of the Stalker's victims."

"Nothing more?" My voice sounded hollow, far away, and completely detached from my body.

"You were just a little kid," Lily offered. "I imagine they were doing their best to protect you."

"And since you were a child, a male one at that, their concern was fully justified. As far as I know, there was never anything to connect what happened to you to the other incidents. I've no idea if I'm right, of course. My guess is Hargrave saw an opportunity to advance his career by connecting your case with the Stalker."

"What *is* this?"

Three pairs of eyes flew to the open doorway and watched as Janet Drake yanked open the screen door and practically launched into the room. Her voice was uncharacteristically harsh, and the accompanying look of shock and surprise were not just a trick of nature and her oddly arched brows.

"I-I couldn't help overhearing the comment about the Stalker." She gave a tentative smile of apology to me, then turned her gaze on Chuck. "Whatever made you bring up that old subject—especially in front of Richard?"

I could tell from the tremor of her voice that she was reliving the horror of what happened to me that night nearly twenty-one years ago. I'd been under her care, her responsibility, and somehow it had gone wrong, and I'd been injured. Janet felt the burden of this far more than anyone, feeling she'd betrayed my parents by allowing the incident to occur. Over the years, I'd often observed her reaction of fear and confusion when the subject was broached. She'd look at me with a mixture of sympathy and apology, assuring me that if the good Lord wanted me to remember what transpired that night, I would.

She'd been the only one to ever say that, the only one who said if I felt the need to discuss the incident, I could feel free to do so with her. Her offer made me feel better about things, about the silence I received from all other quarters, but I quickly realized it had been made from a sense of guilt, the subject causing her as much pain as it did everyone else.

"—related to what happened last night to Tara Morgan."

I came out of my trance in time to hear the last of Chuck's explanation. Janet nodded at him, her face calmer, body no longer tensed. The hesitant smile was replaced by a real one as she turned to greet Lily, taking the other woman into her arms for a brief hug.

"We don't see enough of you, dear. That gallery of yours keeping you busy?"

"That and other things." Lily flashed me a sly grin. "Came up to make certain Richard's staying on task. We've got big plans for this young man."

"Let's hope this incident with Tara doesn't delay them." Chuck's dry remark was answered by a sharp glance from both Lily and Janet.

"Nonsense. And that's just what I told that know-it-all detective when he came by the house this morning." Janet wrinkled her nose in distaste, her arched eyebrows creased in a single line across her forehead as she frowned. "He's reaching at straws, and he knows it. Whether the girl sufficiently recovers or not, he hasn't a shred of evidence to pin on Richard."

I went to Janet and, placing an arm about her narrow shoulders, gave her a gentle squeeze. "Thanks for the vote of confidence. No, I mean it," I patted her arm as I released her. "Hargrave is only doing his job, and right now, I'm afraid that means looking at me as a suspect. I don't like it but have to live with it until Tara regains consciousness and proves my innocence."

Janet's eyes narrowed and her voice again held a slight tremor. "And that's possible? She—she's going to be all right?"

I shared the information Dr. Noland supplied, and as Janet questioned me at different times regarding Tara's condition and my alibi for the previous evening, Chuck and Lily slowly gravitated toward the door. At a break in the conversation, Lily said she'd call me later, Chuck flashed me a grin and the peace sign, took Lily's elbow, and they left together. It was a strange sight, knowing how they felt about one another, and I couldn't help but laugh. The laugh worked like a tonic for Janet. The look of concern was erased, replaced by a smile extending from ear to ear.

"That's what I like to see and hear." A thin, long-fingered hand reached to my forehead and brushed back a lock of unruly hair. "You've such a beautiful smile, dear. It lights up your dark eyes making the tiny glints of amber dance about." She ran a hand down my cheek. "Always such a handsome child, so full of promise." She gave an embarrassed laugh as she quickly withdrew her hand. Her lashes fluttered coyly, and she looked down at her hands now clasped tightly in her lap.

"I-I got carried away. It's just, well," she met my gaze and grinned. "You were like my child, too. The one I never had, yet better." She cleared her throat and brushed at the spotless white cotton skirt she wore.

It was an awkward moment and one of rare insight for me. I'd always known how fond Janet and Edmund Drake were of my family, never doubted the connection between us. Yet, while Edmund often referred to me as his foster son, I saw my relationship to Janet more as a favored nephew. This sudden revelation and tenderness, while completely in character for someone like Janet, was far beyond anything I'd expected. As she regarded me with love, tears glistening in the corners of her eyes, thin mouth tremulous, I suddenly realized the extent her devotion ran.

I covered her hands with mine, stilling the involuntary quaking. She met my eyes, a corner of her mouth lifting slightly.

"I imagine you think me a sentimental old fool. But, no matter. I am what I am, I suppose." She withdrew her hands, patting one of mine matter-of-factly. "Now, on to the business at hand. Your mother phoned shortly after you left last evening, requesting I accompany her on her cruise. I was hesitant at first, knowing Edmund couldn't go as well, but you know how persuasive he and Annie can be. I agreed to go, but now all of this has occurred, I feel—"

"No," I protested. "You should go."

"Richard—"

"I mean it. There's no reason to cancel your plans. Or for mother to know what's going on." I gave her a meaningful glance. "Things will work out. Tara will recover, Hargrave will end up with egg on his face, and life will go on as it should."

"You seem very sure about that." Her tone matched her doubtful expression.

"I'm innocent, so why shouldn't I be?"

A shrug of the shoulders as she rose from the couch signaled I'd failed to reassure her.

"What if, what if Tara can't identify her attacker, Richard? Suppose she didn't see him, that all she can see is her anger toward you?"

"I won't say the thought hasn't crossed my mind. And yes, the idea scares the heck out of me. But the fact remains that I didn't do it. We just have to hope the system of innocent until proven guilty actually works."

She seemed suddenly distracted. When next she spoke, she regaled me with her and my mother's plans, her almost black eyes suddenly alight with the prospect of the trip before her. It seemed my mother had procured two tickets for everything long before asking for Janet's companionship. I guessed Edmund made the suggestion, probably insisting mother wait until the last minute to speak with Janet so she would be less likely to refuse. I'd seen this happen before with plans made for the women by Edmund or my father, and while I didn't approve of the method, it appeared to work for them.

The two would fly to New York the day after tomorrow where they would board a ship bound for London. Plans included a motor tour of England and Scotland, a jaunt to Ireland, and a week in Paris. They would be gone for a minimum of six weeks with the return trip by air not yet determined.

"We'll miss your opening at the Arts Festival, though. Do you mind awfully?"

I assured her I didn't, reminding her the exhibition was for the entire month of July.

"You just go and enjoy yourselves."

Janet nodded, apparently satisfied. As we walked to the door, she took hold of my arm, exerting a gentle pressure upon it.

Without looking at me, her voice barely above a whisper, she said, "That talk earlier about the Stalker, did they say anything about—about you?"

The opening I'd been waiting for? I hoped so.

"They said Hargrave believed I was one of his victims." I turned Janet to face me as she solemnly nodded.

"He tried to convince us to let him… for the hospital, to—to—" She shuddered. "When Edmund found you, he thought you were dead. He was so frightened, terrified to move you. He covered you with his shirt and ran all the way back home to phone for the ambulance.

"You can imagine what I thought when he came into the house half naked, hair matted down from the rain, eyes wild. He was nearly incoherent. Can you picture that, Edmund Drake incoherent? But he was." She reached out to the door jamb for support.

"I'd no idea what was happening, just that he'd returned without you and was mad with worry. He didn't stop for explanations, just made the call and dashed right back out of the house. I knew I had to follow him. I mean, he hadn't even grabbed a raincoat off the hall tree. I quickly put one on, got his and ran after him."

Janet's face contorted into a look of pain and anguish. While part of me wanted to recall her from the memories of the past, a larger part was urging her to continue, to break the silence after all these years.

She closed her eyes, her voice rasping as breathing became more difficult. "It wasn't hard to find him. He was there in the center of the park, next to the new foundation, standing straight and tall like a giant oak buffeted by the storm. When I got to him, he grabbed the coat from my hands, but rather than putting it on, started to lay it on the ground." Janet opened her eyes and stared at me. "You were lying there at his feet, so still, so horribly still, Edmund's soaked shirt all that covered you against the storm."

"All?" I asked confused.

She nodded slowly. "You were, were—" She took in a deep breath. "He couldn't leave you like that, so he took off his shirt even though it was already soaked through. When he put the Mac over you, he looked up at me so frightened, I thought I would die. He said you must never know, that it had to be kept a secret. That it was our fault." Janet put a hand to her lips, violently shaking her head. "I shouldn't have told!" She cried. "I never meant to. But all the talk about that—that Stalker, how you were found... I thought it was best you have the truth." Her eyes appealed to me for understanding.

Be careful what you ask for...

The words rang in my mind, bouncing off the sides of a brain deep within the grips of a killer migraine. I may have stood as still as a stone statue, but I felt as fragile as a piece of fine porcelain balanced precariously on a ledge, about to fall and shatter into a thousand pieces.

A coldness on my bare arm and fingers like talons kneading my skin made me jump back in sudden terror. There was a roaring in my ears and darkness closed in around me, a thick, impenetrable blackness that threatened to devour me. I felt myself teeter on the brink of collapse into the nightmare world into which I'd been thrust.

I was forced onto a chair, my head shoved between knees too weak to have held my weight any longer. As my vision cleared, the brightness of the room gradually coming back into perspective, Janet's voice sounded above the tinnitus, a lifeline which I grasped and clung to.

"You always wanted to know, begged us to tell you. It was understandable, yes, but how could we tell, explain to a child the horror? It was better forgotten, left buried in your subconscious. You never seemed to suffer for it—I mean, we watched, all of us, for signs that what that...that monster had done to you wasn't somehow carried over into your life." Janet stroked my cheeks, my forehead, her hands cool and tender. "You matured just as we all thought you would, fulfilling the bright promise you had as a child. Handsome, strong, full of love, life and good humor. No dark side to haunt you, to be concerned about or fear. And, all man. I think that was a major concern, that the r-ra...the way he, er, used you, that you would, well, somehow not be whole."

Janet Drake cupped my face in her strong hands, raising my head to meet her steady gaze.

"You're a good man, Richard. Talented in so many ways, sweet and gentle. Forget what you've discovered here today, don't dwell on it or try to force memories to actually return. Take this information and file it away, determine not to allow it to make a difference to who you are."

"How?" I croaked through a parched throat. "How can I do that?"

She took me by the shoulders and shook me hard. "Because you can, because you're strong, stronger than a nightmare, and that's all these words are to you. A nightmare, a horrible dream that happened to a child long gone. You've gone all these years not knowing—"

"But wanting to know."

"Not knowing and growing resilient and healthy in spite of it all. I wouldn't have told you now if it hadn't been for Lily and Chuck Stinnet frightening you like that. I still wouldn't have said anything, but I got to thinking that sooner or later that detective is bound to make the connection. And when he does, I didn't want you learning about it from him so he could try to use it against you in some way." She drew herself up straight, patted her hair carefully into place, and gave me a weak smile.

"You mustn't say anything to Edmund or your mother, dear. They would be horrified to know I told you, that you even had an inkling of what transpired that night. If you feel the need to talk about it, write your thoughts down and we'll discuss it when I return. All right?"

Still stunned, I nodded absently as Dr. Noland's face flitted across my mind. I knew she'd be interested in what I'd learned, yet I discarded the idea almost as quickly as I'd thought it. After all, Joyce Noland was searching for my memories, and thankfully, I had none to share.

I glanced to where Janet was fussing over something lying next to the door. She bent down, talking what sounded unintelligible gibberish to my ears. While the roaring gradually subsided, there continued a rush of sound, a rising and falling similar to that created by covering your ears and quickly taking your hands on and off them.

My olfactory sense returned with a suddenness that would have sent me reeling had I not been seated. I experienced an assault to my nostrils, Lily's cologne and the bakery smells mixing unpleasantly, causing my already shaky stomach to jerk spasmodically. I closed my eyes, an attempt to cease the rolling and threatened nausea, counted to ten slowly, then reopened them.

Janet had risen and was holding the jacket I'd discarded that morning after Hargrave left. She lifted the garment gingerly, fingering the strips of torn material as though she'd never seen such a thing before.

"What—"

"I'll take that."

I didn't even bother to look up to acknowledge the voice that came through the open screen. Janet Drake, however, started, her dark eyes round as saucers as she clutched the jacket protectively against her chest.

Without invitation, Hargrave entered the apartment with a confident swagger and dropped a folded paper onto my lap. Licking numbed lips, I picked up the search warrant and struggled to regain my composure as I stood and smiled ruefully at Janet.

"You might as well give it to him." I told her. Then to the detective, "I assume that's all you've come for."

"That's a fact. Nice to see you've still got the item, Richard. Mrs. Drake?" He held out his hand for the coat only to have Janet take a firmer hold on the article.

"I would like to know what's going on here, Detective. What purpose have you in confiscating this jacket?" Her eyes narrowed, back straightened, and she threw her head confidently back. "Are you harassing this young man?"

Hargrave threw me a nasty look over his shoulder. "No, ma-am, just trying to collect some evidence. If you'd release it, please."

I was in no mood for the situation to go further. With a wish they'd both go and leave me with my thoughts, I yanked the jacket out of Janet's hands and thrust it and the warrant into the detective's. Both individuals stared at me, startled, Janet still expecting an explanation, Hargrave giving me an appraising look. Behind us, the telephone rang once, the burr of the answering machine kicked in, and the tinny whine of the tape could be heard in the awkward silence that ensued.

Hargrave's head nodded toward the desk on the far side of the room, a corner of his mouth quirked up. "You've a bad habit there, Tanner."

"Perhaps. But it's really none of your business, is it?" I met his gaze evenly. Inside, I felt less solid than a bowl of Jell-O, but I wasn't about to let him see it.

He raised a bushy eyebrow. "S'pose you're right. At any rate, I've got what I came for."

As he turned to go, Janet caught hold of his coat sleeve and tugged hard enough to jerk the man sharply backward. He glowered at her but held his tongue.

"Ma-am?"

"I would like to know what this is all about. Mr. Tanner is one of my husband's faculty, and I feel, as such, we have the right to know."

Someone who didn't know her wouldn't recognize the edge to her voice or the tic in the right cheekbone that signified distress. After our recent discussion, Janet, too, was having considerable difficulty reining in her emotions, perhaps feeling as raw and exposed as I did.

Hargrave gave me a quick glance, then as a smile bordering on a leer spread across his thin lips, he said, "Mr. Tanner is currently being considered the prime suspect in the assault on-"

"That's utterly preposterous!"

"Miss Tara Morgan," he continued. "The search warrant was for the confiscation of this jacket here, as I'm sure you've deduced. It's going to our forensics experts to see if it matches the fibers found beneath Miss Morgan's nails. If there's a match, as I suspect there will be, I'll be returning with a warrant for the arrest of Mr. Tanner." He inclined his head in my direction. "My warning from this morning still stands, Richard. Don't leave town." He gave a slight bow to Janet, then turned on his heel and walked out the door. The screen had only just slammed into place when his face came back to the window.

"And I strongly suggest that you unhook that damned answering machine of yours. As I said before, man, it's a bad habit."

Chapter 7

Bad habit or not, less than two hours after I switched off the answering machine, it was on once again. Though it was nice to find I had so many concerned friends, relating the little I knew about Tara's assault over and over was exhausting. The comfort of reassurances not withstanding, if anyone else wanted information, they'd be forced to get it from the media.

In the end, it was thoughts of my mother, not Hargrave's suggestion, that led me to shut off the machine. Still caught up in the shock and horror of the incident, I hadn't considered the speed such news would travel, or how upset Mother would be if she couldn't reach me. I wanted to call her but was reluctant to do so while Janet hovered at my elbow.

Janet looked as though she was waiting for the other shoe to drop. Her long face contorted, her hands twitching the leather strap of her purse back and forth like a whip, she eyed me dubiously. No words of assurance assuaged her fear of reprisal for having betrayed the silence kept all those years. By the time I calmed her down enough to leave, my own emotions were more under control. But while my solemn promise to keep our conversation secret appeared to put her at ease, it did little to allay my continued tension and curiosity.

After she'd gone, I took Midrin to try to squelch the pain from the migraine, and managed to mix some paints in preparation of filling the waiting canvas. Try as I might, I couldn't recapture the scene or inspiration Lily's untimely arrival disrupted. Some of my earlier passion had waned from all the interruptions, but the beauty and peace of the view from the bluffs managed to ease my inner turmoil—and Jenny's mysterious presence, with the look of contentment on her uplifted face, couldn't help but attract and draw me to it.

Yet underneath it all, the work I was preparing to do, the well-wishers I'd thanked with appreciation for their concern, I was a mass of confusion.

How did I feel about being a victim of this mysterious Linden Stalker, about the rape and beating of the small boy I'd once been? How else could I feel? Angry? Furious, would be a more appropriate term. I was hurt and frustrated by the truth having been kept from me all these years. At the same time, there was an understanding, a comprehension and acceptance that my family only did what they thought was best for me.

They'd watched, as Janet said, for I clearly remembered those hooded eyes, off-handed, sidelong glances and stolen looks. They'd been afraid, as I'd suspected, but their fear of my remembering had a far greater basis than anything I ever imagined.

Was I different?

I asked myself this question as I stared into my reflection after downing the Midrin. I looked the same; dark brown eyes with amber flecks that nearly matched the color of my hair, wide brows and a somewhat angular jaw line like my father's, and the wide, full mouth from my mother's side. My shoulders were strong and straight. I didn't have the upper body development Chuck Stinnet possessed, but I was no slouch, either. Pecs and biceps well-toned, a firm abdomen, and legs conditioned by stairs, long walks, and the refusal to use the car unless absolutely necessary. I was no Brad Pitt, but I'd do.

Visually, I was the same, and while my emotions still churned and crashed on a wild sea within my brain, essentially I felt unchanged psychologically as well. Janet was right to have compared the information to a nightmare. Without any memory of the incident, it seemed little more than that. Disturbing because of the knowledge it happened to me, to who I had been, yet with a sense of unreality.

Ten year old Richie Tanner had gone into the park whole, complete, and awakened from a coma two weeks later and grown into the man I was today. There was no pain or fear connected with that awakening— that I could remember. Even probing my mind as I was now, all I could pick up was the hurt and frustration I'd felt from the way my parents treated me afterward; the fear I'd done something for which they could never forgive me.

And it felt wrong somehow. The others' recollections failed to ring any bells or stir the slightest memory. Surely if something so traumatic had occurred, hearing about it should have produced some recognition. But there was nothing, nothing at all.

Except the rain...

I remembered my vision from that morning, of Tara lying bruised and beaten with the rain pelting her, her small form crumpled in a heap before the gazebo. Could that possibly be a memory from my own assault? And that loud crack of wood slamming against flesh and bone, the dark figure prepared to land another blow—

My face blanched with the memories, and I clutched at the sink to steady myself.

Suddenly there seemed some sense to it, the vividness and certainty I'd felt as Hargrave told me about Tara. I was convinced I now had the answer—it hadn't been imagination, at least, not imagination alone. Without realizing it, I'd recalled the terrorizing events of when I was attacked. It had taken the news of what happened to Tara for my own memories to be released. And now they'd begun, now I had the story, it was surely only a matter of time before the floodgates opened and I would truly remember.

A little shaky, I returned to the living room and tried calling my mother once again. This time she answered, her sweet, high voice anxious as she questioned me about Tara and about my own state of mind. I'd thought it would be difficult not to ask her about my "accident," as she'd referred to it, but it wasn't hard at all. Hearing the concern in her voice and thinking about all the times she'd comforted me in her arms, I felt stronger, even more self-confident than usual. There was no reason to burden her with the past, to overshadow her excitement for her upcoming vacation. She'd earned the peace of mind she'd captured in coming to grips with life without my father, and I refused to disturb that for anything.

We talked for awhile about little things, joking and making one another laugh. Before hanging up, I reminded her to send me some postcards and she wished me luck with the exhibition at the university, promising to come to Linden the moment she returned. I felt a great sense of relief afterward, and as I lay the background color on the canvas, an odd kind of contentment fell over me. I was soon lost under the power of my creative muse.

I spent the next two days in relative quiet, wrapped up in the progression of the painting and taking long, relaxing walks. The warming spring air was refreshing after the smell of paints and turpentine. But I wasn't complaining. The block had been chipped away, and the canvas was slowly coming to life, every brush stroke bringing more and more of the scene into reality.

Imagination had little to do with it. Inspiration, perhaps, even less. It was almost as though the connection between brushes, paints, and canvas had a mind of their own, working in combination to create the blues of the sky and the rich greens of trees, valley, and bluffs. I didn't spend much time looking at the painting, allowed the part of myself that seemed to know instinctively what to do next to just let it happen. I knew that too much conscious thought could bring the creative process to a grinding halt, and after so many false starts in the last few months, had no desire for this to happen.

I never asked myself where my mind went while I painted; that was part of the beauty of the thing. And while I couldn't say I didn't think about my recent discoveries, neither did I mull over them a great deal. Curiosity remained, it had always been there, but the intervening years taught me never to brood on a subject too long.

During this time, Tara drifted in and out of consciousness, basically unaware and incoherent. Joyce Noland kept me apprised of the situation, calling daily to assure me that it wouldn't be long before my ex regained her viper tongue and caustic wit. In moments of lucidity she was already applying them to the hospital staff. A good reason, Joyce stated, to keep her under sedation.

While Joyce uttered these calm assurances, I heard the underlying reason for her calls in the tone of her voice. She knew the added pressure I felt, how the migraines had become more painful and frequent, and was concerned for my health. She urged me to come in for a check-up, and failing that, just to sit and talk—at a reduced charge, she'd joked. I was grateful for her concern but was more content in my solitude for the moment to take her up on the offer.

Lily called the day after her seduction attempt with a half-hearted apology. Her husky voice had been tight, evidence she was uncertain about approaching me. Whether this had anything to do with the aborted effort or the revelation of my part in the story of the Linden Stalker case, I was unable to discern. She hadn't been in the mood to talk and signed off abruptly with a promise to bring the canvases I'd requested on her next visit.

Chuck also phoned, missing me during one of my lengthy treks through the surrounding neighborhood. He left a brief message to let me know I could count on him for support and then asked irreverently how my recovery from temptation was coming along. I enjoyed that but decided against returning the call. I was too involved with my present endeavor to engage in a long conversation—especially when the topic could lead to further distractions, like one of Chuck's women friends. Knowing Stinnet as I did, and his belief that a little female companionship could make any situation better, it wasn't hard to conclude this was most likely what he had in mind.

The following day, Professor Drake stopped by with news that Janet and Mother had gotten off on their trip without any problems. We talked for a while, his occasional questions regarding Tara, and my answers, appeared to ease his mind somewhat. As head of the college to which I was attached, as well as being a lifelong friend, it was especially hard for him being placed in the middle of such a controversy. On the one hand, there was the responsibility he had to the university, on the other, a friendship that spanned three decades. With Hargrave questioning people about Tara's and my relationship and hinting at my culpability, it was making things extremely difficult for the professor.

While my declaration of innocence may be believed by the vast majority of those who knew me, there was always the consideration of what the institution would feel about the matter. The university would not appreciate the innuendo and attempt to besmirch one of its own, and was not likely to tolerate the situation for long. Sooner or later they would have to take a stand, and if it came between defending a lowly instructor and protecting their good name, there was no doubt which direction the wind blew. The question was just how long the professor would be able to defend me to both the Board of Regents and the police before all hell broke loose—it was a position I did not envy in the least.

Still, despite knowledge of what might happen, I went on with my work giving little thought—conscious, anyway—to the "what if" scenarios. Things were progressing well; I had two paintings just past the beginning stages, and there was no end in sight of the urge to continue in the same vein.

The third morning dawned brightly, the air coming in through the open windows scented with the freshness of growing things. I was up with the sun, seated before the canvas, palette in hand, mind lost to whatever dimension it went at such times.

Despite the need and desire for cross ventilation, I hadn't bothered to open the door. Since that eventful day when the screen had become a revolving door, I'd decided to maintain my privacy with the main door closed and securely locked. Perhaps that's why I didn't notice the knocking at first—heard it on some level, I suppose—but was too wrapped up in painting to respond. It wasn't until the door seemed to buckle under the insistent pounding that I finally returned to myself and reluctantly laid aside brush and palette.

Wiping my hands on a clean rag, I opened the door to a red-faced Hargrave. His narrow grey eyes looked like two ball bearings in the craggy face, hard and impenetrable. His mouth quirked up in one corner as he pushed past me into the room.

"Sorry about not calling in advance, Richard, but there wasn't time. The doctor has given the green light, and I didn't want to keep the little lady waiting."

Having talked with Joyce last evening, I knew this was coming, but hadn't expected it to be quite so soon. I welcomed the news but was a little piqued about not being forewarned of Hargrave's visit—especially when he virtually demanded I go to the hospital with him. Looking at the man with his rather smug demeanor, I chalked it up to his desire to unsettle me and received great satisfaction at his distress at not having done so.

It was obvious he was perturbed by my enthusiastic response, and just as obvious there was more on his mind than the upcoming interview with Tara. I wondered what he had up his sleeve, about the results of the forensics tests on my jacket fibers, but decided not to ask. Hargrave wasn't the type to remain quiet for any length of time—not when he thought he could spring it on you suddenly. So I waited, staring out the passenger window and bracing myself for whatever might come.

It wasn't entirely quiet in his car, a big Ford of some indeterminate make and vintage. The police radio chattered constantly with static-filled talk, making me wonder how anyone could understand what was being said. On the seat between us sat the requisite red beacon atop several file folders that appeared to barely hold their contents.

While the floor of the car was virtually spotless, the same could not be said for the remaining surfaces of the vehicle. Small, shiny spots adorned most of the dashboard and door side panels, looking as though something had erupted and spilled throughout the car. It smelled vaguely of stale coffee and spearmint with an overlying odor of mustiness, like something wet had been left in the vehicle to molder away. Wearing the same suit as he had three days earlier—and showing definite signs of wear and tear—the detective looked quite at home among the debris.

"Seen that little gal of yours recently?" There was an edge to his voice, a mixture of triumph and satisfaction.

"Tara? No." I gave him a sidelong glance, then resumed staring out the window, watching him surreptitiously from the corner of my eye.

"Nah, the other one. The one in your drawings." He grinned then, if it could be called that, his lips stretched tight with a show of crooked teeth.

When I didn't answer, he grunted in apparent contentment. "Didn't think so."

At a stoplight, Hargrave turned slightly toward me, his head cocked at an angle, his expression, if not gloating, close to it.

"I knew there was something familiar about your name the other day, but couldn't quite place it. When I saw you, there wasn't any recognition to jog my memory, and I started to wonder if I was mistaken."

The light changed, and the cars in front of us were moving. Although Hargrave returned his eyes to the road before us, I could tell his attention was still on me.

"Hell, I'd been up over twenty-four hours and on duty more than half of them, so it was understandable." He slouched into the seat, his right hand drumming erratically on the steering wheel. "It was Janet Drake, more than anything else, that got me searching. And once I'd started, it didn't take long to find you."

I braced myself for whatever might be coming, silently thanking Janet for having the forethought to prepare me as best she could.

"God almighty." He blew a breath out through clenched teeth. "The Linden Stalker case. I hated that damned thing almost as much as I enjoyed the challenge. He was a vicious bastard, what he did to those girls, and I wanted more than anything to see the creep behind bars—or begging on his filthy knees trying to come up with one good reason why I shouldn't blow the monster away." He stole a furtive glance in my direction.

"Nearly every available cop in a hundred mile radius was primed for killing him. Twelve girls in the space of two years, raped, beaten, and left for dead. He always chose areas close to the towns, places people usually felt safe in—like parks. Victims were most likely chosen at random—there never appeared to be any real similarities between them. They were all young, yes, but he didn't choose a particular girl because of hair color or length, or their body type, like some nutsos do. Naw, this guy wasn't choosey. When the urge hit him, he struck.

"Everyone worked closely together on the case, forming a task force and sharing info and the like, and we'd seemed to finally come up with a sort of pattern as far as locations were concerned. We were fairly certain the next strike would be in Bassington or Harley, and were putting in overtime helping the locals keep an eye out. We never expected another hit so soon in Linden. And we especially never expected the victim would be male."

I drew in a deep breath and nearly bit through my tongue as the light before us changed and Hargrave slammed on the brake. He glanced up in the rearview mirror, threw the car in reverse, and backed up a few feet in answer to the blaring horn from an approaching semi. Muttering something under his breath, his steely eyes followed the tractor-trailer as it crossed the street before us.

"Little Richie Tanner," his voice contained a kind of awe. "Last time I saw you, your face was about as white as the bandages wrapped about your head. No wonder I didn't make the connection."

"And now you have?" I asked dryly.

"Things are beginning to make a little more sense."

"Really? I suppose you believe that what happened made me some kind of deviant." I couldn't help being flip about it. The sarcasm was lost on Hargrave, however. He was headed for something, and he wasn't about to be deterred.

"I'd hate to think that every individual who suffered a traumatic experience turned it around to make others pay, but it's been known to happen. You ever remember that night?" The car started moving again, but I knew from his expression that he was barely aware of the traffic around us.

"No."

He nodded, the grin widening. "Didn't think so. That means you probably don't remember me, either." He snatched a brief look at me as I started in surprise. "That's right, Richard, me. We were sure your attack was related to the Stalker case in some way—it fit most of the M.O. I attempted to interview you shortly after you regained consciousness. Your folks, however, didn't like the direction I was taking and had me escorted out. They'd refused to authorize the rape test, said there was no supporting evidence for it, and the doctors supported their decision. It was very upsetting. Ticked off a lot of people."

"Including you?"

He laughed. "Yeah, especially me. We were close, man. Real close, and having the door slammed in our faces like that, well—"

We sat for a moment in silence, even the police radio ceased to make any noise outside a gentle hum.

"Been listening to the news, Richard?" Without waiting for my answer, he continued. "They've found a body over in Wilmark. A young woman with long brown hair." He heard the catch in my breath and nodded in satisfaction. "They haven't the proper facilities, so they've brought the deceased here. Since no one has identified her yet, I thought you might have a look before we go see your ex."

I swallowed hard, a protest already forming on my lips. "I met Jenny once, Detective. Even if it happened to be her, I wouldn't be much help. All I have is her first name."

"Well, man, that may be all we need to trace her." His mouth formed a thin, tight line. "Ever see a body that's been left out in the open a few days, Richard? It's not a pretty sight. This girl had been somebody, someone's baby. Now she's just a piece of meat on a slab in the morgue. Makes you sick, doesn't it?"

I didn't answer, knew that nothing I said would make a difference, let alone change his mind.

As the scenery flashed by, I scarcely thought about Tara, her anger and possible vindictiveness a little thing in comparison to viewing a body. A shudder at the thought passed through me, and I silently prayed it wasn't Jenny.

"No questions, no curiosity about how the girl died?" Hargrave asked as we finally pulled into the parking lot of City Hospital.

"I figured you'd tell me if you wanted me to know." I responded.

He laughed then, an odd crackling sound that echoed through the musty interior of the vehicle. As he shut off the car, he turned toward me, squinting his eyes against the glare of the sun and giving me a cold, hard stare.

"I don't think you're as tough and calm as you'd like me to believe, Tanner. I think you're over there shaking in your shoes, scared spitless of what we might find out about you."

I ignored his remark, pushed open the door and climbed out of the car. "I'd like to get this over with, if you don't mind." I said evenly. Taking a deep breath of the warm, fresh air, I looked over the top of the vehicle at the man. "I may be a lot of things, but I'm not a murderer."

Hargrave grunted at this but didn't answer. He led the way into the basement of the hospital and through a door labeled in large black letters: Morgue. With my hands clenched tightly at my sides, I waited in an office while Hargrave went in search of an attendant. I knew he wouldn't make this easy for me, accepted he would arrange the viewing to be as shocking as possible. He didn't disappoint me.

Several minutes later, I was led down a long corridor smelling strongly of disinfectant and what I assumed to be formaldehyde. The combined odors and silence had an uncanny effect, sending gooseflesh to cover most of my body. I wasn't squeamish, had done my time in lab sciences in school, but none of it prepared me for what I was about to see.

The morgue attendant waited for us in the cavernous, stainless steel nightmare used as an autopsy room. Before I had the chance to look away, I saw the gleam of tables and instruments and a nude body lying nearby in preparation. Along one side of the room were rows of drawers labeled with names and numbers, one of which the attendant opened to reveal a sheeted form.

Hargrave rounded the drawer, his eyes matching the color of the room as they narrowed over it and leveled on me.

"Ready, Richard?"

The ghoul was enjoying himself at my expense, and as I met his gaze I prepared myself for the worst.

The sheet was lifted with a dramatic flourish, and in the way one has of noticing even the minutest of details at traumatic points in one's life, I became suddenly aware of the clock on the opposite wall slowly ticking off the seconds with a barely audible click. Even the sound of the blood as it rushed in and out of my heart seemed to become loud in that unnaturally quiet room, every intake of breath on behalf of the three living occupants cutting through the silence and piercing my soul.

Half the girl's face had been eaten away by some kind of animal, the raw flesh jagged at the edges and revealing a show of teeth and gum. The bite marks on the discolored flesh were almost as shocking as the gaping hole in her cheek and neck. I whirled around, gagging, every impression burned on my retinas.

There had been a dark bruise about what remained of her throat, and what looked like pieces of flesh which had flaked off around it. The mouth was open in a terrible grimace, what was left of the black lips, pulled tight against her teeth, and the remaining eye looked more like a cloudy marble than anything human. Her hair had been a deep brown, rich and abundant, and the high, unwrinkled forehead spoke of youth which would remain unfulfilled.

Putting a hand over my mouth, I stumbled toward the door, hearing the drawer squeak shut behind me. As I made my way into the corridor, I heard Hargrave mutter something to the attendant, and as the door swung shut behind me, they both laughed.

A water cooler was located just beyond the office, and I set my sights on it, forcing back the memory that tried to overwhelm me. The water was only lukewarm, but it was a relief to my overheated face. I hung my head over the spray, soaking my neck and hair.

"That wasn't so bad now, was it?"

Hargrave came up behind me so quietly I hadn't heard him, his voice startling me and causing me to jump involuntarily back. He clapped me across the shoulder, smiling his ghoulish smile.

"Well?"

I shook my head. "No, it's not Jenny." The words squeezed past a throat that spasmed in preparation of throwing up. I was sure I'd turned a nasty shade of green, and the absurd look of pleasure upon the detective's face confirmed the fact.

He headed me in the right direction, and I made it to the toilet in barely the nick of time. Afterward, my empty stomach aching, throat raw, I rinsed my mouth out in the sink and cursed Hargrave aloud. An orderly coming out of a nearby stall glared at me, then backed out of the bathroom as though he thought I might attack him. I was still trying to collect myself when the door swung open and Hargrave's voice came from behind me, booming in the quiet and bouncing off the tiled floor and walls.

"You wanna shake a leg, Richard? We're due upstairs."

I turned to scowl at him where he stood in the doorway, one large foot holding open the door. With slow deliberation, I splashed more water on my face and across the back of my neck. I stood dripping over the sink for a few minutes, then tugged some paper towels from the dispenser and dabbed at the remaining droplets.

Nothing, not even the slow pace I adopted upon joining him in the corridor, seemed to disconcert Hargrave in the least. He was still riding high from the scene in the autopsy room, his smug expression not having changed an iota since the morgue attendant removed the sheet from the dead girl's face. It was one of the few times in my life that I felt like hitting someone, and suppressing the urge to smash my fist into that craggy, over-confident mug took all the strength I possessed. The grim satisfaction of feeling his nose crush beneath my fist would hardly be worth an assault charge and jail, and I refused to take the bait and fall into the trap he was so obviously setting.

Tara had been moved into a private room just down the hall from the ICU wing. There was still a guard posted outside her door—a different man from the one before—and as we approached he nodded at Hargrave in recognition.

"They've been waiting for you." The officer said, rolling his eyes heavenward. "I don't think she's very happy with the delay."

Hargrave snorted in answer, squared his meaty shoulders, then strode past the guard. Pushing open the door, he stood aside motioning for me to enter.

As the door opened, Tara's shrill voice rang out in anger. Hargrave and the guard shoved past me, rising to the moment and ready to defend the "helpless" victim in the bed. For all their courage and preparation to do battle, it immediately became evident their assistance would not be required.

A nurse hovered over Tara's bed, hypodermic in hand, gently trying to persuade her patient to cooperate for the injection. The tubes and IVs I'd seen several days before were gone, and apparently Tara wasn't too keen on the idea of baring her hip. Her face was mottled, beet red and various shades from black to purple as she did her best to thwart the nurse's attempts with limited range of movement. Her head was still swathed in bandages, strands of her pale hair sticking out at odd angles giving her the look of a scarecrow. Both eyes had been blackened and were now a deep purple making her dark brown eyes take on an odd yellow-black appearance. There was a bruise across the bridge of her nose, and I thought for a moment it might have been broken, but realized it was only an illusion of shadow.

She was propped up in the bed with pillows arranged on either side of her, the light beige hospital blanket folded neatly beneath her breasts. Her present agitation added to the battered appearance but also lent a fierceness to the features.

The shrieking came to an abrupt halt when she noticed Hargrave and the guard advancing toward the bed. The glare that followed included the nurse and the two men. Spotting me, she blinked twice rapidly, her eyes blazing.

"Wot the 'ell is 'e doin' 'ere?" She demanded, her swollen mouth making her sound a bit like a Cockney. She shot daggers in my direction, the look she turned on Hargrave little better.

The detective dismissed the guard then went to stand beside the bed, motioning the nurse aside. With a sigh of reluctance, the nurse sat in a nearby chair, placed the hypo on a table, and picked up a magazine. She gave the two one last look, shook her head with apparent exasperation, then lowered her eyes, ostensibly to read.

"Ah assed you a ques'un." Her voice was stern in spite of the comical ring, a clear sign she was on the road to recovery.

He gave her a tolerant smile, speaking softly. "Don't you remember our conversation yesterday afternoon, Miss Morgan? I mentioned bringing Mr. Tanner by."

Tara eyed him suspiciously, glanced over his shoulder at me, and began to shake her head only to stop and wince in pain.

"Ah don' 'member you sayin' anythin' 'bout 'im." She stated firmly. "If you 'ad, Ah'd a tol' you to stuff it!"

Bending forward, Hargrave muttered something to which Tara responded with an unladylike snort. They exchanged a few more words, Hargrave's barely audible, Tara in full voice. Occasionally, one of them would glance in my direction or the nurse's, but mostly they regarded one another with an odd intensity.

I resisted an urge to laugh, knew it would only exacerbate the already existing problems. Instead, I remained where I was, barely inside the room, watching and thoroughly enjoying Hargrave's turn at discomfiture.

It was evident from the thrust of the man's shoulders that he was uncomfortable. The tips of his ears had turned a bright scarlet, and while it didn't show on his face, the erratic tapping of his fingers against the side of his leg proved he was having a hard time maintaining patience. If he'd wanted a cooperative witness, he wasn't getting it—something I could have told him had he cared to ask.

"Ah tol' you, dammit!" The shrill voice sounded on the edge of breaking. " 'e's too much of a wimp to 'ave done dis. 'Side which, Ah woulda rec'nize 'im." She cocked a critical eyebrow at me. "Not 'is style."

Hargrave drew in a deep breath and slowly exhaled. "Stop a minute to think about this, Miss Morgan, Tara. It was dark, you were walking through the park, and someone—"

"Ah may look like 'ell, 'Argrave, but they didna 'mash my brain in, though they tried." A hand went to gingerly touch the back of her head. "Ah know where Ah was an' wha' Ah was doin'! So stop treatin' me like Ah'm some kinda retar'." She flashed him a look that might have shriveled a lesser man, then turned her green-black eyes on me once again. "Rishar' can be a bastar', but 'e didna do dis. Ah know it wasna 'im 'cause Ah know everythin' abou' 'im. An' Ah do mean everythin'."

There was no kindness in the look she gave me, and I knew without a doubt that she would have liked more than anything to have said I'd been the one who assaulted her. Yet, the honesty and integrity she usually kept hidden had somehow won out over her usual vindictiveness. I gave her a weak smile—guess there was hope for her yet.

"Miss—Tara, just—"

"Will you ge' them the 'ell outta my room!" She glared at the nurse. "Ah'm tire' and Ah jus' wanna sleep." She peered at me from the corner of her eyes as they were closing, and I saw the tears she blinked back. I had a sudden urge to go to her and try to comfort her but knew better than to try.

Without waiting for Hargrave, I turned and walked quickly from the room. He followed a few minutes later, the smug expression gone, replaced by a deep scowl. After whispering something to the officer, he joined me across the hall.

"She wasn't in very good form this morning." He said half under his breath.

"For Tara, it was perfectly normal."

If looks could kill, I'd be dead.

"Yeah, well, she was a lot more cooperative yesterday. From what I got out of her, I thought she might be able to recognize her attacker. Today I'm not so sure." His steely gaze narrowed on me a moment longer, then looked abruptly away.

"What is it, Tanner, why didn't she finger you?"

"Perhaps because I didn't do it." I answered simply.

Hargrave started off down the corridor without answering. I caught up with him in a couple of strides, and giving him a sidelong glance, asked the question that had been burning in my mind since his arrival at the loft.

"What about the results of the forensics test on the jacket fibers?" Knowing the answer already, my voice was calm, and I couldn't resist the almost gloating tone. It wasn't lost on Hargrave.

"No match—*this time*. But that doesn't prove a thing. Besides," he stopped at the entrance to the hospital, the automatic doors sliding open behind him with a slight swoosh. "There's still the little girlie in the morgue." With a grim smile, he turned on his heel. "This isn't over, Tanner. Not by a long shot."

Chapter 8

I elected not to ride back to the loft with Hargrave, the decision based more on my own ability to remain in check rather than his thinly veiled hostility. There was little doubt left regarding his motives—it seemed obvious he was out to get revenge for the injustice he felt dealt him by my parents long ago. He'd admitted the anger and frustration at being refused access to me, his inability to definitively connect my "accident" to the crimes of the Linden Stalker thwarted by my parents' refusal to fully cooperate. I wondered if this may have adversely affected his career, if he saw the incident as coming between him and his apprehension of the Stalker. It was, at least, one explanation for his attitude toward me. Though it didn't explain his behavior on our first encounter when he'd already pegged me as the guilty party. Perhaps he still thought I was guilty of the assault on Tara. I wouldn't dare presume to know what he was thinking. He'd made it clear he wasn't letting go. Despite Tara's conviction I wasn't guilty, he considered me fair game.

Gazing out across the parking lot and watching Hargrave's car pull onto the main road, I thought again about the girl in the morgue. It had been an unsettling experience, designed by the detective to be even more so. I wondered what he'd hoped to gain. Did he truly believe me capable of such a thing, or was it some form of scare tactic orchestrated to convince me to confess to the assault? The message that he wasn't messing around was loud and clear—had been from the beginning. Revenge or not, Hargrave would be a formidable enemy, and the thought was not one I relished.

I rubbed the back of my neck feeling the strain of the morning start its slow ascent to an already overcrowded brain. A search of my pockets turned up nothing but lint and an old roll of Certs that looked even less appetizing than the balls of fuzz. It was ironic, being in a hospital full of drugs and not having access to the one necessary to relieve the starting migraine. The thought led to a solution, and a quick call to Joyce Noland's office confirmed she was not only there, but free at the moment.

I took my time walking the short distance between the hospital and medical building, filling my lungs with long, deep breaths of the fresh air in an attempt to clear my nostrils of the stale, medicinal odor of the hospital. The day was bright and clear, a few clouds, white and puffy as cotton balls, were drifting in from the northeast along the trail of a gentle breeze. It would be a good day to find a spot in the sun overlooking a valley and allow my mind to wander as my fingers sketched out the scene before me. The thought brought me back to the painting of the bluffs, and I felt a longing to return to my work.

The medical building was dim after the brilliance of the sun, and I stood for a moment in the entryway to allow my eyes to adjust. Joyce's suite of rooms was on the second floor in the rear, and rather than taking the elevator, I jogged up the stairs.

The receptionist smiled and waved me in, informing me that Joyce should be in her office beyond the examination rooms. She was waiting for me there, the blue eyes behind thick-lensed glasses carefully concealing her thoughts as she indicated for me to take a seat.

"I assumed from the spontaneity of the call this wouldn't be a professional consultation." She raised an expressive eyebrow. "Decided to take me up on the offer to talk, huh?" Her thin lips spread in a wide grin.

"That, and the fact I've a nasty migraine started with no medicine on hand." My light tone made her laugh, and regarding me with amusement, she reached into a drawer and pulled out a key.

"Midrin, right?" In answer to my nod she said, "I'll be back in a moment."

Alone, I felt suddenly at a loss. We were friends, yes, but our relationship had been built on a mutual respect borne from our original professional status as doctor and patient. We were familiar with one another to a degree, but there wasn't the kind of intimacy as I shared with other friends. So what brought me here—aside from the migraine?

Dr. Joyce Noland possessed a friendly nature that made her easy to talk to. Whether this was the result of years of medical training and practice, I couldn't say, but her ready wit and willingness to truly listen had drawn me to her from my first office visit.

In her late forties, Joyce was married to the plant manager of a local diaper factory. The few times I'd seen them together I thought they made an excellent pair—her husband a confirmed talker, Joyce the avid listener. Perhaps it was the look of intent I'd often seen on her face that confirmed the decision to come today. Or maybe it was the realization that I really had nowhere else to go.

I made a mental list of friends and acquaintances, Chuck Stinnet and Professor Drake topping it.

Chuck would be sympathetic, or as much as he could be. Considering his irreverent, flip outlook on life, it was hard to imagine his taking anything too seriously—especially when it didn't affect him personally. Still, despite his faults, he was a good friend. Maybe too good. It had been hard for him to tell me about the Linden Stalker and what he knew happened to me; I'd seen the pain and indecision in his eyes. The idea he'd known all along bothered me, made me reluctant to share my thoughts and emotions now.

Then there was the professor. He was the one to whom I would really like to turn, the one who would have answers to the questions that remained after Janet's confession. And it was my promise to her that kept me from his door.

Joyce returned with the capsules and a glass of water, handed me both, then stood before her desk, arms crossed.

"What's happened, Richard?"

How to begin?

I felt self-conscious beneath her intense gaze, and shifted uncomfortably in the chair.

"Did you know about the body they found in Wilmark?" That seemed as good a place to start as any.

She nodded. "They brought her in last evening. Why?" One look at my face gave her the answer. "He didn't, Hargrave didn't—"

"Bright and early this morning." I grimaced. "I'm afraid I didn't handle it very well. Guess it's a good thing I never became a doctor."

"Why, in God's name?"

I told her what happened from the time Hargrave picked me up at the apartment right through the interview with Tara, leaving nothing out. Joyce listened raptly, interrupting only once or twice for clarification, her expression becoming more and more outraged.

"It's nice to know we're supplying our police department the funds to carry out their personal vendettas." She remarked dryly. "Are you going to report it?"

I shrugged, my shirt suddenly feeling too small. "I've no proof any more than he does." I stood up, stretching my arms above my head. "Being innocent helps, of course." I said. "But his persistence isn't going to be looked on favorably by the university. Not to mention what it might do to the exhibitions."

"I see your point." Her eyes narrowed thoughtfully, brows drawn in speculation. "So, what are you going to do?"

"Talk to Drake, let him know what's going on. Now that Hargrave's told me about that night, Janet's off the hook. He doesn't need to know she said anything to me, and I keep my promise." I looked past her out through the bank of windows which encompassed most of the wall behind her. The deep blue of the sky was streaked with feathery clouds through which the sun played hide and seek, creating shadows in the field beyond the hospital grounds.

"It should be easy enough." I said.

"And what about you, Richard? Do you feel comfortable with the story now that you know it?" Her voice was soft, inquisitive.

The million dollar question. "Not entirely. But I suppose that's to be expected."

She cleared her throat, shifted her position, and sighed. "I'm not a psychologist, you know, only possess a layman's interest in the analyzation process. I suppose that goes along with being a brain surgeon. After all, I know the physiology of the brain, the nerves linking it to the body, its functions and processes; it only seems natural to also want to know what makes an individual tick." She glanced thoughtfully at her feet, then met my gaze once again. "I haven't been totally honest with you, Richard, and I feel badly about that."

I raised an eyebrow in question, to which Joyce smiled and moved to take a seat behind her desk.

"I think this requires a bit more distance." She laughed nervously. "You remember my mentioning Dr. Astin the other day? Well, it seems he treated you twenty years ago."

"I see." What else could I say? It made sense after all. I'd been in the hospital for more than a month, and it wasn't so far-fetched to think that the doctor who'd taken care of me might still be on staff. "So what did he say?"

"Nothing, really. Just that you'd been found in the park by Drake and there had been some discussion about it relating to the Linden Stalker case. He didn't confirm or deny the rumor—he wouldn't, professional ethics and all."

"Had you already known about this Stalker thing?"

She shook her head. "I've only been in Linden ten years, and I don't imagine it's something people enjoy dredging up. When Tara came in, I suppose it brought back memories, and some of the hospital personnel starting reminiscing. Nasty business." She shuddered. "Now you have the story, any memories of your own return?"

"No. Janet compared it to a nightmare, and to some extent, she was right. I have the information, know the child they're talking about was me, but feel totally unconnected to it all. I've no idea what a psychiatrist would say about that," I laughed. "I don't think I want to know. What their opinion would be, I mean. I suppose I should be reeling from the impact, but I don't feel any different. The curiosity is still there as it always was but, I don't know—it's like I haven't gotten the whole story. Like something's missing."

Joyce nodded. "I think that's understandable under the circumstances. It's different to be told of an incident as opposed to having the actual memory of it." She paused, appeared to be considering something, and having made a decision, drew back her shoulders. "Would you like to meet Astin? I could arrange it if you would."

I let my breath out in a slow, steady stream. "I think I'd prefer to wait on that for a while, give myself an opportunity to become more comfortable with the information before I start delving into specifics." I gave her a half-hearted grin. "Don't want a brain overload, and with all that's going on at present, I believe I'm already dangerously close to one."

We talked a while longer, both of us becoming increasingly relaxed in one another's company. The ease of conversation, the air of serenity and companionship, worked to relieve the stress and tension of the morning. The sense of relief was so great, I almost mentioned the phenomenon of the changed sketches, but something held me back. A few minutes later, as Joyce gradually worked around to the subject of my migraines, I was glad I hadn't said anything.

I only managed to half convince her that coming in for testing wasn't necessary, that as things settled down, so would the migraines. She was doubtful, donning her best doctor's attitude in an effort to change my mind, but I wasn't buying any of it. I still had a vivid memory from my teens when my parents, worried about the recurrent headaches, had taken me to a specialist. The poking and prodding which resulted left a bitter taste in my mouth—and my head. I had no desire to repeat the experience only to be told there was really nothing they could do beyond the continuation of the medication I currently took.

Despite this difference of opinion regarding my health, by the time I left her office, I was glad I'd stopped in. It was an understatement to say that a lot had happened in the last few days, and I was consoled by the fact that even the strongest individual needed a confidant now and again. I may not possess the solutions to my dilemmas, but I definitely felt better equipped to handle things after sharing my thoughts with Joyce.

My Citation was parked beneath the stairs to the apartment when I returned, the bill tucked into the handle of the screen door. Its delivery meant there was no longer a reason to put off cleaning out my office, and after lunch, I phoned Mrs. Winston and let her know I'd be right over.

Dorothy Winston is a quiet little woman in her early sixties, very grandmotherly, a sweet disposition, and the most efficient secretary I'd ever dealt with. Always the soul of discretion, she still managed to keep her fingers to the pulse of university activity. If there was something worth knowing, it was likely Mrs. Winston had been in on it from the beginning. While she may not be an instigator or contributor to the gossip pool, neither was she one to hold back when she had something important to say. And she had volumes when it came to Detective Hargrave.

She greeted me with enthusiasm and followed me into the office I shared with two other professors. As I boxed my few belongings, I was regaled with tales of the detective's campus interviews. I'd been right to assume the university was quickly losing patience in the matter, Hargrave's persistence almost to the point of being rude.

"He had the audacity to imply you'd made lewd remarks and advances habitually!" Mrs. Winston exclaimed in alarm. "He asked if we'd ever witnessed any scenes between you and that young woman, if we thought you capable of committing a violent act upon her. Well," she exhaled deeply. "I let him know that the only scenes around here were ones Miss Morgan created herself. That seemed to shut him up."

I was sure it did. Whether Tara or I had been the instigator, Hargrave would see the situation as just another motive for me to silence her once and for all. I doubted he would stop to consider the finer points or look at my unsullied reputation as an instructor, or as a human being; he'd already made up his mind I was guilty.

I did my best to calm down Mrs. Winston, assuring her I still intended on contributing my work to the July exhibition. Mention of the Arts Festival got her going on that subject and all the additional work that would be required.

"Not that I mind it a bit," she said firmly, her round face beaming. "Nothing's more exciting than to see my faculty's work appreciated by the general public. I mean, we all know what you're capable of. It's the excitement generated by the outside that gives one a special thrill." She eyed me warily, balancing first on one foot and then the other. "This isn't, er, I mean," she drew in a deep breath, and letting it out set her double chin wagging. "You're not having difficulties with your painting because of all this hoopla, are you?"

"That's one thing that doesn't seem affected at the moment." I told her. "To the contrary, I think I've tapped into some wellspring I hadn't previously known existed."

The smile that spread across her face was beatific, causing her small dark eyes to crinkle into near nonexistence. "That's wonderful, Mr. Tanner. Truly wonderful. I so look forward to viewing your work. And what with that professional showing in Kansas City next winter, why, oh dear," she looked suddenly crestfallen. "I hope that won't mean Linden will be losing you."

Convincing her that I'd no intention of quitting my job in the near future was no easy matter. Once she'd gotten the notion into her head, it was as good as done, and it didn't help having to watch as I loaded the last of my belongings in the box. Still, something I said must have finally gotten through, and by the time I was ready to leave, she was back to her congenial self, looking forward to the upcoming exhibition in the Arts Festival, and assuring me that the extra work would all be worth it.

Back at the loft, I tried to return to my painting, but the necessary creative impulse was no longer there. I toyed around with a few unfinished sketches but finally decided to call it an early night. Unfortunately, I was unable to sleep.

Every time I closed my eyes I saw the gory remains of that poor girl's face, the scene in the morgue repeated again and again. After a couple hours of this, I got up and returned to the studio, grabbed another canvas, and attempted to start a new painting. It was sometime in the wee hours of the morning that the migraine hit with such a vengeance that I threw down brushes and palette in surrender. Rather than the medicine cabinet, I reached for the radio, found an easy listening station and turned the volume down low.

I switched off the lights, realizing only after I'd sat down, that the one above the sink in the kitchen remained burning. It hardly seemed to matter, I thought, staring intently at the green dial of the radio; I didn't figure I'd sleep anyway. Still, I stretched out on the couch, and closing my eyes, began some deep breathing, relaxation exercises. They must have worked, for the next thing I knew, it was mid-morning and sunshine was pouring in through the opened windows.

I lay still for a moment listening to the sound of muffled traffic in the distance and the birds just outside my windows. They were peaceful sounds, and coupled with the delicious fragrance permeating the apartment from the bakery below, I felt an odd contentment.

Reaching up to run a hand through my hair, I stared in amazement at my blackened fingertips. I looked at them for some time before the implication began to sink in.

I rose from the couch and hesitated on the step to the studio, curious and a little frightened of what I might find.

The large drawing sheet attached to a cardboard backer was set on the parson's table, the picture done in various shades of black and grey charcoal. It was a dark, phantasmagoric image in abstract, the exaggerated outline of a woman's form distorted with strange lines and shadings. The mouth of the image contained sharp, canine teeth, its protruding tongue of serpentine length, wrapped about the narrow throat.

In the center of the figure, which neither head nor body was distinguishable, was drawn a single eye. Its elongated shape seemed to encompass most of the image, the grey orb contrasting strikingly with the black pupil whose shape was reminiscent of a cat's eye.

It was like nothing I'd ever done before, and drawing back in shock and disgust, hoped I would never do anything like it again.

Sweat poured down the back of my neck and sides, yet I shivered, covered with gooseflesh. My hands were clenched at my thighs, the fingers growing white and numb from the lack of blood and oxygen. I stared down at them in wonder, then looked back at the drawing asking myself how.

There wasn't any more of an answer this time than there had been the last; an overworked mind, a too active imagination that even when asleep did not shut off. Were these acceptable explanations, or were there any?

I flexed fingers that tingled as though stabbed with dozens of tiny needles. The dampness from my palms had smudged the charcoal, imbedding residue into the lines and creases in an odd crisscross pattern. My eyes were mesmerized by the images created there, following first one line and then another, across one hand to the next and back again. I searched for answers there, wondering if they were mixed into the creases of hands that somehow did the work without the benefit of a conscious mind. But whatever story they had to tell was hidden deep within the crevices, covered or shielded by the charcoal smudges as surely as the veil that blocked the knowledge held in my subconscious.

Perhaps Joyce was right; maybe I should go in for tests. I'd suffered from migraines for more than half my life but never had experiences like this before. So far, these fugue states seemed limited, occurring at night while I believed I slept. What was the possibility of their becoming worse, expanding to daytime hours and taking over my life? That didn't bear thinking of.

Heedless of the charcoal stains on my hands, I clutched my head, demanding myself to think as I sank onto the single step that separated the living room and studio.

Taking stock of the past four months, it would be a vast understatement to say a lot had happened in my life. Beyond the consideration of the last week, the stress and tension had begun at the time of my father's unexpected death. Dealing with my own emotions had been difficult, helping my mother deal with hers, even more so. Not so much time had elapsed, after all, and in the interim was the preparation for my leave of absence from the university, the finalization of the one-man exhibition at Art Magic, and the concern that I wouldn't have the time or inspiration to fill the canvases that warranted such an honor. If these events weren't enough to boggle the mind and add to the general confusion, there was always the increasing tension between Tara and myself to complicate matters further. No, I wasn't going crazy, nor were these works of my subconscious a sign that something physical was wrong with me. I was an artist, so what would be more natural than for my dreams to manifest themselves in the form of my art?

The explanation was so simple it should have come to me long ago. On each occasion, I'd been under a great deal of pressure throughout most of the day. The first time occurred after a sleepless night spent grading finals and an eventful day culminated with the strain of dealing with Tara. I'd met Jenny in the park, her shyness and beauty the one bright spot in an otherwise depressing afternoon. She'd captured my imagination, drawn me in with those brilliant violet eyes, and left me wanting more after her sudden departure. My subconscious held onto this, transferring it to the sketches while my conscious mind slept. And, in essence, the same thing happened last night.

I glanced over to where the charcoal drawing sat on the parson's table, the darkness and grim reality of the scene reaching out to enfold me.

It was there, the horror of the unidentified girl's death, the stark coldness of the morgue, and the shock of her violated body. An abstract because the graphic depiction of the truth would have been too much, too horrifying to reproduce. The charcoals were not my usual choice, had rarely been used, but some part of me had known they would be right for this picture. The thick lines and dramatic difference between them and the drawing paper giving the proper depth and dimension, compelling one to look even as it shocked and repelled.

My breathing returned to normal with the determination that the incidents were an extension of my creative talents—albeit a subconscious one. It was only then that I realized the radio was still on, the low hum overlaid with a static crackle not there the night before. I got up to change the station, finding one that was just beginning their news and weather. I turned it up so the sound would follow me down the hall as I cleaned up.

Sometimes life can be sweet, rendering justice so swiftly and exacting as to make one believe in miracles. I'd only just shut off the tap in the bathroom when the mention of Wilmark caught my attention. Quickly grabbing up a towel, I was in the hallway blotting the water from my face, as the details were broadcast; within twenty-four hours of the body's discovery, they not only had the girl's identity, but her murderer as well.

The details were sketchy, something to do with S and M carried to extreme, and a boyfriend too frightened or ashamed to come forward. He'd finally done so, however, turning himself over to "a detective from the Linden City Police Department. Detective Jack Hargrave refused further comment on the case..."

I didn't need to hear more. I shut off the radio and prepared to enjoy the beautiful day.

Chapter 9

I wasn't totally surprised when I received the call, supposed that on some level, I'd been expecting it. Nagoochi returned home to Japan leaving Tara all alone. Whether it stemmed from actual loneliness, or some strange longing for my company, she asked a nurse to phone me, requesting a visit. Without hesitation, I agreed to come right away.

It had been nearly a week since I'd last seen her, a week in which my life seemed to finally return to normal. There'd been no further incidents of waking and finding some unexpected artwork to greet me; my conscious efforts were coming along well. And more importantly, Hargrave stayed out of my face.

Professor Drake assured me the detective had ceased his inquiries at the university, and as a result, there was no further talk of making my leave of absence permanent—which was a huge relief to me. We'd a good, long discussion of the state of affairs I found myself in, the professor's wisdom and insight in the matter a great comfort. While he insisted no one ever thought me guilty of the assault, the Board had convened early last week to decide what was best to do under the circumstances. As Mrs. Winston told me, Hargrave's interviews set the university on its collective ear, and innocent or not, it all boiled down to trying to keep scandal from touching the school.

If not for Tara's wild, ill-mannered reputation, I may have been handed a pink slip at the first sign of trouble—not being tenured. Though the Board saw no reason to take undue risks, a small group of my colleagues, Professor Drake and Chuck Stinnet among them, interceded on my behalf, changing their minds. I thanked God for the reprieve and was grateful for such steadfast friends.

Still, it was like I'd been tried and convicted without benefit of counsel. The experience taught me a valuable lesson: it's not always innocent until proven guilty as we've been taught to believe, but quite often the other way. A sobering thought indeed.

Chuck handled the whole thing with a laugh, joking about the absurdity of it all. Scandal, he stated with a smirk upon his Paul McCartney features, was the standard operating procedure of the school, with its backbiting and rumors rife among faculty and staff alike. The only difference this time was Hargrave's untimely and most unwelcome appearance.

"It made too many people nervous," he'd laughed again, holding his side and nearly doubling over in response to his own joke. "They were afraid he'd discover the skeletons in their closets as well."

This lack of reverence and respect was typical of Chuck, and while I might not agree with his perception, his comic reenactment of the Board meeting was good for a chuckle—especially with the knowledge of what they'd been about to do to me.

I had about two hours before I was expected for lunch with Professor Drake, plenty of time to visit Tara. While the call hadn't been unexpected, I'd no idea what she had in mind. On the drive to the hospital, speculation and possible scenarios played themselves over and over again. I doubted this experience mellowed her, thought I might be subjecting myself to more tongue-lashing, but knew the visit was necessary—at least for me, for closure.

I pulled the Citation into the hospital parking lot, the vehicle coughing and sputtering almost as badly as before its recent repair. I didn't like the idea of replacing the car but expected it would be necessary in the near future. A mental rundown of my current financial condition brought a grimace to my face, and on that happy note, I went in to see Tara.

There was no longer a guard outside her door, nor was a nurse inside her room. I was a little surprised at first, but the explanation soon became clear.

The sun slanted in through the partially opened blinds in the single window, illuminating the bed with a soft halo of light. She lay propped slightly at an angle, probably the most comfortable position for the broken and bruised ribs. The turban of bandages was gone from her head, replaced by a smaller strip that went across her forehead to hold the pad at the back in place. Her golden hair was slightly matted, its long, soft tresses spread out across her pillow and shoulders, making her appear innocent and childlike.

She held out a hand when I entered the room, and without a second thought, I went to her. Entwining my fingers with hers, I gave them a gentle squeeze.

"I wasna sure you'd come." Her speech was hindered by her still swollen lips, but it no longer had the sound of a Cockney. She gave me a weak smile that trembled slightly at the corners of her mouth.

The area around her eyes had changed from that sickly yellow-black, but their deep color and bland tones of the room made the puffiness and discoloration surrounding them even more apparent. The bruise across the bridge of her nose had faded to a pale yellow, and her skin was pasty and in stark contrast to the bright red of her swollen mouth.

I hadn't been this close to her that last time with Hargrave, and, therefore, not seen the chipped and broken teeth. I winced at the sight and obvious pain, recalling the white, even teeth and seductive smile of the past. She seemed to sense what I was thinking, and turned her head away—but not before I caught the look of distress and self-conscious flood of color that tinged her cheeks. She'd always been proud of her appearance, way beyond the point of simple vanity. The thought of what this must be doing to her now made me pause to reevaluate the situation.

"I'm here, Tara." Reaching behind me, I groped for the bedside chair, found it without releasing her hand, and sat down.

"How are you feeling?"

"As though I've been run over repeatedly." She gave a little laugh, her face contorting with pain as she quickly clutched her side. "No jokes, they hurt too much."

We exchanged a long, appraising look, each weighing the other with caution. Discounting the visit with Hargrave, the last time we'd been together had been explosive, the memory still painfully vivid. The scene in the Snack Shack stood between us now, a hurdle too high to jump in a single bound.

Tears shone in Tara's eyes, brightening the dull color with a shining silver.

"Are you all right? Do you want me to get someone?" I started to release her hand, but she firmly retained her grasp.

"Don't, I mean, no. It's not that, it's I, I just," she paused, looking at me with a plea in her eyes. "I don't suppose if I apologized and told you it would never happen again, you'd believe me and take me back. It's too late, isn't it?"

I nodded warily. I wasn't sure where this was heading, had no desire to hurt her or cause her more distress but had no choice other than to tell the truth.

"We've hurt one another too often, Tara. It's time we accept the fact we can't make it together. Face it, we make one another miserable most of the time. And the rest of it, well, we can't spend our lives in bed."

A wry smile touched the swollen lips. "That would be nice, though, wouldn't it?" She turned her head away with a sigh. "Deep down, I know this as well as you, but, but—"

Our eyes met, her gaze revealing a lost and broken spirit. "All this time, I've known that if I needed someone to rely on, someone to hold me and tell me everything would be okay, that you were there for me. Sometimes it infuriated me that you could be so damned forgiving, and I told you it was a sign of weakness and abused you because of it. But, the truth is, it wasn't your weakness I hated, it was mine. Mine, for not being able to get on with things, for turning to you the moment I messed up again. Mine, for treating you with disrespect." She made an odd snorting sound, a form of derisive laughter. "Mine, for always wanting and demanding far more than it was possible for anyone to give.

"I—I've been talking to this—roving pastor and decided it was time to, I don't know, turn over a new leaf, change. At least give it a try. So I thought maybe you might want to clear the air, talk it out or something." Her free hand plucked nervously at the sheet and blanket neatly folded just below her breasts.

"Kick you while you're down? Doesn't sound like the best advice."

"No, but to make peace." Some errant strands of hair flew across her face. I reached over and gently removed them from her forehead, then cupped her cheek in my hand. She moved her head enough to lightly kiss my palm.

"After interviews with that nasty detective, and his even nastier insinuations, I-I guess I was ready to listen to the preacher, decided it was time to take stock of my life. There hasn't been much else to do in here but think. I didn't want to, didn't want to accept I might be to blame somehow." A small frown creased her forehead, wrinkling the strip of bandage across it.

"Hargrave tried to get me to change my mind, say it was possible you hurt me. I got tired of the bastard bugging me, so I called his captain. Killed two birds with one stone; got Hargrave out of my life and the guard off my door." She squinted at me, raising a hand to shield her eyes from the sun shining through the window behind me. "I don't know what that guy's got against you, Richard, but I'd watch my back.

"Anyway, the idea that someone I knew tried to bash my brains in, well, if that's not a good enough reason to try to realign one's thinking, I don't know what is."

I gave her what I hoped was an encouraging smile. "Good. I always knew you had it in you."

"What? To be good and kind, filled with honor and integrity?" Despite her warning against laughter, she laughed, once again clutching her ribs in pain. "I've my doubts. It's only in those damnable dreamy eyes of yours that I'm even a fourth as good. No one else sees it. Not even me."

My hands clasped hers tightly. "You have to stop being so hard on yourself."

Tara Morgan rolled her eyes heavenward then looked at me with an almost comical expression on her bruised and battered face. "And you're losing your resolve." She tugged at her hand and, reluctantly, I released it.

She was right, as much as I hated to admit it, and I felt the flush of embarrassment rise into my face. It wasn't a sign of weakness, this strange inability to let go of something easily and without a fight. No, it was something else, something far stronger and unexplainable.

I returned Tara's look, stare for stare. And this time when we regarded one another, the caution was gone.

"I've also been talking with one of the shrinks here," she continued. "He, he thinks it would be good for me to get into therapy. Not just because of this, but, but because I—I'm a self-destructive, histrionic personality." She scowled. "It's a lot worse to say it yourself than hear someone else say it to you. While I'm not entirely certain I agree, I figure it can't hurt. I suck at relationships, and I've had enough of them to know it. I suppose if I ever want to get beyond point A, I'll have to back up a bit and change the negative habits of a lifetime."

We talked a while longer, Tara alternating between her former caustic sense of humor and this new self-deprecating attitude. Finally, a nurse came in insisting I leave so Tara could have lunch and get some rest. Tara's protests were silenced by a stern look from the nurse—a first for her and proof of this newly adopted attitude. As I rose to go, I leaned over, kissed her gently on the forehead, and promised to come see her again. One of her arms snaked around my neck and held me to her for a moment, her tension flowing into my body. She let me go reluctantly and watched with tear-filled eyes as I headed for the door.

"You—you'd better not come back. Things are just too close right now. I—we, uh, might not be able to handle it." A single tear rolled down her cheek, and I had to hold myself back to keep from gently wiping it away. Instead, I eased the door open, silently nodding my agreement.

"There was a time I could sell you anything. Even the Taj Mahal, if I'd wanted." Her voice was barely a whisper, but the meaning was perfectly clear.

I stopped then, turning to face her once more. "And I would have bought it and more." I told her sincerely.

We exchanged a long, knowing look, one filled with more meaning, more emotion than had been between us since the beginning of our relationship.

I turned away without a word, walking quickly down the hall and concentrating on placing one foot in front of the other. I knew what was needed—to put as much distance between us in as little time as possible, giving neither of us the chance to falter in our resolve.

Cruel? No, just necessary.

My heart thudded loudly within my ears, a pulse beat so erratic it may have been frightening under different circumstances. At the end of the hallway, I stopped for a moment to draw in a deep, cleansing breath.

"Are you all right, sir?" A young nurse peered anxiously into my face, her hand going reflexively to my shoulder.

"Fine, thanks." I gave her my best imitation of a smile and continued toward the hospital entrance, my mind gradually returning to its senses.

We'd done it, perhaps not well, but we'd made it just the same, ending our relationship on a note of friendship rather than hate. It had cost us and was something I'd not soon forget. For in that one sentence, that one look, I'd known just how easy it would have been to go back to her. And if I had, we might have been lost forever.

Chapter 10

It had grown considerably cooler while I was in the hospital, and by the time I dropped the car off at the loft and walked to the professor's, storm clouds had begun to roll in. While the sun still peeked out between darkening clouds, the dampness in the air spoke strongly of the coming rain.

I was greeted by the Drake's part-time housekeeper who, confirming the storm prediction, shuddered as she closed the door behind me. It was "tornado weather," she said in ominous tones, and the idea frightened her considerably. With another glance out the window, she let me know where to find the professor, then hurried off to the kitchen to finish luncheon preparations.

In his den/office, Edmund Drake had cleared the top of his desk of paperwork, covered it with a thick drop cloth, and set out brushes, paints, palette, and turpentine. His grey head was bent intently over a small black serving tray, his thick fingers deftly holding a #5 round-tipped brush. I watched quietly as he dipped it into a prepared cadmium yellow mixture and returned to the serving tray to lay on the color with a single quick stroke.

Spotting me from the corner of his eye, he looked up and grinned broadly.

"My latest hobby." He waved his free hand at the items on the desk. "Tole painting. I thought perhaps I might get Janet interested—you know how she likes antiques—and it would be something we could do together." He gave a good-natured laugh. "But, alas, she found interest only in purchasing the items, leaving the refurbishing up to me."

A form of Folk Art, the relatively simple designs of tole painting were done basically with a single brush stroke, and had been used for years to decorate both tin and wooden household items. Almost a lost art, interest had been revived in recent years as collectors worked to preserve designs on antiques. Soon, it became an affordable hobby—one that could be enjoyed with little investment of time or money and which required more desire than talent to perform.

As a professional art instructor, the professor's talent and ability went beyond what was necessary, of course, but he'd always been a hobby enthusiast—especially when it came to painting.

I glanced over his shoulder to look at the item in question more closely.

"Janet found four of these at an auction in St. Joseph a while back. They were in pretty sad condition, let me tell you." Professor Drake explained how the serving tray had been refurbished, its original fruit basket design carefully traced so it could later be transferred back onto the tray.

"She was all right through the first couple of steps but just couldn't get the brush strokes down." He shook his head, amused by the thought. "I suppose I should know better by now. She's never been crazy about the mess created by painting anything and couldn't understand why I'd prefer it over a novel." He chuckled, rubbing his chin thoughtfully with the tip of the paintbrush.

"For me, sitting for hours upon hours reading a detective novel, barely moving a muscle during all that time, seems an utter waste of time and energy. No exercise of anything but the mind and eyes!" He exclaimed. "While I love a good book as much as anyone, I read in moderation. Give me something like this to stretch the imagination and stimulate creativity, and I'm happy. Janet, however, is bored to tears."

I remembered this discussion well when visiting during the summers years before. As a compromise, rainy days had been spent divided between what each of them thought more important: the professor encouraging my raw talent for drawing and painting, Janet introducing me to the limitless wonder and imagination offered through literature. He provided sketch pads, paints, and small canvas boards, instructing me in simple techniques and styles, versing me in the magic to be found watching your visions come to life with a stroke of a brush. She enticed me with books about faraway lands and heroes that set the imagination soaring. The end result was a total love of the arts, the ability to envision scenes never actually visited, and the desire to transfer them into a story on canvas.

"Anyway," Professor Drake continued. "It was either find another outlet for my art, or start making the rounds of craft shows to unload some of my work." He glanced around the room at the various oil miniatures on the walls. From painted saw blades and clock faces, to the wild birds and animals on small canvases, the room was filled with his work—as was nearly most of the house. Understanding the obsession well, I smiled in sympathy.

Lunch was served, and although he declared it a "simple fare," it was more like a banquet to me: baked chicken with all the fixings, mashed potatoes, and apple cobbler for dessert. After spending the last two weeks more intent on painting than filling my stomach, my taste buds were startled into wakefulness.

During lunch, I told the professor of my visit with Tara. He listened, his face etched with disapproval, his bushy grey eyebrows drawn in a tight line across his forehead. Gradually, as the story unfolded, a reluctant smile broke through his frown.

"I was beginning to wonder at the wisdom of seeing her again, but perhaps it was best after all." He ate his last bite of cobbler and dabbed at his chin with a napkin. "Perhaps this, er, truce between you will avert further difficulties." Professor Drake raised an eyebrow in speculation as he peered at me over the top of his coffee cup. "It's truly over?"

"With Tara, yes." I nodded. "As far as Hargrave is concerned, I'm not sure. I don't see how he can pursue a case against me when the victim denies my guilt and refuses to testify, so I'm hoping he'll crawl back under whatever rock he came out of."

"Well, as far as the Board is concerned, barring further unpleasantness, we should have no more trouble from them. The current issue appears to be whether or not one can trust the young lady in question." His brows knit together across his forehead. "What do you say, Richard, can we trust her this time?"

"Yes." I said without hesitation. "Sometimes it takes a knock on the head to get our attention and make us aware of what's going on around us. In Tara's case, it was literal."

"Um, well, if Miss Morgan sticks to her story and refuses to allow the detective to sway her, I believe you'll be out of the woods."

It seemed a sort of providence that he chose that particular phrase. I took a swallow of water and gathered my words carefully.

"Which brings me to a question I've been meaning to ask." From the sudden tenseness of his shoulders, I was fairly certain he knew what was coming.

"Hargrave told me about my "accident," that he believed it was related to the Linden Stalker case."

Edmund Drake's usually ruddy complexion faded to a pasty white before my eyes. His hand, trembling slightly, reached for his water glass, and clutching it tightly, both hand and glass remained glued to the table's surface. He drew in a breath between closed teeth, exhaling raggedly as his eyes met mine.

"I was afraid of this, hoped he would have the decency not to say anything," he snorted at this, "but should have realized that particular attribute was something he did not possess."

A touch of sadness crossed his face. Tossing the napkin aside, his shoulders squared, and his mouth was drawn into a thin, taut line.

"I suppose there's nothing for it then." He sighed in resignation. "Ask your questions, son," he said softly. "I'll do my best to answer them."

This sudden acquiescence took me aback, and struggling for my own composure, I sat quietly for a moment to organize my thoughts. There were so many questions it seemed to take a form of physical pushing and shoving to keep them locked away and filed in an orderly fashion.

"You found me in the park." Despite only just having taken a sip of water, my throat was parched giving my voice a rasping sound.

Professor Edmund Drake, imminent scholar and proud Head of the College of Arts and Humanities of Linden State University, lowered his eyes and nodded dejectedly.

"God help me." He pushed his chair away from the table and paced about the room. The mock chandelier above the table sent crazy shadows leaping erratically with every lap the professor made.

"I had an appointment and was late. We never had much of a dinner schedule during summer; it wasn't unusual to wait until eight or nine, so Jan decided to hold it until I got home. She said she'd given you a snack in my office around seven and left you curled up on the window seat, absorbed in *Tom Sawyer*." He glanced up at me. "You know how hectic summer sessions are, twice as much to prepare and grade. She went to see about dinner, then into her office to work. It wasn't until I returned at nine that anyone realized you were missing."

After a quick search of the house, Janet started making calls to neighborhood friends. It hadn't taken long for panic to set in.

"She was beside herself with worry, terrified you'd gone to the treehouse. You'd been fretting for the last several days that they'd

PORTRAIT OF JENNY

bulldoze it before you had the chance to remove your things." He explained. "Because of the work going on in the park, we'd made you promise to stay away from that area, and I, in turn, had promised to get you there before it was too late. But, work piled up at the school, and one thing led to another, and well," he raked a hand through his thick grey hair making it stand on end.

"The storm had come in fast, totally unexpected. It was dark far too early for the first of July, and getting darker and wilder all the time."

Still, the professor felt I'd enough sense to come in out of the rain and refused to give in to Janet's panic. But when another hour passed and I still hadn't shown up, he'd run out into the storm to look for me.

It was as though a dam had burst, all the years of silence had built up a pressure so intense that the tiniest crack in the foundation had loosed an entire flood. I listened raptly as the information poured forth, so caught up in his emotion that I had to remind myself to breathe.

"You loved playing in the back woods. The place was so overgrown and wild, you claimed it was like being in another country." He stopped his pacing to look at me then, his eyes bright with memory. "Do you remember, Richard, do you remember telling me about your imagined battles? That summer you were Robin Hood."

I nodded as the vague thread of memory surfaced. I smiled up at him.

"Stealing from the rich, giving to the poor, and defending Maid Marion's honor."

The professor answered my smile with one of his own. "As I recall, that was little Mary Rogers who used to live down the street. And what an unwilling damsel in distress she was! You came home with more skinned knees and bruised ankles than any young hero should have to stand." The smile changed slowly to a grimace as he waved away the lighter memory.

"The Rogers' hadn't seen you since that afternoon, and the Murray boy, I forget his name, was sick with the chicken pox, so that left the woods."

He knew I hadn't cared about the renovations being made in the front half of the park, so he'd rushed through the area without bothering to call out or search for me. There were, after all, no places to hide with most of the trees thinned out, and beyond a slight curiosity regarding the new foundation of the proposed gazebo, it was of little interest to me.

As I'd feared, work had already begun in the back woods area. Much of it had been cleared, but there were still downed trees blocking old pathways creating unseen hazards, and it was filled with surveying equipment and heavy machinery. Surprisingly, the small grove where the treehouse was built had not yet been touched.

"The rain was blinding, coming down in sheets, and was occasionally mixed with hail. It was a wild night, and I'd come out totally unprepared. There were no lights, and without a flashlight, I had to rely on bursts of lightning to help me see." He looked up again, his gaze seeming to settle on some point beyond my shoulder.

"During the entire search, I occupied my mind with all the possible punishments I could settle on you—it was probably the only thing that kept me from giving in to my own panic."

But when I hadn't been found tucked safely in the snug confines of the treehouse, his general calm had begun to erode.

The professor started suddenly at the appearance of the housekeeper in the dining room's doorway. He stiffened slightly, making a visible effort to relax as he gave her permission to clear away the remnants of our meal. As we moved back across the hall to his office, I could hear the clink of the dishes being gathered—an oddly normal sound in the midst of the story being told.

The smell of the turpentine in the office assaulted my senses, pulling me out of the past with a sudden jolt. I looked about the familiar room, my eyes coming to rest on the window seat and bay that looked out upon the front lawn.

I'd wondered why my mind hadn't been reeling from the information Janet provided, had said as much to Joyce Noland. I'd taken what Janet gave me and filed it away, taking it out and examining it only to find it lacking, not quite touching me. I believed I now had the reason for that detachment.

Janet's account of that night had been simplified with only the essential details related. She'd been more concerned about the end result, how I would be affected now, rather than with the raw emotions of that time. Perhaps it was the guilt and responsibility she still felt that prevented her from telling more. Or, maybe she didn't feel the same need that so obviously gripped the professor.

I searched my memory for that small boy, for some inkling to that night so long ago, but all I could see were the images the professor just described.

We sat facing one another in the twin chairs before his desk. I was surprised when he sat; after his earlier restlessness, I didn't think it possible for him to remain calmly seated as he continued his tale. Nor did it take long for him to prove my assumption correct.

Professor Drake's mouth curled wryly on one side as he stood abruptly and began pacing once again.

"I suppose I would have found you immediately had I really looked." He rubbed his hands briskly down the legs of his trousers. "You were no more than ten to fifteen feet from the gazebo's foundation, lying in a rut that was partially filled with rain."

He had been kept from stepping on me when a sudden flash of lightning illuminated my still body, immersed from the waist down in a puddle of water.

The professor turned his back on me then, his voice breaking emotionally. With great difficulty, he reiterated what Janet told me.

Seeing my nude body, he'd stripped off his already drenched shirt and draped it over me. He'd searched frantically for a pulse, breathing a sigh of relief when he found it.

"I wasn't sure what to do, whether or not to move you myself, and finally decided it would be best to get an ambulance there as quickly as possible."

On an adrenaline high, he'd run all the way home. Janet had been anxiously waiting for him, but he'd flown past her, ignoring her frightened questions, his mind fixated on what he must do.

"Do I notify the police as well?" He asked, as though suddenly thrust back into time. He shook his head forlornly. "I didn't know the answer to that one. The ambulance was the important thing. Once you were safely in the hands of professionals, the other decisions could be made."

With the call taken care of, he'd dashed back out into the storm without a thought for his frantic wife.

"I'd heard her, of course." He gave me a grim smile. "One cannot help but hear Janet when she's determined to be heard. I just didn't have the energy to answer her."

He hadn't realized Janet followed him to the park until she'd placed the raincoat across his shoulders. Not even sparing her a glance, he'd immediately whipped it off and laid it over me. Then, without a word between them, Janet and Edmund Drake stood guard over my prone body until the ambulance arrived.

"There were a lot of questions, which was natural. I only half listened to what was being said, all my thoughts were for you and what we must tell your parents. Later, when things were a bit more settled, Janet told me she'd fended off inquiries by pleading shock. Not that it was far from the truth."

He sank onto the chair opposite me, leaned his head back, and with eyes turned toward the ceiling, sighed deeply. In the sudden quiet, I could hear the sound of the wind whistling through the screen and rattling the windows as it picked up velocity. Branches of shrubs in front of the house scraped the siding with an eerie sound that added to the haunting reality of the story being told.

Professor Drake rubbed a large hand across his face, then met my eyes.

"From the moment Hargrave showed up at Lambert Hall I knew it was only a matter of time before the story would come out. Aside from the time you were in the hospital, these have been the longest weeks of my life." He gave me a half-hearted grin. "The events have been replaying in my mind constantly—as I'm sure you've already guessed from my treatise."

I nodded. My mouth felt as though I hadn't had a drink in days; even the act of swallowing was difficult.

"When did the police become involved?"

"I believe it was radioed in from the ambulance." He shook his head. "There were a lot of people involved in taking care of you that night. More than I'd ever imagined there would be. It was the mention of the Stalker case that led the doctor to ask us about the, er, tests. As it turned out, they had enough on their hands trying to keep you stabilized. Worrying about whether or not you'd been raped didn't compare in importance." He met my eyes squarely. "I'm sorry, son. I know this can't be easy for you."

"Nor for you." I said softly. My emotions having run the gamut in the last several minutes, I was surprised to find my voice steady in spite of my dry throat.

"No, it's not easy for me, either. But then, I've had almost twenty-one years to live with it, you haven't." He cocked an expressive brow. "It was never proven, Richard."

It wasn't difficult to figure out what he was referring to. "But Hargrave believed it was possible."

"Oh, yes. He believed it enough to force himself onto your parents, Janet, and me while you were still in a coma, and refused to take no for an answer." The professor rose again and went to stand behind his chair, his large hands gripping and kneading the back of it. "He hung around the hospital for those two weeks, lurking in the hallways and waiting for you to come around. And, by God, the bastard had the audacity to try to question you within the first few hours after you'd regained consciousness! But your father took care of him. Had the man booted out of the hospital and followed up with a call to the Chief of Police. I don't imagine the detective's forgotten about that."

My father had rarely lost his temper, but when he did, he'd held nothing back. A quirk of fate and a strange combination of the gene pool had given him a stern face that barely saw relief even when he'd smiled. Flushed with anger, his forbidding appearance was taken that one step further into the danger zone—"The wrath of God on overload," as my mother once put it. I would have hated to be in the detective's shoes.

"So this might have something to do with revenge—this desire of his to frame me for Tara's assault—it does have some basis?"

Professor Drake nodded, a lock of his grey hair falling across his forehead. "I wouldn't doubt it. Oh, I'm sure he felt justified pursuing you in the beginning. After that row in the Snack Shack earlier that day, and Nagoochi's testimony that you and Tara had become bitter enemies, you would seem a likely suspect. But once he'd made the connection, well, I'm sure the detective would deny it, but I've no doubt the additional pressure was based on the past."

No longer feeling capable of sitting still, I jumped up from the chair and strode to the window. The last rays of sunlight had been blocked out and the clouds hung dark and heavy in the sky. Bits and pieces of debris flew past the window, and the branches of the old maple at the side of the lot whipped back and forth in the wind as though they were no more than twigs.

"Looks like we're in for a hell of a storm." I commented idly. Rather an inane sort of response considering the subject of our conversation.

Goose bumps prickled the length of my arms to gradually be felt all over my body. As I looked out upon the ever increasing darkness, I pictured another afternoon almost twenty-one years before and the child that sat in this very room on the window seat before me, innocently reading *Tom Sawyer*.

Yes, I could see it now. Clearly. Reality was setting in with a vengeance. This time enough of the story had been told to give it the ring of truth, to make me see and feel that day so long ago.

I turned slowly back toward the professor, not surprised to find him watching me.

"So," I cleared my throat. "We know what Hargrave believed happened, that I was raped by the Stalker and left in the storm to die. What about you, Professor? What do you believe?"

His eyes grew large and twitched slightly at the corners in time with the pulse at the base of his throat.

"It—it was my greatest fear that he was right and some day you would remember and not be able to live with what happened." His hands tightened their grip on the back of the chair. "We all talked about it, your parents, Janet and I. We had little else to do those two weeks but try to anticipate what would happen once you regained consciousness." He swallowed convulsively, his eyes darting around the room as though he wished to escape the intensity of my gaze. "When you finally came around and had no memory of the event, we took it as a sign, a true godsend. We didn't have to deal with our fears—or yours. It was a reprieve, a chance to discuss what we knew, speculate on what we didn't, and try to come up with a conclusion we could all live with. We needed alternative plans in case your memory should suddenly return, some explanation for you, for us. The first decision was to get you away from Linden as soon as you were well enough. The second, I always regretted, and that was to put an end to your summers alone with Jan and me."

So that hadn't been a decision of my parents alone. I'd often wondered.

Now, seeing his look of dejection and remembering all the nights of sharing adventures before bedtime, I realized just how much our time together had meant to him. Never having children of his own, he'd taken his friend's child into his heart and home, living the life of a parent in those three short summer months and attempting to capture and hold onto that intimacy until the next time we would be together. The plans he made—the time spent building the treehouse, hours of catch, museum field trips—all of it had come to an end because of that night in the park.

"We always anticipated your visits here with pleasure, planning our days around you." He said, echoing my thoughts. "You were the son Jan and I never had, Richard. A real joy and bright spot in our lives. As time passed, and your memory failed to return, I wanted to ask about your coming back to us in the summers. Jan was skeptical, concerned your parents could never fully trust us again, but finally agreed we should try." He returned to the chair, sitting wearily on its edge.

"I have to give your parents credit. They never once blamed us for the incident. Never held it against us. Our friendship remained strong, as you know. But where you were concerned, time only made their fear fade a bit, never took it completely away. I suppose they were afraid if you were to come stay with us, something might happen to jolt you into remembering." He shrugged. "We didn't handle it very well, I know. Maybe if we'd run the tests, known for sure, perhaps gone to a therapist—but we didn't. We hid what we knew and prayed to God you'd never remember and make us have to face it or our inadequacies. I'm sorry."

I waved away his apology. "Sorry for what? Trying to protect me? You did what you thought was best. I'll admit it drove me crazy not knowing what happened. I mean, waking up in the hospital and seeing everyone looking so sad was weird. I didn't have the vaguest idea what was going on, and for a long time thought I'd done something horribly wrong that couldn't be forgiven. I was confused, and it hurt to be left in the dark. But even worse was feeling unable to talk about the nightmares because of the pain I saw enter your eyes." I sat on the window seat and stared at the professor thoughtfully. "I couldn't justify causing anyone more problems, so I decided to keep quiet about it, and eventually, the dreams faded away." I cleared my throat and ran my tongue over parched lips. "I wanted knowledge, and I've gotten it. It took a long time in coming, but I can't fault anyone for what was or wasn't done. If there's blame here, I suppose it should be on my shoulders. After all, what was I doing out in the middle of a storm anyway?"

"I wish to God I knew!" He looked at me earnestly. "It's a question I've asked myself, asked Janet, a thousand times. Perhaps it was the treehouse, perhaps something else. I don't know, will never know unless your memory returns. And after all this time, that seems highly unlikely. But the one thing you need to know, son, what you need to remember, is you're not to blame here. You're the innocent in all of this."

I rubbed the palms of my hands briskly across my jean-covered thighs. The denim felt rough, almost foreign, to the sensitive skin.

"There's something here we're missing. Something important."

The wind beat at the window, rattling the screen and whining through the minute cracks of the casing.

"Jan and I have gone over that afternoon more times than I could count, Richard, analyzing it down to the minute. There's nothing, no sound explanation for your action. You were contentedly reading on that window seat one minute and gone the next." His pale eyes regarded me intently. "You were ten years old and very impulsive. Perhaps even more so than usual that night. The explanation? You got a notion into your head and acted on it. We'd forbidden you to go to the park during the daytime because of the work going on there, so you decided to go that night. We hadn't told you about the Stalker, there didn't seem any reason to, so you had no sense of the possible danger.

"Let it go, son." He said softly. "No good can come from your brooding on something that happened so long ago."

"In a nightmare world?" I asked, using Janet's terminology.

He nodded. "A nightmare, yes. That's certainly what it was. If—if it's haunting you, maybe you should try speaking to a therapist. Perhaps they could lay the ghosts for you, help you to come to terms with it."

"Help me remember?"

"If that's what you want, what you feel you need, yes. Hypnotism might aid in that regard." He looked up questioningly. "I've wondered why you never tried it before."

I shrugged. "It was only a curiosity before, something odd about my past. The big question mark." I laughed wryly. "Until I began getting bits and pieces…"

"And now? Now that you know?"

"I want the rest. All of it—eventually. First, I want the chance to digest it, get used to the idea. Everything still seems so unreal to me, as though what you've described happened to someone else. There's a ring of truth in it that makes a connection for me, to me, but, I don't know. I'm still detached. Perhaps that's a good thing."

Detached, but not impervious. How could I be when the incident had changed not only my life, but the lives of my parents and the Drakes as well? Since the initial disclosure by Chuck and Lily, and Janet's enlightening of their sketchy details, my thoughts had continued to return to the subject in spite of everything else that was happening around me. Tara's assault, Hargrave's conviction of my guilt, the mysterious fugue states that had produced the drawings of Jenny and the charcoal of the girl in the morgue—all of it was overlaid by the knowledge that had been so long in coming. The thought that someone had beaten me and left me to die was bad enough to contend with, but the additional, shocking information that I may have been raped could have easily blown my mind had I allowed it to do so.

So, I dealt with it the way I knew best, throwing myself into my work and concentrating on all the intricate details involved. From the mixing of paints for the right values and textures, to the correct choice of brush and size of canvas, I gave myself to my art. In return, my creative muse had taken possession of mind and body, bringing to life my thoughts, ideas, and dreams, and giving me the opportunity to stand back from the events of the first of July nearly twenty-one years ago.

As with the production of any piece of art, perspective was needed, a time to compare and contrast what I knew to what I'd learned. I must take into consideration the child I'd been and graduate to the man I'd become. Only then could I confront what happened and ease it into my life and learn to live with it.

I knew these things, accepted them and their importance to my psychological health. Why then did I continue to harbor that niggling doubt, that deeply rooted belief that this wasn't it, that the true story was still waiting to be told?

Watching as professor was gradually restored to his normal, good-humored self with the mantle of silence drawn at last from his broad shoulders, the questions and inability to accept this as the whole truth remained. Oh, I knew this was the story, the chronology of events as the professor knew them from that stormy night long ago. The terror had been as real for him now as it was then—as was the disgust and regret he felt for having failed both my parents and me.

But for all the raw emotion, for all the shock that came with the revelation of the facts, there remained the belief that something was missing. Not just my own memory of that night, but that somewhere, somehow, a very large piece of the puzzle had been left out. And, until that final piece was at last inserted, what happened to little Richie Tanner could not touch or connect with me. I would not escape unscathed, but neither would I be destroyed.

We talked a while longer among the smell of paints and turpentine from his discarded tole painting paraphernalia. With the subject changed, Professor Drake's mood steadily lightened. A weight had been lifted, a burden that hadn't decreased its load through all the years of silence. But the telling had created a new challenge; I saw it in his eyes as the afternoon wore on. He was prepared for this one; his eyes and attitude told me he felt equipped to handle anything that was to come. No longer feeling the necessity to protect me from what I did not know, he let me know with a look and a word that I was not alone; there were now two of us to fight the demons of the past and face them here in the present. He'd helped me slay imaginary dragons and enemies years before when I was child but had been unprepared to protect me from one very real monster. Now, he was prepared and offering to help me lay that final demon to rest.

Chapter 11

It was nearly four o'clock before a lull in the storm gave me an opportunity to head back to the loft. But, as I stepped outside, the idea of shutting myself up in my apartment was far from appealing. The air was sweet and heady with the scents of spring and rain, the wind had died down, and despite the lowering sky, I didn't believe I was in immediate danger of being caught in a sudden downpour. And if I were, it wouldn't be the first time.

Whether it was from some strange sense of morbid curiosity, or the normal course of my obsession, I found myself at the edge of University Park without conscious thought of having walked there. Because of the storm, the area was deserted, which suited my purposes completely. With no distractions, and a little luck, I might be able to bring back a memory or two.

I looked out across the park trying to recall what it looked like in the midst of renovation. The precision with which the park's department had designed it made it difficult to see what I knew had been relative chaos at that time, so I closed my eyes to shut out the uniformity and encouraged my mind to drift back to that summer.

I'd seen the equipment and crews swarming through the park,

remembered the noise that could be heard at the Drake's beginning early every morning and running until dark every night. Mary Rogers, Frank Murray, and I had watched from across the street—still marveling that the summer before, the road in front of us had been a pathway through the woods.

By that June, most of the east side, or park front as it was always referred to, had been on its way to completion, with designated sections all carefully laid out for the garden areas, playground, and, most importantly, the gazebo. There hadn't been sidewalks that first summer, but I remembered the survey crews that patiently set out their strings before the workers began to dig and put in forms for the cement.

The majority of action had been around the gazebo—or, actually, what was to be the gazebo. Frank, whose father was foreman of one of the crews, had been full of stories on how the workers had been forced to set and reset the gazebo's location site because the Council had insisted it be placed in the direct center of the park. As no one had yet determined exactly where that would be, pouring the foundation had been pushed further and further back, resulting in construction being far behind schedule. It had taken what Frank referred to as "an act of God," for the final decisions to be made. The surveying crews were given the go-ahead to set the western boundary of the park, and the center had finally been determined. Toward the end of the month, with a great deal of overtime, the groundwork was completed, the forms were set, and the foundation was ready to pour. A week of rainy weather held things up, and by the time the crews were back in the park, they'd been working with a vengeance.

A sudden, involuntary shiver passed the length of my spine, and I opened my eyes with a start. Without explanation, I was finding it hard to catch my breath, yet, at the same time, was breathing far too fast.

Hyperventilation. The word sprang to my head and with it came the cure. Without a paper bag available, I placed my hands tightly over my nose and mouth and made the conscious effort to breathe slowly in and out. As I did so, my eyes strayed toward the gazebo, my heart skipping a beat as I spotted the tiny figure looking out in my direction.

Jenny.

I lifted my hand in a wave and smiled when she returned the gesture. My breathing was still somewhat erratic, but it didn't seem to matter; Jenny was in the gazebo, and I wasn't about to stand there like a fool and miss seeing her.

I walked quickly, dodging puddles and skirting around mud that had washed up over the sidewalks. After that first skipped beat, my heart began pounding in anticipation of the meeting, increasing in tempo and strength until I could hear it thumping loudly within my head. I felt as giddy as a schoolboy on his first date, with my palms growing cold and beginning to sweat.

I hardly took my eyes off her and was pleased that she looked as happy to see me as I was her. I wasn't more than ten feet from the gazebo when I spotted Chuck and a young woman coming across the park from the other direction. I hoped he would be too preoccupied with his companion to see me, but it wasn't to be. The sound of his voice as he called out my name broke not only the silence that surrounded me but the spell as well; from the corner of my eye, I saw Jenny withdraw into the interior of the gazebo. I mentally crossed my fingers that her shyness would not prompt her to leave before I was able to get there.

Chuck Stinnet's latest companion was of Asian descent with the most appropriate name of Jet. Her long, dark hair of that very color hung down to a nearly nonexistent waist, dwarfing her tiny facial features under a cloud of pitch. She stared up at him with adoring, almond-shaped eyes of burnt umber, her small hands clutching at his arm possessively. An exotic little figure as delicate in appearance as a porcelain doll, she was the complete opposite of his last conquest, a nearly six foot Swedish import with white-blonde hair and the palest blue eyes I'd ever seen.

"We're on our way to Murphy's, Rich, want to join us?"

Jet made a sound of protest to which Chuck responded by pulling her even closer—if that were at all possible—and kissing her firmly on the mouth. He winked at me over the top of her head, patted the small mound of her bottom, and gave her a nudge to continue on her way.

"I'll join you in a moment, sweetheart." He told her with a grin and an appreciative look that caused the girl to giggle. She glanced at me with doubt, obviously none too pleased with his invitation, shrugged, then drawing a hand up to her full red lips, kissed the palm and blew lightly across it. Chuck played her game, reaching out and "catching" the blown kiss to her delight.

"Scoot." He watched her turn, licking his lips and grinning like the proverbial Cheshire cat.

"Possessive little vixen." He commented when she was out of earshot. "But for what she can do to a guy..." He gave a long, low whistle. "So, Rich, ole buddy, what are you up to this rainy afternoon?"

"I had lunch with Professor Drake and decided I needed a walk before going back to the loft." I said simply, my eyes straying toward the gazebo.

Stinnet followed my gaze.

"Someone waiting for you, or is it just wishful thinking?" There was a humorous twist to his mouth. "Not hoping to see your rainy-day gal, are you? Or is this more on the definite side?"

I ignored the light tone of sarcasm. "Something like that." Turning to look in the direction Jet had gone, I said, "You'd better get moving. She's almost to the street."

"You may be right. Look, man," he clapped me across the back. "I'm sorry for teasing you. The invitation to Murphy's stands. If you'd like, I'm sure Jet could find one of her friends—"

I raised an eyebrow, gazed back to where Jet stood waiting impatiently at the edge of the park, and shook my head in what I hoped appeared reluctance.

"It's tempting, but I think I'd better pass. She doesn't look as though she'd like to share your company with anyone just now."

"No," he agreed. "She doesn't. But hell, I'm feeling particularly magnanimous, sated at the moment," he said with a salacious grin and cock of his head in the girl's direction. "And thought we might find someone to knock those old headaches of yours right out of the ballpark. Believe me, Richard, an hour—half hour with someone like Jet, and, well, I'll leave it to your imagination." With a wide smile, and a wave of his hand, he jogged off to rejoin his companion.

I didn't bother to wait or watch them, my attention drawn back to the gazebo and the girl I hoped still waited there.

The wind started to rise once again; a gentle breeze lifted the fronds of a nearby willow and sent a shower of raindrops across my face. I wiped at them with the back of my hand, closing the remaining gap between the gazebo and me in a couple long strides.

The quiet had returned to the park, the only sounds made by the soughing of the wind as it passed through the branches of trees and bushes along with the chirping of birds that had come out to feast on worms forced from underground because of the rain.

A robin darted out from behind one of the rose bushes around the foundation, flying past with a ruffle of feathers. It drew my attention to the newly opened blooms of yellow, white, and red, carefully cultivated and pruned to perfection. While some of the bushes were tall, they could not hide the fissures and ugly gashes webbed in the cement behind them. The spidery forks spread steadily upward, with some of the worst damage along the base at ground level where chips of cement had been loosened and perched precariously against the whole. As Hargrave stated nearly two weeks before, it seemed odd nothing had been done about the damage. I'd never before seen the foundation in such a state of disrepair.

As I rounded the gazebo to the steps, I called out to Jenny, and receiving no answer, felt my heart sink within my chest. As I'd feared, the interior of the building was empty, and a quick look around revealed that once again, she'd left nothing behind, no clues to her identity.

The wind continued to rise and was now moaning through the latticework with an eerie, off-pitched cry of protest. Dark clouds scudded across the sky, and branches of nearby trees tossed to and fro in a macabre kind of dance. There was a sudden absence of birdsong and activity, a sure sign, if I'd needed one, of another storm approaching. With a final look around the empty gazebo, and a sigh of disappointment, I quickly started for the loft.

It was difficult not to dwell on the frustration of being unable to speak with Jenny after seeing her once again. I could have blamed Chuck and his companion's untimely arrival but decided the fault lay more with Jenny and her lack of patience and/or debilitating shyness. No, I didn't have anything definite to account for my suspicions, but it did seem rather odd that on both occasions it was the sudden appearance of Chuck Stinnet that led to her abrupt departure. Maybe I'd been close to the truth when I joked about his reputation being the reason behind her avoiding him.

After all, what did I know about this strange girl? She was beautiful, enigmatic, seemed painfully shy, and had a habit of disappearing at the most inopportune moments. She'd held me with her eyes, capturing my attention in a way that led to almost obsessive behavior—a good explanation for the sketches done in the middle of the night without cognizance of the action.

While I felt strongly that Jenny was everything I described and more, I had no doubt there had been a man, or men, in her life. It was simply thinking of her in connection with Chuck Stinnet that didn't correlate.

My thoughts strayed to Inge, the beautiful Swede who'd managed to hold Stinnet's interest for nearly two months the previous semester. I'd never seen her replacement, heard bits of raunchy description of the affair from Chuck, but that was it. The relationship hadn't lasted long, her tastes too eclectic even for Chuck. Which led to his present conquest, the exotic Jet.

While I didn't agree with or condone Chuck's behavior, nor did I feel it my place to judge him—how could I, after all, when I'd been involved with Tara who was considerably like him. He seemed happy with his chosen lifestyle. My desire to find permanence in a relationship caused him to break into gales of laughter, as did my belief in romance and insistence on monogamy.

Chuck may be cynical and irreverent about life in general, but he wasn't stupid.

Nor was Jenny.

The incongruity of the two individuals was so vast, it had been crazy to even think of them in the same context. If Tara wasn't his style—the female version of himself—then Jenny most certainly wouldn't be.

A couple of fat raindrops exploded on the sidewalk in front of me as I ran across the street to Weisher's. They'd be closing within minutes, and I wanted to pick up some bread for supper. I was reaching for the doorknob when I noticed the dirty green car parked before the bakery—the nondescript Ford belonging to Hargrave. This time, the model sunk in, an LTD from the middle seventies, and from the looks of it, it was in no better condition than it had been nearly two weeks before.

I backed down off the step as a customer came out of the shop but not before I saw Hargrave himself, deep in conversation with Mrs. Weisher. As curious as I was, avoiding him was more important at the moment. I turned and quickly started by the large display window, hoping to make it past without his noticing me.

It nearly worked. I was just rounding the corner of the building into the side alley when I heard a tap on the window and, without thinking, looked up. Hargrave stood on the inside staring out at me. He raised his hand in a mock salute, which I chose to ignore, and laughing, turned back to his conversation with Mrs. Weisher.

When he made no move to follow me, I breathed a sigh of relief, hoping that I'd seen the last of the implacable detective. But the professor's description of the man's relentless pursuit of me following the assault was a grim reminder of the resentment he might continue to harbor toward my family for thwarting his investigation of the Linden Stalker.

The momentary reprieve from Hargrave and small triumph I felt was short-lived; beneath the stairs leading to the loft was a navy and white Blazer with a license plate that read HTSTUF. I recognized it immediately as belonging to Matthew Marzetti, and the implication was too much to contend with at the moment. I was about to turn back into the side alley when the heavens let loose with a vengeance; I was soaked to the skin by the time I threw open the door to the loft.

I stood just inside the doorway, dripping on the balled-up rug laid there, eyeing Lily with a mixture of relief and skepticism—relief that it was not an irate Marzetti waiting for revenge, skepticism about Lily's presence and what she was up to this time.

It was obvious she'd been going through the stacks of completed paintings; some of the later ones were propped in various places along the walls of the studio. She had switched on all the lights, removing the shades to spotlight some paintings and moving the lamps to strategic points on the floor to highlight others. Her back was to me, but I could see she was holding the canvas of St. Joe's Krug Park. Startled by my arrival, she turned around to face me so quickly she nearly dropped the painting, catching it just before it hit the floor.

"Oh!" She glared at me as she set the painting on my work chair, which was pushed tightly against the parson's table.

Flipping a mass of soggy hair from my eyes, I said with exasperation, "Have you got a key or what?"

She waved a hand toward the storeroom. "I brought the canvases, all stretched and mounted to your specifications. Mrs. Weisher was kind enough to offer her husband's assistance in getting them upstairs during the storm's brief intermission." She regarded me with a mixture of humor and dismay. "You're drenched and getting everything around you drenched as well."

I cocked an eyebrow in her direction. She appeared to read my mind.

"Don't worry. Your virtue is safe from me, Richard. I've learned my lesson."

"Really?" I found that hard to believe, and it must have shown in my voice.

"Really." Lily Reston's full, sensual lips pursed wryly. "If I was unable to tempt you last time with my best teddy, I sincerely doubt you'd go for me in a ratty pair of blue jeans and a T-shirt. Now, go get changed before you catch cold."

"Ratty" was hardly the term I'd have given to the form-fitting Calvin Klein's that sheathed the lower half of her body. As for the T-shirt, it appeared at least a size too small and was stretched tightly across her ample bosom. She'd pulled her long, blond hair back into a ponytail, leaving a fringe of bangs across her forehead. She looked young and attractive, and I was sure she knew that as well.

Noticing my appraising glance, a smile touched the long corners of her mouth.

"If you're finished with the examination, Richard, I'd suggest you go before I decide to throw caution to the wind."

A few minutes later, dry, with the exception of my hair, I returned to the living room. She hadn't heard me approach in my sock feet, and I was able to observe her as she studied the Krug Park painting.

Her eyes were intent as she stood back to gain some perspective, an unreadable expression upon her face. Then, surprisingly, she went to kneel before it, her fingers reaching out to touch the canvas tentatively as her long mouth worked from side to side as though she was chewing on the insides of her cheeks.

"Something wrong?" I asked, briskly rubbing my head with a towel.

She jumped back, startled, landing on her rear and frowning up at me.

"Don't do that," she said harshly.

"Sorry." I tossed the towel onto a nearby chair and pulled my comb from the back pocket of my jeans. Combing my still damp hair, I went to help her onto her feet.

Lily made a show of brushing off her jeans, her eyes remaining shielded by her long lashes. She seemed in a strange mood, more thoughtful and reserved than I'd ever seen her, and I idly wondered if something was wrong.

"I've never known you to do figures." She said finally. "Is she the latest woman in your life?" Lily kept her eyes averted, returning them to the study.

"No. But she does add interest, doesn't she?"

I stared down at the scenic depiction of Krug Park, still marveling at how easy it had been to start and finish the picture. Without explanation, I'd become blocked while working on the bluffs view as I came closer to the inclusion of Jenny. The more I tried to break through the block, the worse things had gone, until I finally set that painting aside and opted to begin another.

My muse had taken over once again, and without an awareness of a choice having been made, I'd soon found myself in the middle of Krug Park, the pond and ducks bringing life to the surrounding trees and amphitheater in the background. Adding Jenny had been just as easy.

As with the rest of the composition, Jenny's inclusion was done with little thought, the mixing of paints for the right hues and the delicate brushstrokes to convey the barely discernible features, flowing without effort. The work had gone so well that I finished it in record time—and found myself still unable to return to the bluffs scene.

There were several plausible explanations for the sudden impasse, but recognizing them did nothing to overcome the block. Comparing the two paintings, the differences between them was obvious: in the bluffs study Jenny was in the forefront of the painting, the apparent focal point; but in Krug Park, there was little more than a hint of the face beneath the chestnut hair. There was nothing definite about the tiny features, just a suggestion of the whole, which was totally unlike the detail that would be involved with the bluffs depiction.

I'd always steered away from portraits, keeping to landscapes, seascapes, even an occasional still-life to avoid including people in my compositions. Now, here I was attempting it on a rather grand scale—especially with the view from the bluffs.

"She seems familiar." There was an odd ring to Lily's voice, and staring at her thoughtfully, I recalled Hargrave's comment when seeing the sketches.

"Perhaps you've seen her around town." I watched for a reaction and was rewarded with a slight shrug of her shoulders.

"She's from around here then?" She peered closely at the painting then finally turned to me. "I'm not in Linden enough to notice the locals, so I'm probably wrong. There was just something…" Another expressive shrug. "Oh well. It doesn't matter. What does is that it's really good, Richard. Not like your normal pieces. I'm very pleased. Especially with the charcoal."

"The charcoal?" It took me by surprise. "You were in the storage closet?"

"Um. When Mr. Weisher and I brought in the canvases. That *is* where you store them, isn't it?"

"Yes. I, uh, just didn't expect you—"

"To notice something so overwhelmingly incongruous to the rest of your work?" She seemed incredulous. "You've been hiding some very interesting aspects of your talent, and I hope we'll see more of it in the future."

I know I shouldn't have been offended, but I was. I knew she liked my work. She had, after all, become my staunch supporter and fan after viewing the few pieces I'd contributed to the Fine Arts showing five years before. It wasn't just this sudden expression of desire to have me add to my repertoire that disturbed me, which was something any artist would want. Rather, it was the idea that what sparked her enthusiasm appeared to come from a piece I didn't feel able to lay claim to. There was nothing I could say and continue to sound sane, so I just smiled and thanked her for the compliment.

"It wasn't meant as a compliment." She gingerly picked a clean rag off the parson's table and wiped her hands on it. "I'm simply telling the truth. You'll need the diversity for the exhibition to keep people's interests. If you continue to work in the same vein as these, you'll do wonderfully."

"People's? You mean Marzetti, don't you?"

Lily gave me a sidelong glance, but didn't answer. Instead, after tossing the rag back onto the table, she carefully gathered the paintings she'd spread throughout the studio. Following her example, I turned off lamps and replaced the shades before returning them to their accustomed places.

"Is he still giving you a hard time about the show?"

Lily's back was to me, but I saw it stiffen slightly. She drew in a deep breath but didn't respond.

"We're still on, aren't we?" Though I'd said it as a joke, her continued silence caused me to wonder if something had, indeed, gone wrong. Surely not even Matthew Marzetti would consider calling off a contracted exhibition.

"No, I mean yes, it's definitely a go." She turned to me, pushing aside a lock of hair that had come loose from her ponytail. "Look, Richard, it's not you. It's me. I—I've told Matthew that we're through, that I'm tired of a dead end relationship. He's not about to leave his wife, and I'm sick of sneaking around behind the woman's back." She folded her arms protectively across her chest. "Married thirteen years and *now* she's pregnant, and he's walking around like a proud papa or something! What do I get after six years of waiting and promises he'd dump her? Nothing. Zilch."

I reached out to comfort her, but she shook off my hand.

"It's my own fault, of course. I know it, Matt knows it, and his precious little wife knows it as well. So, we've made a deal. Art Magic becomes mine the first of the month, and if I don't see a profit within a year, it reverts back to him and I'm out. In the meantime, I have total autonomy." Her eyes appealed to me for understanding. "Do you see?"

"I think so." I said evenly. "Now you're in total control, you're having second thoughts about the young artist you've decided to back so heavily." I shoved my work chair into place with a little more effort than was needed. It hit the parson's table with a loud bang, nearly upsetting the partially opened bottle of turpentine in the center.

She nodded reluctantly. "I kind of put all my eggs in one basket and am scared as hell of getting them broken." She gave a derisive laugh. "Doesn't sound much like me, does it? Always so poised and extremely confident. That's me. Yeah, right." She picked up a discarded sketch that had fallen out of the recycle can, unfolded the paper, and looked down at it absently.

"Before, it was like a game—not my belief in your ability, Richard, please don't think that. It was just that I knew I could try new things with the gallery, choose new artists and give them the chance they might not get otherwise. Matt was always there if I fell, knowing what to do, taking that discerning eye of his and saving my rear when necessary. But with our deal..." She wadded the sketch back up and tossed it toward the can. It missed.

"We've agreed to no contact, so my butt belongs to me, and I'm not so sure I can handle that."

"I don't know what to say." Which was a vast understatement. She was right when she'd said this current attitude wasn't like her. I'd never thought to see the day that her confidence in herself would be shaken enough to allow doubts to infiltrate, let alone overcome her to such an extent. Lily had always seemed unshakable in her resolve—case in point, her continued determination to seduce me after numerous unsuccessful attempts. Whatever transpired between her and Marzetti had left her full of uncertainties about herself and her abilities to manage the gallery. One thing was certain, if she was to succeed with Art Magic, she had to snap out of this mood of self-doubt immediately, and I told her as much.

She dismissed my concerns with a flick of her hand, her large blue eyes narrowing thoughtfully. "I've let this get to me, and I refuse to allow it to do so any longer. I haven't been sitting on my hiney these last six years, you know. I may not be the connoisseur Matthew believes he is, but I'm not completely without the talent necessary to pick winners. I chose Autumn Hargis a year ago, and look where she is today, receiving national recognition! And you, Richard," a smile returned to her long, full mouth. "You're the ace in the hole. You've talent, imagination, and you know how to use them." She walked past me into the living room and began pacing its length, her shoulders squared, head thrown back, and eyes wide with determination.

"What I want from you is a little more diversification. Perhaps a few more of those charcoal sketches—and stay in tune with whatever dark side of your soul allowed the emergence of that first one. It's eerie and compelling, the type of thing that will grab the younger set and mesmerize the rest."

In the pause that ensued, I considered telling her how the charcoal had been produced, and once again, changed my mind. Even if I told her, I doubted she would give the story any credence or believe that I would be unable to tap the same creative vein to do more like it. Besides, in a matter of minutes she'd seemed to come out of her depression, and I had no desire to do anything that might alter her present state of mind. Instead, I remained where I was, alternating my glances between the pacing figure and the easel where the scene from the bluffs waited patiently for completion. My palms were itching—not the sign of money some people might believe it signified but a sign of inspiration that made me anxious to return to work.

I pictured Jenny as I'd briefly seen her today, her long chestnut hair blowing in the breeze, her face lit in anticipation.

Anticipation, maybe, but not enough to have kept her waiting for me.

"...and then, with the new pictures intermixed, it will show your true range of talent." Lily was saying. "What do you think?"

Lost in my thoughts, I hadn't heard the first part of the conversation, but the look of enthusiasm on her face gave me enough of an impression to smile and nod, safe in the knowledge that it didn't make any difference whether I'd heard or not.

"Good. See, I knew I could do it if I set my mind to it." Her ponytail swung gaily as she bounded to me and kissed me on the cheek. "Thanks for being a sounding board. Matt and I had that horrible confrontation just before I left KC to come up today. Needless to say, I brooded all the way here. What made matters even worse was knowing I had to drop the Blazer off at his house when I got back. Talk about rubbing salt into the wound!"

A sudden crash of thunder startled us both into laughter. Lily clapped her hands together like a child and grinned sheepishly.

"I—I'm supposed to meet my parents for dinner, but I've enough time for a drink at Murphy's if you'd like to join me. No funny business, I promise." She added hastily.

I gave her a grin and a half-bow. "I wish I could accept such a gracious invitation, my lady, but, alas, I feel it imperative to return to my work. After this miraculous recovery of yours, I wouldn't want to fail you."

She pursed her lips in disappointment. "Rain check?" Another boom of thunder gave the term a humorous twist.

It was agreed that the next time she was in town we'd not only have a drink, but dinner as well. Then, loaning her an umbrella, Lily went out into the storm. I remained at the screen door until I saw the Blazer head down the alley.

The rain was coming down heavily, the afternoon darkened to a deep slate as the heavens let loose their fury. A bolt of jagged lightning pierced the sky and appeared to touch the ground a few blocks away. It might have been my imagination, but I swore I could feel the static electricity surge through the metal screen and into my hands. Whether it was real or not, it was too close for comfort. I shut the main door and turned toward the studio.

Just as I'd suspected, it didn't take long for me to become fully immersed in the painting once more. Maybe the inspiration had come from seeing Jenny in the park, or perhaps all I'd needed was a little space to regain confidence in myself. Whatever the case, as I stood before the canvas with brush in one hand and palette in the other, the lights carefully trained on the partially finished painting, I knew there would be no further delays.

Time and circumstance again worked in my favor. For the present, I wouldn't have to worry or brood about the past, my relationship to it, and/or my acceptance of what might have happened to me. Contrary to my former belief in a policy of action and facing things as they came, I allowed myself to be carried along in much the same fashion as I'd permitted Tara's frequent intrusions in my life. If this was a sign of weakness, I was guilty as charged—though I preferred to think of it as another necessary tool of survival. I was dealing with the information in my own way, giving it the chance to seep into my brain cells and stimulate the desired response: memory. Once that elusive item was sparked, I knew it would return in full force, and I would be ready and waiting for it. In the meantime, I gave in to my imagination, offering up my heart and soul for the sake of my work, my art.

I looked from the sketch to the painting and back again, the small area where Jenny would be placed fixing itself into my mind.

It was all there, just like the sketch, the view from the bluffs with the hawk soaring in a rich azure sky. In the valley below ran the tiny silver thread of a river bounded on one side by a lush green field, on the other by a thick stand of trees. In the distance, almost obscured by the atmospheric perspective of colors gradually softening and blending together to add depth, was the outline of an old barn and farmhouse. It was beautiful and tranquil, the perfect idyll.

Another glance at the drawing, at the tiny uplifted face, and I closed my eyes and drew in a deep, cleansing breath. A simple pause, an interlude of wonder, and my hands began to work independently of my body and mind just as it should be. Brushes were exchanged for others more suitable for detailing work, paints were mixed and applied without hesitation, and slowly, almost like a miracle, Jenny emerged onto the canvas even more lovely and vital than she had appeared in the sketch.

The thunder and lightning continued throughout the remainder of the afternoon. Hail was interspersed with rain, the pellets beating against the glass of the skylights like tiny BBs, clicking and snapping, adding to the racket of the storm. The wind steadily picked up and howled in through the cracks and crevices of the loft, whistling through the small opening in one of the living room windows and sending the curtains billowing out before it only to be sucked tightly back a moment later.

I was acutely aware of all that was going on around me, my senses fine-tuned to both atmospheric and creative energies. I worked without stopping, without concern for the day as it moved into night or the storm that shook and rattled the windows.

As I neared completion, I moved from Jenny to put in highlights, methodically going from the hills and trees to the hawk, then to the grasses and wildflowers, and finally returning to Jenny's beautiful hair. Shadows were placed accordingly, adding proper depth to make the scene and figure three-dimensional and bringing just the right touch of reality. Another pleat to Jenny's skirt gave the illusion of texture, and a strand of chestnut hair across her forehead made me feel the gentle breeze that had blown it there.

Six hours later, I put down the brushes and palette and stood back to examine my handiwork. I couldn't help the way my breath caught in my throat or the little sob that was finally released with it. I knew I was standing before some of the best work I'd ever done—the "remarkable" I'd been after—and I owed it all to a girl I knew nothing about save her first name.

The rap on the door surprised more than startled me. It was late, nearly eleven, and the storm was still raging without. This was evidenced by a flash of lightning that streaked across the skylight above my head, illuminating the darkness with an eerie glow that vanished in an instant. It was rapidly followed by the hollow rumble of thunder that quickly escalated into an earsplitting roar, blotting out the muffled female voice that came from beyond the door.

She stood on my narrow porch with the screen door pushed back, rain streaming down into eyes that blinked rapidly trying to adjust from the blackness of the night.

"Swan?"

The word was muffled by another clap of thunder, but I didn't question it or the providence that brought her to my door.

Recognition dawned in the familiar face, and biting her lower lip, a beatific smile lit up her countenance.

"Richard." The soft voice said in wonderment, her violet eyes shining brightly just before they dimmed, and she collapsed in my arms.

Chapter 12

It wasn't a true faint; she never lost consciousness, simply crumpled against me like a rag doll. I swung her easily into my arms—she couldn't weigh more than ninety pounds—and by the time I'd closed the door, she'd asked politely to be set down.

As pleased as I was to see her, I couldn't help wondering why she was out so late in such a storm, and who, or what, was "Swan."

Jenny was soaked, the water in her hair sending rivulets down her face, dripping from her clothing and making puddles on the floor. She seemed totally unaware of her condition; the smile remained fixed, her beautiful violet eyes sparkling as they took in her surroundings.

"You'd better get out of those wet things before you catch a chill." I said, practically repeating what Lily told me a few hours before. My own shirt-front was soaked from our brief contact and felt cold against my skin, so I could imagine how Jenny must feel with not an inch on her dry. The situation was amusing if one stopped to think about our first encounter and this present reversal of roles.

She lifted the damp fabric of her skirt and looked up at me in what appeared to be amazement. Without a word, she nodded her assent and took my offered hand.

"There are towels in the closet here," I told her when we reached the bathroom. "I'll go find something for you to wear while your things dry."

She nodded again, still not speaking, looking intently around her. She stopped her inspection when she got to the medicine chest with its large mirror, a curious expression on her face. Turning back to me, she lowered her eyes as a blush deepened the color already staining her cheeks.

"Do you live here then?" Jenny asked quietly.

It seemed an odd sort of question, but considering the little I knew of the girl, hardly out of character.

"For nearly six years. I'll take you on the grand tour once you've dried off. I've a robe that might fit you." I told her. "Be back in a moment."

Going to my bedroom, I pondered her question. Could she have known the previous occupant of the loft? I supposed it was possible, though according to the Weishers, the place had been empty nearly five years before I moved in. Taking this into consideration, and my estimate of her age at no more than twenty-five—which was probably stretching things—she would only have been fourteen at the time. It seemed an awfully long time between visits, especially before ascertaining the party you wanted still resided in the same place. Coupled with the present weather conditions and the late hour, it was even less prudent.

Unless she was in some kind of trouble.

This seemed the most likely explanation, perhaps even the answer to why she'd disappeared so quickly this afternoon.

The idea kindled my damsel-in-distress-hero-syndrome, and as I tugged open the doors of my closet, I wondered what I was getting involved in this time. I pushed back the thought as I shoved shirts, jackets, and slacks aside, and finally found what I was looking for. It was still in its protective garment bag, the fluffy white fabric of plush terry cloth taking on an off-grey color beneath the plastic wrap.

The robe had been a Christmas gift to Tara two years before—one she'd not had the good grace to accept. She hadn't cared for the simplicity of the fabric, the color was dull and ordinary, it washed out her complexion, and couldn't I "have at least gotten the right size?" She'd shoved the robe back into my arms, rolled her eyes in exasperation, and stormed out of the loft into a blizzard. It had been three months before I'd seen her again and neither of us mentioned the incident then or in the future. As a matter of fact, until now, I'd forgotten all about the robe and the events involved.

I removed the plastic from the robe and lifted the soft fabric to my nose. There was only a slight odor lingering from its long confinement

PORTRAIT OF JENNY

within the wrap; the smell of new material was stronger. I cut off the tags, and after tossing them into a waste can, returned to the bathroom.

I don't know what I expected—Jenny to be waiting impatiently on the other side of the closed door or perhaps standing in the doorway swathed in towels, watching for me to reappear. What I had not expected, however, was to find the young woman still fully clothed, standing before the bathroom sink, staring fixedly into the mirror above, an expression of bewilderment on her face as a puddle formed beneath her. She didn't hear my silent approach, and afraid to embarrass her, and fascinated by what I saw, I didn't call attention to myself.

Observation of individuals, events, and everything surrounding you is as important to the artist as it is to a writer, policeman, or even a doctor. You watch to catch every nuance, each minute element and particle that goes into making up the whole. The more acute your observations, the better chance you have of recalling the details later for reproduction. In most professions, interaction is as essential as the keen attention being given to your object of reference. For my part, as an artist, it had always seemed most effective when done undercover—without my subject's knowledge of being watched. Just as a cartoonist studies their object of interest to reproduce movement and expression in the art of animation, I studied to discover form, texture, and the relationship to items around my subject. Whether inanimate or part of nature, animal or human, everything possessed an inner secret that needed to be understood before it could be successfully transferred onto the canvas. And with my current project before me, the opportunity to quietly observe Jenny while she was unaware of my presence was more like homework than spying.

She continued to gaze at her reflection with a kind of awed fascination, touching the mirror with one hand while the other went to her face. There was a quizzical expression in those lovely, violet eyes, with the brows cocked at right angles as she continued to stare intently into the mirror.

She lifted a strand of soggy chestnut hair, darkened by rainwater but still possessing a healthy sheen. The mirror reflected her action as it should, and her joyful response added yet another dimension to her already unusual behavior.

Kicking off her sandals, she whirled around the small bathroom, laughing and hugging herself in glee, the soaked fabric of shirt and skirt—were they the same ones she'd worn that first time?—molded to the generous curves of her body. Her tiny feet splashed in the puddle of water, and she wiggled her toes with delight, her entire being glowing from the inside out.

With a sudden flush of color, she glanced toward the door just as I backed out of sight—but still able to see her. She twirled about one last time before resuming a sense of decorum. She walked sedately to the linen closet, pulled out a towel, and buried her face into its downy folds.

I suddenly felt ashamed for having invaded her space, my excuses and fancy explanations for what really did amount to spying making me feel even worse. But my sense of shame for betraying her confidence didn't lessen the pleasure it had given me to witness the intriguing scene and her strange and unexplainable actions. It added to the enigma of the girl, the overall sense of mystery that drew me like a magnet.

Not wishing to embarrass her, I backed up a few paces, lightly tapped against the wall, and loudly cleared my throat before proceeding slowly forward. Jenny's head almost immediately appeared in the bathroom doorway. She had a towel slung around her neck and was gently squeezing water from the ends of her hair.

"Find it?" She asked, beaming at me.

I held the robe out to her. "It's been stored for a while, but I think you'll find it more comfortable than what you're wearing."

She giggled, looking down at the long, wet skirt that continued to drip on the floor.

"I look like a drowned rat, don't I?" She shrugged her narrow shoulders. "Oh well, it was worth it." She took the robe and smiling her thanks, went back into the bathroom and shut the door.

"Would you like something hot to drink?" I called out.

"That would be groo—great. Um, do you have stuff for hot chocolate? No, no, wait. How about tea? Really hot, sweet tea with just a touch of lemon?"

It was like talking to a child when giving them the choice of anything they wanted, their natural inclination being unable to decide between all their favorites. I couldn't help smiling.

"Which would you prefer?" I asked, hoping my amusement didn't show in my voice.

"Oh, uh, this sounds horribly childish, Richard, but they both sound so lovely, I can't decide. You do it for me."

As I continued down the hallway to the kitchen, Jenny started to hum quietly to herself. It was an old, familiar tune, but I was unable to put a name to it at the moment. A crash of thunder distracted me, and by the time the racket ceased to sound overhead, Jenny appeared in the kitchen, no longer humming.

She'd wrapped her long hair in a white towel, and the robe, also white, brought out the rose of her cheeks, brilliance of her eyes, and made her small, bow-shaped mouth red and enticing. Even belted tightly about the waist, the voluminous quantity of the oversized robe refused to remain upon her narrow shoulders. It would slip first down one, then the other, revealing the hollow at the base of her throat, collarbone, and cleavage where the silver and gold chain of her pendant lay nestled then disappeared beneath the folds of fabric. Each time she attempted to rectify the problem, the opposite shoulder slipped even further, nearly exposing her on that side. She finally clutched the folds together just below her chin and padded over to the kitchen table.

I set a cup of hot water and a spoon before her, then lined up a packet of instant cocoa, tea bag, sugar, and lemon behind that.

"Take your pick." I told her with a grin. "And whichever you choose now, you can have the other later on."

She laughed with delight, her lovely violet eyes sparkling as they passed over the items in front of her.

"You'd think this was a major decision or something the way I'm going on. It's just..." Her voice trailed off as she fingered first the tea bag, then the cocoa packet. She finally settled on the tea and started preparing it to her specifications.

Watching her, I wondered again what led her to my door.

"Jenny," I began hesitantly. "Are you in some kind of trouble?"

Her eyes shot up in alarm, the hand holding the teaspoon trembling slightly.

"No. Why?"

Even though she held my gaze steadily, I could swear I saw a shadow of doubt or fear pass over her face.

"I'm sorry, I don't want to pry, but your showing up like this—I—I just want you to know that if you need someone, you can count on me." I'd botched it. I couldn't believe my schoolboy nerves made me sound like a babbling idiot.

But that's what she did to me. She was just so incredibly beautiful, so intriguing...

I sat opposite her at the table, placed my hands upon it and determined they wouldn't shake, that I'd regain my composure before she noticed.

An awkward silence ensued as Jenny continued to fiddle with her cup of tea. I didn't want to say anything that might lead her to run back out into the storm, especially before I had the opportunity to discover a little more about her—like her last name and what led her here tonight. It was a good bet she hadn't expected me to answer the door, and while she didn't appear overly disturbed I had, it had definitely been a surprise.

So, for now, here we were, sitting across from one another, Jenny toying with the spoon in her tea, avoiding eye contact, and me idly examining the smudges of paint adhering to the cracks and crevices of my hands.

"I hung my clothes on your shower rod and put the bathmat and a towel down to catch the water." She peered at me from beneath her dark lashes. "I—I'm sorry, Richard, for showing up like this. I'm sure you've better things to do than harbor a fugitive from a rainstorm. It's just..."

You didn't have any place else to go, I finished for her in my head. Aloud I said, "I'm glad you came."

She gave me a broad smile that lit her entire face. The hand that had been clutching the folds of the robe shyly covered mine where it lay on the table between us. She squeezed gently.

Her hands were as small as a child's—completely in proportion with the rest of her body. I marveled at her size, a petite five foot, and every inch a woman.

She would be a portrait artist's dream with the smooth, clean lines of her forehead, the small, straight nose offset by wide eyes of a color so clear and vibrant they brought the entire face to life. Even with her hair covered by the towel, she was beautiful—a tiny bit of perfection amid the disorder of my unkempt apartment.

One of her long fingers traced the faded color embedded in the crease of my hand.

"You were painting." She carefully turned the hand palm up and continued to draw a line across the center. "You've strong hands, Richard. Well-shaped. See your lifeline? There are a lot of forks in it. A lot of life already lived, adventures, dangers, and more to come. You'll live a long time, I think, have a good life and an enduring love." She folded my hand and patted the closed fingers.

"So, you're a fortuneteller." I joked. "Are palms your specialty?"

She blushed, her smile deepening to reveal dimples in each cheek.

"Just a good judge of character." Her violet eyes studied me frankly. "You show a lot of what you are on your face. You've been having some troubles lately, something related to a long time ago. It's there in the furrows of your brow, making them deeper than they should be for someone so young."

Considering the shoe had been on the other foot just a short time before, I shouldn't have objected to this sudden reversal of roles.

Can dish it out but can't take it, eh, Tanner? My subconscious chided as Jenny continued to study me.

There was a difference, I answered the taunting. She hadn't been aware of my observation.

True. You spied. She's doing it to your face.

I shook my head to rid myself of the unwanted thoughts and turned my attention back to Jenny. She'd been watching me closely, her eyes wide, waiting for a reaction. She could tell she'd struck a chord, and the look of satisfaction on her face deepened the dimples in her cheeks.

"You're not used to being on the receiving end, are you?" She asked, disconcerting me once again with her ability to read my thoughts.

"No, I'm not." I grinned. "Am I that readable?"

She shrugged, and without the hand to hold together the folds of the robe, it slowly slipped apart. With more amusement than embarrassment, she drew the robe back upon her shoulders, her eyes remaining locked on mine.

"Have you a safety pin handy? I don't think we'd better trust this thing any longer."

When the robe was modestly fastened into place, Jenny left her tea on the table and began to roam about the loft. I stayed at the kitchen table as she examined the contents of the living room, watching as she fingered different items in interest, acknowledged others with a nod, and smiled her secret smile as she looked out across the whole.

"I like what you've done." She spun about the room much as she'd done in the bathroom. "You've allowed the space to remain uncluttered with too much furniture, so it gives you room to move, to breathe without feeling confined. And the studio—" She stepped down into the room, walking the length and then the width, stopping occasionally to study a canvas on the wall or floor, then moving on.

Where my easel stood in the center of the room beneath the skylight, Jenny came to a halt. She leaned slightly against the parson's table, her eyes sweeping across the supplies it contained, then on to the distant wall with its special adjustable lamps. As her examination continued, she looked up at the skylight at the same moment a burst of lightning split the dark sky, causing her to laugh with delight.

"Heaven's fire." She said quietly. "And there's quite a bit of it tonight."

It was as though it had been a cue, for at that moment, there was a tremendous crash of thunder, and all the lights went out. Jenny emitted a cry of alarm, to which I offered instant assurances and set out to remedy the problem. Within a few minutes, with the aid of a trusty flashlight, an old lantern, and several candles, the loft was bathed in a soft yellow glow.

Jenny hadn't moved during the entire process; she'd remained transfixed, hands tightly clutching the neck of the robe, eyes wide in alarm.

It wasn't until the last of the candles was lit that she finally seemed to come unglued to that spot on the floor and apologized for her reaction.

"I—I'm not crazy about the dark—especially the black dark." She turned away from me with a rueful smile. Hugging herself, she moved closer to the painting I'd just completed.

"Could you bring the lantern closer so I can see this better?"

I did as she asked and held the lantern slightly above her head so the full extent of the light hit the painting. I waited, holding my breath for her reaction.

"It's me!" Her voice echoed her surprise. She looked at me quizzically, then returned her attention to the painting. "But how? Why?"

"You seemed to belong there." It was hardly an adequate explanation even in my book, but she seemed to accept it.

"I—it's beautiful." She put out a hand as though to touch it, stopping inches before the canvas and tracing the outline of the scene in the air in front of it. Closing her eyes, a dreamy expression settled on her face.

"It's as though I'm really there." She whispered. "I can see the hawk swooping up and down, fighting against the wind to gain altitude, then using it to his advantage to soar across the sky. Far off, perhaps beyond that little stand of trees, there are cows. I can hear them lowing." She opened her eyes and smiled at me. "Thank you. It's a wonderful gift."

I wasn't quite certain what she meant, and my confusion must have shown on my face.

"Your including me in such a beautiful scene." She explained. "That's one of the best presents I could ask for." Standing on her tiptoes, she urged me to bend so she could kiss my cheek.

Her lips were cool, the touch of them no more than the brush of a feather. She walked past me into the living room and sat on the edge of an overstuffed chair. Turning back to me, her face glowed in the candlelight.

"Would you like to paint me? Do my portrait?" Her eyes were unreadable dark orbs, but I knew they watched me intently.

"I'm not, I mean, I don't do portraits." I cursed myself for faltering, for throwing away an opportunity without even attempting it. After all, what could I lose? True, the hours involved would take me away from continuing my real work, yet there was a very big plus in the proposal—the time would be spent with Jenny.

Fortunately, she didn't give up.

"You do, though. What do you call that? I know it's not exclusively a portrait," she rushed on, "but it is a representation of me. So why can't you do it on a larger scale?" As if to convince me, she whipped the towel off her head, shook out her long hair, and combed through it with her fingers. The chestnut tresses fell seductively around her shoulders, framing her small face with a mass of soft curls that enhanced her beauty.

As further evidence of her being a good subject, Jenny undid the pin at the top of the robe, pulled down the shoulders to expose a generous amount of cleavage before repinning it, ran a hand through her hair one last time, and struck a pose. As she turned into the light of a nearby candle, the ankh pendant and chain glistened against the creamy white skin of its owner and reflected a tiny flame in the darkness.

"Now what do you think?" Her voice was like honey, thick and sweet, and as her small tongue slowly wet her lips, I thought I would lose my mind.

I felt the breath catch in my throat and was once again caught in the enchantment of the girl before me. She drew me to her with the intensity of her eyes, and without thought, I was lifting her from the chair.

Her skin was like alabaster, smooth and milky white, cool under the heat of my hands. I caressed her face, her shoulders, the hollow below her neck, marveling at the wonder of her. She trembled at my touch, uttering a small cry as I kissed one shoulder and then the other.

She tasted and smelled as fresh as the spring rain, so soft and cool to the touch that the sensors on the tips of my fingers seemed charged with the life beneath them. I held her to me, kissing and caressing, cradling her small body against my own.

Even on tiptoe she was still at least a foot shorter than me, so I lifted her onto the chair where she stood slightly above me. My hands encircled her small waist to steady her, and she cried out once more, a sound that sent the blood thudding through my veins. Tenderly cupping her small oval face in my hands, our lips finally met.

Her mouth was soft and curiously cool, but mine held enough heat for both of us. I felt her arms go around my neck, her hands holding the back of my head as my fingers became entangled in the silkiness of her long hair. She seemed so delicate, so fragile within my arms, as though the slightest pressure could crush her.

My heart thumping, my brain beyond reason, I was startled when Jenny withdrew from the embrace. Balancing awkwardly on the cushion, she put a hand in the center of my chest; a subtle request for me to keep my distance.

"No, Richard. I—It's not right…" She climbed off the chair, moved past me to the bank of windows at the front of the loft, and clutched the robe tightly at her throat.

With her back to me, she inhaled deeply. "I'm sorry. I—I shouldn't have let it go this far." She shook her head, and this time the cry was in the form of a sob. "Things aren't as they seem. I'm not," she turned to me, tears glistening in the corners of her eyes. "We don't even know one another." She said finally.

"It's all right, Jenny." I told her softly. "I'd never force—"

"I know that. It's not you…it's…. Please believe me." She faced the windows again, watching the rain and the lightning that streaked across the night sky. "It's late and we're tired, caught up in the romance of it all." She shook her head again. "In the idea of saving one another."

Hail drummed against the walls of the apartment, beating its own mysterious tune as the wind played at the windows and skylight, whistling and whining its musical accompaniment. The symphony was joined by the crash of thunder and highlighted by a brilliant display of lightning as it streaked across the night sky, flashing in an almost syncopated rhythm.

"I should go."

I heard the doubt in her voice and called her on it.

"Is that what you want?"

She turned back to me, and even in the dim light, I could see a pleading in her eyes.

"No, I mean—" Her hands went to her face, like she was trying to hide from me—or herself.

"Jenny." I gently removed her hands, tilting her head until our eyes met. "If you'd like to stay here, you're welcome for as long as you want. I'd like to help you, Jenny, if you'd let me."

"Help me?" She gazed up at me, hope shining from her beautiful violet eyes.

I nodded. "Trust me. I won't hurt you or force you to do anything against your wishes. I promise. Just tell me what you want, what you need."

She pulled slightly away, and brushing the tears from her eyes, stared at me intently.

"Richard." She whispered my name, not as an address, but as though she was testing it in some way. Her eyes glazed, going somewhat out of focus for a moment, returning a moment later even more brilliant than before.

As suddenly as it had gone out, the electricity came back on. We blinked at one another in the glare of the lights, but neither of us turned away or commented on it. The storm seemed to have finally passed, making the silence that surrounded us complete.

"Let me help you." I said again, emphasizing every word.

Slowly, she nodded, and the tears began to flow once again.

I wanted to go to her, to enfold her in my arms, to comfort and protect her but knew should I do so, I would not want to stop.

"How, Jenny? What do you want me to do?"

With a wistful smile, she held her hand out to me and whispered, "Remember."

Chapter 13

I not only remembered my promise to Jenny, but kept it—though within twenty-four hours I seriously doubted my ability to maintain control. While she neither said nor did anything that could be misconstrued or taken beyond the friendship she offered, her sensuality aroused a need so great I felt pushed to the limits of endurance. From the raising of her brows above those deep violet eyes, to the smiles that made her dimple, she reeled me in. Add to that the luxuriant tresses of chestnut hair which surrounded her perfect oval face and pronounce her guilty of stealing both my breath and my heart; guilty of being too attractive, too alluring to a fool who fancied himself falling in love.

The alternative to physically touching the girl was to paint her. In this way, I was able to comfort and reassure her with my presence, caress her with my eyes, entice her with the vibrance of color, and make love to her with every stroke of the brush. While the portrait of Jenny rapidly progressed, I became increasingly uncertain of the wisdom of remaining under the same roof day and night. I wasn't a saint and abstinence was not my vocation or choice. Call it instinct, nature, or what have you, I couldn't look at Jenny and not want to make love to her. It was as simple as that.

By evening of the third day, confinement to the loft and inability to follow through with my baser desires made me feel as though I might go insane. Frustrated, I discarded palette and brushes, and no longer trusting myself to look at her, grabbed up a rag and went to the west bank of windows.

Other than a small exclamation of surprise by my sudden departure from studio to living room, Jenny remained quiet. She neither left the studio nor moved from the high-backed chair on which she was posing. I gave her a quick sidelong glance, the best I could muster as a form of reassurance, then turned toward the windows.

The sun was just beginning to set in a sky aglow with the warm, rich colors of a late spring evening. Mauve, violet, and rose tinged the western sky with a backdrop of soft yellow against the darkening azure as the sun sank beyond the horizon. The sight, along with the cool breeze coming in through the loft's open windows, helped temper the burning inside me, yet created a restlessness which cried to be answered.

It had been three days since I'd last left the four walls that surrounded me, three days spent fighting my natural urges to provide the distance, comfort, and protection Jenny appeared to need. I was anxious for diversion and activity, and unable to answer the call of my body, needed to find what solace I could in nature. Taking a walk was hardly an appropriate exchange, but it was the best I could think of at the moment.

Jenny declined the invitation to accompany me, which was just as well, and as I left the apartment, she called out that I should take my time.

I had no real destination in mind, it was the air and separation I was after, the chance to clear my head and allow my libido to come to grips with the reality of the situation. So, I wandered aimlessly, away from the park and off in the direction of the university. The campus would be abuzz with activity in preparation for the start of summer classes the following day, and with a sudden insight, I knew the students' energy and excitement would offer just the kind of diversion I badly needed.

As dusk of our fourth night together approached, I thought about the last three days I'd spent with Jenny and had no regrets—beyond the obvious. For more reasons than I could readily enumerate, I knew that a physical relationship after such a brief acquaintance would be ridiculous. Knowing this and accepting it, however, were entirely different matters.

I took a shortcut through the campus proper coming out before the residence halls. Cars filled with students of both sexes whizzed past unheeding the 15 mph speed limit, yelling out obscenities and catcalls to one another and me. There was a pervasive odor of beer and liquor about the area, as well as the smell of burning charcoal, wood smoke, hot dogs, and hamburgers. A couple of teens ran by in pursuit of a wayward Frisbee; laughter surrounded me on all sides, yet in spite of it all, my mind returned to thoughts of Jenny.

Despite my protests, the morning after her sudden arrival on my doorstep, I'd begun her portrait. I'd awakened on the couch to find her sitting opposite me in the overstuffed chair, her eyes on me but lost in thought. She hadn't noticed I was awake, and in that moment, I perceived a sadness in Jenny so profound it tugged at my soul.

She was wearing her long, gauzy print skirt and was sitting with her legs tucked beneath her. I recognized the sweater she wore as something I had shrunk long ago and never gotten around to discarding. It was a deep midnight blue that enhanced the color of her eyes, her creamy complexion, and brought out the red and gold highlights in her hair.

While I watched, she put a hand to her neck in search of her pendant, and when she didn't find it on the outside of the sweater, a look of alarm crossed her face. With trembling fingers, she reached beneath the neckline and gently tugged on the curious twist of silver and gold chain until the ankh came free. As it swung from beneath its confines of the sweater, she clutched the cross tightly, closed her eyes, and mouthed silent words of thanks.

When her eyes finally met mine, it was as though some of the electricity from the night's storm had remained trapped in the loft. It crackled in the air between us, an unspoken promise, a vow necessary to fulfill. So, after breakfast and a fresh change of clothing, I chose one of the larger canvases Lily had delivered, and began the portrait.

Throughout that first day, conversation remained on neutral subjects: the improved weather conditions, the preliminary sketch, and music. Jenny had shown a particular fascination to my old record collection and had been absolutely mesmerized by the shiny CDs and player. She'd examined everything carefully, exclaimed over *The Beatles*—both their ensemble and solo efforts—*The Rolling Stones*, Elton John, and numerous others popular in the middle sixties/early seventies.

Watching her enthusiasm, I casually remarked that considering her affinity for this kind of music, she should have been born twenty-five years earlier. Jenny stared at me blankly for a moment, the color drained from her face, then delved back into the CDs. She'd deliberately bypassed the music we'd just been discussing, and withdrawing Dan Fogelberg's "Greatest Hits," stated she'd never heard of him before. While I thought this a bit odd—though no odder than her reaction to the CDs—I took the disc and showed her how to load it into the player. She had watched, entranced, and with the start of the music, settled back to work. That disc had since become a standard for our day of posing, played at least twice during the day. *The Beatles'* "Abbey Road" and Simon and Garfunkel's "Greatest Hits" were among others she couldn't get enough of.

While I'd discovered that her taste in music tended more toward older rock and roll, it said very little about Jenny's overall personality. She was quiet to the extreme, curious and observant with a kind of childlike wonder to things, and forever evasive. She seemed uninterested in television, listened raptly to radio news broadcasts, yet never picked up the newspaper. She was able to sit in the same position for hours without so much as a twinge and didn't complain once or ask to be excused for the bathroom or to grab something to eat. She quietly watched me work, appeared to trust and enjoy my company, and absolutely refused to leave the loft even to sit on the porch.

I was drawn from this reverie by the sound of my name and looked to find a group of former students huddled around a grill, munching on hot dogs. They invited me to join them, and realizing I'd eaten nothing all day, gratefully accepted the hot dog thrust into my hand. Two beers and a good forty minutes later, I bade them goodbye and headed back toward the loft considerably more in control, as well as in a better frame of mind.

I'd offered Jenny my help, and if that meant keeping my hands off her, then that was the way it must be. After our brief conversation yesterday, I knew she was in trouble of some kind, but pressing her for information simply turned her into herself. As much as I wanted the answers, I was forced to accept her silence and hoped it was only a matter of time until she let me know what was going on. While there was a special allure to the mystery surrounding her, Jenny's reticence was also frustrating—further evidence why our becoming lovers at this juncture would only complicate things.

The thought brought with it the lyrics of Fogelberg's *Make Love Stay*, a song Jenny had become particularly fond of. I considered the words in connection to my present situation—all about the mystery of love and the difficulty of keeping both the mystery and the love alive. The sentiment held far more truth than one might care to admit.

Twilight had gone and darkness rapidly approached as I departed the university grounds and headed back toward the loft. The night was alive with activity; crickets chirped, birds sang their evening songs, an occasional rabbit could be spotted as still as a statue on an empty lawn, and people of all ages were out enjoying the cool evening breeze. It was a beautiful night with the stars sparkling like diamonds against the darkening sky, the half moon bright and looking deceptively near—a repeat of the night before.

After we'd finished another three-hour sitting last evening, I tried to get Jenny as far as the porch. She'd stubbornly refused, muttering something like "if I leave, they won't let me come back." I'd called her on it, attempting to draw her out, but she'd pursed her lips tightly, refusing to say more on the subject. The opening finally came later while she looked over my shoulder at the rudimentary beginnings of the portrait.

She'd examined it for some time, and watching her as I cleaned the brushes, I finally asked what she was thinking.

"I was just marveling at how much it already looks like me." She'd said, continuing to stare intently at the painting. "There are just hints of color and texture, barely defined lines, but even someone who hardly knows me could recognize who it was."

"You're a good subject. Distinctive features, your coloring, it makes it easy."

She'd grinned at me. "I'll take that as a compliment."

"Just fact, Jenny. You're a very beautiful girl."

"Woman, Richard, not girl. When you get as old as I am, one has to make the distinction. Or so my father would say." She'd wrinkled her nose at the memory. "He was always very particular about how people were addressed or referred to. It used to crack me up." She'd laughed.

There it was again, that strange sense of déjà vu that I'd had the first time I saw her. I'd no idea where it came from, couldn't explain the sense of familiarity that came over me at such times, but it was there just the same. I'd searched Jenny's face for a similar response but found nothing. Still, I couldn't let it go so easily, not without giving it a chance, without taking advantage of the opportunity to discover more about my beautiful companion.

I'd watched her, weighing the pros and cons, keeping in mind her previous reluctance in revealing more about herself. Maybe if I could find the right mix of subtlety and concern I could push the door wider and her secrets would tumble out. Jenny had, after all, provided the opening, so if I was careful, it just might work.

It wasn't difficult to play my part, to look interested and concerned. What was difficult was trying not to show just how eager I was for the information. So, with as much nonchalance as I could manage, I'd picked up on her statement and asked, "Was? Is he gone then?"

"Gone? You mean dead?" She'd shaken her head, her eyes still glued to the painting. "My mother died when I was very young, but Father's still around."

Returning to the high-backed chair we were using for the portrait, she regarded me thoughtfully. "He's getting up there, though."

"I take it you haven't seen him for a while."

As usual, Jenny had chosen to ignore my question and countered with one of her own.

"What about you, Richard? Are your parents still alive?"

Don't press, I'd told myself. "My mother is. Dad died a few months ago."

"I'm sorry." After pulling her legs under her, she'd taken great pains to smooth her skirt over her knees. "When my mother died, I was too young to understand what had happened. It was so strange. She was there one moment and gone the next. I missed her terribly, and as a result, Father tended to over-compensate."

"Spoiled you?"

"Rotten." She'd returned my smile. "When I was little, it was all right. But as I got older, it felt as though he was smothering me. Sometimes I swore that if I didn't get away, I'd shrivel up and die from lack of oxygen."

"Is that why you didn't go to him?" I'd thought it worth another try.

Rather than ignoring me this time, Jenny looked directly into my eyes, staring pensively.

"Something like that." She'd shifted her position but didn't take her eyes from mine. "If I could have gone, I would. To see him and—"

"And?" I prompted gently.

"My daughter." The whispered words stunned me, and as I tried to assimilate this revelation, Jenny blinked rapidly and turned away.

"I'd never have left her if I could help it. There was just nothing I could do. You understand that, don't you, Richard? That circumstances of fate can interfere?"

"The business of living gets in the way," I'd said, recalling the words from something I'd once read.

"Exactly. I was sure I could manage things, that what I was doing would make our lives better in the end. I didn't stop to think, to consider that, well, that my plans might interfere with someone else's." She'd shrugged her narrow shoulders and leaned comfortably back in the chair. "The best laid plans. I suppose we have to accept and hope things work out in the end."

The wistful expression on her face was touched with the sadness I'd noticed in her before. I felt the urge to go to her, to enfold her in my arms and comfort her, but I'd held back—as much from my promise as for the hope of satisfying my curiosity. Jenny was finally opening up, and the slightest distraction would be all that was needed to shut the door on communications once again. So, I remained where I was at the parson's table, using the paint and turpentine soaked rag I'd used to clean the brushes to scrub at the residue remaining on my hands. I'd watched Jenny covertly, careful not to stare, and waited to see if she would go on.

"My one big hope was to give her what she needed without caging her in." She'd spoken quietly as though her thoughts had somehow found their way to her vocal cords of their own volition.

"She was so bright, ready to learn anything and everything." She'd laughed. "Not at all like me. I knew right away she would make something of herself, that she had the energy and drive for success I'd always lacked. My father saw it too, even though she was so little, and he convinced me that her best chance in life would come through him. So," she'd tossed her head so that a cloud of chestnut hair hid the side of her face. "I decided to stop running and come home. That's when Father insisted I stop acting like a girl and become a woman. He never asked me about her father, and I never volunteered the information. I've never told anyone."

"Is that who you were looking for the other night?" I asked, a light coming on in my brain. "Swan, isn't that what you said? Is he the child's father?"

As she pushed back her hair, I saw her mouth the word, a secret smile playing about her lips.

"I came looking for a friend," her violet gaze fastened onto mine. "And I found you."

There had been no more reminiscences, no further sharing of her past. She'd closed the door, at least for the moment, leaving me ridiculously in the dark.

Sensitivity for her feelings was one thing, acceptance and inactivity another. I was determined to know immediately if the media was contacted about her. I listened to news broadcasts, scanned both articles and the personals in the paper, and kept eyes and ears open for any slip, any nuance that might give me a clue to her identity or the trouble she was in. In the meantime, I would continue to offer my friendship and protection, such as they were, and watch helplessly as my heart and soul fell for the mysterious young woman I'd opened my home to.

While I may not know much about Jenny's past or the circumstances that led her to my door, I learned that whatever else she was, she was a good listener. Without my being aware she was doing it, Jenny quickly had me talking about myself in a manner I'd never done previously. Before long, she practically had my life story, including the most recent additions regarding Tara and the incident almost twenty-one years ago.

Jenny showed concern and sympathy for Tara's ordeal, her gentle questioning skillfully extracting all I knew about the incident. There was nothing morbid about her interest, no request to dwell on gory details, just a simple desire to have the complete story. As we'd continued talking, I'd felt compelled to relate the tale in the hope that sharing the details of those harrowing days would cause them to no longer have power over me. Even her fascination for my childhood trauma seemed to have a strange cathartic effect. Yet, as comforting as it was to tell her my stories, a confession of her own would have made me feel even better.

As I rounded the corner of the Weisher building that led into the side alley, I felt again the odd tingling along my spine that I'd experienced while relating what the professor told me. The brightness of Jenny's eyes had intensified as I'd spoken, and she'd leaned toward me with interest, her lunch forgotten. She'd shivered at the mention of the Linden Stalker, a reaction that graduated into a tremor when I'd related how the professor found me unconscious in a puddle of water. She'd watched me in absorbed fascination, a deeply penetrating violet gaze from which I could not escape.

"And you remember nothing? Nothing at all?"

"Not a thing. That's what makes me feel there are still pieces missing." I'd laughed wryly. "Of course, no one knows what was going on inside my head, why I'd gone out in the storm. It's just..." Shaking my head, I'd pushed out of the chair and restlessly walked the length of the room. "There's this feeling I have that someone knows something that would spark my memory, but they're holding back." I'd shrugged my shoulders and felt the slow ascent of pain from my neck rising to meet the pounding that had begun in my head. Jenny saw me wince and questioned me about it.

"And that's all that remains, the headaches?" She'd asked quietly.

"As far as I know, yes. My life has been rather undramatic since—until recently. I'd always been curious about my accident, wondered if it would affect my life in some way, but knowledge of the incident hasn't changed the way I look at myself or things around me. I thank God for that."

"Memory's a funny thing." She'd mused. "Ordinary things can stick with us for years and details remain intact. Other times, we're lucky if we remember exactly what we did several hours before, let alone days or months." Jenny had risen from the table and stretched. She'd flashed me a smile, then slowly walked to the stereo.

"You know," she'd said, thumbing through the rack of CDs. "A trauma like that has the potential to damage someone for life, yet you've been fortunate enough to come out of it unscathed. That alone should tell you something." She'd plucked out an early Neil Diamond CD and loaded it into the player as I'd shown her.

"Your head injury has acted like a shield all these years, protecting you from the shock. But I wouldn't worry." She'd cocked her head on one side and turned to me with a brilliant smile.

"You've the key right inside here," she'd tapped a finger against her temple. "And when the time's right, you'll remember what happened."

The music came on, and we'd gone back to work, the remainder of the day uneventful. Very little was said, communication was done with glances rather than words, and after working until ten with intermittent breaks, Jenny had retired to my bedroom, and I'd taken up residence on the couch.

At first I hadn't thought I'd be able to sleep, but it didn't take long for me to find myself locked once more into that blackened nightmare world from which there seemed no escape.

The darkness that surrounded me rendered my eyes useless, and with out-flung hands I searched frantically for a way out. Even in my terror and confusion I remembered what was ahead, that—that *thing* was watching, waiting to claim me.

I felt a tremor of fear course through my body as I recalled the cold, clammy skin, its groping arms that held me locked in a band of steel. I knew it was coming, that I must flee or be doomed, yet just like the last time, I was unable to get away before it found me.

With a suddenness that shook the breath from my body, I felt its claws digging into my arms. Slowly, I was drawn backwards, the agonizing slow-motion effect increasing my fear and restricting my breath as I was held tightly in that final, terrifying embrace.

I must have cried out, for when I awoke, my head was cradled on Jenny's lap, and she was pushing back the damp, heavy hair from my forehead and gently rubbing it. She'd spoken to me softly, soothing words fit for a child, her tender hands comfortingly cool against the heat of my skin. I couldn't remember if I'd spoken to her, didn't know if I'd responded to her presence in any way. The next thing I knew, it was morning, and Jenny's bright face was peering at me anxiously from across the room.

Today had been even quieter than the others. Jenny had been pensive, disinclined for conversation. She'd gone through records and CDs during our breaks, selecting older, melancholy tunes that were depressing to listen to. In the early part of the day, she'd been restless, unable to sit still for more than a half hour without the need to get up and move about the loft for a while. Several times I suggested a walk, and each time she'd refused, becoming more and more agitated. When I'd asked what was wrong, she'd shaken her lovely head and sighed.

Later in the day, I caught her watching me, a longing in her eyes that

I yearned to answer. As my own urges had increased with our prolonged company, when given what I believed to be encouragement, I decided to answer the call—which Jenny quickly halted.

"Your fascination with me is just an illusion, Richard," she'd told me, her tone gentle but firm. "What you want, what you need is real, everlasting love. Not me. Not this...infatuation."

I hadn't known how to respond, simply returned to the portrait while Jenny resumed her statue-like ability to remain posed. It had worked until, frustrated, my neck and shoulders aching from overwork, I'd thrown down my brushes and come out for a walk.

Now here I was, returning to the loft, to Jenny, calmer, but still no closer to answers than before. I'd offered her my home, protection, and assistance, respecting her wishes and asking nothing in return.

I was surprised to see Professor Drake coming down the steps from the loft. Spotting me beneath the security light, he flashed a big smile.

"Just been playing delivery boy for our girls. Annie included a package for you in something Janet sent, and this was the first free time I had to bring it over." He inhaled deeply. "Beautiful night for a walk."

I nodded my agreement. "So, what do you think of her?"

The professor looked confused.

"Jenny. My, uh, house guest?"

Professor Drake shook his head. "I'm sorry, Richard, but I've no idea what you're talking about." A slow smile spread across his face. "Are you trying to tell me you've taken up with a new young lady?"

"More like she's taken up with me." I grinned.

He raised a shaggy eyebrow and descending the remaining steps, paused before me.

"I'll explain later." I lifted my head and stared thoughtfully at the door. "So, you didn't meet her?"

"I knocked, there was no answer, but the door was ajar, so I went in. I thought you must be around somewhere because I couldn't imagine after everything that's happened you'd go off leaving your door unlocked. Anyway, I called out, and when there was still no answer, set your package on the coffee table and left." He laughed. "I have to admit my curiosity regarding your latest canvas, but I kept a tight rein on myself and came away without looking."

"That *was* an accomplishment." I joked. "Actually, I'm glad you didn't peek. I'm doing something different, expanding my horizons, so to speak."

"And?" He prompted.

"The girl I spoke of, Jenny, I'm doing her portrait."

"That *is* a surprise! Do you intend to show it at the Arts Festival?"

His encouraging tone had the effect it always did on me.

"If all goes well. On second thought," I glanced back toward the loft. "Would you like to come up for coffee and take a look? You could tell me if you think I'm headed in the right direction—I believe I am, but—"

"But you've become so enamored of your subject that you feel you've lost your objectivity." He nodded. "I've heard that happens—especially when the model is of the opposite sex. However," with a look at his watch, he declined the invitation. "I must get back to preparations for tomorrow. Reports state we're to have a record enrollment. Besides, son, you know that's not my area of expertise. Perhaps you should ask Lofgren or Seitz. I'm sure either of them would be happy to be of assistance."

While I never believed in the "limited" range of the professor's talent, I knew better than to attempt to change his mind once it was made up. Edmund Drake was an excellent teacher, an inspiration to students, and the perfect mentor for an aspiring artist. He was also an extremely talented painter, one, I'd always been certain, who possessed a wide diversification of ability. Why he chose to hide his light under a bushel and contain himself to hobby activities was beyond my realm of understanding.

I thanked him for his suggestion of Lofgren and Seitz to confer with, yet even as I did so, knew I would never consult with them. Both were colleagues at the university, were good artists in their own right, as well as fellow contributors to the upcoming exhibition. But while I liked and respected them as instructors, I didn't value their opinions as I did the professor's.

I watched until he turned into the side alley and slipped out of sight, then climbed the stairs to the loft.

When I entered the apartment, Jenny was standing at the west bank of windows. She looked toward the door somewhat cautiously, breaking into a big smile when she recognized me.

"You've had company." She nodded to the package on the coffee table. "I—I was in the bathroom when I heard someone come in. I," she lowered her eyes. "I was a little frightened, so I didn't come out until he'd gone. I'm sorry."

"Don't worry about it. He's an old friend."

She nodded. "When I saw the package, I figured that, but—" She gave me a shy smile. "You had a call, too. I just let your machine answer it like you always do." Jenny returned her violet gaze to the window. "I watched the last of the sun go down from here. The sky was so beautiful it," her voice broke and she sighed as she turned back to me. "It almost made me cry. Silly, huh?" She cleared her throat and waved a nervous hand toward the coffee table. "Aren't you anxious to see what's inside?"

I grabbed up the package and started to peel off the brown paper wrap as I strode to the desk and pressed the play button on the answering machine. While the tape rewound, I turned up the volume then read the short note from my mother taped to the small box which stated it held a miniature of Stonehenge.

She and Janet were having such a wonderful time, they'd decided to extend their trip.

"So we won't be back until the last week of July, dear—still plenty of time to see your exhibition."

I grinned at the message, pleased their vacation was going so well. Just as I was about to open the box, the answering machine kicked in, and Tara's voice broke the silence.

"Hi, Richard. I won't keep you, just wanted you to know that I'm going away for awhile. I called my mother and she's actually making time for us to spend together. Might even do some therapy sessions as a team. How's that for a turnaround?" Tara laughed. "I suppose stranger things can happen. Anyway, I wanted to let you know that I'm off to the Windy City first thing in the morning. Oh, and Richard, Hargrave called me a little while ago. It seems they've found what was used to knock me senseless—or some sense into me, if you get my drift." A wry laugh was followed by a sound that could have been a muffled cry. When she continued, Tara's voice was shaky.

"Some kid found the top part of a baseball bat in the shallow end of Moss Creek. When he showed it to his old man, who just happens to be a cop, they decided to pass it along to the detective. By now you've guessed they performed some of those magical tests and discovered it was the weapon in question. What they didn't find was fingerprints. Nor have they found the bottom half of the bat. Hargrave assured me they were still looking, though, and then he, well..." She paused and I could hear her breathing into the phone.

"Look, Richard, the guy may not be after you like he was, but I don't think he's given up the notion. He, uh, he asked if you owned a Louisville Slugger—I assume that's the bat—and then he asked if I was sure I wanted to hold to my story. When I told him I wasn't about to change my mind about you, whether you owned one of those damned things or not, he kind of laughed, real eerie-like. Then he, well—Oh hell, Richard, he said things, weird things that led me to believe he might be following you. And, Richard, if, well, if any of what he was implying is true, I think you might need some help.

"Hey, there's the other line. I'm expecting a call from Akiro, and I don't want to miss the little bas—I don't want to miss him." There was another pause, this one so long I was surprised the machine hadn't automatically kicked off.

"You haven't started talking to yourself, have you? I mean, it's related to your work, right? Or have your headaches gotten so bad tha— Hell! I've gotta run. Take care!"

The machine beeped, clicked off, then went into rewind. I stared down at it with a cross between shock and anger.

Hargrave was following me?

I strode over to the west windows and looked into the street, scanning up and down the block for any car I didn't recognize.

"You think he's out there?" Jenny came to stand next to me, her cool hand feather-light on my elbow.

The street lights and security lamps in front of the businesses lit the area fairly well, making it easy to discern the cars parked along the street. I searched the length of the avenue twice and breathed a sigh of relief when I failed to spot Hargrave's battered LTD lurking among the familiar vehicles.

"I don't see his car. Though he might use a different one…"

I moved to the far end of the windows and pulled the drapery cord until the night was completely blotted out. In all the years I'd lived here, it was the first time I'd closed the drapes.

"Now, unless he's planted a bug," Jenny started at that, and I quickly went on to reassure her. "Don't worry, as nervy as he is, I don't think he'd go that far."

Despite the hour and my weariness, I jumped at Jenny's suggestion that we return to the portrait. I'd left most of my supplies out, and after a few minutes of arranging and rearranging, was once again poised before the canvas.

"The man in the park the other day, is he a friend, too?"

She could have knocked me over with a feather! For three days I'd wanted to ask her what had happened, why she'd left without a word. Now, here she was bringing the subject up from out of the blue. I hoped it was a good sign.

"Chuck Stinnet," I nodded. "Do you know him, Jenny? Was that why you left so quickly?"

She lowered her eyes to where her hands fidgeted nervously in her lap. "You looked pretty intent on your conversation and I—I didn't want to be caught in the storm." She finished quickly.

I stepped back from the canvas, watching her and wishing with all my heart that I could help her overcome the sadness that weighed so heavily upon her. My urge to comfort her had no sexual overtones this time; it was simply the desire of one human being to help another.

"Can't you tell me what's wrong? What I can do to help you?"

When she raised her eyes, they glistened with tears.

"You *are* helping, Richard." She said quietly. "My being here, the painting, your desire to save me, it's more than I deserve."

"Jenny, I—"

Without any warning, the brush in my right hand fell abruptly to the floor. Both hand and fingers felt as though an electric shock had surged through them as they tingled painfully.

I stared in fascination at my abused limb, brain trying to make it function normally, but it refused to obey. The tingling changed to numbness, the elbow gave out, and I felt an enormous dead weight extending from my right shoulder downward.

I continued to stare, dumbfounded, the pressure from my arm connecting to the ever increasing pain in my head. Like some strange creature, the numbness seemed to creep up the useless limb, past the shoulder joint, up the side of the neck into the jaw, and on to the right eye. A fog appeared to descend over the eye, and I closed both of them and tried to blink rapidly in the hopes of dispelling it. Instead of helping, it only seemed to make the fog denser, and the eye became as useless as my arm.

I'd had a stroke!

That was the single coherent thought I had before I felt gentle hands ease me into the old, paint-stained desk chair. Those same caring hands were tenderly massaging the taut muscles at the back of my neck and following the course of numbness down the arm to my fingers.

"Relax, Richard. Breathe deeply. Close your eyes," said a soothing voice.

But how could I relax? And if I closed my eyes, would I be able to see at all when I reopened them? My mind screamed.

I tried to tell this ministering angel that I needed to get to the hospital, that she should call for an ambulance, but the words wouldn't come.

I felt Jenny untie the lace that held my hair in a queue at the nape of my neck. She urged my head forward, her fingers massaging my scalp and neck.

"You've been working too hard, Richard, and you're all tied up in knots. Your poor head and shoulders. I shouldn't have encouraged it, but the time—"

Slowly, the numbness seemed to evaporate and there was an almost pleasant, tingling sensation from my right shoulder down to my fingertips. Opening my eyes, I found the fog had lifted, my eyesight nearly normal. I told Jenny this, but she continued her ministrations, gently rubbing my temples, following the line of my jaw into the top of my shoulder, then down the length of my arm. As she massaged, an overpowering weariness took hold of me, and I slumped back into the chair, longing for sleep.

"You'll have the bedroom tonight, sleepyhead." She laughed, tugging me to my feet. "But you've got to help me get you there. I can't carry you."

Like an automaton, I followed her and allowed her to assist me into bed. I sank into the comfort of mattress and pillow, waiting for sleep to swallow me up.

I didn't have to wait long.

Dreams came in fragments, images of my mother, father, Janet, and the professor floated in and out like ghosts with too little substance to allow them to remain. Chuck was there, his laughing, McCartneyesque eyes taunting me, his voice grinding out the facts in the Linden Stalker case. Lily was present as well, her augmented breasts bulging out of their flimsy wrap, a long, manicured nail pointing at me.

"It was you, Richard!" She screeched. "It was you! You! You!"

In that strange way you know you are only sleeping, that it's just a dream, I fought against the images, pushed at them in an attempt to dispel the dream. But I only succeeded in replacing one torment with another.

Hargrave now stood before me, laughing sardonically. Someone was behind me, pushing me, and I stumbled into the detective who shoved me brutally aside, then yanked me further into the darkness beyond.

Suddenly, a blinding light assaulted my eyes, and only when I tried to shield them against it, did I realize that my hands were cuffed behind my back.

As my vision gradually adjusted, I could see I was once again in City Hospital's morgue. The brightly polished, stainless steel surfaces reflected our blurred images like funhouse mirrors, grotesque and shapeless, adding yet another reason for apprehension.

While I'd been taking in my surroundings, Hargrave opened a drawer to reveal a still, sheeted form. His cold, calculating eyes watched me with unguarded amusement.

"Want you to take a look at this, old buddy." He cackled.

Without further ado, he whipped back the sheet and I gagged at the pulpy mass that had once been the side of someone's head. I turned away only to be forced forward by the unseen person behind me.

"Look, Richard, old buddy. Take a gander at this!"

My head was shoved ruthlessly down until I was within inches of the ruined face on the slab.

I screamed then, hysterically, my mind feeling as though it could no longer maintain its grasp on sanity.

"No! No!" I cried, trying to break free, to escape the iron grip that held me.

I struggled, helpless against their strength, their cruel, taunting laughter.

"Yes, yes!" Hargrave shouted angrily. "That's what you have to look forward to." He lifted his hands, and I saw he was holding the top of a broken bat in one, a large, flat board in the other, both stained and dripping blood.

Finally, inexplicably, I was free and backing away, yet still unable to take my eyes from the form on the slab.

"Not a pretty sight," Hargrave was saying. "But death seldom is—especially violent death. You know that, though, don't you, Richard?"

"But it's not too late." Came a softer voice.

I tore my eyes from the body, *my body*, and stared in shock at Hargrave's companion.

Jenny stood at his elbow, her sweet face smiling up at him. She glanced briefly at the corpse, her smile fading into sadness, and as those violet eyes turned to me, I felt as though I was fused to the floor.

"It's all right, Richard. Everything will be all right if you—"

Her voice called me from the nightmare, and she was there on the bed beside me, her gentle hands and soothing voice working their magic. I reached out to her, my leaden arms clutching at empty air as Jenny's voice continued to sound softly in my ear.

"Remember me."

Chapter 14

When I awoke the following morning, Jenny was gone. There wasn't a note of explanation, but she hadn't departed without leaving behind a sign; she'd unpacked the miniature of Stonehenge and placed it on my dresser. A Post-It note from my mother read: "Thought you could use a little magic." How aptly it applied to my mysterious visitor.

There was an instinctive feeling I'd never see Jenny again, and while I was disappointed by her abrupt departure, I really wasn't surprised. She'd remained in character to the end, an enigma, a puzzle that I could not solve. I wouldn't deny I'd hoped our three days together meant as much to her as they did to me, but somehow I'd known she could never belong to me, that she was merely "on loan" for a time. The portrait had formed a valuable link between us that would remain, but it wasn't binding.

Looking back, I should have recognized the signs—her sudden restlessness, the furtive looks, and her even more closely guarded conversation. She'd seemed to fade throughout that final day, her exuberance and inner glow of warmth and vitality guttering like a candle in the wind. With each passing hour, her anxiety had increased in much the same manner as my desire for her had reached a feverish pitch. She hadn't said anything, but I should have been tuned in enough to have guessed. Hindsight, as they say, is better. But not any more comforting.

I was forced to accept I might never know what brought Jenny to my door that stormy night, or what, in the end, had driven her away. A mistake of providence? Maybe. Fate? Perhaps. Whatever it was, I reveled in my good fortune and the brief opportunity allotted me.

I wasn't afraid of being unable to complete the portrait without her— I knew I could do it with my eyes closed. Her sudden departure only made the vision inside my brain more acute, more vivid in every detail. I knew her face as well, or better, than I knew my own. Which, at present, wasn't surprising.

Whether it was a sense of impending change, a sudden aberration in my character—or Jenny leaving as she did—I'd begun to feel particularly Bohemian and let my hair and beard grow. The first week the whiskers itched like fury, but as my skin became less sensitive, the itching decreased, and I gradually became accustomed to the new visage I beheld in the mirror. The Weishers joked that I looked rather wild and more than a little unkempt, while Professor Drake shook off my appearance, opting for his usual tolerance for the "stage" I was in. For myself, I saw it as fulfilling a small part of that age-old dream of becoming a hippie; I may not live in a commune or Greenwich Village, but it didn't mean I couldn't look the part.

When I wasn't painting, I rented old movies and sat before the TV lost in the trials and tribulations of others, or laughing at the timeless jokes and tongue-in-cheek antics of Nick and Nora in *The Thin Man*. I walked a good deal, mostly after dark, steered a course away from University Park and the school, and explored areas of Linden I was less familiar with. In spite of myself, I couldn't help being startled by cars approaching from the rear, Tara's warning about Hargrave a constant reminder that the detective might be following me.

Chuck Stinnet and I met at Murphy's a couple of times for drinks, his usual sagacious wit the kind of diversion I needed after a day or two of seclusion. He commented on my appearance with more than a hint of sarcasm but quickly changed his tune when it became obvious the female patrons of Murphy's didn't agree with his opinion.

The strange appeal my new look had on the ladies amused him, as did my more aggressive manner toward the fairer sex. He questioned me about this sudden reversal of attitude and I called him on it, demanding why it was all right for him to seek a replacement for Jet so soon after their breakup, yet it was not all right for me. This uncharacteristic flare of temper surprised him, amused him still further, and disturbed me a good deal. The next time he called to suggest we go out for drinks, I graciously declined the offer. He took the refusal in stride, telling me to go ahead and become a hermit; it left more women for him.

It wasn't that I no longer wanted the companionship, just felt I had neither the time nor the energy to waste. I supposed it was the lull after the storm, the "coming down" from the high I'd ridden while at the peak of production. Like a manic depressive's low period, I seemed to have crashed into such a state where everything outside my work required more effort and energy than I possessed. I tried to link it to the disappointment of Jenny's departure or my uncharacteristic and embarrassing flirtations, but in the end, dismissed the ideas as ludicrous. If I was running on empty, it was because I'd done it to myself, expecting to accomplish and achieve beyond what I was capable of. Jenny wasn't to blame, neither were the young women I'd sought as a diversion.

Nor were the migraines I'd lived with the past twenty-one years.

Still, as the days wore on and the cool spring days were rapidly replaced by summer heat, my headaches grew worse. I attributed it to a mixture of excitement and dread for the upcoming show—once again making excuses and explanations for things for which I hadn't any answers.

While I'd regained full use of my right arm and hand with no residual symptoms of numbness, I'd refrained from returning to work for a few days after that unusual attack. By the time I picked up brushes and palette again, the incident had become a dim memory, a gentle reminder of what pushing beyond the limits of endurance could do. It wasn't until the week before the exhibition, when a particularly vicious migraine was accompanied by that same odd numbness that I began to worry about what had and might be happening. Though this incident was less severe than the first, it was enough to convince me to call Joyce Noland's office. With news she was away on vacation until after the first of July, I made an appointment for the middle of the month, set the incident aside, and got back to work.

The last week of June was spent framing the chosen exhibition pieces and selecting the right spot to hang each canvas. Mrs. Winston, as usual, was a godsend, overseeing preparations for the opening of the Arts Festival with the same efficiency and attention to detail she had in her normal secretarial duties. She expressed her enthusiasm for each work, whether it belonged to Lofgren, Seitz, or me, rated them according to the stated importance to our overall collection, then discussed placement for proper effect.

The Fine Arts building at Linden State University is a complex, modernistic structure with a clover-leaf design. The central "leaf,"

Lambert Hall, houses the art department, with Bretton Hall—music—to the right as you enter the main hub, and Davis Hall—drama—to the left.

The Gallerie de l'Art in Lambert lies directly before the main entrance of the building in the very heart of the surrounding classrooms. It is a tastefully designed gallery with soft cream walls that do not distract or detract from the displays, specially designed lighting, and grey marble floors specked with black. The semicircular construction of the gallery is divided by a single wall which runs down the center of the vast room with another dividing wing extending back from the wall on either side. The design was carefully arranged for optimum use and effect, providing plenty of wall and walking space, as well as offering, in the broad, flat surface that faces the gallery entrance, the perfect focal point for a particularly special work of art.

Tradition held that the Wall of Honor would remain empty until opening day of the Linden Arts Festival—the position voted on by the three department chairs of the Fine Arts as well as the contributing artists. Competition was always stiff but friendly, the collections of each participant studied throughout the preceding week during final preparations. Vote was by secret ballot with Mrs. Winston as the unbiased counter. It was under her direction that the selected work was mounted and lit to its best advantage prior to the doors of the gallery opening to the public.

The presentation of this honor was done with much pomp and circumstance, strictly for the benefit of giving special recognition to contributing university artists. A bottle of champagne was on hand for the occasion scheduled an hour before the official opening, and toasts of congratulations, pats on the back, and general kudos for a job well done were exchanged. It was with great reverence that I accepted my due when I entered the gallery Friday evening to find "A Portrait of Jenny" hanging proudly on the Wall of Honor.

From the time of its unveiling, I'd been fairly certain the portrait would be chosen. Among the land and seascapes, still-lifes, occasional abstract and pastoral, the portrait stood out like a beacon by contrast. Both of my fellow contributors had commented favorably on the painting, and both had been seen standing before it time and again, studying the beautiful face that smiled out at them.

I was pleased and excited by their reactions, thrilled to see that my conviction and belief in the portrait were being confirmed. Jenny's mysterious pull had somehow transferred itself onto the canvas, her timeless beauty captured for all to see and appreciate.

It had taken longer than anticipated to complete the painting. Every time I thought I was finished, I'd come up with something else that simply must be added. By the time I finally laid my paints and brushes aside, the portrait seemed to glow with Jenny's warmth and vitality, her beautiful violet eyes shining with life and laughter.

Somehow, I'd managed to convey her enigma, the magnetism and aura that surrounded her and made her seem so ethereal. The paints appeared to have taken on a phosphorescent glow, a shimmer I couldn't recall deliberately trying for, adding a curious depth and luminescence that radiated its own special light.

Jenny looked out from the canvas with a smile somewhere between shyness and that of a temptress perfectly aware of her allure. The delicate line of forehead, jaw, and chin, the slight indentation of a dimple in each soft, pink cheek, was there for the observer to marvel and wonder at how so much perfection was possible in a single woman. Her shining mass of chestnut hair curled about her face and shoulders with a casual air that added to her seductiveness, the violet eyes inviting; "Beauty too rich for use, for Earth too dear!" Romeo, too, had known such a woman.

Even Jenny's ankh pendant turned out well, the silver and gold twist of chain contrasting sharply where it touched her alabaster skin, the ankh itself glistening brightly against the deep blue of the sweater as it rested between the hollow of her breasts. If you looked long enough, you had an overwhelming feeling that at any moment you would see the pendant move with a sudden intake of breath, that the girl would lift one of those delicately tapered fingers and beckon to you—so well had I caught the three-dimensionality of the model that she looked as though she might step from the painting. It was, without question, the best work I had ever done.

So Friday, June 28 arrived; I was toasted for my remarkable accomplishment by colleagues and distinguished guests, and then the doors of the Gallerie de l'Art of Linden State University were finally thrown open and the weekend "festivities" began.

It would be a long, exciting, and hopefully productive weekend. Situated as it was between the largest cities in the tri-state region, Linden always attracted large crowds on these occasions, and from the general information gathered beforehand, this year would be no exception. As the guests of honor, Lofgren, Seitz, and I were expected to spend most of the initial three days on hand to greet visitors and mingle with the crowd. Refreshments were provided during the Arts Festival's Grand Opening, and the normally subdued atmosphere of the gallery would be transformed into that of a party.

I always found it interesting and fascinating to listen to patrons' comments on various works, remaining in the background so their true opinion could be heard rather than the often polite comments they were more likely to say to the artist's face.

"A Study in Black," the rather inane title I'd given my charcoal abstract, was heralded as being the most unusual piece in the entire three collections. Most people commented on how uncomfortable it made them. Others found deep, almost reverent meanings behind the large, knowing eye, the misshapen head, and erratic movement of lines. It was the former group of individuals who held my attention—the way they lingered before the charcoal, tiny shivers running the length of their bare arms raising gooseflesh as they passed. These reactions, and their repeated attention to the sketch despite their avowed aversion, spoke of their true opinion.

"A View From the Bluffs" and "The Duck Pond" both garnered favorable comments on detail, form, and color, while "A Portrait of Jenny" won hands down in the category of the most people before the canvas at any given moment. The fascination the portrait held was not limited to the male population in the gallery, either. Several times I noted groups of women standing before the canvas, studying the painting from various angles, smiling, nodding, even frowning at one another's remarks. Whatever they thought or felt about it, or the girl depicted therein, they were repeatedly drawn to it, resulting in a perpetual crowd before the Wall of Honor.

I thoroughly enjoyed myself, talking with individuals who knew nothing at all about art and those who spoke with more knowledge than I ever hoped to possess. Among the lavish attention, genuinely kind words and pats on the back, I couldn't help scanning the in-coming crowd for my friends. I'd long ago given up hope that Jenny would make a dramatic appearance but found it rather disconcerting that neither Chuck nor Lily had yet to show up. Professor Drake had been called out of town the evening before and been considerably upset about missing the Grand Opening since he'd decided against viewing the collection beforehand. Without him, I had no family representation, and while I understood his commitment to responsibility, that child we retain inside ourselves felt hurt when the final moment came, and we were presented in all our glory.

Still, I did my duty, joined people I didn't know in discussions of the work on display, politely danced around controversial issues involving my two esteemed colleagues' collections, accepted compliments—sincere and not so sincere—and smiled until I felt my face might break. From eight until midnight, a steady stream of visitors poured into the Gallerie de l'Art and wandered through the marble-tiled hall, visiting with one another and stuffing their faces with the appetizers and punch presided over by Mrs. Winston and a long-faced graduate assistant.

It was close to eleven-thirty when I saw the girl standing before the portrait. I probably wouldn't have noticed her at all if she hadn't been alone, the single observer as opposed to the crowds that gathered there all evening. But there she was, standing quietly before the painting, her shoulder-length brown hair touched with golden highlights accentuated by the gallery's discreet lighting.

She was of medium height with a long, lithe body and shapely legs. Her small feet were bare, thrust into a pair of clog sandals that dwarfed their size and seemed totally incongruent to the beige linen culottes and jacket she wore. Without seeing her face, she was familiar in a way I couldn't explain. Perhaps it was the way she moved, the graceful lift of her hand, or the manner in which she tossed her head to free her face from a curtain of hair. That twinge of recognition reminded me of Jenny and my persistent sense of déjà vu experienced in her presence. The feeling was so overwhelming, that I knew I had to meet her. Yet before I had the chance to do so, I was whisked away among a crowd of well-wishers who were intent on hearing my personal interpretation of the haunting "A Study in Black."

I collapsed gratefully onto my bed that night, pleased with the way the evening had gone and looking forward to the following day. My curiosity about Chuck and Lily's absence was satisfied by messages left on my answering machine, and other than not having the opportunity to meet the girl with the sun kissed brown hair, I felt totally content.

My body was lulled by the softness of the mattress and comfort of no longer being on my feet, but my mind remained active despite the exhaustion. I reran the images of the evening through my mind, smiling at its success as I buried my head into the pillow. The tranquil thoughts were disrupted by the sound of Lily's voice, high-pitched and anxious as she related a multitude of excuses and apologies for not being at the opening night festivities.

Lily's obvious case of nerves and hesitant starts and stops failed to assuage the fear I maintained in regard to February's Art Magic exhibition. It explained why my imagination now ran wild, the nagging thought that something might have transpired between her and Marzetti to throw a wrench in the works. I didn't have a lot of faith in the man keeping his word to Lily about the gallery. And it was a sure bet that if she was out, so was my exhibition.

I turned from Lily's worried tone to the lighter note of Chuck Stinnet's voice as he apologized for his inability to attend the opening. He'd given a hearty laugh before continuing his explanation.

"I just got a call from Lily with a request for my help. Can you believe it? The woman practically begged me to come to KC to pick her up!" There was more raucous laughter. "Looks like you've lost your appeal, my friend. I think the lady's hot for me, Rich. I can see myself nibbling on those luscious curves already. Sorry, pal—like I said before, leaves more for me."

He'd signed off with another laugh followed by a lewd comment that even now made me blush. While I doubted Lily's call had anything to do with her sudden lusting after Chuck, I did find it curious. If something happened to her beloved Porsche, I would've thought she'd phone for a rental—but second guessing Lillian Reston was not a subject in which I had much luck.

I tossed restlessly on the bed, urging my mind to relax and drift into the void that would inevitably induce sleep. When it came, so did the dreams that had now become as much a part of my nightly routine as brushing my teeth before going to bed.

There was a series of dreams that would visit me; some were the nightmares from which I'd awaken in a cold sweat; others were curious pictorials, a hodgepodge of images that evoked a myriad of emotions ranging from intense fear to intense pleasure. They never came in the same order, nor was there any sense in their random appearance. I could be dreaming of a dark and driving rain with flashes of lightning and crashing thunder one minute and the next find myself in a cool green meadow much like the one in "A View From the Bluffs."

Sometimes Jenny would be there beside me, watching the hawk as it soared high in the rich azure of the sky, her chestnut hair blowing in the gentle breeze. It was a peaceful scene, one I never minded visiting—until that final moment when Jenny would turn to me, one side of her beautiful face crushed into a pulpy mass of tissue and bone. Her thin arms would reach out, a hideous smile lifting the remaining corner of her mouth as the brilliance of the single violet eye beckoned to me. I would awake screaming, my heart pounding in my head and chest as I gasped for breath and the reassurance that it was only a dream.

A dream.

Nightmares were something I thought I'd left behind in my childhood. Now they were commonplace; I couldn't sleep without one or more every night. As a result, I was often groggy in the morning, longed for a nap in the afternoon, and dreaded the thought of bed at night. Here I was, nearly thirty-one years old, a man for God's sake, and I was being terrorized by bad dreams!

But the nightmares didn't come that night, and while my sleep was filled with dreams, they were not of a terrorizing nature. Jenny was in one, her face intact, her smile as warm and soft as I remembered. She was leaning out of the gazebo in University Park, calling to me across the wide expanse between us, telling me to hurry because she must go soon.

As I ran to the gazebo, I noticed the fissures in the base had grown in length and breadth to form dangerous crevices between the foundation and structure itself. They seemed to grow before my eyes, the cement cracking and popping louder and louder as I drew near. I tried to call out to Jenny, to warn her of the impending danger, but my voice seemed locked in my throat. So I continued to run, my feet barely touching the ground, praying I would reach Jenny in time.

I swung around the corner to the steps, gasping for breath as I leapt into the gazebo. It shifted back and forth as though suddenly caught in an earthquake, and I grabbed the newel post to steady myself until the motion stopped. Jenny was nowhere to be seen, and the only remaining sound was that of the wind whining eerily between the lattice-work as it kicked up small dust tornados between the picnic tables.

The dream faded, and I found myself in the gallery at the university, people milling about in aimless patterns, pushing and shoving past me until they vanished from sight and I was alone. The quiet was almost deafening in the deserted gallery but a welcome change after all the noise of a moment before. I recognized where I was, at the back near the emergency exit, and with a sudden desire to view the portrait of Jenny, quickly made my way to the entrance.

But I was not alone. Standing before the portrait was a young woman of medium height whose shoulder-length, light brown hair gleamed beneath the lights like rich honey.

Her appearance neither surprised nor frightened me, but it did evoke a powerful curiosity. As I neared her, she turned away and headed for the gallery doors. I tried to call out to her, wanted to entreat her to stay, but once again my voice seemed frozen in my throat. I started after her only to be intercepted at the last moment by Hargrave and a tall, somber man I didn't recognize. They both seemed to be speaking to me at once, their words mingling into unintelligible garble I could not understand. Try as I might to excuse myself and make my way past them, I could not, and over Hargrave's shoulder I watched helplessly as the girl with the golden brown hair drifted out of sight.

I walked away from the two men, heading back toward the rear exit, disappointed not to have made contact with the girl and determined to be alone in my misery. But that was not to be. Both of them followed me, both continuing to harangue me in words that maintained a foreign sound to my ears. I couldn't shut out their voices, or escape their presence—no matter where I went in the gallery they remained my faithful shadows. It was my alarm that finally freed me from them and a dream that seemed riddled with questions. Shutting it off, I thanked God for small miracles and the ultimate escape into wakefulness.

There was already a handful of people in the gallery when I arrived that morning at eleven sharp. Mrs. Winston was directing the campus caterers on the placement of the cheese and vegetable platters while three young people, properly attired in black slacks, white tailored shirts, and black bow ties, looked on with bored expressions upon their collective faces. My frazzled secretary greeted me with a smile and wave of her hand, then returned her attention to the bewildered looking caterers with a sigh of exasperation.

Custodial had done themselves proud; the marble floor gleamed beneath the lights of the gallery, everything in sight a pristine elegance. Voices from beyond the center wall led me to the small group gathered at the rear of the gallery where Edmund Drake, Seitz, and Lofgren appeared deep in conversation. The sound of my footsteps caught their attention, and I was hailed with excitement by my fellow contributing artists.

"There's our esteemed colleague now." Greg Seitz grinned conspiratorially. "Professor Drake was just informing us that the guest register indicates we entertained a record crowd last evening. If it's indicative of what is to come over the next two days, we may very well exceed that of the Hollister Exhibition eight years ago."

Lofgren nodded in excitement. "And that's quite a feat when one considers Hollister had international recognition."

I caught the professor's curious stare as he took in my appearance. He gave me a somewhat hesitant smile, then returned to the conversation at hand.

"Definitely an accomplishment to be proud of, gentlemen." Drake's silvery voice echoed through the gallery as he bestowed his most enigmatic smile on those before him. "And if I'm right, the boost to your reputations will result in guest lectures and exhibitions at other institutions." He continued to beam at them. "We are indeed proud of you all."

The news and sincere compliment widened the grins on both Seitz and Lofgren's faces, each of whom considered themselves instructors first, artists second. While they were busy digesting the information and formulating it into visions of the future, Professor Drake skillfully excused himself, nodded to me to follow his lead, and steered a course away from my fellow artists.

"You know, of course, what the success of this exhibition could mean to your own career, my boy." He gave me a sidelong glance that once again took in my long hair, which I'd chosen to wear loose today, and the full beard and mustache that covered the lower half of my face in a thick mass of dark brown whiskers.

"I'm sorry, I don't mean to stare, but the effect is quite startling." He shook his head. "Ordinarily I would have said the resemblance between you and your father was minimal at best, but now—just let me say that if your mother should see you like this, she would probably have a stroke."

Once again his heavily browed eyes regarded me intently, scanning my face with something of amazement. A little self-consciously, I rubbed the wiry hair on my chin.

"It's only temporary. A kind of aberration, I suppose. And as far as my career is concerned, I hope you're referring to a success of a different kind from that of my colleagues." I grinned and received one in return.

"You're making a name for yourself, Richard, supplying a reputation that Matthew Marzetti cannot ignore. This success should provide Lillian with the confidence and ammunition necessary to convince the man not to interfere with your February show."

It was my turn to look surprised. "You know about that? About the trouble Lily's been having, I mean?"

The professor released a heavy sigh and nodded. He stopped before my "A Study in Black," and staring at the charcoal, said, "She asked my assistance should it prove necessary, and I was only too happy to assure her she would have it." He turned briefly to me with a similar look of assurance, then resumed his study of the charcoal before him.

"It's a very dark piece, Richard. Different from anything you've done previously. Haunting and intense. Interesting." He stepped back from the sketch to gain more perspective. "The depth and understanding of a fragmented existence. A dreamscape, perhaps? Um, no, the production doesn't surprise me. I've always known there was that kind of intensity inside you. The lines, the shadings, the abstract itself is like something out of a nightmare. Am I right?" His pale, hooded eyes regarded me thoughtfully.

"Inspired, you might say, from my visit to the morgue." I told him. "I have to admit that it came as rather a surprise to me." I didn't bother to relate how the charcoal had truly been a by-product of a nightmare. There wasn't any reason to bring it into the discussion.

"Ah. That would do it. I'm impressed."

I murmured the proper words of thanks which he simply brushed away.

"What I'd really like to discuss is the portrait." He averted his eyes, glancing down the long hall as though studying the many paintings that graced the walls on either side. When he finally turned to me, his bushy eyebrows were drawn into a thick line across his forehead, his eyes hidden.

"So, that's the young woman you've been entertaining." The words were spoken with a strange and slow deliberation that accentuated every syllable.

As the statement was rhetorical in nature, I simply nodded my head in agreement. With what was likely an equal amount of deliberation, I asked the professor what he thought of the portrait.

"Remarkable. I can well understand why it was chosen for the Wall of Honor." He smiled then, a strange smile that barely touched the eyes. Those same eyes twitched slightly as they continued to regard me.

"So tell me, Richard, what's her name, and where did you meet the lovely young lady."

Though it was said casually enough, I sensed a kind of command behind the words. It registered as odd, his attitude guarded rather than anything general in nature. Still, after holding it in for all this time, there was something cathartic in telling about meeting Jenny in the park, the pouring rain, and the odd sense of déjà vu I'd felt from our initial meeting on. I related how she had shown up on my doorstep during the storm several weeks earlier and how she had remained with me for the following three days only to disappear as suddenly as she had arrived. He listened intently, though with a sense of detachment, his face a mask through which no emotion showed.

"I started the portrait at her suggestion. She'd seen "A View from the Bluffs" and recognized herself. I suppose that gave her the idea."

"And you know nothing about her beyond her first name?" There was surprise as well as disappointment in his voice.

"I know how odd it must seem, but if you'd met her, you'd understand. She seemed frightened of something, or someone. It didn't feel right to press her." The explanation sounded as inadequate aloud as it had inside my brain all this time. I couldn't help feeling foolish, and wasn't very successful at covering it up.

Professor Drake took in my discomfiture and patted me on the back. "I do understand, son." He spoke quietly. "Sometimes a woman can take one that way, beguiling us with their beauty, their air of mystery or tragedy, luring one into believing anything is possible." He paused, clearing his throat. "After what you've said, and seeing your depiction of the young lady, I fully accept the lack of information. She is quite—beautiful." There was a catch in his voice, something which might have been indiscernible to someone less familiar with him.

"Are you all right?"

He flushed slightly at my concern. "Fine, fine." Once again his eyes scanned the length of the gallery, lingering on the various paintings displayed. "I'm just overwhelmed." He said quietly. "And proud. Extremely proud."

His words touched me profoundly, giving me a small sense of the approval I'd always yearned to receive from my father. This glow of warmth and pride sustained me through the rest of what proved to be a trying, hectic day.

Saturdays and Sundays were notorious for being particularly busy during the early part of the day. It was a time when families chose to take advantage of the free entertainment; parents glorying in the diversion of a grown-up activity that could also bring a sense of dignity and culture into their children's lives. Oftentimes, such a group would isolate the artist, insisting he accompany them throughout the gallery on their own personal tour. These little excursions could be brief and entertaining, or drug out mercilessly as answers to questions went unheeded or had to be repeated because little Johnny or Jane constantly interrupted or insisted on "behavior unbecoming in a place like this!" At the end of such a tour of duty, you had no idea whether you'd managed to convey any information they could hold and take with them or if it had been a total waste of everyone's time.

By mid-day, the reactions to various pieces in the three collections were becoming increasingly predictable. "Night Moves," a seascape by Lofgren depicting a tiny craft caught in a storm at sea, was praised for its sense of danger and peril, while "The Home Farm" by Seitz was lauded as being the idyll of farm living—the return to a simpler more serene way of life. "A Study in Black" continued to shock and intrigue, and "A Portrait of Jenny" maintained its ability to mesmerize even the youngest visitor as they passed before it into the gallery proper.

Each of us took turns at "stations" throughout the gallery, making ourselves available for the inevitable questions that arose. Some of my former students drew me into a deep discussion on line, form, and texture, questioning my technique with the charcoal and the three-dimensional quality of Jenny's portrait. When Seitz came to inform me that he'd spotted Chuck Stinnet, I gratefully relinquished the discussion to him and headed toward the front of the gallery.

As I made my way through the interspersed crowds of families and the typical artsy lot, I could hear the strains of some sort of commotion near the front entrance. This was an ordinary enough occurrence on family day, the inevitable protests of a disgruntled youngster who would rather be anywhere else than a stuffy old art gallery. The thought amused instead of rankled me as it might another artist—memories of childhood and being dragged along at a parent's whim still fresh enough for me to sympathize with the hapless child.

I was brought up short by the sight of Detective Hargrave standing before the Wall of Honor. I searched the area for a sign of Chuck but failed to spot him in the crowd on the other side of the room. Whatever caused the disturbance had left people clustered in small groups near the entrance with heads huddled close together in anxious whispering, throwing occasional glances over their shoulders. This posturing hinted that it was not the usual childish tantrum as I had suspected, but something of deeper interest, and I wondered what could have happened to create such a response.

I returned my attention to Hargrave, trying to decide whether I should risk an encounter or backtrack and approach from the opposite direction. While debating the issue, I watched as the detective studied the portrait, his steely eyes drinking in every detail.

He was dressed in a light-weight shirt with a loud Hawaiian print and navy twill trousers. Despite the casual air the clothes implied, the aura surrounding the detective spoke otherwise. The intensity of his interest in the portrait, the rigid set of his shoulders, and the quick sidelong glances were evidence he hadn't left his badge at home; he maintained that edge to his personality that screamed out his profession to anyone who cared to notice. This visit to the gallery might appear unofficial, but that didn't mean it was. Perhaps it was my strange dream of the night before that led me to interpret his presence as the prelude to something malevolent, but after the way he'd hounded me, I didn't believe I was overreacting.

During the periodic shifting of his gaze away from the portrait, I'd managed to remain well out of his line of vision. With the constant buzz of conversation and activity throughout the gallery, there was no way he could have heard my approach, yet something seemed to alert him to my presence. He turned to meet my stare with a steady, appraising look.

In spite of my transformed appearance, he had no trouble recognizing me; he didn't register the least bit of surprise. Was this corroborating evidence of Tara's warning that he was keeping an eye on me?

"I'd say she translated well into the larger form, wouldn't you?" His voice held the slightly mocking tone that I'd begun to believe was the man's trademark. "Nice use of color, proper mix of lights and darks to bring her out of the canvas."

"I'm glad you like it." I answered evenly, trying not to show he'd astonished me by his remark. The man must know more about art than he'd previously let on.

A slow smile lit the detective's craggy features.

"I'm duly impressed, Richard. Even without seeing more of your work, I'd say you've hit your mark with this one. 'Course that's my opinion. Can't say I speak for everyone, however." The smile gradually changed to a smirk as he continued to regard me with unconcealed amusement.

"Know any reason why a woman would take one look at this painting and cry out in alarm, forcing her companion to escort her from the gallery?"

The commotion I heard earlier? Somehow I doubted it.

"I haven't time for your games, Detective." I started to move past him, intending to check the other side of the room for Chuck, but a hand on my arm stopped my progress. I looked coldly down at the offending limb, then raised my icy stare to its owner.

He released me with a chuckle.

"Aren't you even a little curious what I'm talking about?"

My lack of answer failed to discourage him.

Again the laugh. "Guess you're just one of those people," he said, shaking his head. "A kind of pivot point with stems radiating out around you. Involved, yet not involved, still somehow a principle player."

"If you've something to say, Detective, why don't you just say it and get it over with. This is not exactly the time—"

"No, it isn't." He threw a look over his shoulder and nodded to a woman who was passing by. "Hi, how are you Mrs. Simpson?" He smiled and listened politely to the answer then returned his steel grey eyes to me. They were as cold and hard as the glare I gave him.

"Ever own a Louisville Slugger, Richard?" Here was the question I'd been waiting for, and thanks to Tara's call, was prepared. But he didn't wait for an answer. "One of those can do a helluva lot of damage to a person's skull," he continued, shaking his head. "But then, you saw that for yourself, didn't you? Your ex was pretty messed up—"

Someone called my name, and with a triumphant smile, I turned my back on him to respond. But Hargrave wasn't finished with me yet. Like his dream version, he followed closely behind me, remaining my faithful shadow until I was alone once again.

"What?" I demanded impatiently in response to his stony expression.

With a shrug of his shoulders, he scanned the faces of people as they passed.

"I was just wondering why a painting of that girl would make a friend of yours react so oddly." Hargrave's voice sounded loudly above the din of the gallery. His eyes narrowed as they bore into me. "Strange, man, real strange. Almost as though she'd seen a ghost."

The remark was so absurd it didn't bear a comment. I moved purposely past him and back toward the gallery entrance. I was only a few steps away when I saw Chuck come through the doorway. His clothes and hair were somewhat disheveled, and his movements seemed jerky, not at all the fluid, precise, even cocky manner he normally displayed. Drawing nearer, I took in the paleness of his complexion and the almost wild look in his eyes as he gazed quickly up at Jenny's portrait before scanning the crowd. When he spotted me, he made a brave attempt at his usual jaunty smile.

"Are you all right?" I asked as we retreated into an unoccupied area just inside the doorway.

There was a visible effort of his trying to pull himself together as he looked away and pretended to greet some passers-by. When he returned his attention to me, the smile was more firmly in place, his hair smoothed back, and a sparkle of amusement was in his eyes.

"So that's the little lady from the park." He nodded his head in the direction of the painting. "I can see why you didn't need my company."

With a sense of pride, I looked up at the portrait. "So, do you think she was worth it?"

The sound that emitted from Chuck Stinnet could hardly be described a laugh. I looked at him sharply, concern for my friend returning when I realized he appeared to be choking on something.

"For God's sake, quit pounding on my back!" He jerked away from me out into the main hallway of the Fine Arts building. The glance he threw me was more suspicious than friendly, and confused by his attitude, I began a slow burn.

"What the hell's the matter with you?"

He didn't respond immediately but continued to stare past me to where the portrait hung just inside the doorway of the gallery.

"Tell me about her."

The tone made it a demand, not a request.

"What is it you want to hear, Chuck? That when I wasn't painting her, I was screwing her brains out?" Despite my growing anger, I managed to keep my voice low enough so no one else would hear our exchange.

Stinnet raised a single eyebrow in surprise, his mouth quirking at the corner. "Vulgarity? Quite out of character for you, Rich. But I like it." The leer turned into the more familiar grin. "Actually, I was curious about the girl herself. Like, for instance, her name."

Embarrassed by my angry outburst, I felt the heat rise from beneath my collar and into my face.

What was wrong with me? I'd never been so easily riled, had always been able to keep my temper under control. Now it seemed the simplest thing could set me off.

I took a deep, cleansing breath, forced a smile when another colleague passed by on his way out of the building, then turned back to Chuck.

"Jenny, that's all I know." My voice had regained its normal tone. "She wasn't exactly the most forthcoming with information about herself. I know how odd that sounds, considering the volume of work in which I've used her image, but..."

"She *is* beautiful." He met my eyes with a genuine smile. "I'm impressed. Surprised, but very impressed."

He waved away my question before it could be asked.

"The surprise isn't for the quality, Richard. That's always been a given. No." He shook his head, glanced briefly through the doors at the portrait, then looked at me. "It's the girl. She's—familiar."

There was a strange note in his voice, something akin to the tone the professor had used. Before I had the chance to question him about it, he was already heading toward the main entrance of the building.

"Look, Rich, I gotta run. I left Lily in the car. She—uh, got sick right after we arrived, and I had to take her outside. I didn't want to leave, though, until I had the opportunity to let you know we'd been here. I'll try to get back later on to see the rest of the collection, and I'm sure Lily will be here as soon as she's feeling better."

Without allowing me a word, he was out the door and down the steps. I watched in confusion as he headed across the parking lot. Then, with a heavy sigh, I turned and went back into the gallery.

Chapter 15

The tone of the exhibition seemed to change after Stinnet's departure—or perhaps it was my perception that changed. Since the earlier disturbance and my encounter with Hargrave, there was a tenseness in the air, and I didn't believe I was the only one who felt it. For some time afterward, voices seemed more hushed, conversations subdued. The party atmosphere basically continued, but it paled by comparison.

Even less encouraging was the thought Lily may have been the cause of the disturbance. While I preferred Chuck's brief explanation of her illness over Hargrave's belief it was a reaction to Jenny's portrait, as the day wore on, I began to have some doubts.

There appeared an increase in the amount of people questioning Jenny's "true" identity, commenting on her familiarity. It wasn't impossible or even improbable for someone to recognize the girl; I'd hoped that might happen and eventually lead me to her. What was so unusual about the situation was the vagueness of the individuals, as though they were searching their memories of the past for an answer.

My solution to their dilemma was the old standby that everyone has a twin somewhere in the world, and Jenny reminded them of someone they'd once known. The answer seemed to satisfy, and the popularity of the painting continued throughout the day. Yet despite the satisfaction others appeared to derive from this explanation, it failed to convince me. I felt as though I was missing something.

I was also certain that had any one of these people met Jenny, they would not have forgotten her so easily.

Late that evening I was stationed in direct view of the gallery entrance. When not occupied by those already present, I enjoyed watching the response of individuals as they came into the room and their eyes first fell on the Wall of Honor and Jenny's portrait. Perhaps it sounded odd, but the looks of wonder and fascination of that initial viewing gave me far more satisfaction than any words of appreciation could.

Positioned thus, I spotted Lily within moments of her arrival. She kept her eyes carefully averted from the Wall, giving credence to Hargrave's claim that something about the painting disturbed her. She looked about the area, her face a strange composite of calm and anxiety all mixed into one. She didn't appear ill, the only outward betrayal of her usual serene composure a nervous twitch at the corner of her mouth. I'd seen that twitch before when she'd told me about the break with Marzetti, and I wondered what was causing it now.

I excused myself from the small group of people who had clustered around me, meeting Lily halfway across the expanse seconds after she spotted me.

"It's a good thing Chuck warned me about the beard or I'd never have recognized you." She gave me an appraising glance.

I grinned, rubbing my chin in amusement. I started to welcome her, but she beat me to it.

"I take that back. Your eyes give you away." She gazed around the room feigning an interest I knew she didn't feel. "I wondered if I'd have the chance to speak with you. Have the crowds been like this since last evening?"

I told her they had, and taking her by the elbow, drew her gently out of the main aisle to an area currently devoid of people.

"Are you feeling better?" I watched her closely, trying to figure out what might be bothering her. But Lily has always been a cipher to me—her true personality hidden behind those large blue eyes and air of sophistication. Only when she'd been trying to seduce me had her thoughts and intentions been clear—and this wasn't one of those times.

She asked if I'd mind giving her a guided tour, and tucking her hand within the bend of my elbow, we began.

Lily's attention wasn't fully engaged on the activity, I knew from the almost banal remarks she made from time to time. Occasionally she would stop before a canvas and make a rather insightful comment but mostly it was cursory. She was here because she felt she should be, not because she wanted to be. This in and of itself might not seem so unusual; she was, after all, my friend. But considering her line of business, one would have thought she might have shown more interest in the work around her—especially in that of the artist she was a sworn benefactress.

It was the fastest tour I'd made around the gallery. As we neared the main entrance, I could feel the sudden tenseness in Lily's hand. She was anxious to be gone, and equally anxious not to view the portrait again. With an effort that was far from subtle, she pulled me out of the gallery and into the hallway and a nearby alcove. She gave me a brief smile that held only a hint of her usual brightness, pushed back a wayward strand of hair, and shrugged her shoulders.

"I know that couldn't have been very satisfying, and I apologize." Again the weak smile. "It's nothing to do with you, Richard. Honestly. I just haven't been up for this. Matthew had me sign some papers yesterday giving me temporary custody of Art Magic, then proceeded to tell me he was pulling the lease on the Porsche." She gave a little laugh that seemed to border on hysteria. "Better the car than the gallery. Still, it does tick me off. I'm trying very hard to be good and not confront that witch he calls a wife, but..."

I took her hand and gave it a reassuring squeeze.

"I'm sorry—"

"Oh, don't be." She said sharply, followed by an apology. "I'm not my best at the moment. But now things are final, put into writing and all, I know where I stand. Business is great, and I have every reason to believe it'll keep on getting better. Matthew believes that, too, and already had his lawyer draw up the transfer papers. I'll bet his little wifey really hates the thought I'll come out with anything at all, but Matthew won't go back on his word; Art Magic will be mine. I know it, he knows it, and even the witch knows it."

Watching her, I had the feeling she was stalling for time, that all this information about Marzetti and the gallery was just window dressing. She was avoiding the moment when she would be required to say something about the show, and even given her half-hearted perusal of the collection, it made me uneasy.

I couldn't understand her aversion to the portrait, and curious as I was to know the reason behind it, her current agitation kept me from questioning her.

I listened attentively, managed to say the proper things at the right times, but the longer she avoided the issue, the more uncomfortable I became. When she finally came back to the subject, it took me a moment or two to realize what she was talking about.

"—and where did you say you met her?"

It was the nod in the direction of the gallery that made me realize she was referring to Jenny.

"I didn't, actually." I responded. "But we met one day in University Park, and things went from there."

Lily lowered her eyes, suddenly intent on the toes of her shoes.

"Is she, I mean, she is the same one I saw in the other painting? The one of the duck pond."

I nodded. "She seemed to belong there." It was a rather inane statement, but considering Lily's present mood, I doubted she even noticed.

She hadn't.

"Creates more interest. But the portrait," she swallowed loudly, excused herself, and went to a nearby fountain for a drink.

"I think I knew her mother." She said into the basin of the water cooler.

The comment took me by surprise, and thinking back to the little Jenny had said about her family, my curiosity got the better of me.

"Really? She'd mentioned that her mother died when she was very young."

Lily nodded without looking at me. I waited for her to say something further, and when she didn't, tried again.

"It's rather embarrassing, really, but she was very secretive about herself. I've been trying to—"

"Mr. Tanner?" One of the servers, an anxious young man who fiddled nervously with the bowtie about his neck, stood just a few feet away. "I hate to bother you, sir, but a Mrs. Fordem is asking for you." He grimaced slightly before he continued. "She has a group of people with her and was upset about being unable to find you."

Knowing what I did about the formidable Mrs. Fordem, I could well understand the lad's discomfort.

"Just what I needed." I muttered, hoping it was said quietly enough he hadn't heard. To him, "Would you tell her I'll be right there? And," stopping him as he turned to go, "Try not to let her intimidate you. It gives her too much satisfaction." He grinned at the remark, gave me a mock salute, and departed far more relaxed than he had arrived.

When the young man had gone, I turned back to Lily. "The wife of a Board member. After all this crap with Hargrave and Tara I have to keep on my toes."

"Kiss ass, you mean." It was the first real smile since her arrival.

"Unfortunately, yes. Until Tara's assault case is solved, and they have the creep in custody, I'll have to play it close to the vest."

"Isn't schmoozing fun?" She laughed. "But seriously, how *is* Tara?"

"Good. She met her mother in Chicago a few weeks back, and they've been going to counseling together. She still can't recall anything that might help the cops locate her assailant, but she doesn't seem to care. It's not really in character for her, but I think the assault made her take stock." I shrugged. "The postcard I got last week didn't say much, but I got the feeling she wouldn't be coming back to Linden."

"That might be wise under the circumstances." Lily made a show of checking her watch. "Look, Richard, you'd better run before Mrs. Whatsername has a tizzy. Besides, I've got to get moving." She patted my arm. "The collection looks good."

The remark was more of an afterthought than anything sincere. Rather than taking it personally, I chalked it up to her general state of distraction.

"Will I see you tomorrow?"

She shook her head, releasing long strands of her blond hair from the too sedate bun at the nape of her neck.

"I've got to get back to KC. You know how it is. I'll try to get back soon so I can give your collection the attention it deserves. Until then, don't kiss too much ass—remember, mine's awaiting its turn."

With a dazzling smile and a jaunty wave of her hand, she was gone.

~

Sunday dawned with the promise of rain, a promise that was fulfilled by mid-afternoon. This led to an increase in the crowds, which not only kept us all hopping, but also managed to avert questions and introspection on the conspicuous absence of Edmund Drake, the head of the College of Arts and Humanities.

My own curiosity regarding the professor's whereabouts were one thing, my colleagues' yet another. It wasn't as though the Arts Festival demanded his presence throughout the weekend, but it was rather unusual his attendance was only in the brief morning hours of the day before.

Had something happened that necessitated his absence, or had the success of the Festival seemed so secure he didn't feel his continued presence important? These questions were uppermost in both Seitz and Lofgren's minds, with my own remaining unanswered because of interruptions each time I went to phone him.

Breaks were not easy to come by. Unless you chose to shut yourself in a bathroom stall, you could be found no matter where you decided to spend those few precious moments alone. Even Mrs. Winston's marvelous stamina was sorely tested, and by five that afternoon, her smile and hairdo had wilted considerably. My offer to oversee the refill of the refreshment table while she grabbed a few minutes for herself was greeted with hesitation, but she finally relented. With a weak smile of thanks she tottered unsteadily for the exit. At the door, she looked back at me uncertainly as another group of people pushed past her, only leaving after I'd waved her on.

The servers knew their jobs well, so I stayed out of their way and let them do it. One of the kids asked if I thought the evening would be as busy as the afternoon, and my hesitation in answering led them all into despondency.

"I think people are coming just for a free hand-out." One of them commented wearily. "Sorry, Mr. Tanner, I didn't mean, I mean, I just never saw so much food disappear this fast."

As I assured the young man that no offense had been taken, I smiled at the patrons coming through the food line.

"Just watch," the same young man said quietly at my elbow. "See those people that just came in? They'll stop before the Wall of Honor for a moment then make a beeline for the food."

It was just as he said, and I looked on in amusement and some consternation as one by one the same pattern was followed.

Mrs. Winston returned groomed and rested after her fifteen minute respite. Her smile was back in place as was the twinkle in her small, round eyes.

"Bless you, Mr. Tanner." She patted my arm. "I feel ever so much better."

She resumed her place behind the table, her arms folded across her ample middle, prepared to greet and serve all who entered. With my own energy level flagging, I admired her resilience, realizing in my brief turn at the refreshment table that she'd dealt with far more people than I had.

Seeing everything was once again under her able control, I turned to go, only to be stopped by a sharp whisper from my secretary.

"She's back again." Mrs. Winston nodded in the direction of the entrance. Turning, I saw the girl with the golden brown hair enter the room.

"She can't seem to stay away." Mrs. Winston commented behind me. "Wait and see. She'll look around for a moment, pause, then slowly move forward to the Wall of Honor. Now she'll stand before the painting for what," she seemed to be conferring with the servers. "Five, maybe ten minutes before she begins her tour. Within the half hour she'll be back before the Wall for another look at the painting before she leaves."

I gave my secretary an appraising look which she seemed to misinterpret.

"I know I shouldn't be so forward, Mr. Tanner, and I wouldn't have said anything, but it's been the same thing two or three times every day. Right kids?" She looked to the servers for confirmation which they readily gave. "She seems totally entranced by that portrait—even more than most people. Has she sought you out to speak with you about it?"

I shook my head, then turned back to study the girl.

"Then perhaps you might—"

I didn't need my secretary's prompting to go to her. In spite of the constant buzz of conversation, the gallery seemed to suddenly become very quiet. People entering the room did not stop before the Wall as they usually did, but moved into the gallery proper leaving the area free of crowds for the first time in the last three days.

"Do you love her?" She asked without turning, some sixth sense making her aware of my presence behind her.

She had a beautiful voice, soft and melodic with a gentle lilt.

The question took me by surprise, and gazing up at the portrait, I stared into the depths of those engaging violet eyes.

"I thought perhaps—but, no." I answered honestly. "I—I hardly know her."

The girl before me turned then to regard me frankly, with a ghost of a smile touching her full, pink lips.

She had eyes like sapphires, a rich blue with uncloudy depths, high cheekbones with a healthy rose tingeing the lightly tanned skin, a small, pert nose, and a softly rounded face. She was attractive, even pretty in an ordinary sort of way, her shoulder-length brown hair shining with golden highlights accentuated by the gallery lighting.

I returned her gaze, smiling thoughtfully.

"I—wondered. There's something there, though. Something very strong, intense." She said softly.

Taking my eyes momentarily off the girl, they flicked briefly over the portrait then came back to rest on the young woman before me.

"A fascination, perhaps. A kind of obsession." I felt myself blushing self-consciously at the admission.

"Um." She eyed me speculatively. "Honesty. That's refreshing." She grinned, bringing her face to life and destroying my previous low assessment of her looks. In her own way, she was as beautiful as Jenny.

She seemed about to say something else when someone came up behind us and interrupted. Without demur, she stood aside, and before I had the chance to excuse myself, I was ushered away within a group of admirers. When I was finally able to extricate myself, I searched the gallery for her, but she was nowhere to be found. It was so reminiscent of my dream from a few nights before, that I couldn't keep myself from looking over my shoulder, fully expecting to find Hargrave and his mysterious companion ready to dog my steps for the remainder of the afternoon.

We were scheduled to close the gallery at nine that evening, and by seven, I was already marking the minutes as they passed. Professor Drake still hadn't made an appearance, but apologies were sent by way of messenger, alleviating any doubts my colleagues had while adding to my own curiosity. Still, on the whole, the three days had proved successful, enjoyable, but trying as well.

There is a certain anonymity for someone working in the arts; you present your work, be it a novel or a painting, then place it where the public has the opportunity to view it, your performance held in the privacy of home, office, studio, or wherever the creative process takes place. When your work sells, you can then assume it was appreciated and enjoyed. When it doesn't, then it's back to the drawing board for another try.

While there was a certain amount of satisfaction in actually seeing the responses of others to your work, it also tended to take a great deal out of you. I was exhausted, tired of explaining technique, of dissecting each piece until they were reduced to nothingness, and of the perpetual smile that had been plastered to my face for the past three days. Though I was appreciative of the graciousness and attention extended by the university and hundreds of guests that passed through the gallery, I was ready to return to my own quiet, perhaps mundane, existence where I could choose when and to whom I smiled at or visited with.

Promotion and selling oneself may be the price of success, but sometimes it seemed too high to pay.

Shortly after eight, Mrs. Winston sent one of the servers to tell me that the "peculiar young lady" had returned. Thanking him, I managed to excuse myself from my current fan and made my way to the Wall of Honor.

She had indeed returned, but this time she was not alone. A tall, white haired gentleman with a deeply lined face and somber expression stood beside her, their arms linked. Spotting me, the girl smiled, then whispered to her companion. He turned watery blue eyes to me, a frown settling upon his thin lips as he released the girl's arm and started toward me. When she moved to follow him, he turned briefly, said something in a very deep voice that I could not make out, then resumed his advance.

With a shrug of her narrow shoulders, the girl wandered off along the other side of the gallery and was soon out of sight.

"I take it you are the artist of that painting." He had a supercilious attitude that I found particularly annoying after my long day. Still, I managed to hang onto that fake smile and adopted an equally false enthusiasm for his attention.

"Yes, sir, I'm Richard Tanner." I held my hand out to him only to have it ignored. The man continued to regard me in his superior manner, the long, thin face and square chin reflecting a look of even greater distaste.

"I wish to speak with you about the model. In private." It wasn't a request. The watery blue eyes were hard and cold as they bore into me, the deep voice firm. It was obvious this man was used to being obeyed without question.

"I'm sorry to disappoint you, Mr.—"

"Grant." He supplied impatiently.

"Mr. Grant." I nodded, still smiling that idiotic smile. "But I'm rather tied up at the moment. I'd be happy to tell you anything I can, but I'm afraid it won't be much. As I told the young woman you were with, I hardly know the girl."

There was a look of disbelief on Grant's face, and he set his jaw firmly in an angle of persistence.

"I shall be the judge of that. Now, I suggest you cooperate or—"

As usual, the conversation was interrupted by someone who just *had* to speak to me at that moment. Mrs. Fordem was back with another group of friends and expected me to help her impress them. Noticing my companion, she smiled brightly and held her hand out to him.

"Why, Robert, how delightful to see you." She exclaimed. "I was just commenting the other day how long it had been. How are you?"

Grant took her hand within both of his and brought it to his lips in a rather continental gesture to the even further delight of Mrs. Fordem.

"Evelyn. It is good to see you as well. You're looking as lovely as ever."

Evelyn Fordem was an imposing-looking woman, tall, big-boned, and quite wide. She had a high, grating voice, a pushy attitude, and an outrageous taste in clothing. Today she was wearing an orange and black rayon dress which reminded one of Halloween more than summer, its large floral print accentuating the size of its wearer. In her ears dangled earrings of a similar pattern, and an ornate orange hair tie drew the sides of her short grey hair into a knot on the top of her head. Lovely was not the word I would have used to describe her.

After exchanging a few pleasantries, she agreed to relinquish her claim on me in exchange for a promise from Grant to attend a dinner party the following week. When she'd finally gone, Robert Grant returned his cold eyes to me.

"As I was saying, I would like some information."

My good humor was slowly evaporating, as was my patience. I didn't like his high-handed tactics and had no desire to be grilled about Jenny by a man I knew nothing about. Looking at him, at the sparse eyebrows that stuck out at odd angles, the wide eyes, and heavily lined face, I judged him to be in his late seventies. Surely this couldn't be the father Jenny had mentioned.

I knew the trap of judging people by their appearance alone—I was often taken as being stuck-up rather than shy—but I didn't believe my judgment of the man before me was incorrect in the slightest. The way he held himself and spoke, looking down his nose at me, showed how highly he thought of himself and how little he thought of those around him. Even the niceties spoken to Mrs. Fordem had been said in a condescending manner, the woman too innocent to notice. It made me even less anxious to impart the little knowledge I had of Jenny—the desire to protect her as strong as ever.

Robert Grant drew himself up, his back ramrod straight, the watery blue eyes piercing. His hands clenched and unclenched several times at his sides before he brought them together before him.

"You'll have to forgive me if my manner is a little brusque." He took a deep breath, and letting it out slowly, forced a smile that I believed was meant to be apologetic. If that's what he intended, it fell short by several degrees.

"Mr. Tanner." The tenor of his voice had not changed. Nor had the general expression on his face in spite of the smile. "I have every reason to believe that the young woman in that painting is my daughter."

Now it was my turn to take a deep breath. My reaction had not gone unnoticed.

"I can see you understand the implication." His eyes bore into me. "I would appreciate your telling me where to find her."

"I'd like to help you, but until this moment all I'd known was her first name."

"You can't expect me to believe that, Tanner." He said through clenched teeth. "I've been told about the volume of work which includes her. You cannot spend that much time with an individual and claim ignorance."

"Whether you choose to accept it or not, I've told you the truth."

The man's jaw tightened, and mentally I heard the grinding of his teeth. Despite his age, I sensed a violence beneath the surface that was being restrained by considerable effort. Still, for propriety's sake, I calmly continued.

"When I met Jenny, I was so taken with her that I immediately began to sketch her. Long before the idea of the portrait was suggested, I'd already intended to include her image in the other works. It was simply a case of adding her to already drawn sketches then transferring the total onto canvas. It's not such an unusual thing to do. Especially when something, or someone, makes such an indelible impression."

"And who suggested the portrait?" He asked evenly.

I hardly saw this as relevant, but answered just the same. "Jenny. But—"

"No buts, Tanner." He loomed over me, and in spite of the fact we were of similar height, he suddenly seemed much taller. "My daughter has been missing for some time, and I'm in no mood for equivocation. I need to know precisely where she is, and I do not intend to leave until you tell me."

People were beginning to stop and stare. With as much grace as I could manage, I backed away from Grant, still making the attempt to smile as though nothing untoward was happening.

"I told you the truth. Jenny was very withdrawn when it came to her personal life. So much so that I had the feeling she might be in some kind of trouble."

"Trouble?"

"She mentioned that her mother had died when she was very young, and that she'd left a daughter in her father's care. That was the extent of her revelations. She never mentioned her last name, much less her address. I can't tell you what I don't know."

"You said she was in trouble. What kind, exactly?" I could tell from the way he spoke that he was having a great deal of trouble maintaining control—and the way his hands had balled into fists, I was waiting for the moment it gave way, and he let one of them fly in my direction.

"It was just a feeling I had. I can't cite anything definite. Now if you'll excuse me—"

As I started to walk past him, he grabbed my arm.

"I intend to have my answers." He seethed.

Jerking away from him, I readjusted the sleeve of my jacket and stared him straight in the eyes.

"I hope you find them, Mr. Grant." I said evenly, but my sincerity was lost on him. He still didn't believe I was telling him everything I knew, and in an odd sort of way, I understood the fury and frustration driving him. I, myself, found it difficult to accept that the time Jenny and I spent together garnered so little information about her life.

I turned from the intensity of those watery blue eyes to find Detective Hargrave standing just a few feet away, watching us intently. He nodded slightly to me, his attention fixed on Robert Grant. This was not a time to question providence, and while the two men continued to regard one another with something akin to animosity, I made my escape.

The air in the gallery seemed suddenly stale and thick. I loosened my tie, drew in a deep breath, and found myself coughing spasmodically. Within moments, Mrs. Winston was by my side with a glass of punch and the excellent suggestion that I step outside for some fresh air. Rather than risk a further encounter with Grant, I continued toward the rear of the gallery, carefully avoiding contact with patrons along the way. Spotting Seitz, I drew him aside and asked if the alarm on the emergency exit was still off so I could use that door instead of the main one.

"I believe so." He looked tired and confused. "You going to try to grab a few minutes alone?"

"If at all possible. I shouldn't be gone long, but if anything important—"

"Don't worry. Things should settle down soon." He assured me. "We close in less than an hour."

With as much discretion as possible, I slipped out the emergency exit and into the parking lot located directly behind the building. As I'd hoped, the area was deserted—only a couple of university cars occupying the spaces. The air was hot and close, the afternoon rain having raised the humidity making it muggy. It was little better than the stuffy atmosphere of the gallery, but with one important difference: there were no people here to contend with.

I tugged off my jacket, flung it over the bicycle rack perched on the edge of the sidewalk, then proceeded to walk the perimeter of the lot in as quick a pace as I could muster. Pent up emotions of anger and frustration, days of being unable to take my normal walks, the stress of preparing for the Festival, and the resultant command performances had all taken their toll on me. Bursts of energy surged through my body demanding release.

I was only dimly aware of the setting sun, the streaks of rich azure contrasted by clouds that had turned from gray to pink, lavender, and white, visible only at fleeting intervals because tree branches nearly formed a canopy over different parts of the parking lot. I ran to the musical sounds of insects and civilization that could be barely heard in the distance. I attempted to clear my mind, rid it of tension and allow the air to cleanse and purify it with every breath I took.

I was so preoccupied with trying to relax that I didn't hear their approach, didn't even see them until they were already within a few

PORTRAIT OF JENNY

paces of me.

Robert Grant and a man who could have been Mr. Universe, his arms as thick as tree trunks, watched me with expressions of smug satisfaction. There was no use trying to avoid a confrontation with them; I wasn't about to run away. Besides, Mr. Universe blocked the gallery door.

"Perhaps now we have a little privacy you will feel more comfortable giving me the information I asked for." Grant's deep voice reverberated across the empty lot, the echo lending it a menacing sound.

I stopped just a few yards in front of them, staring at the two men thoughtfully and wondering how I was going to convince Grant I'd already told him everything I knew.

While I contemplated the best approach, Mr. Universe was getting antsy. He began to move slightly back and forth, his massive hands balling into fists which then released with a snap and crackle as he stretched meaty fingers before clenching them tightly once again. Grant put a restraining hand on his companion's arm, observed me watching them, and flashed me a deadly smile.

"Jim thinks you're trying to avoid answering me, Mr. Tanner, and he's getting impatient." The voice was smooth and cold, the implication of a threat audible.

"I'm not avoiding anything, simply trying to figure out how to make you believe what I've already told you." I crossed my arms in front of me and adopted a stance which I'd found successful when dealing with unruly students. I had my doubts it would work on Jim but was hoping Grant had the intelligence and insight necessary to see I was serious.

It didn't work.

Robert Grant drew himself up, back ramrod straight, head high, watery blue eyes attempting to bore right through me. He wasn't buying what I was selling, and he made it clear with every movement that he had no patience left.

"Jennifer has been missing," his voice broke on the last word, but he refused to allow the momentary weakness to lessen his resolve to drag every piece of information from me that I possessed. "She has been missing for t-twenty-one years—"

"Well, sir, unless she was four or five years old at the time, the girl in the portrait could hardly be your daughter." I hadn't meant it to sound insolent, but there was no other way it could have sounded under the circumstances.

Mr. Universe continued to clench and unclench his massive fists, not really listening to the conversation, rather standing and glaring at me, his heavy features distorted and threatening. When Grant jumped back as though startled by my statement, the man of steel reached out to steady the older man, throwing me an even deadlier look.

While Robert Grant seemed momentarily taken aback, I decided I should try to further my position.

"Look, Mr. Grant, I'm sorry to disillusion you, but you've obviously made a mistake. Jenny, the girl in the portrait, couldn't be more than twenty-five at the most. Therefore, it stands to reason there's no way she could be your daughter. It's just one of those strange coincidences that sometimes happen."

Grant moved purposely away from his companion, closing the gap between us by several steps.

"I am not mistaken, and you know that perfectly well." He said, his jaw so tight I was sure I could hear his teeth actually grinding together this time. "How dare you imply that I wouldn't know my own child!"

I wasn't prepared for what happened, despite the crazy way the conversation quickly became less and less civilized. Still, I didn't see it coming.

My cheek stung from the force of his blow, my ears rang. I looked at the old man before me with amazement, stunned beyond belief.

Before I had the chance to fully recover, "Jim" was behind me, jerking my arms back painfully.

"Just tell him what he wants to know, dirtbag, and you don't have to get hurt." His gravelly voice came from so close to my ear that I could feel the heat of his breath on my neck. He tugged on my arms, emitting a chuckle when I winced.

"If you don't cooperate, I might have to break something. Then how would you continue painting, huh?" There was a sound of glee in his voice, a daring to defy and see what would happen next.

I had no desire to antagonize either man. Indeed, had no idea how this had gotten so out of hand. My cheek hurt, and there was the taste of blood in my mouth.

Blood, for God's sake! What the hell was going on here?!

I'd been in scrapes as a kid, though nothing serious, and the incidents were so rare and unimportant that I couldn't have given detailed descriptions of them now. My aversion to violence, to hand-to-hand combat, left me sadly lacking, especially when my opponent was a muscle-bound jock who looked as though he was itching for action. I had to keep my wits, try to appeal to Grant's intelligence and hope to make him see reason.

Robert Grant stood before me, a smug expression on his lined face, his watery blue eyes tinged with cold fire.

"Since you refuse to be cooperative, Tanner, you've forced me to resort to extreme measures. It's not the first time I've had to deal with scum like you, thinking you know what's best for my daughter."

With a nod of his head, Mr. Universe tightened his grip on my arms until I thought they would pop loose from the shoulders.

"I've told you all I know about the girl." I gasped against the pain. "Assault is hardly—"

"Civilized?" Grant offered with a smirk. "Perhaps not, but it can sometimes produce results one is unable to get otherwise." He grabbed hold of the front of my shirt and yanked it upward until the underarm seams dug uncomfortably into my skin. His narrow face was inches before mine.

"Let's try this once more, shall we? And I suggest that you think very carefully before you answer. *Where the hell is my daughter?*"

There was a sense of unreality about what was happening, a strange sort of belief that the melodrama unfolding around me could not be real but a joke of some kind. These thoughts flashed through my brain even as it was recording the pain of the next blow inflicted. The side of my face seemed to burst into flame, my eyes stung as my vision clouded over, and the taste of blood increased.

Grant was no street fighter; his was a more refined method of inflicting pain. With a large signet ring turned palm ward, the hand straight and flat, he scored and seared my flesh, taking satisfaction from his handiwork.

I watched helplessly as the next blow neared the side of my face in a crazy sort of slow motion, tried to open my mouth to say something, but was unable to get the words out before Grant's open hand came into contact with my already bruised cheek. I felt the stinging sensation, heard the sound reverberate inside my skull, and then the world burst into a kaleidoscope of color. Just before the world went black, I heard a woman's scream.

~

It was as though I was emerging from a great fog; my ears were functioning, hearing voices raised in anger all around me, but my eyes, while open, could see nothing but a dim light in what seemed a vast distance before me. There was an odd tingling sensation throughout my body, little pinpricks that teased the nerve endings with sparks of electricity. Was this another dream, another nightmare designed to confuse and frighten me? What would suddenly appear out of the fog...

"Lie still." A soft voice sounded just above me.

A cool hand on my brow, flesh against flesh. Not a dream.

As the periphery of my vision gradually increased, my other senses began to react. I seemed to be lying on a hard surface, curled on my left side. My head was slightly elevated, resting on something firm but far softer than whatever held the rest of my body. Movement took too great an effort, and since the gentle voice reiterated the command to lie still, I decided it best to obey.

The right side of my neck ached, sending shooting pains upward into my brain—a migraine of monumental proportions, but something I was familiar with. Still, I had to wonder what was going on, how I'd come to be lying down. Trying to force memory made the pain in my head increase, but I continued to try anyway.

The voices went on around me, the words indistinguishable, but the tone of extreme anger clear. Now and again I caught a word or two and gradually, as I was able to piece together what was being discussed, memory returned.

"Jenny?" I croaked.

"Sh-sh." Again the hand stroked my brow. "Just lie still, Richard. Help's on the way."

Despite the agonizing pain and effort, I moved my head, and blinking, gazed up into the face above me.

She was backlit by the twilight, by the dim phosphorous glow of the security lights, a halo surrounding her head. It wasn't Jenny but an angel with golden hair. She had my head cradled in her lap. While one cool hand soothed my brow, the other dabbed lightly at the corner of my mouth.

I settled more comfortably onto her lap, trying to focus eyes that were clouded with sweat and blood, yet content to remain within the gentle arms that held me with such tenderness.

Slowly, the face of the golden haired girl came into focus. She gave me a tentative smile as she once again encouraged me to remain still.

"Will you two please be quiet." The girl/angel said firmly. "Don't you think it would be far more constructive for one of you to wait out front so the ambulance can be directed back here when it arrives?"

The voices became distinctive then: Robert Grant and Detective Hargrave. It was the first time since having met the detective that I was actually glad he was around.

A great wave of pain sent shock waves throughout my brain, and I cried out as my body drew up into the fetal position of its own accord.

Something was happening inside my head. I could feel my brain pulsating and shifting, growing and then shrinking. I grasped onto the hand that tried to soothe me, clutching it as though it was a lifeline.

"What's going on? What's happening?" Hargrave's voice was closer now, and I squinted out through eyes that refused to stay open to find him kneeling next to me.

A heavier hand on my arm, Hargrave's rough voice in my ear. "Tell me what day it is, Tanner. Give me your address. Talk, say anything, just stay awake, damn you."

He sounded so anxious, it made me want to laugh in spite of it all. But I couldn't laugh and had no idea how I was supposed to stay awake when unconsciousness seemed so inviting.

"What's the date?" The detective demanded again.

"July first." I slurred obediently in an effort to get the man out of my face. But somehow, I knew what I'd said was wrong.

I didn't understand his response, but the tone said he wasn't pleased. As I nestled closer into my angel's lap, I fought off another wave of pain, knowing there was some significance in the two words I'd uttered.

"Just hang on, Richard Tanner. Do you hear me? *You stay awake!*" The girl/angel peered anxiously into my face. "I'm not about to lose you now."

Despite the firmness, the voice was warm, soft, and gave me a tingle of pleasure. I had no idea what was happening to me, and even though I was frightened, I also felt a strange kind of security and contentment.

I snuggled closer, inhaling her scent as the darkness once again closed in around me.

Chapter 16

Sounds.

White noise, like that of a TV channel without a broadcast, pierced my brain, forcing itself into every minute particle therein. Images flickered among the din, pictures that had no voice, no animation, no sense of reality in this strange realm of discordance.

I drifted in and out of consciousness, floating at times within the comforting arms of peace, slamming at others against relentless shores of pain and fear. Sometimes things came into sharp focus, like the starkness of the hospital and the glare of lights as they quickly moved above me. There were voices of nurses, their faces wavering before me, and my golden-haired angel reassured and comforted me.

I had a vague sense of knowledge, cognizance of what was happening, what had gotten me to this point in time. I felt there was something I needed to tell these people who bent over me, their fingers poking and prodding my head, neck, and shoulders, but words failed to form. Instead, I found myself adrift in a vast sea where thoughts of past and present converged, and memory and dreams became one...

~

Nothing was the same this year as it had been in the past. It wasn't just that the park was being demolished, the heavy equipment tearing it apart and making it smaller and smaller as the days wore on. That was a large part of it, the absence of the special freedom of running from dawn to dusk in the best playground anyone could ask for.

But there was more to it than that, something he could sense but not quite put a finger on. And it didn't help that Aunt Janet and Uncle Edmund seemed constantly at odds.

That was an expression he'd heard his mother use when she didn't want to admit she and his father were fighting. But he knew what it meant. There would be odd silences, cold shoulders, and looks that could send a chill right through you. He was smart for his age; they'd always told him that. He knew about strained relationships, about nerves that were stretched so taut by disagreements that it could be felt by others not even involved. And that was exactly what was happening here.

It was abnormally quiet in the Drake house whenever the couple was alone together. There were no raised voices or angry looks like he'd witnessed between his parents; that was part of what made it so weird. Aunt Janet and Uncle Edmund were very polite to one another and to him—perhaps too polite. They smiled smiles that didn't seem to come from deep inside but were more for show and spoke in measured tones in a way that made him think they were treading on glass, afraid to rile the other one. But it was more of what they didn't say during those times that made him aware something was wrong. And try as he might to figure it out, he was unable to do so.

Richie leaned back in the window seat, propping his legs up in front of him. He could hear the sounds of the heavy machinery at work in the park, and it made him angry they were destroying what he'd always thought of as his special playground, a wonderland of fun and adventures. It was only a matter of time before they got to the grove of trees where he and Uncle Edmund built the treehouse two summers before. When it was gone, the memories would go with it—or so he thought. That made him even angrier.

He'd been forbidden to go to the treehouse, told to watch the renovations from across the new road, a road that just the summer before had been a brook which ran right through the center of the parkland! Now, the brook was gone, and houses and businesses were going up all around in areas that used to belong to nature. He wondered where the animals had gone. The rabbits and squirrels could always find homes, but what about the deer and raccoons? How would they feel having their homes bulldozed and civilization intruding on what really belonged to them?

"Just as rotten as I do." He grumbled as he put his head onto his knees.

Nothing was the same...

~

It was almost embarrassing to admit that a blow to my jaw landed me in the hospital. And I'm sure I would have protested the situation more had I been able to remain conscious for more than a few minutes at a time. Instead, I was incapacitated and completely at the mercy of the hospital staff. Fortunately, during one of my more lucid moments, I managed to give Joyce Noland's name and was subsequently assured she would be notified.

After what seemed an eternity of being stuck with needles, x-rays, and questions I didn't understand or was unable to answer, Joyce's familiar face loomed above me. Her expression was anxious, but warm, her voice an anchor in a sea of uncertainty.

"I wanted you in for tests, Richard, but I didn't expect you to go to such extremes to oblige me." She grinned at me over the chart she studied. "It's a good thing I decided to come back from vacation early or where would you be?" She signed and handed a piece of paper to a technician, then pulled up a stool and sat next to my gurney. "So, how are you feeling?"

"Like I've been hit by a Mack truck." I tried to return the grin but couldn't tell if the correct signals were sent.

She nodded gravely. "Never expected you to be in a fight," she said, gently moving my head to one side. "The guy wearing some kind of ring?"

I tried to nod but decided against it when a bolt of pain shot up my neck. I settled for a verbal response.

"Um, well it did a number along your cheekbone."

The technician returned to her side, spoke to her quietly, and Joyce nodded.

"I've set you up for an MRI. Hank here is going to take you in for the test. I want you to try to relax, and do what he says. When it's over, we'll see you settled down for the night." Dr. Joyce Noland squeezed my shoulder. "Looks like this time of year isn't lucky for you, kiddo. Hang in there, and I'll see you in the morning."

I closed my eyes as I was wheeled away.

This time of year... Was it July first? I'd been trying to remember since Hargrave insisted I tell him the day. But I was in too much pain to care. Still, there was something...

July first, twenty years—no, *twenty-one* years ago. The day of my accident in the park...

~

The place had always been like Grand Central Station, everyone moving in and out of both his aunt and uncle's home offices at all hours of the day and night. Today had been particularly busy, especially considering that Uncle Edmund had left for the university sometime after nine and hadn't been back home since. It was already past noon, the day half over, and it seemed as though a record number of people had passed through the house.

"Ought to install a revolving door." He'd said sheepishly to his aunt, a remark that earned him a huge grin and a good-natured pat on the back.

Even with whatever was bothering them, the Drakes continued to maintain a kind of open house. This was something he was used to, the excited voices echoing through the rooms, the benevolent smiles of Aunt Janet and Uncle Edmund as they gave freely of their private time. They didn't mind sharing, and neither did he.

There was something thrilling about watching all the people, their differences another dimension of the life he was anxious to participate in—that of a grown-up. It was never quiet like it was at home, and he liked the liveliness, meeting new people, and having them look at him as though he were something special because of his aunt and uncle.

Of course, some of the students and others that came by weren't so nice. They would talk down to him and treat him like a baby, and he really hated that. But most weren't so bad. Like that guy Charlie who'd come by earlier. Richie liked him from the moment he'd met him.

He'd quietly followed behind his aunt and her latest advisee, waiting at the end of the hallway while Janet Drake ushered the young woman out the door. When she'd turned around, Aunt Janet hadn't noticed Richie at first, and he'd gotten a close look at how tired she was. He started to step from the hall shadows when the weary sigh stopped him.

"Now who's around to solve my problems?"

The whispered question startled Richie as much in its fervency as the sudden admission to what he'd been feeling since his arrival over a month before. He burst out from the hallway shadows and grabbing his aunt's hand, held it tightly. She smiled down at him, her strange eyebrows taking away some of the sincerity and warmth he knew she felt.

"Not much time for recreation today is there, my boy?" She gave

him a quick hug then started down the hallway. "I promise to make it up to you, Richie. Just be patient."

Just then the doorbell sounded, and Aunt Janet asked him to show whoever it was into the den—Uncle Edmund's office—and entertain them until she had the chance to make an important phone call. Still concerned about his aunt, Richie was happy to do anything that might help her and determined to be as charming as possible. Charlie made that vow easy to fulfill with his bright smile and light-hearted attitude. They'd begun talking right away, and pretty soon, Charlie was offering some sage advice.

"Wonderful people, girls, but difficult as heck." Charlie grinned, winking over at Richie. "Can't live with them, can't live without them. Not that I'd ever want to be without one, mind you. No, I can't picture myself without a lovely lady hanging on my arm."

"You got one in mind?" Richie asked politely, realizing immediately that this must be the trouble he needed to speak with his aunt about. Maybe he could help the guy out, he thought. After all, he'd watched his aunt and uncle plenty of times, and it didn't look like such a hard thing to do.

"Have I ever!" Charlie whistled. "Prettiest little thing you ever saw, Richie, old man. The problem is, I am, or was supposed to be, engaged."

Even Richie knew you couldn't get married to one girl and go out with another one. This was definitely a problem. What could the guy be thinking?!

"So why don't you just tell the one you don't want that you have someone new?" The solution seemed simple enough, even to a ten-year-old.

Charlie laughed long and hard. Wiping tears from his eyes, he smiled over at Richie companionably. "You make it sound so easy, my friend. Now why didn't I think of that?"

For a moment, Richie thought Charlie was laughing at him, that he'd said something foolish, but the guy reassured him. They continued to talk for awhile until his aunt came in, and when she started to send Richie away, Charlie objected.

"Nah, go ahead and let him stay. Rich and I are old buddies now, and I think he has a stake in what's going on."

Richie knew all about sarcasm, he'd heard his mother refer to it often enough, and he knew Charlie was putting him on. Still, it made him feel good to sit and listen.

After a gentle warning to remain quiet, Aunt Janet encouraged Charlie to describe his problem. She listened patiently, her face gradually settling into a frown that made her oddly cocked eyebrows *give her a fierce look. Richie knew from the expression that she was deep in thought, pondering the situation to come up with the best solution to Charlie's dilemma.*

Charlie told his story with quips and laughs thrown in to make it sound far less serious than even Richie knew it to be. He could tell from the way the words were used just how worried his new friend was, and it kicked in a kind of protective instinct in Richie. He leaned forward on the window seat, concentrating and watching, wishing he had the experience and years necessary to help.

"I'm sorry, Charlie. As I've told you before, it would be inappropriate for me to interfere, especially with an individual who isn't even attending the university." Aunt Janet said finally. "As it is, if you weren't a friend, and I didn't know your fiancé—"

"Former fiancé." Charlie quickly interjected.

Janet Drake gave him a tolerant smile. "Former fiancé, then. Knowing Lillian makes the difference. I simply can't approach a young woman I don't know. We've discussed this before."

Charlie got up and paced the room. The impatient gestures of his hands as he spoke emphasized his concern. "I never meant for anything to happen, you know. It was entirely coincidental—fate, kismet. The moment I met her, I knew what I had to do, and I did it. I broke it to Lily as easily as I could."

Aunt Janet's weary expression deepened, and she'd rubbed her face briskly before responding.

"I know you did. But you can't blame the girl, Charlie. She's still very much in love with you. So much so, she's desperate."

*"So desperate she's claiming she'll do anything, **anything** to get me back!" Charlie raised his hands in a helpless gesture. "She's wild. I've never seen her like this." He shook his head. "I can't handle this and graduate school as well. Something's gotta give."*

Richie watched as his aunt went over to his new friend and placed a comforting arm about the young man's shoulders. She gently turned him toward the doorway, flashed a look at Richie that told him to stay put, then led Charlie out of the den.

"If only she wasn't interested in someone else." Charlie's pitiful voice gradually diminished as he was led down the hallway to Aunt Janet's office and privacy.

Richie scooted back against the window, his imagination working overtime.

Problems and solutions. It was almost like the games Uncle Edmund designed, adventures in the disguise of a form of a scavenger hunt, surrounded by fascinating story lines that always captured Richie's attention.

Puzzles to solve, dragons to slay, damsels in distress to save.

Only this summer, the damsel seemed to have developed a dislike for boys, his dragon or partner, whichever the scenario called for, had developed chicken pox, and Uncle Edmund, the Master of the Game, had been far too busy to devise any new adventures. It was no wonder Richie found the students' problems a welcome diversion!

"I wish," he crossed his fingers and closed his eyes. "I wish for the biggest, best game Uncle Edmund has ever come up with." He said fervently into the empty room.

Real dragons were what he needed. A lady, or even a man in danger, and a monster that only he could destroy...

~

Most of the poking, prodding, and tests I'd wanted to avoid in the past were conducted while in my semi-conscious state. I recalled Joyce's voice and reassurances, the tunnel-like MRI procedure, and wondering which was louder: the pounding in my head or that of the machine. Throughout, I maintained that odd sensation of my brain tissue shrinking and then growing so large that it seemed to push against my skull, the cavity inside my head too small to contain its mass. There was confusion, frustration, fear, and the welcome and comforting words of a nurse as I was finally tucked in for the night.

A return to consciousness brought with it a bone-wearying exhaustion. Sleep was a refuge, a temporary escape from the pain and worry. But who's allowed to actually sleep in a hospital? Being a pin cushion seemed more important than rest. Having a blood pressure cuff Velcroed on and off, a penlight shined in my eyes, and expectant faces waiting for me to answer their questions, disrupted my sleep every few hours.

My head hurt like hell, and my pride was running a close second. When I was awakened for the morning blood draw and pressure check before breakfast, I snapped viciously at the aide before submitting to yet another invasion of my body. After the promised meal was set in front of me, I waited until the departure of the cafeteria staff member before I pushed back the bed tray and closed my eyes against the too bright overhead light. Sometime later I awoke to the sun filtering in through the partially opened blind in a nearby window. My eyes did not remain open for long; even the blind couldn't block enough of the sun to keep it from piercing my brain.

"You really should try to eat something, you know."

The voice seemed disembodied, pleasant in tone and consideration but completely without the substance necessary to form a human being. I had no desire to open my eyes again and be forced to explain myself to another nurse or aide. But there was something familiar about the voice that urged me to respond.

I opened my eyes slowly, bit by bit, allowing them to gradually get used to the brightness of the room. It was still painful, but tolerably so, and detecting a slight movement from one corner, carefully turned my head until the owner of the voice was within view. She smiled widely, her deep, sapphire eyes crinkling slightly at the sides.

"I hope you don't mind my watching you sleep. They told me you were all right, but I needed to see for myself." She glanced quickly toward the half-opened door, then returned her gaze to me. "How do you feel?"

"I've been better." I croaked as I regarded the young woman before me. Her eyes looked a little sunken as though she hadn't slept, her demeanor anxious. "I'm not entirely certain what happened last night, but I do seem to remember your intervention and assistance."

She laughed slightly. "Considering everything, that's some speech." She tossed her golden brown hair back over her shoulders. "And before you say it, don't bother to thank me. If it wasn't for me, it never would have happened in the first place."

"I hardly see how you could be responsible for your companion's actions." I told her, my voice a bit harsher than I'd meant it to be. I attempted to lighten the tone, softening my next words with an answering smile. "Perhaps you should see about getting the gentleman some psychiatric help, though."

This time when she laughed it was full-bellied.

"That's rich." She said as she wiped some tears from her eyes. "Robert Grant asking for help in any matter would be something to see." She sobered up and shook her head. "A nice thought, Mr. Tanner, but it would never happen. And," she swallowed audibly as she leaned toward my bed. "He isn't just a companion. Robert Grant's my grandfather. Nicole Grant, at your service," she said, holding out her hand.

I took the small, proffered hand, studying her intently.

"Your grandfather?" Releasing her hand, I leaned back upon my pillows and closed my eyes against the glare of the sun. While I was busy searching my memory for any resemblance between the Grants, I could hear Nicole get up from the chair and move about the room. A few seconds later came the distinct sound of the blinds being closed.

"Thanks." I told her as she returned to the bedside chair.

No, looking at her, I didn't see any similarities. Her open, honest face was a study of innocence, far different from the lined and craggy hauteur of her grandfather's. Still, the revelation surprised me. Perhaps it was the idea of someone's grandfather behaving as abhorrently as Grant had done last night. He'd been aggressive and ruthless, over the edge in a matter of minutes—and something about the story of his daughter hadn't rung quite true.

Studying Nicole Grant, an awkward silence ensued. While I was reevaluating my former assessment of her angel status and wondering if she was here to run interference for the old man, she shifted uncomfortably in her chair. She drew her jean clad legs up beneath her as a sudden understanding entered those beautiful sapphire eyes.

"No, I won't ask you not to charge my grandfather. If anything, I'd encourage you to do so. Don't get me wrong," she added quickly, a deep crimson rising up from her neck into her cheeks. "I love him very much but have never been overly thrilled with his high-handed tactics."

"High-handed? I'm not sure that quite covers it. The guy went off the deep end."

"I know." She grimaced. "I should never have told him about the painting, let alone taken him to see it."

Robert Grant's reaction to Jenny's portrait had been totally irrational, his claims that she was his daughter who'd been missing for twenty-one years, outrageous. I told this to his granddaughter as she sat humbly before me, shaking her head and apologizing again for her part in the incident.

"As I said before, the man needs help." I concluded as I carefully rearranged my position in the bed.

Nicole's rich blue eyes gazed deeply into mine. "He's never accepted her disappearance." She said quietly. "That doesn't excuse what he did. Nothing could. But I should have guessed, *known* what his reaction would be when he saw the resemblance. I suppose I believed he accepted my explanation, thought he'd be pleased by my discovery." She sighed deeply. "It was too much for him. I think it took him back, made all these intervening years dissolve."

"You're not," I started, narrowing my eyes on the young woman before me, trying to gauge what she might be thinking. "You don't believe as he does, that the portrait is his—your aunt?"

"Mother." She corrected soberly, shaking her head and sending a cascade of golden brown curls over her narrow shoulders. "No, I don't. But—"

"Good morning." Dr. Joyce Noland pushed the door to my room fully open, her commanding presence calling a halt to our conversation. She acknowledged my visitor with a nod of the head, cocked a questioning eyebrow at me, then included us both in a smile.

"I thought you'd gone home." She said, addressing Nicole Grant.

"I had. But I came back about an hour ago." Nicole grinned. "I've been watching your patient sleep."

"Oh?" Joyce picked up my wrist, checked her watch, then returned her attention to Nicole, peering out at her over the top of her thick-lensed glasses. "And what about your grandfather?"

"Big Jim's got orders to keep him under wraps for the day. I'm not sure how he liked receiving directions from me, but when I reminded him of the trouble they were both in, he agreed readily enough." She grinned, extending the warmth to me. "If there's one thing the galoot is afraid of, it's the police. And the way that detective was throwing his weight around last night, I think Jim will try to melt into the background for the next several days."

Joyce nodded, set my arm gently on the bed, then began to carefully examine my face and head.

"Speaking of Detective Hargrave, he's already called four times this morning." Joyce said as her fingers checked out my bruised cheekbone. "I told him he'd have to wait his turn to see you. I didn't figure you'd be up for visitors for a while." She looked from me to Nicole, then back again. "Guess I was wrong."

"I really didn't give him a choice, I'm afraid." Nicole responded, the hint of a blush entering her cheeks. "I was here when he awoke, and he was too kind to send me away."

"Really?" Joyce raised her expressive eyebrows, continuing to probe my skull as she directed her conversation to my visitor. "Did Robert take the sedative I sent?"

"I take it you two know one another." I said, more than a little annoyed with the discussion going on around me.

"Mr. Grant was a patient of mine a little over a year ago." Joyce said, tilting my head back and shining a light in my eyes.

"A stroke." Nicole offered in explanation.

"With his tendency to go off like that, it doesn't surprise me." I muttered so low that I could tell his granddaughter hadn't heard me. But my doctor had.

She poked me lightly in the shoulder and whispered, "Be nice."

"So, how are you feeling?" Joyce Noland finally stood back from the bed, pursed her thin lips, folded her arms in front of her, and regarded me intently.

With an attempt at bravado, I smiled. "Aren't you supposed to tell me?"

Her mouth twitched at the corner in a hesitant smile, but she didn't say a word.

"After all the tests last night, I'd say you're in a better position to tell me what's going on inside my head and body than I am." I continued in the same vein, hoping to evoke a true smile from the woman.

Joyce Noland patted me on the back, her face remaining noncommittal.

"Dr. Astin will be done with rounds in fifteen to twenty minutes. When he's finished, we'll be in to talk with you."

I didn't like the sound of this. No smile, completely sober expression, and a tone that sent a shiver of apprehension down my spine.

"Joyce—"

She shook her head. "Soon, Richard. In the meantime, do yourself a favor and rest easy." With an "I'll see you later" to Nicole, my doctor and trusted friend headed for the door, leaving me feeling far less confident than when she'd arrived.

She was at the doorway when I spoke.

"Tell me something. Could what happened to me last night break free hidden memories?"

Joyce regarded me thoughtfully. "You mean, could what you lost by one knock on the head be returned by another one?"

"In essence."

"There have been those who believe so. Why?" Again her eyes narrowed, lips pursed. "Have you remembered something?"

A quick glance at Nicole and back to Joyce told her this was a subject I'd rather not discuss at the moment.

"Fifteen minutes." She said firmly, then breezed out the door.

I turned to find Nicole studying me, her fair eyebrows arched over intense blue eyes.

I'll give her credit for not questioning me about what that last bit of conversation regarded, but the longer she sat there, and silence ensued, her consideration for my privacy failed to earn her any favorable points. I felt anxious, the rather ominous tone of Joyce's visit once again setting in motion the fears I'd felt so strongly the night before.

Last evening I'd seen this lovely young woman in the role of a guardian angel. Today, with the knowledge that she was Robert Grant's granddaughter, I began to look for an underlying reason for her being here.

As she began talking about the Arts Festival and all the works on display in the gallery, I was fighting two parts of myself: one who still wanted to get to know this girl who'd fascinated me in the gallery, and the other who was furious with her part in what inevitably landed me in the hospital. Despite her obvious charm and sincerity, anger built on fear and frustration won out.

I held up a hand to stop her in mid-sentence.

"I don't want to be rude, but you heard what my doctor said about me getting some rest." As hard as I'd tried, I hadn't been able to keep the edge from my voice.

Nicole's face fell, the blush that seemed to come so readily into her already rosy complexion stained her cheeks.

"I'm—I'm sorry. I didn't think, I mean—" She unfolded her legs from the chair, stretched, then stood up. "I guess I should leave."

She lowered her eyes to the floor, grabbed up the bag propped against the bedside chair, and tucked it under her arm.

"I didn't mean to intrude. It's just—" She gave me a wan smile when she saw I wasn't relenting. "Maybe when you're feeling better we can talk."

Heaven help me, I almost retorted a nasty "Fat chance," refraining from doing so just as it was about to issue from my lips.

She left without another word, a simple turn of the head and wave of her hand before she disappeared through the still open doorway. The moment I was alone, I regretted my behavior, damning myself for my irritability and wishing for some way to call her back.

Still, there was that other side of me, that newly discovered dark half that didn't see my actions as unreasonable, and in the end, it was this part that won out. As I sat there and stewed about the interview yet to come with doctors Noland and Astin, I fumed, unable to feel anything other than resentful and used.

My interest in Nicole Grant had been obvious the day before. She'd seen it, and after her grandfather's irrational behavior, sought to use it to save his worthless hide. She'd tried to impress me by urging me to pursue charges against the old man, and, for awhile, succeeded in making me believe in her sincerity.

A trick, pure and simple, not so unlike one Tara might have instigated. But I was older, and hopefully wiser, and not about to fall into such a trap. She could use her feminine wiles to her heart's content and still would get nowhere with me. I was stronger, more resolute.

And my damned head hurt like hell.

I'd no sooner closed my eyes and laid back against my pillows when I heard the sound of scuffling feet and the rustle of papers nearing my door. I looked up anxiously as the two doctors entered the room, Joyce Noland hanging back a step to pull the door nearly closed after they were both inside. With a smile that did not erase the concern from her eyes, she introduced Dr. Jerome Astin.

When Astin enclosed my hand in a firm grip, I had the impression I was seeing a near double to the actor Raymond Burr. Tall and robust, though perhaps not as heavy as the actor, he had the full round face, beard and moustache—a black tinged with grey—that I recalled from the later *Perry Mason* movies. I'd always liked and enjoyed Burr's work, and there was something comforting about Astin's looking so much like the amiable and ever ingenious television lawyer.

"Richard," Joyce began, Astin deferring to her as my physician. "I've called in Dr. Astin for a second opinion. He's taken a look at the MRI and the results of the other tests we've gotten back and has offered his services."

I didn't like the sound of this or the way Joyce refused to meet my gaze straight on. She nodded at her colleague, and with this sign of concession, turned the ball over to him.

"The MRI shows a growth—"

"Growth?" My stomach sank clear to my feet.

"A tumor," he continued. "We have no evidence of it being cancerous, of course, but you must understand that all brain tumors are serious because of the buildup of pressure and compression in the surrounding areas as the tumor expands."

"Those headaches of yours have been the warning sign." Joyce interjected. "And last night you spoke of an episode of numbness that you couldn't explain."

"The lesion may be nothing more than a meningioma, a benign tumor, or an aneurysm—" his voice droned on and on until he finally hit on the worst case scenario: cancer.

I was fortunate to be a candidate for surgery; I was told so seriously that I nearly began to laugh, the fear and hysteria having built up inside me so strongly it was eager to burst forth.

"Because of the potential danger, I'm sure you would like the opportunity to—"

"To get my life in order?" That was a joke, surely.

"I know your mother is in Europe with Janet Drake," Joyce broke in, the discomfort she felt at having to deliver such news evident on her face. "I thought you might like to call her."

And give her the chance to watch another member of her family die? I thought. Not hardly.

"Professor Drake is in the outer waiting room, has been most of the night," Joyce continued calmly. "Perhaps it would be a good idea for him to come back—"

"No." I answered firmly.

But Astin was nodding his approval, their act seeming so precise it might have been rehearsed.

"His support would be invaluable. And it wouldn't be out of line to contact your lawyer, get things squared away—"

My God! First they tell me it might not be that serious yet were now behaving as though I had just been handed my death sentence.

"We know this is a lot to take in," Joyce apologized for something she could not help. "But we feel that to delay would be a major mistake. It would be best to schedule the surgery within the next couple of days. I wouldn't recommend waiting any longer—"

Screaming, if I were a person prone to that, would be what I would recommend, I thought. As I listened, their words washed over me, drowning me. Don't delay. Allow us to saw through your skull, cut into your brain, and extract—extract what? A disease? A piece of me? Would I come out of it whole or minus some very important part of who I was? Perhaps even minus a few more memories.

"That's it." I said evenly, surprised to find my voice held so much control when I felt so completely out of it. "You've told me all I want to know, enough to make a decision."

"Richard—"

"No, Joyce." I looked directly into her pleading eyes and recognized what it had cost her to have to tell me about the tumor. "I appreciate both of you, but right now I have to be alone."

"Of course." Astin nodded in understanding. "You must have time to digest what we've told you."

"Would you like me to send in the professor?" Joyce asked.

I shook my head, closed my eyes and leaned heavily against my pillows.

"Please feel free to contact either of us at any time." Astin spoke quietly, the confidence in his voice meant to convey the same to me.

"Thank you." I spoke without opening my eyes.

"Richard?" A hand on my shoulder urged me to respond to her voice, but I couldn't force my eyes open even for Joyce at that moment.

"We'll take good care of you. I promise."

I listened to their footsteps recede, to the sound of the door swinging closed behind them. When I was certain I was alone, I swung into action. Fear and frustration propelled me out of the bed, kept me from giving in to the nausea, and helped me into my clothing.

I had to get out of the hospital, needed the fresh air and freedom of a wide open space and the communion with nature. Even before I made my way stealthily down the hospital corridor, I knew my destination.

One of Linden's three cabs was just dropping off a fare, the driver assisting an elderly woman from the rear seat. I asked if he was free, received a nod of affirmation, and climbed into his vehicle to await his return.

As we finally drove away from the curb, the driver asked for an address.

"University Park." I told him firmly, then settled back against the seat for the ride.

Chapter 17

It was difficult not to be contemplative under the circumstances. With all I'd been forced to deal with in the recent past, why should a life-threatening diagnosis surprise me at this point? From coping with the death of my father, I'd rushed headlong into the excitement of my first big showing while struggling with the rapid downhill progression of my relationship with Tara. When she'd been assaulted and Hargrave began his none too subtle investigation of me, nightmares started haunting my sleep, leaving behind their residual effects: altered sketches, the eerie charcoal piece that received rave reviews at the Festival, and a mind frequently muddled from a lack of rest. The discovery that my "accident" twenty-one years earlier had been the result of some madman terrorizing the area had been revealing, yet strangely not as troubling as the relationship I'd developed with one mysterious girl who'd come in and out of my life like water dripping through one's open fingers. The analogy was not lost on me, but in my present mood, I was not amused.

I'd been so caught up in my thoughts during the doctors' visit, that after their initial words of doom, I'd failed to listen to their full diagnosis. What I heard, however, was enough to set my mind spinning as those words were repeated over and over again within my brain:

tumor, cancer, surgery—death.

Aneurysm, meningioma, what did they really mean? Then again, what difference did it make in the long run?

The difference between life and death.

Don't think! I told myself harshly, attempting to divert my attention from within by observing the passing scenery. It was only a momentary diversion, however, and soon my mind was quickly trying to process the little information I had.

A tumor. Perhaps that was the answer I'd been seeking, the explanation to the changes in the original sketches where Jenny had been added, to the charcoal that I'd awakened to find after my disturbing visit to the morgue—even to the subtle changes in my own personality. I'd never been easily angered yet, during the past several weeks, there'd been an almost constant irritation gnawing just below the surface. I'd been aware of it, tried to sluff it off or explain it away with the added stress of the Arts Festival being imminent, but it continued to grow within me like some separate being.

I shook myself mentally, the shock of the news feeding my rage. This was a normal reaction, the fury I felt, the frustration and helplessness. Explanations were unnecessary. And besides, after everything I'd been through, it seemed a rather appropriate epilogue.

The driver stopped at the north side of the park, and after paying him, I made my way over to the gazebo, slinking past the few people populating the area. It had become a dark, gloomy day for July, the lowering clouds blotting out the sun and earlier promise of a bright summer's day. I couldn't help but be thankful for the turnaround, knowing it meant most people would avoid the park, decreasing the possibility of my being bothered.

As I neared the gazebo, I noticed sawhorses bordering the outer perimeter. Several of the rose bushes had been removed, and fresh mortar covered some of the worst cracks within the base. It was obvious more work was planned; the small trench dug close to the foundation contained forms ready to receive additional cement required for reinforcement. While caution signs warned of staying away from the work area, they offered assurance that there was no danger in the use of the structure.

I saw everything with eyes borne of familiarity, taking in all that was new or different then tucking away the information with little interest. Climbing the steps, I looked out across the expanse, seeking something I could neither identify nor explain yet knowing it was here somewhere. With a heavy sigh, I slunk over to my usual bench, sat, and leaned my head gratefully back against the support post. I breathed in deeply, closed my eyes, and concentrated on my heartbeat while wishing away the memory of the doctors' words. But the tranquility I'd hoped to find was refused me. The crunch of gravel on the diagonal walk had my eyes flying open in time to see Nicole Grant's golden brown head coming around the side of the building in the direction of the steps.

"Damn it all to hell!" I stood facing her, a frown punctuating my greeting.

She raised her eyes to mine, a hesitant smile on her lips, her head thrown confidently back, her steps resolute.

"You followed me!" I glared at her. "Like your grandfather, you'll stoop to anything."

The lift of a pale, expressive eyebrow, and the smile was more firmly affixed to her face.

"I felt someone should keep an eye on you. After all you stole out of the hos—"

"As if it's any of your business what I do!"

"You left the hospital without bothering to tell anyone." She continued, her voice soft, controlled.

"So you took it upon yourself to become my keeper—out of concern for me. No ulterior motive?"

She came forward to take a seat just a few steps away from me, her gaze unwavering.

"Perhaps my reasons aren't so pure, but then, these are special circumstances."

Special circumstances. I would have laughed if I hadn't been so utterly exhausted. Instead, I sank back onto my bench and stared wearily at her.

"I don't suppose I could convince you to leave me the hell alone. That out of consideration for what your grandfather did to me, you'd just go."

I saw her take a deep breath as she folded her hands in her lap.

"What Grandfather did was outrageous, but surely you can't blame him—"

"Can't blame him? Why the hell not? If it wasn't for him—"

"If it wasn't for him you may not have found out about the tumor until it was too late." She answered reasonably.

"Really? So now I'm supposed to thank the old coot, huh?" I seethed. "I guess I can add eavesdropping to your other, er, attributes. I was right; you *are* as bad as the old man." I turned my back on her, determinedly looking out across the park.

"You're upset; that's only natural. If it was me, I'd be frightened beyond reason." She paused as though waiting for a response. When it didn't come, she continued.

"You're right." She spoke to my stiffened back. "I don't know how you feel. How could I? But, I do know what I sensed from your paintings. Anyone who could produce such wonderful works of art has to possess a sensitivity not only to his own emotions but to others' as well. Someone like that doesn't rely or exist on being cold and unreasonable but looks beyond the facade into the very heart of things."

"A pretty speech, but what's it supposed to mean?" I said, still refusing to turn around.

"That you know my grandfather's not the cause. That it was only as a result of what happened that the discovery was made. Look," her voice pleaded with me. "I know you're hurting, that's understandable. You've a right to lay the blame wherever you want, just please don't push me away?"

"Why? Because you want something from me?" I turned then, meeting her face to face, eye to eye.

"There's that, yes. But—" She sighed heavily as she shrugged her shoulders. "I've no right to ask you any favors, I know, and I can't blame you for not wanting my company."

"But?"

A grim smile touched her incredibly beautiful lips and I found myself relaxing as I focused on them.

"If you promise to give me a chance, hear me out, I promise to leave you alone if that's your ultimate decision. At least I'll try, anyway."

I raised my eyebrows in question.

"That's complete honesty. I admit to having an almost irrational tenacity to hold on to anything or anyone I become involved with. I got the impression you were very similar."

"Oh? My paintings again?"

She nodded. "When someone is able to build their dreams on canvas for the world to see—well, I'm not so imaginative, but I am determined." She leaned forward, gazing at me thoughtfully. "My art, my magic, is teaching young children, those wonderfully wise individuals whose souls are so pure, imaginations so fully developed that often it seems they are doing the teaching, not the other way around. It's from them I've learned my patience and diligence, the tenacity and fortitude to hang on despite all odds." Nicole Grant sighed deeply as she propped her elbows on her knees, her chin resting between the knuckles of her joined hands. "You want to find your Jenny and so do I. Why not join forces, hear me out?"

As badly as I wanted to surrender the anger I still felt, it wasn't so easily accomplished.

"Because she's your mother?" I sneered.

"No." She said evenly, without a hint of temper in her voice. "Because it's highly possible she's my sister."

It was easy to see this young woman before me as a teacher of children, her calm, considerate attitude, the open, honest face, and tone of reason and sanity that did not rebuke or speak down to one but remained level and flexible to the moment. She was special, this girl with the golden brown hair, perhaps even unique. A wonderful and rational voice in the world of unreality I'd been thrust into. I sensed all these things with one part of my soul while the other half, that crazy, unforgiving, angry-with-the-world part of my being, wanted to retain the unreasonable fury that had built to a feverish pitch. That part wanted to lash out at the girl, misuse and abuse her until she cried out in pain and in as much distress and frustration as I myself felt.

Where had my true personality gone? Had it been blighted by those years with Tara, the accusations from Hargrave, Jenny's defection, my father's death? Or was this the personality defect my parents and the Drakes always looked for and feared, the result of that night in the park twenty-one years ago when I might have been raped and beaten by a madman and then left for dead? Was this my legacy of that childhood trauma finally come to haunt me? Or could it be the result of the growth in my brain?

Tears filled the corners of my eyes, angry tears that I refused to shed for emotions so raw and exposed that anyone passing by could see. I felt sorry for myself and disgusted at the same moment for giving in to such weakness. This wasn't me. It was the fear that caused these reactions—a fear of the unknown.

Fear of the worst case scenario: cancer and death.

Nicole shook her head, freeing her beautiful hair from her face. A light breeze played with the tendrils, lifting them gently and rearranging the strands into a becoming disarray. I couldn't help being moved by her allure, those deep sapphire eyes peering at me in earnest. It seemed useless to fight her; indeed, I was so lacking in strength at the moment that I would have been unable to do so had I tried, all the fight seeming to have suddenly abandoned me.

"What do you want from me?" I asked wearily.

Her expression lightened, a slight smile flitting across her lips. She recognized her victory in this round, but was insightful enough to realize there could be greater conflicts ahead.

"It's a small thing, really," she told me in a steady voice. "And something I'm sure you'll be interested in."

My expression must have revealed my uncertainty, but she strove on, determined not to lose what little ground she'd gained.

"If you'd come to my house—"

Alarm bells sounded. "I don't see what that can accomplish."

"Please," she rushed on. "You act as though I'm trying to kidnap you or something equally as underhanded. I'm really not that deceitful or cunning. Look," her voice softened, the melodic tenor that I'd found so entrancing before attempted to lull me. "I'm not trying to pull anything, Mr. Tanner. It's very simply a case where "a picture is worth a thousand words." Literally."

I raised a quizzical brow, my curiosity piqued, but still wary.

"I'd rather not say anything else for fear of giving you any preconceived notions. You just have to trust me, take my word this is all above board." She leaned forward again, her manner conspiratorial, her engaging eyes holding a silent plea.

Lately, it seemed every time I was engaged in conversation with someone it was interrupted by an unwelcome intrusion. So it happened while I considered what I might have to lose in going along with Nicole's invitation, I heard my name being called from the sidewalk behind me. I recognized the voice instantly, just as I perceived the anxious tone.

Realizing the import of the intruder's arrival, and having no desire to be forced into explanations, I jumped up from the bench, practically dragged Nicole off her perch, and steered her toward the steps.

"Are you all right?" Nicole's voice trembled slightly, her alarm apparent.

"You wanted me, you got me. Now let's get the hell out of here."

Still curious, but unsure of questioning me, Nicole Grant managed to disengage my groping hands from her shoulders, captured one within her own hand, and led me thankfully in the opposite direction from Chuck Stinnet. I calculated that we were in her car before he even realized we'd left the park, and most likely driving off by the time he started searching the walkways for me. Perhaps I should have felt some guilt for my actions, but I felt nothing. Why should I? With a virtual death sentence hanging over me, I'd become a hospital runaway with no real place to go. And having been issued a curious invitation by yet another enigmatic young woman, why should I feel any remorse for accepting it?

"There's no need to worry about encountering my grandfather," she assured me with a sidelong glance as we headed to the north edge of town. "Last night's, uh, excitement has left him rather subdued. Not to mention the fact that Big Jim has orders to see that he remains confined to his rooms." She grinned, and I recalled her conversation with Joyce. It was obvious Nicole Grant was pleased with herself on this point.

Not having to deal with more of Grant's irrational outbursts was definitely a plus, but the idea of being in the same house as the man and his beefy bodyguard was a little disconcerting. I tried to analyze these feelings as well as my reactions to everything that happened since I'd awakened that morning but found the effort too exhausting. That was one of my flaws, long ago pointed out by my darling Tara, the over-analyzation of things. Perhaps she was right.

I continued my silent vigil of the passing scenery, noticed the wind had picked up velocity since we'd left the park, and watched as the clouds grew increasingly darker as they scudded across the sky.

Storm clouds, high winds, sultry weather. The Midwest in early July, weather that could turn on a dime from hot and sunny to cool and threatening with high, damaging winds and possible tornados. It seemed all too fitting to my present mood, and as I had welcomed the disappearance of the sun earlier, I urged the worsening weather to strike out with a vengeance.

Nicole didn't press for conversation, just drove on, her hands lightly encircling the steering wheel, her eyes remaining on the road ahead. There were several times that I thought she would speak, her small mouth would open slightly as she'd take in a deep breath, but she continued to honor the silence between us.

Surprisingly, the drive helped release some of my pent-up emotions, and a good deal of the pain in my neck receded, leaving behind a kind of comfortable lethargy. I soaked up the scenery that flashed by, noted the turn onto Elmwood Drive, the prestigious neighborhood where the moneyed of Linden lived, and gloried in the first drops of rain that eventually led to a downpour.

Nicole pulled into a long driveway that led to a fairly large sandstone house with a pillared front porch. The drive circled completely around with a garage bigger than most houses, situated to the far left. I was too weary to take in many of the details, and by this time, the rain was coming down in sheets, battering the windows of the car and blocking out the view.

She parked directly before the main entrance, grinned at me sheepishly, and said, "Ready to make a run for it?"

She jumped out of the car and was under the protective cover of the porch roof in no time. I followed a bit more slowly and succeeded in soaking myself to the skin. Pushing back my lank hair, I drew it to the side to squeeze out any excess water before we continued on into the house. Nicole waited patiently, excused herself just inside the doorway, and returned moments later with a couple of towels. She flashed me a brilliant smile as she handed them to me, those lovely eyes of hers completely guileless. For the first time that day, I actually felt like smiling back, and did so.

"Good." Was all she said as I took the towels from her outstretched hand.

"Nice place." It was a stupid comment, but under the circumstances, the best I could manage. She accepted the small olive branch, her smile widening.

"I can't take any credit. All of this," she waved a hand toward the rest of the house, "is a result of my grandfather's wheeling and dealing in real estate over the years. He and my grandmother bought the land more than forty years ago. He had the house built for her. Unfortunately, she didn't live long enough to enjoy it."

"And your mother?"

Nicole Grant shrugged. "That's another story altogether."

The touch of sadness in her voice confirmed my thought that tragedy seemed to run in the family; one young woman had died before she'd had the chance to enjoy a home built especially for her, another disappeared several years later never to return.

I studied Nicole carefully as I handed her one of the wet towels. She didn't appear to have been too deeply affected by either woman's loss, however. At least not visually. Aside from the slight tone of sadness of a moment ago, this young woman's eyes were clear and direct without a hint of the tragedies clouding her vision. She regarded me with interest, some impatience, holding nothing back. Perhaps my original assessment in the gallery had been correct after all, and it was my own unhappiness and fear that caused me to suspect the worst of her.

"Done?"

I slung the remaining towel around my neck to catch the water that still dripped from my hair, nodded, then followed her across the entryway to a hall that ran the length of the house on the right side. We had no need to traverse its distance; what she'd brought me here to see lay behind the first door we came to.

"My grandfather's office. He usually keeps it locked, but—" She took a deep breath as her hand went to the doorknob.

"There's nothing I can say to preface this—not if I want your honest reaction." For the first time, her smile wavered. "I know how mysterious this must sound," she said, laughing nervously. "But you'll understand in a moment." She turned the knob, looked back at me, and paused. "Ready?"

The question seemed more than a little rhetorical, but the look on her face told me she needed a verbal response before we could continue with this unusual game of show and tell.

"Go ahead. I figure that at this point, I'm ready for anything."

The fleeting shadow that passed over her features revealed her uncertainty, and I felt her hesitation as her hand lingered on the knob. But I refused to be deterred. My curiosity had definitely been aroused, though it was strongly underlined by irritation from her cryptic remarks and secretive attitude. Still, that glimpse of lightheartedness she'd given me had seeped into my soul, and I grasped onto it, refusing to allow myself to sink back down into despair. Despite the fact that I was growing steadily wearier and tired of what was beginning to seem a cruel game, I was determined to reach its conclusion.

I laid my hand gently on top of hers, and together we turned the knob and pushed open the door to Robert Grant's office.

There was no need for Nicole to point out the object she wished me to see; it was apparent the moment we entered the room. My breath caught in my throat as I stared up at Jenny's portrait, my painting, yet not mine, somehow.

Jenny smiled down from the wall above a beautiful red brick fireplace, her shining mane of chestnut hair flowing about her shoulders like a mantle. Those entrancing violet eyes drew me across the room as a thin, tapered hand beckoned to me, a hint of amusement behind the smile that slightly curved her full lips.

As I neared the fireplace, I was vaguely aware of Nicole's presence nearby, heard her comment about the similarities of the portraits, the words seeming to come to me over a vast distance. I could no more have carried on a conversation with her at that moment than I could have taken my eyes off the painting before me.

Similarities? That simple word could never begin to describe the unbelievable parallel between the two portraits. It was like the comparison of mirror images, so closely related that for one brief, idiotic moment, I wondered how these people had gotten my painting out of the Fine Arts gallery!

But as my heart gradually settled back into a more regular rhythm and my initial shock had passed, I began to see subtle differences between the portraits. Concentration took over as my trained eyes reexamined the evidence before me—evidence that led to an astounding, even outrageous conclusion. As my mind quickly assimilated the variations of form and technique, rejecting that which my eyes were trying hard to convince me of, Nicole's voice seemed suddenly in my ear.

"Meet Jennifer Diane Grant, my mother."

"This is your mother?" My eyes flew to hers, the impact of her affirmation resounding like a blow. "It's not possi-"

"That they're one and the same, no. This was painted shortly before my mother's twenty-first birthday—about a year before her disappearance. So, while it's not possible for the girl in your painting to be my mother, I feel it highly likely that your Jenny might be my sister."

The explanation was not only plausible, but as she'd said, quite possible.

I returned my attention to the portrait, a sense of awe and wonder enveloping me. Now I noticed the broad, bold brushstrokes that were so different from mine and spoke of an accomplished and confident artist. There was a slight turn of the model's head not depicted in my painting, and while the ankh pendant was present, it lacked the sparkle and life that my portrait of Jenny had given it.

There were other differences as well, now that I examined the work more closely. While the shade of the sweaters worn in each was the same, the texture depicted here spoke of something soft, fuzzy. Angora, I guessed from the wisps and softening technique. Where my painting had seemed to capture Jenny's sensuality in an ethereal sense, it was obvious from the expression in Jennifer Grant's magnificent violet eyes and delicate curve of her mouth that this portrait was of a woman in love—and loved in return by the artist. The exquisite depiction captured the very essence I had imagined and thought of while painting Jenny but had been unable to reproduce. The artist who had painted this portrait had no such trouble with her counterpart.

Satisfied that I'd not been presented with a hoax, my eyes sought the artist's signature, but my search was interrupted by yet another unwelcome intrusion.

"Nicky, is that you?" A weak masculine voice sounded from the hallway, followed quickly by the appearance of its owner at the door to the room.

Robert Grant, dressed in a long silk bathrobe loosely cinched around his waist, entered the room a little uncertainly. He didn't notice my presence, indeed, he seemed somewhat disoriented. Still, I backed away from the fireplace, watching him warily as I went to the far end of the room.

Gone was the man with the piercing eyes and cold, calculating gaze. In his place was a bent and wizened figure whose white hair floated in disarray about his head. The firm jaw line had slackened, the hands that dealt me some wicked blows appeared gnarled and completely unusable.

"Nicky? I've been calling for you, child. Jim said you'd run an errand and that I was to take a nap. The man is treating me as if I were some sort of child, or an idiot." There was more hurt than reproach in the revelation. "You know how I hate inactivity. I simply cannot lie in bed all day when there are so many things that need to be done."

As Grant spoke, he'd walked to where his granddaughter still stood before the fireplace. Nicole's back was to me so I couldn't see her expression, but from the tenseness in her shoulders, I was able to determine how anxious she was. I remained where I was, immobile, hoping she would find a way to divert his attention and draw him out of the room before he spotted me. But once again, Lady Luck refused to smile upon me.

Grant's eyes lit on me, and the sudden recognition in them drew us both into fighting positions.

"What's that whoreson doing here?" He demanded harshly, his features doing a quick transformation that oddly reminded me of a movie with computer enhanced special effects.

Nicole didn't wait for further reaction, and with an arm about his still stooped shoulders, attempted to turn him away and diffuse the situation.

"It's all right, Grandpa. Mr. Tanner's with me."

This hardly seemed to reassure him and offered little comfort to me.

"You won't let him take the portrait!" He said, horrified. "Not my Jennifer, please not my Jennifer." His eyes bore into me, then moved to the painting. "She belongs to me." He intoned stonily. "No one ever understood that. Not even Jennifer herself."

There was a kind of amazement in this last statement, as though such a doubt should never have entered his daughter's mind. But even while the words were spoken harshly, the rapturous look on his face softened his features into one of glowing and undeniable love for the child who had chosen to leave him so many years ago.

"It's all right. Really, Grandpa. Mr. Tanner's going to try to help us find mother through the portrait he painted of—"

"Jenny?" Grant said the name doubtfully, shaking his shaggy head. "Poor, sweet Nicky." His large hand reached out to gently cover her free one. "Looking at life through rose colored glasses. Even I know that's not possible."

There was a strange finality to the statement, especially after the incident of the night before. I found it difficult to believe that after what transpired, I'd finally managed to convince the man I knew nothing about the mysterious girl I'd painted. This made his pronouncement even harder to accept at face value.

I had no idea what was going on here but was thankful when Nicole used this sudden gentleness to turn her grandfather and lead him out of the room. Once they were in the hallway, I heard her call out for the burly bodyguard, and after several moments passed, there was the sound of heavy feet running down the hall. Voices echoed back to me, their tones of anger the only thing recognizable at that distance.

Though I could not bring myself to forgive Grant for what happened, I found myself sympathetic to his loss. In those few moments when he'd gazed longingly at the portrait of his daughter, I'd seen the love he'd had for her and what her loss meant to him.

Feeling relatively safe from further interruptions, I moved back into position to study the portrait of Jennifer Diane Grant. I tried to block out the sounds of arguing in the hallway, my eyes fixed once again on those of the entrancing model. I needed to find the artist, needed to ask him...

~

It was the sharp, shrill voice that pulled him away from "drawing" his alphabet and down the dim hallway toward his aunt's office. Concerned, he'd quickly discarded his tablet, forgetting the professor's assignment, and rushed toward the sound.

The door was slightly ajar, and although he couldn't see the people inside, the tension radiating from the room seemed almost visible from where he stood.

"For God's sake, Lily, calm down. Hysterics won't do anyone a bit of good." Aunt Janet's voice sounded cold and harsh, not at all like herself.

Richie drew himself protectively against a tall wooden file cabinet that stood just outside the office, his ears on the alert for sounds that might indicate they were coming toward the door. If that happened, he'd be back in the den like a shot, without a backward glance. Things had been too weird today to risk being caught eavesdropping. Under the circumstances, he couldn't even count on his explanation of concern for his aunt's safety to be taken seriously, and he was certain the punishment for such an offense would be unreasonably hard.

He drew in a deep breath, reflecting that since Charlie left a few hours earlier, his aunt had not been in a particularly benevolent mood. And now, having to deal with this crying, ranting girl, her usual good humor was certain not to return for the remainder of the day.

Rather than stand there brooding on what a lousy summer he was having with people he'd always considered his most favorite in the world, Richie fine-tuned his senses to what was going on behind that partially closed door.

"How can you expect me to calm down when my entire life is going down the toilet?" The girl cried out sharply. "You've no idea what I'm up against. She's a witch, that's what she is. One look, one smile, and they're hooked."

"If it's a mere physical attraction, it's bound to wear off. Charles is made of tougher stuff—"

The laughter that followed made Richie's spine crawl.

"Chuckles is weak in the knees! Her name turns him to jelly—with the exception of one part of his anatomy, which he'll be lucky to keep if I ever get my hands on him—"

"Lillian Reston! Not only must you get a firm hold on yourself, young woman, but I suggest you refrain from making further threats. Crude or otherwise."

"The calm, clear voice of reason, huh?" The girl's tone changed in an instant from raving and out of control to cold and full of derision. "How can you remain so serene, so confident and self-assured of all the answers?"

There was an odd rustling sound within the room as though someone were sifting through papers.

"What are you implying?"

The silence was just long enough to make Richie wish he'd stayed closer to the doorway so he might've been able to catch a glimpse of what was going on inside the room. He was about to move from his hiding place when movement near the door stopped him.

He could see the long blonde hair of the girl inside and one trim leg protruding from beneath a brown mini skirt. She had a hand on her hip and her head cocked to one side.

"Nothing, dear Mrs. Drake, nothing at all." The voice was smooth and sly, a clear indication she hadn't meant what she'd said.

"Did you come here to ask for my advice, Lillian, or taunt me with unfounded rumors?" The anger in Janet Drake's voice turned Richie's blood to ice. He'd never heard his aunt speak this way before, and something about it terrified him.

He'd heard enough. Too much for his liking. Being shut up in the den reading **Tom Sawyer** and doing simple drawing assignments might get boring, but it was better than this uncomfortable piece of reality.

"Of course they're unfounded, just as all that talk a year ago about him and—"

"Stop it! Stop it right now, Lily. Not one more word. I've no idea what's gotten into you today, but I'm in no mood to suffer your petty insolences. I think you'd better leave now before either of us says something we'd later live to regret."

The sound of feet nearing the doorway sent Richie like a bolt of lightning down the hall and safely back into the den. He grabbed up his sketchbook from the chair where he'd discarded it earlier, crawled onto the window seat, and closing his eyes, willed his breathing to steady as he took a swipe at the perspiration running down his forehead.

He had no idea what was going on, and while his natural curiosity *was piqued, he was scared to death of what he might find out. He'd wished for problems to solve, for the thrill of adventure, but that was the game. He was no longer certain he was ready to face the grown-up reality of such things...*

~

The memory slammed into me like being blind-sided by a pro linebacker. I stumbled backward, fell over the arm of a chair, and sat stunned, lost somewhere between the past and the present. As I drifted slowly in a kind of limbo, the warm, homey smell peculiar to the Drake's house was still in my nostrils.

What caused this sudden intrusion of the past? I could understand the previous experiences after Grant knocked me unconscious, but what brought about this latest one?

These questions were minor in comparison to the thoughts that were now running through my head. How was it that neither Chuck nor Lily ever mentioned knowing me as a child? It was understandable that I might not have remembered them, but after what happened to me in the park, considerably less likely they would have forgotten meeting me—and I already knew how accurate their memories were regarding the attack on me. That left one alternative, and it seemed unlikely that the secrecy my parents and the Drakes perpetrated through the years had extended to people outside the family. Which brought me back to my original question: if they hadn't been asked to remain silent about the past, why had nothing ever been said?

The memories, though vivid, had come in such a hodgepodge sequence that it would take some time to assimilate and to decide what, if anything, they had to do with that fateful night so long ago. I was still trying to recover from the impact when Nicole reentered the room.

She rushed over to me, fell on her knees before the chair, and with concern etched across her face, peered anxiously up at me.

"Oh dear God! Are you all right?" Her warm, gentle hands stroked my face, the mist of the past lifting enough for me to recognize that I was still in her grandfather's office.

"I should get you back to the hospital." Nicole was saying as my eyes roamed about the room. "Do you think you could stand, Richard? You can lean on me if you want."

Kindness, warmth, sympathy. A true compassion radiated like an aura from the lovely girl before me. Still caught somewhere in between the mist that clouded my brain and the present, I could see a golden halo surrounding her. I gazed into her clear, blue eyes, yearning for the peace and tranquility I was sure could be found there.

I reached out to her, touching, caressing the smooth planes of her face, fascinated by the fullness of her lips, the curve of her chin. I didn't know, didn't even care what made her so tender and caring to me, simply accepted that unseen force that had drawn her to me and me to her.

Unseen, yes, but not unfelt. There was something here, something emanating from the tips of my fingers as they lingered on her lips, a strange magnetic power that seemed as tangible as tiny threads linking us together.

"It's okay, Richard. Come. Give me your hands."

Her voice urged me to obey, and remaining in a kind of trance, I willingly complied. I gave myself into her hands, peering out of my eyes as though I were detached from the scene before me, an out-of-body experience that only added to my confusion.

She led me from the room, down the hallway, then out onto the porch. As she was drawing her keys from her pocket, the wind blew a shower of rain across us, making Nicole shiver as she once again took my arm.

"I hate storms." She said as we made our way quickly down the steps to her car.

I continued to allow the sound of her voice to guide me, climbing into the car and watching as she closed the door. Pressing my forehead against the window, the coolness of the glass seemed to plunge me further into that vortex of unreality. Although the mist and rain continued, somehow, for me, they seemed swept away, revealing a clear glimpse of the porch as Nicole rushed into the car and started the engine.

This time, when she called to me, I was unable to respond, my eyes transfixed on the scene outside the window.

As we drove away from the Grant's house, I watched in fascination as the dim outline of a girl in a peasant dress slowly evaporated from the edge of the porch.

Chapter 18

It was wrong to think I hadn't been affected by the past—these dreams, or visions, were enough to make me realize the truth. But as weak as I felt physically, by the time Nicole Grant got me to the hospital, I was strong enough mentally to take control of my life.

I refused to be lectured by the nursing staff as they reinstalled me in my room. I didn't regret leaving, and even though the fear remained that the tumor was malignant, I wouldn't give in, was determined to fight the odds. My life was only beginning to take the turn I'd always worked toward, and I wasn't about to let go so easily.

Bravery had nothing to do with it. I was terrified of the surgery, of what it entailed, but as I discovered on the return drive to the hospital, I was even more terrified of the alternative.

Nicole's soft, soothing voice had slowly brought me out of the fog into which I'd descended, her words reaching out to pull me back to sanity.

"People aren't generally given the choice between life and death." Nicole said as she peered through the driving rain. "Faced with the decision to have an operation that could possibly save your life or allowing nature to take what might be a destructive course seems a fairly easy choice to me."

"I don't—" Mist still lingered on the outer edges of my mind, but I tried hard to focus on her words.

"You're not the kind to give in or give up. Your determination as an artist proves that. I know you're afraid, Richard," she continued softly. "I would be, too."

The thought of someone sawing into my head, slicing away a piece of my brain, seemed an abomination. Thinking straight or not, I knew brain surgery was risky under any circumstances.

"Isn't it worth the risk?" Nicole asked as though able to read my mind. "Life. Isn't that better than the alternative?"

"It isn't—that easy. If it's cancer, malignant—"

"But if it isn't? Either way you'll know and deal with it from there. Waiting, even for a short time, would be like walking around with a time bomb inside your head, never knowing when it could blow." Pulling up to a street light, she glanced over at me. "Perhaps I'm being presumptuous talking to you like this. It's just, I, uh, after the way you left the hospital, I don't know what you're thinking."

"Why do you care so much? Because you're hoping I can help you find Jenny and ultimately your mother?"

The light changed, and after another brief glance, Nicole turned back to the road.

"I'd be lying if I said no. But there's more to it than that." She shrugged her narrow shoulders. "I've always relied on instinct. A little crazy perhaps, but that's my way. Sure, you might be the key that opens up my mother's past to me, but—"

She pulled out of the main stream of traffic onto a side street, then over to the curb. Putting the car in park, she turned slightly in her seat, her sapphire eyes meeting mine.

"From the moment I walked into the gallery, I knew I had to meet you. Jenny's portrait started it, but the incredible energy I felt from the rest of your paintings clinched it. With each one came this amazing feeling that I already knew you. All that was missing was the preliminary introductions." She shook her head, and a strand of hair fell across her face. Before she had the chance to remove it, I'd gently tucked it behind her ear.

"I felt it too." My voice was little more than a whisper. "The sense of knowing you. I imagine it's your connection to Jenny."

"That explains you. But what about me?" Her eyes seemed to cloud over as she struggled with her words. "I, uh, you don't need any extra burdens at a time like this, and you owe me nothing. I just want to help, be there for you if you'll let me. And don't ask me why, because I couldn't explain if I tried." She smiled a little. "So what do you think?"

I looked out upon the rain-sodden street, at the rivulets of water running rapidly toward the gutters, and the limbs of trees as they whipped back and forth in the wind. I hadn't left the hospital because I was trying to escape the reality of surgery; I'd gone in search of something. Answers, yes, but also the strength to put my life back together.

There was no tender moment of self-realization; Nicole saw the dawning of acceptance in my face and continued our journey without another word. And although nothing had been confirmed between us, there was an unspoken understanding that she would remain close at hand.

It was a trial to keep my raging emotions under control throughout the additional tests, but one I battled successfully. Just the knowledge that each time I returned to my room, Nicole would be waiting, a smile upon her face, seemed incentive enough to cooperate. Her support helped me become more relaxed and far less anxious than I imagined possible. With the anger gone, some of my former good humor returned. My future might look bleak at present, but I was determined to live for the moment.

It was a novelty to be on the receiving end, the one who was "saved" not doing the "saving." The classic distress syndrome I was so used to but in the reverse—at least that's how I perceived it. Perhaps it was chauvinistic, but the scenario felt wrong somehow. Still, it was comforting to have Nicole by my side, offering her support just by being there.

I signed the release papers, allowed Joyce to reprimand me for running out on her, and agreed to Dr. Astin's suggestion of surgery first thing the following morning. They made it clear that ordinarily they wouldn't have pushed for it quite so soon, but my two hour disappearing act spooked Joyce, and she didn't want to risk a repeat. By late afternoon I was enduring the last of the pre-op preparations.

Nicole stood by quietly as I directed the male nurse who'd come in to shave the right side of my head to go ahead and complete the job. I watched as the hair piled up in the tray before me, trying hard to erase the anxiety I felt. It didn't take long to go from fashionably long hair to bare as a baby's behind, and once we were alone, I completed the transformation by painstakingly removing my beard and mustache.

While I shaved, Nicole stayed in the doorway of my tiny bathroom. Catching her eye in the mirror, I smiled through the shaving cream and received one in return. There was a hint of mischief in her expression as she studied me.

The flash of déjà vu wasn't as strong for me this time as it had been with Jenny, but I still felt as though I'd been drawn tightly back against a bow and then flung loose. As I tried to assimilate this feeling, Nicole began the promised story of her mother.

"My mother kept a kind of diary," she began slowly, "which is the only reason I can tell you anything at all." She gave a little laugh. "She kept them hidden inside a corner of my toy box. I suppose that once I'd gotten older and able to read she would've moved them, but as you know...

"Anyway, she was an only child. After her birth, my grandmother's health was never very good. She died when mother was seven or eight. You've met my grandfather, can see how autocratic he can be—"

"I think pig-headed and dangerous are more appropriate terms."

She conceded with a grin. "This is my story, so if you want to hear it, behave yourself. Okay?"

I agreed, returning her grin. Her response was instantaneous and gratifying, and once again I found myself marveling at how unique she was.

"Anyway, Grandfather was very strict, spoiled her in some ways, but from what I was able to glean, she felt stifled. When she was sixteen, she ran away, hooked up with a guy named Cole, and headed for California. They were together a couple of years before Grandfather's detectives found us—it was only Mother and me by that time. He offered to bring us back to Linden and she accepted. Neither of them mentioned my father—all I know about him is the one name—first or last...there was only that one mention of him in her diary."

"Have you tried to find him?"

She shrugged. "Thought about it a time or two. But, I don't know..."

I'd finished shaving, so we moved back into the room. Nicole fussed with the sheet once I'd gotten situated on the bed, her eyes misting over with unshed tears. I caught her hand and, holding it tightly, drew it to my lips. The kiss brought a blush to her cheeks, but she made no attempt to withdraw from my clasp.

"I was told I could come back now, but I see you're busy. Perhaps I should—"

Professor Drake's voice startled us both. Nicole gently disengaged her hand and stood slightly away from the bed to give me a better view of the doorway.

"Dear God, Richard, what's happened?" He gasped as he caught sight of me, grabbing the doorjamb to steady himself.

I motioned for him to come in as I self-consciously rubbed my bald head.

"I guess it's a little overwhelming after all that hair."

Edmund Drake remained in the doorway, looking at me with a mixture of shock and fear. As I started to rise from the bed to help him to a chair, Nicole put a hand on my chest to stop me and went to him herself.

"Professor Drake, I'm Nicole Grant. I've heard a lot about you, sir. Here," she reached out to him, "Let me help you to a chair."

Drake took her hand uncertainly, his eyes remaining on me. Although he'd never seemed to age in all the years I'd known him, he suddenly looked far older than he was.

"Richard," he croaked as he took a seat next to the bed. "What?"

"A tumor. It was discovered when they brought me in last night after an, er, altercation."

"Behind the Fine Arts." He nodded. "Greg Seitz called saying you'd been taken away in an ambulance. He said some crazy man waylaid you in the parking lot and had beaten you up."

"That's a simplified version of what happened, yes."

Professor Drake looked from me to Nicole then back again.

"I don't understand."

"It's a long story and—"

"And I'm not about to let him go into it at this time." Dr. Joyce Noland entered the room and surveyed us with a critical eye. "I thought you promised he'd get some rest." She said to Nicole. And to me. "Go a little overboard here?"

Joyce examined my appearance as she crossed the room.

"If you were hoping for a disguise, it won't work. I'd know those eyes anywhere." She came alongside the bed and lifted my wrist to check my pulse.

"There was a nurse here not ten minutes ago, and she did that." I protested good-naturedly.

"And now you've got the doctor." As she proceeded to inspect the bruises on my face, she directed her conversation to my visitors.

"I see you've finally gotten the opportunity to check on my willful patient, Professor Drake. I hope you will use your influence to convince the young man to adhere to his physician's advice and rest."

"Of course." He said in obvious confusion. "But what's this about a tumor?" The worry and concern in his voice drew her attention from me, and after a slight frown for my benefit alone, she turned to him.

"If it's all right with Richard, I'll be happy to explain everything to you."

He peered around her to me. "I was given the impression that what happened had to do with Tara. I mean, Hargrave has been in and out of the hospital all day grumbling about wanting to talk to you and I just assumed..."

"And he can continue to grumble. He's banned from seeing Richard for the time being." Joyce assured us both. "Besides, the man's a bane to society, at least as far as Richard's concerned. I'm not about to let him get his hands on my patient."

"Thanks for small miracles." I told Joyce with a wink. "As for the incident involving Tara, it doesn't. Trust me. It's part of that long story we'll have to put off until later."

The professor nodded uncertainly. He'd remained perched on the edge of the chair, his hands locked on the narrow wooden arms. Nothing said appeared to put his mind at rest enough to relax his hold. Indeed, it seemed that with each passing second, his tenseness increased.

Every now and again I caught him stealing a glance in Nicole's direction, the expression on his face curious. Nicole must have seen it, too, and from the way she fidgeted, I knew it made her uncomfortable. For some reason, this made me angry with the professor; angry at his unwelcome interruption of the story about Jennifer Grant; even angry at his worry and concern for me.

The thoughts were ridiculous, and guilt gnawed at me for having them in the first place. This was my friend, my lifelong mentor and companion, yet I felt a strange uneasiness in his presence.

"So how are you feeling, son?" Professor Drake's bushy eyebrows formed a thick line across his forehead.

I might have been looking into the eyes of a stranger, these odd thoughts of mine interfering with the normal connections in my brain.

"Other than the fact that I look a little like a cue ball, I'll do." I said, trying to cover up my discomfort with an attempt at humor. The remark seemed lost on the professor yet was rewarded with a snicker from Nicole and a sharp glance from my doctor along with an unpleasant poke in the shoulder.

"Don't let him fool you. There was no reason for the radical haircut. The incision will be made about here." Joyce traced an invisible line across the upper right of my skull at the back. "The tumor appears to lie directly beneath. If all goes well, the extraction will be completed in very little time. If there's no sign of metastases, recovery will be quick—as long as he behaves himself."

"And if it's malignant?"

Having already discussed this with the doctors earlier, I really didn't want to hear it again. Joyce was aware of this but also sensed the professor's desperation. Placing a hand on my shoulder, she squeezed it gently before she continued.

"That's a bridge we'll cross if necessary. Richard knows the risks, and we've talked about treatments." She went to stand near the foot of the bed, closer to where the professor was seated. "Why don't you come along with me, Professor Drake, and I'll give you a run-down of what we know and exactly what's going to be done."

Edmund Drake nodded, his thick, gray hair bouncing about as if filled with static.

"What about Annie?" He asked as he rose, his pale hooded eyes filled with concern. "Have you called your mother?"

"No, and—"

"Good God, Richard! She should at least know what's going on."

"Professor," this time it was Nicole who broke in to save me an explanation. "Richard believes that under the circumstances it would be best to wait until after he's out of surgery before she's contacted."

"No, I don't think—"

"She's already had to sit in a hospital and watch one member of her family die this year." I broke in, speaking more harshly than I'd meant to. "I don't intend to force her to relive those final moments of my father's life. Once I'm in recovery, and we have some idea what's going on, Joyce and Nicole have agreed to get a message to her. That is, unless you would care to do it."

He didn't like the idea of waiting but reluctantly agreed. With his heavy heart showing in his face, he hugged me tightly.

"If you need anything, son, I'll be close by. Don't hesitate to let me know."

The dampness of his cheek against mine stirred me deeply, and letting go of the uneasiness I'd felt a moment before, I fiercely hugged him back.

"There is one thing you might do." I told him as he withdrew from the embrace. "Chuck's bound to show up sooner or later and want an explanation." I threw an accusing glance in Joyce's direction which failed to affect her at all. "I'd rather not be forced to give one."

The professor nodded.

"Will do. And the moment you're in recovery, I'll get a message through to Janet and Annie. Neither will be pleased by the delay." He gave me a slight grin that seemed an attempt to deny the tears that slowly rolled down his cheeks. "You'd better be ready to pay the price."

With a quick clasp of hands and a final look filled with more emotion than I'd ever seen in his face, he turned away and allowed himself to be led from the room. At the door, Joyce turned back to Nicole.

"Watch him." She said with a meaningful glance in my direction, a look that said she was still uncertain about trusting me to stay put. I doubted my smile did anything to regain that trust, but I found the act itself appeared to lighten my tenseness.

When we were alone once again, Nicole released a long, deep breath and pulled one of the chairs closer to the side of the bed.

"He cares a lot about you." She spoke quietly, the soft, melodic sound of her voice singing strangely in my heart.

Just as I'd always found it difficult to account for my continued attraction to Tara, I was now unable to explain the sudden closeness I felt to Nicole Grant. In the last twenty-four hours, I'd run the gamut of emotions, going from one end of the spectrum to the other. Questioning what I felt would not lead to answers, and for once in my life, I decided to let it go at that. I accepted Nicole as a friend, knew instinctively that I could trust her.

I smiled, and holding my hand out to her, settled back to give her a brief history of my relationship to the Drakes, telling the story of a lifetime in the matter of a few minutes. I let her know about the friendship between the professor and my father that started it all, the introduction of my parents by the Drakes, and their eventual marriage. I spoke of summers spent with Edmund and Janet, their encouragement to develop my artistic talent and love of literature, and the wonderful freedom they'd given to a boy whose desire for adventures had to be reined in nine months of the year.

"When I was about seven, the professor developed a marvelous game that would last at least a week at a time." I told her, smiling at the memory. "It wasn't an ordinary kind of game, but a sort of scavenger hunt enclosed within the form of a great adventure. There were always dragons to be slain or someone who was in grave danger that needed to be rescued. You name the scenario, we probably played it out.

"The task was to search for clues while gathering a list of items outlined by the professor. Usually there were the three of us, Frank Murray, Mary Rogers, and myself. They lived close by and seemed to get as big a kick out of the game as I did." I readjusted my position against the pillows, reveling in the memory of those happy-go-lucky days. "We played the game every summer. It was a lot of fun."

"Sounds terrific. He must have loved you very much to go to all the time and trouble necessary to create such an intricate game. And think of the imagination that would have to go into it!" Nicole leaned forward against the bed, propping her feet along the bottom railing. "The answer to a kid's dream."

She looked thoughtful for a moment, then shook her head.

"Although I'm sure I've never met him, he seems familiar to me. I suppose it's the stories the children have told me."

Seeing I didn't understand what she meant, she went on to explain.

"He's been teaching art at my preschool twice a week. You'd think after two years I'd have met him, but since the kids go straight from music to the art room," she shrugged. "He's great with the kids, and now I know why. It comes naturally."

Though this was news to me, I wasn't surprised to learn the professor had been teaching outside the university. For the last several years, the additional responsibility as head of the college gradually decreased the amount of time he spent in the classroom. And as Edmund Drake was a natural born teacher, it was only logical he would need to find an outlet elsewhere. Still, with as close as we'd always been, it seemed a little odd he hadn't mentioned it. Now, remembering the fun I'd had with his lessons all those years ago, I knew how perfect he would be for such a job. It was yet another facet to a man I'd always admired, and I made a mental note to ask him about it.

We sat in silence for a while, the professor and Joyce's visit reminding us that we were really just strangers. However brief the interruption, it succeeded in creating a gap which left us feeling a little awkward with one another.

Nicole's hand gradually inched over to mine, and we laced our fingers together, seeking to regain familiarity and build on the tenuous relationship we'd begun.

I gave her hand a gentle squeeze. "How about continuing your story?"

She flashed me one of her shy, secret smiles and nodded.

"Sure. Um, where was I? Oh yes, I remember now." She shifted slightly in the chair, careful not to disturb our still linked hands.

"My grandfather brought the two of us back to Linden and agreed to certain concessions regarding Mother's behavior as long as she agreed to act like the adult she claimed she was." She laughed. "The way her diary tells it, she was finally allowed to fraternize with the young gentlemen of Linden, providing she adhered to the golden rule: Grandfather must first approve his lineage. I don't believe she ever took the decree too seriously, there were hints she knew how to get around her restrictions. She even became involved with one of my grandfather's chauffeurs/jack-of-all-trades—"

"Henchmen?" I offered.

"Nice term, but I'm not sure it applies." She wrinkled her nose at the idea. "But she did cause quite a stir with this guy. If I've interpreted it correctly, I'd say he was spying for my grandfather, and Mother figured the best way to eliminate the problem was to make a play for him. If that's what she intended, it certainly worked. He was dismissed and threatened to get back at my grandfather. I know how that sounds, but I got the impression there was more to it than met the eye."

"You're saying your mother wasn't just a wanton woman. Right?"

Nicole laughed, a light, tinkling sound full of gaiety.

"No, she wasn't. According to her diary, there were only two men she ever really cared for or made love to. Rather an odd remark coming from an avowed hippie."

Here was something else I could associate with. Rather than comment from my own life experiences, I picked up on the conversation in regard to Jennifer Diane Grant.

"One, of course, was your father. And from what you've said, I gather the other was definitely not the guy who worked for your grandfather."

The identity of Jennifer's other love had been apparent the moment I'd seen her portrait. Though I was certain I already knew the answer, I decided to play along, enjoying the diversion of Nicole's story so much I didn't want to see it end too soon.

She pouted prettily, completely aware of what I was doing.

"The last two years she was home, when she even bothered to write in her diary, it was all in code. Initials for names, that sort of thing. I don't know how long she was involved with the man, but her love for him absolutely shines from her writing."

"As it does from the portrait." I said quietly.

She nodded. "What I remember of my mother is this beautiful, laughing creature who was always happy. She seemed capable of charming everyone, even Grandfather at his sternest. But having read her diaries, I know she was very vulnerable as well. Living in the shadow of her mother's death, and her father's terror of losing her, made her lose out on life because of his protectiveness. Running away gave her a chance for freedom, but it was short-lived. I think she found some semblance of it again when she met her artist."

The artist. I felt an icy finger run the length of my spine, halting the question I wanted to ask.

While I was lost in thought, Nicole sat further back in her chair, gently releasing my fingers, yet not completely breaking contact between us. As she traced the lines of my palm with her index finger, a shadow descended over her features, and I felt that all too familiar urge to comfort her. But something held me back. Instead, I sat quietly by, watching as she struggled with her emotions before she continued her story.

"When she dis-disappeared, I couldn't believe it would be forever. I knew Grandfather would find her, bring her back to me. But most of all, I knew how much she loved me. She would never leave me behind." Her voice started to break, and she cleared her throat, clenching her free hand tightly as she fought to regain control.

"One of my most vivid memories is sitting on Mother's lap, hiding behind the curtain of her hair while twirling her ankh pendant round and round my fingers. That little girl, the child that I was, never felt anything but loved. Safe and secure." Her eyes glistened with unshed tears as they met mine. "I've always felt she meant to come back to me, that something happened to prevent her from carrying through. I don't blame her for going, I know what a tyrant Grandfather can be. So whatever her reasons are for not having contacted me in all these years, I understand. I just need to know what happened, and perhaps, through your Jenny, I can find that out."

She came into my arms, and I held her tightly, promising that together we would find the elusive young woman who so resembled her mother.

It was completely natural, the feel of her body against mine, the fragrance of her skin and hair filling my nostrils as I caressed and soothed her. And her response to me was just as normal, beginning with tiny kisses along the side of my neck that gradually became more fervent as she neared my mouth. When our lips met, our emotions were so intense they overwhelmed both of us.

A few minutes later, when Nicole slowly pulled from the embrace, her lovely face was flushed. She appeared both surprised and embarrassed by what we'd experienced, but after a moment the look changed to one of contentment. We'd more than passed through the awkward stage, had advanced to another level of understanding far more quickly than either of us would have guessed possible.

Nicole stayed with me long past visiting hours. Each time we heard steps in the hall outside my room, she'd wink playfully, then quietly steal into the bathroom until the danger of discovery was past. I was amused and touched by her insistence to keep me company, her constant presence leaving me little time to brood on tomorrow's surgery.

Shortly before eleven, I was given the sedative I'd been avoiding all night. The nurse insisted we'd put off doctor's orders long enough and that a good night's sleep was essential for the upcoming ordeal. Though I figured I'd get plenty of sleep during surgery and afterward, I knew it was useless to argue and gracefully relented.

"Good, Mr. Tanner." The woman carefully rearranged covers and pillows, then patted my shoulder. "Now everything's in order."

A crash of thunder and the sudden rush of wind at the window made the nurse jump, startled.

"That's some storm brewing out there. The radio is warning of high winds and damaging hail." She shuddered. "Glad I'm inside. Well, you get some rest now."

After closing the blind in the small window near the bed, she switched off the overhead light and left, partially closing the door behind her. Within seconds, Nicole reappeared, blinking rapidly as I switched on the bedside light.

"Guess I should go before the storm fulfills the nurse's prophecy." She wrinkled her nose as thunder rumbled across the night sky. "I'm not crazy about storms, and the thought of being caught out in one doesn't thrill me. So while it's just all noise and bluster I'm going to run. Besides, you're already becoming bleary-eyed."

She was right. Whether it was the sedative, ordinary exhaustion, or a combination, I was having difficulty keeping my eyes open.

"Thanks." There was so much more I wanted to say but was unable to find the words.

"Don't mention it." Nicole smiled. She leaned down and kissed the top of my bald head. "Never kissed a cue ball before," she told me, grinning. "I kinda like it."

After assuring me she would return bright and early in the morning, she headed for the door.

"I'll be here," she said, a gleam in her eyes. "Don't worry, Richard. Everything's going to be all right."

After checking the corridor, she blew me a kiss, and, with a wave, was gone.

As I closed my eyes, I thought about all that transpired the last couple of days. Some inner sense told me I was missing something, but no matter how hard I concentrated, the solution remained elusive.

I turned instead to the decision not to contact my mother. While the reasoning behind it was flawless, I had to admit it would've been comforting to know she was nearby.

The thoughts were fleeting, passing in and out of my sleepy brain like dream images, each replaced rapidly by another. If, or how long I slept, I cannot be certain. I was just suddenly aware of an uncomfortable draft and movement near my bed. Groping for the blanket, I had an uncanny certainty that someone was standing over me, watching as I struggled to come fully awake. At first I ignored it, remembering perfectly where I was, and realizing it was likely a nurse or aide come to check my vital signs. But there was no checking my pulse or blood pressure, yet the sensation of being observed persisted.

With considerable effort, I opened my eyes and stared at the dim form standing near the side of my bed. The individual made no move toward me but remained as still as the proverbial statue.

My body felt heavy, laden under the influence of the medication. I knew there was no possibility of my getting out of bed, and with a shudder of apprehension, considered my nearly helpless condition.

There was no movement from the phantom image, and as I forced myself onto my side to try to get a better look, there came the almost certain insight that I was still within a dream state. That's what I believed until a flash of lightning brightly illuminated the room, and in those couple of moments, I recognized my visitor.

"Jenny?" Though I managed to keep my voice low enough not to attract outside attention, I hadn't succeeded in hiding my utter amazement.

She came forward slowly, a finger to her lips. The sliver of light from the partially opened door offered little penetration of the room's incredible darkness. Yet as she advanced toward me, there seemed a kind of glow about her, and I was reminded of the unusual phosphorescent quality in her portrait.

"I wasn't sure I should, but felt I had to come one last time." Her lovely violet eyes seemed to shine in the darkness as she reached out and clasped my hand.

"Last? No, Jenny." My voice sounded as though dredged from the bottom of a deep well, the words cumbersome. "Whatever is wrong, we can deal with it. I've met some people who might be your family, and they're dying—"

Her fingers touched my mouth, stilling the overflow of words.

"I haven't long, so you must listen." She leaned down so our faces were just inches apart. "Poor Richard," she gently stroked my head seemingly unaware that it was now absent of hair. "I never meant for you to become involved, but it happened. And now it's time to let go."

"Jenny, it's all right, I—"

"Sh-sh. You mustn't be afraid, Richard, just let it come." She cupped my face within her cool hands, the intensity of her words frightening me a little. "All this time you've been seeking something you can't even name. But you've never been lost, Richard, you've held the answers to your questions all along."

While I pondered her riddle, a noise from outside the room made her quickly draw away from the bed. She turned toward the door, the tenseness of her posture communicating her fear of discovery.

I watched in wonder, my mind and body too leaden to move, my thoughts jumbled and confused. When the sound of footsteps retreated down the hallway, Jenny once more came out of the shadows.

"I have to go now, but first," her hands went to her neckline. There was a sense of urgency about her movements as she lifted the ankh pendant over her head. "This is for Colie," she said, pressing the necklace into my hand. "Keep it safe."

Another flash of lightning revealed the tears coursing down Jenny's lovely face.

"I don't understand—"

"Sleep, Richard." She told me softly, her hands tenderly stroking my forehead. "Sleep and find the key that unlocks our past."

Chapter 19

*H*e was still on the window seat when she came into the room. At first he thought she was just a kid like him, but when he got a good look at her face, he knew she was an adult, likely another university student.

Still shaken by what he'd witnessed from outside his aunt's office, Richie was more than a little reluctant to face the girl.

"Hi," she said brightly.

When she smiled, even someone as young as he was could recognize she was beautiful. She had dimples in her cheeks that were so deep that he bet a pencil eraser could get stuck in them. It was a dumb thought, but he'd seen his friend Kevin Hallet try that at school and then swear when the pencils wouldn't stay put. This girl wouldn't have that problem. Too bad he couldn't show her to Kevin.

"No one answered the door." The girl came further into the room, still smiling at him. "I started to leave, then saw you through the window."

"Reading." He held up the book.

He felt funny inside, couldn't understand why his voice stuck in his throat or why he couldn't seem to take his eyes off her.

"**Tom Sawyer**." She nodded. "A good book. But I'm surprised *you're not outside. Now the clouds have come in, it's really very pleasant."* She lifted a hand and pushed back a strand of her long brown hair.

He looked the girl over from the top of her head down to her sandaled feet. Her hair reached past her waist, and she was wearing the kind of clothing his parents would have referred to as being "hippie attire."

"Are you a hippie?" He asked in awe, hoping it wasn't too rude of him to express his curiosity. Besides, if she was, it would be the first one he'd seen for real, not just on TV or in a magazine. Boy, this was great! He just might have something really important to share with Kevin Hallet when he went home at the end of the summer.

The girl laughed. It was such a happy sound that he found himself laughing with her.

"I used to be." She leaned toward him and put a finger to her lips. Looking over her shoulder as if to make certain they were still alone, she leaned even closer and spoke to him quietly.

"When I was younger, I lived in San Francisco for a while. I was a true flower child." Her eyes sparkled.

That's when he noticed their color. They were like the wild violets that used to grow all over the park, deep and rich in tone—tone, that was an artist's word. Uncle Edmund would be proud of him for thinking about it like that.

"Wow," he said, continuing to study her.

She laughed again, but he knew she wasn't laughing at him, so it didn't matter.

"You must be Richie. I've heard a lot about you." She held out her hand, and he gave her his very shyly. "I'm Jenny, a friend of your uncle's."

~

Within forty-eight hours following the operation, my fears about cancer had been laid to rest. The surgery team, headed by doctors Astin and Noland, managed to successfully extract the tumor—details of which I chose not to recall—and confirmed there were no malignant cells. I should suffer no residual effects and, according to my esteemed physicians, my recovery was right on schedule. The news thrilled me, of course, but in my present condition, celebrating was hardly possible.

I was weak and fairly out of it when my mother arrived more than a little upset about the delay in informing her. Nicole was nearby as she'd promised and somehow managed to take the sting out of the neglect, an accomplishment that earned not only my appreciation, but the respect of my mother as well.

Other faces and voices drifted in and out of my range of comprehension, some of which seemed more dreamlike than reality-based. I struggled with nightmares and memories that seemed jumbled together in such a manner that I believed I might never unravel them. But mostly I concentrated on getting well and regaining my strength, anxious to once more be in control of my life.

By evening of the third day, the hospital was abuzz with news of the storm damage Linden suffered the night before my surgery. High winds had downed power lines, uprooted trees, and strewn debris from one end of the city to the other. Golf ball-sized hail had dented cars, broken windshields, loosened or damaged shingles and siding, and broken windows in several homes. What the wind and hail hadn't ruined, the torrential downpour did, flooding numerous basements that never leaked before.

As widespread as it sounded, the concentration of the storm that whipped through Linden had been along a narrow strip in the eastern part of town, with the greatest part of the devastation in and around University Park. The swing sets had been mangled, one of the slides still hadn't been found, and the gazebo had been virtually reduced to matchsticks. It was believed that a tornado touched down in the park long enough to create general havoc and then lifted before it reached the nearby residential area. It would take days to assess the damage, even longer to clean it up. All of Linden was pulling together to get back on its feet.

My apartment, on the edge of the path of destruction, had come through with only one of the west windows broken. Before I was even aware there'd been a problem, the Weishers and Professor Drake had the window replaced and the mess cleaned up. Others were not so lucky.

As I listened in sympathy, I remembered Nicole's comment about getting home before the storm became worse and thanked God she had done so. These thoughts led to the vague memory of Jenny's late night visit, and a sudden fear washed over me that she may have been caught out in the storm. I expressed this worry to Joyce the following afternoon as she painstakingly led me down the hallway, my first jaunt since surgery.

"And Jenny would be the lovely young woman of the celebrated portrait hanging in the Fine Arts gallery?"

We stopped for a breather on the return trip, just a few doors down from my room. I glanced quickly in that direction, thinking how far off it still seemed.

"Um. I can't even be sure she was actually here, to be honest." Which was the reason I hadn't mentioned anything to Nicole. "From the time Nicole left that evening, until about yesterday afternoon, things have been a little hazy. I haven't known when I was awake or simply dreaming."

"That's normal. And you're coming along nicely." Joyce urged me forward slowly. "There have been no fatalities, Richard. As a matter of fact, we've even had fewer injuries than would be expected. The park suffered the brunt of the storm. From the way it tore through that area," she shook her head. "We're blessed the tornado set down there. I'd hate to think what would've happened if it had been in the middle of a residential community."

A nurse passed by, acknowledging Joyce with a smile followed by a curious sidelong glance. Dr. Joyce Noland waited for the other woman to disappear into one of the rooms down the hall before she broke into a fit of laughter.

"You've just seen how very lucky you are, young man, and I hope you don't forget it." She tugged gently on my arm as I stopped by the door of my room.

"Excuse me?"

"This little turn of yours down the hall. Ordinarily the task would fall to one of the nurses or an aide, even to a friend or relative. Rarely does one of the esteemed and mighty doctors of Linden Community see to the job themselves. Thanks to my special attention, your importance as a patient will vastly increase."

"That's what I like about you, Joyce," I smirked. "You've not only a marvelous sense of yourself, but a great sense of humor as well."

We were still laughing when she helped me into bed.

"On a much more serious note, what about those memories you mentioned before surgery? We never had the chance to discuss it before, but I have a little time now if you'd like."

"I haven't said anything to Mother," I told her, glancing through the open doorway. My mother and Nicole left a little over an hour ago to meet Janet for a quick tour of the gallery before dinner. Knowing my mom and how concerned she still was for me, they could return any time.

"For now," I continued. "I'd as soon she know nothing about it." I settled back against the pillows, careful to avoid the bandaged right side of my head.

"That's understandable." She nodded. "Have you anything you'd like to talk about?"

I gazed through the thick-lensed glasses into my doctor's pale blue eyes.

"Although I think most of it's memory, there are times when dreams seem to be interlaced. I'm not sure I can distinguish between the two."

Joyce regarded me thoughtfully. "I can see from your expression they confuse you. Do you think the reason you're having trouble differentiating between them is because you're not ready to accept them as memories?"

Shrugging my shoulders, I waited for the usual bolt of pain to shoot up through my neck into my head. When only the slightest of twinges came in response, I couldn't help but smile.

"Is that a yes?"

"Actually it's a "thank you." I can't tell you how long it's been since I could move like that and not be rewarded with pain."

"You're welcome." Joyce grinned. "Now quit stalling."

I closed my eyes for a moment and reached for the visions that had recently crowded my brain.

"I can see myself as a kid, can watch the events unfolding around me, yet am removed from it somehow. Kind of like the omniscient third person of novels."

"That makes sense. So why the feeling of dream intrusion?"

"Because sometimes they're just too close for comfort." I spoke in a near whisper. "When I was a kid, for years after my accident, I'd have these nightmares that I was running in the rain. It was dark, not just night, but pitch black. The rain seemed to lash out at me, stinging my skin and blinding me. I was terrified, certain that if I stopped running for even a moment, I was doomed." I sat up more in the bed and leaned slightly forward. "I'd awaken soaked through with perspiration, afraid to move, to go back to sleep. When the dreams finally stopped after a couple of years, I forgot about them. Or thought I had. But they came back with a vengeance the night Tara was assaulted."

"I—see. Richard, surely you don't think you could be involved in that nasty situation after all. I mean—"

"No!"

I raised my eyes slowly to hers, and our gazes locked.

"I didn't hurt Tara. I know that. Maybe I had some kind of premonition, or maybe it was coincidence. I don't know." I could see she knew where I was headed. "But what I do need to know, Joyce, is how much of it is just a dream, and how much of it is reality?"

"That's a sobering thought and quite evocative. I suggest we probe this a little deeper—"

I put a finger to my lips and pointed toward the open door.

"My mother." I mouthed.

Seconds later she and Nicole entered the room. I could tell from the look on my mother's face that she was bursting with excitement, but it quickly paled when she spotted Joyce. It took several minutes to reassure her that the doctor was there as a friend, not my physician, and that I was fine. When she was satisfied nothing was being kept from her, and after a good deal of fussing with my blanket and pillows, she launched into a description of their visit to the gallery.

Analisa "Annie" Tanner is an open, gregarious individual who literally thrives on gossip. It is one of the few failings of a woman who is ordinarily sane and completely sensible. My father found the trait endearing, looking to her stories as a form of entertainment, while I'd often thought it rather annoying. When she wanted to, Mother made an excellent storyteller, but that was only as long as she concentrated hard enough to stay on track and keep from embellishing details. Other than the professor who knew how to create marvelous games with his imagination, I'd never known anyone quite like my mother who could take a two minute event and turn it into a novella. Now, as she embarked on her tale, I shifted uncomfortably on the bed and prepared myself.

"We picked Janet up then decided to grab a sandwich before going to the Arts Festival, and boy did that turn out to be a good thing." Mother smiled and nodded to Nicole who simply smiled in return as she pulled up a chair for the older woman.

"Thank you, darling. That's sweet of you." She seated herself on the edge of the chair, leaning forward in anticipation. "Edmund was still at the university, you know, so it was just us girls. Anyway, we went to the Snack Shack because it was closest, downed our sandwiches, then rushed off to the gallery. Nicole told us about your wonderful collection, giving us a preview of what we would see, and as she was talking about it, Janet seemed to become rather nervous. I asked if there was something wrong, if she felt okay, and she just pooh-poohed it the way she does." Mother inhaled deeply as excitement and nervous energy propelled her from her chair.

"I know you've never been particularly fond of the way I drag out stories, dear, so I'll try to be brief." She strode to the foot of the bed, whirled back around to face me, and grabbed the railing.

"I think your collection is wonderful," she cried. "From the moment I entered the gallery, I knew who owned the show." She glowed with pride as she looked down at me.

"The portrait of that lovely girl is genius. I could tell Janet thought so as well. I heard her utter a little cry as her hand went to her throat. Nicole and I nearly had to drag her away. With each painting, we became more and more touched by your talent, Richard dear. Your father would be so proud. And Janet," Mother clapped her hands together in joy. "She was so overwhelmed by it all she didn't think she could face you right now. Isn't it exciting, darling? To touch someone to such an extent is surely a wonderful gift."

As she came up for air, I grinned at Nicole who was trying hard to suppress a giggle.

"That's high praise, indeed." Joyce said, rising. "I suppose I'd better go have a look."

"You haven't?" I asked, surprised.

"No time. Patients, you know. So if you'll excuse me, perhaps I can get in a tour before they close for the evening."

Mother saw Joyce to the door, asked again if I was really okay, then practically bounded back to the end of the bed.

"I'm just so thrilled for you, darling!"

"I appreciate your enthusiasm." I told her with a grin. "Are you sure Janet's all right?"

"Oh completely." Mother responded. "I saw her into the house, and she told me that it just broke her heart to think of all you've had to go through. She started talking about when you were a child and the art lessons Edmund had given you. She said she'd always known you had it—I assume she means what it takes to become a truly great artist. Well, living with someone as talented as Edmund, she would know."

I smiled at my mother tolerantly, took Nicole's proffered hand, and settled back to be entertained.

~

Jenny made herself right at home. She pulled up a chair near him and seemed to regard everything he said with interest.

"What's this?" The small girl stood long enough to pull his drawing tablet from beneath her. Reseating herself, she examined the sketches before peering back up at him. "You've quite an imagination, young man."

Richie felt himself blush. It was obvious she was impressed with his handiwork, and the thought made him puff out his chest as he glowed with pride.

"Uncle Edmund taught me. It's just the alphabet. He gave a slight shrug, hoping she would be even more impressed by his modesty.

She was.

"Why, it's not just anything, Richie." Her pretty eyes gazed back down at the book. "Not everyone can make animals into letters. I mean, look at what you've done! Apes, bears, cats, dogs, elephants, foxes— and you've drawn them so well. My daughter would love this."

"You have a daughter?" Richie found it difficult to believe she could

be that old. She wasn't much bigger than Mary Rogers, at least in height.

"Yes, I have. She's a bit younger than you are, but I'm sure you'd get along. She likes to draw, too."

He and Jenny continued to discuss drawing, **Tom Sawyer**, and the possibility of his meeting her daughter. She never once gave the impression she was bored by his company, and the more they talked, the more he grew to like her.

He wasn't sure how long she'd been there when his aunt came into the room, but the moment she did, he knew there was going to be trouble of some kind.

"I heard voices—" Janet Drake's face went from her usual rose to white in a matter of seconds when her eyes fell on Jenny. One hand clutched at her throat as though she were choking while the other sought the doorjamb for support.

"What are you doing here?" She demanded of the girl, her tone even angrier than it had been earlier when Lily was there.

Jenny appeared unaware of the rage that seemed to pour from his aunt. She slowly turned toward the door, smiled sweetly, and answered in the same friendly manner she'd been using with him.

"Hello, Mrs. Drake, I was just looking for the professor. I was told at Lambert that he might be home, so I thought I'd stop by." Jenny rose from the chair, stretched her arms high over her head, and threw the boy a wink. "Your nephew and I have been having a lovely conversation."

Aunt Janet frowned at him then, the expression so fierce it made him shrink back against the wall.

"As you can see, my husband is not home." The voice was like ice, and Richie could tell Jenny felt the chill as well. She wrapped her small arms protectively about her as she gradually moved away from the chair.

"Yes, well, then perhaps I could leave him a message?" Jenny tried to remain undisturbed, but Richie could tell she was upset. The moment her arms returned to her sides, she'd started to clench and unclench her hands.

Aunt Janet nodded toward the desk. "Suit yourself." She told the girl stonily. "Write your note and I'll escort you to the door."

It was a dismissal, plain and simple. Janet Drake made it known that she did not approve of the girl and was anxious to see her leave. This was something Richie couldn't understand at all. His aunt always seemed to like everyone, even some of the most boring teachers and students that would drop by. Yet here she was, standing like a stone statue, her eyes cold and hard as she watched Jenny dash off her note.

When Jenny was finished, she tore the paper from the pad, neatly folded it, then tried to hand it to his aunt. Again, Richie couldn't believe

Aunt Janet's frosty expression or the hostility with which she regarded Jenny.

"Just place it on the desk," Janet said, refusing to touch the paper in the girl's outstretched hand.

The smile remained fixed on Jenny's pretty face. With a shrug of her shoulders, she did as she was told, then turned back around to Richie.

"Keep up the good work, kiddo. Maybe you'll be a famous artist one day."

Richie grinned back at her, nodding. He'd wanted to talk to her some more but knew better than to even suggest it. Whatever was between this girl and his aunt, he wanted to stay out of it. Besides, if she was friends with Uncle Edmund like she'd said, he'd see her again sooner or later.

The moment the two left the room, Richie found he could breathe a little easier. He knew better than to eavesdrop, but having already gotten away with it once that day, didn't see why he shouldn't break the rules again.

Once the sound of their footsteps receded far enough along the hallway that he was certain they wouldn't return, he jumped up from the window seat and tip-toed to the open doorway. Like before, he felt a little guilty for this breach of privacy, but his curiosity was just too strong to be denied.

The voices were too low for him to hear most of the words, and the little he could hear only added to his confusion. His aunt was not simply angered by Jenny's visit but downright furious. Nothing that was said seemed to shed a light on the problem between the two, so Richie was still in the dark as to why his aunt reacted so strangely to the girl.

Just as he pulled his head back inside the den, his aunt's voice rang out shrilly.

"I've no idea what you're trying to pull with Charlie and Lily, young woman, but you shan't get away with it. And stooping so low as to try to involve my husband will only work against you."

So this was the girl that was causing all those problems for Charlie, Richie thought, a smile upon his face. He might be just a kid, but after the little while in her company, he could easily understand how a guy like Charlie might get involved with Jenny. True, he hadn't gotten a good look at the other girl, but somehow he didn't believe she could begin to compete. Lily had seemed nasty and vindictive even when his aunt had been trying to help her. Jenny, on the other hand, had maintained her cool despite the way Aunt Janet spoke to her. This alone gave her high marks in his book.

Grown-ups!

Shrugging, he started back to the window seat when his eyes caught the folded paper on the top of his uncle's desk.

Did he dare look at it? Eavesdropping was one thing, opening someone's private letters something else.

He went back to the door, peering quickly out into the hallway to make sure everything was safe. There was no sign of either woman, no sound coming from the house except for the constant tock, tock of the grandfather clock in the nearby living room.

Returning to the desk, he stared at the neatly folded paper for a moment, then snatched it up. Turning it over and over again in his hands, he weighed the consequences of what he was considering.

Maybe if the summer hadn't been so boring, if Frank hadn't gotten the chicken pox and Mary had been more inclined to play spy and adventure games than kick him, he would never have thought about it. But it was too late to turn back now.

He carefully unfolded the paper, keeping the crinkling sounds to a bare minimum. After casting a glance over his shoulder, he turned his attention to the words printed on the paper, a huge smile enveloping his face.

Maybe Uncle Edmund hadn't forgotten his promise to set up a spy adventure after all. It was the same kind of message he always used for the games, so maybe he'd asked Jenny to join in since his other friends had copped out on him.

He read the cryptic message once more before refolding the paper and placing it back where Jenny left it. As always, he'd carefully memorized every word, and the thrill of excitement had him humming as he half-skipped to the window seat and picked up his book. But instead of going back to reading, he started imagining all the wonderful possibilities the game may have in store for him.

He was still in the midst of his daydreaming when his aunt came quietly into the room. She didn't even glance in his direction, just went straight to the desk and picked up Jenny's note. He saw her look of confusion and frustration as she read the words, couldn't help but notice the anger that followed when she refolded the paper and tossed it back upon the desk. She left the den without a word, her feet sounding heavy as they carried her down the hallway toward the back of the house and her office.

Part of him believed he should have told her that it was just the beginning of another adventure game. But after the day they'd been having, and this unusual show of temper in his aunt, he wasn't about to own up to his deceit. Naw, he'd wait, let Uncle Edmund fill them both in on the details that night at supper. By then Aunt Janet was sure to have returned to her normal good humor, and he wouldn't have to run the risk *of being punished for peeking at the message. In the meantime, he would have a head start trying to figure out the clues.*

Jumping up, Richie carefully placed the note on the desk so his uncle would immediately see it when he came into the room. Positioning it as strategically as possible, he tried to erase his aunt's anger from his mind and concentrated instead on the upcoming game and the hidden meaning of the words that kept replaying within his brain:

"The tree flowers, the swan sings,
And the white lady cries no more.
Darkness nears at eight o'clock,
Pluck a rose from off the stalk,
And head for the distant shore."

Chapter 20

The television awakened me the following morning long before the nurses had begun their rounds. I'd been asleep, wrapped deeply in memories of the past, prepared to play one of Uncle Edmund's wonderful games, when the blast of the TV rudely brought me to consciousness. There was no time to ponder the dream or try to figure out how much of it was based on actual events; even the warmth of nostalgia was quickly erased as I fumbled with the remote control and reduced the sound.

My mother gazed at me apologetically from a nearby chair, flushed from embarrassment when a couple of nurse's aides flew through the door. She shrank back in her seat without a word. Since she couldn't sleep, she'd decided to come in early to keep me company. She'd become bored waiting for me to awaken and switched on the TV. But in the quiet hospital, the volume was far louder than she'd expected. In trying to remedy the situation, she'd pushed the wrong button. This succeeded in not only awakening me, but also half the patients on this end of the hall.

She sat properly contrite as I submitted to the hospital routine, waiting until we were alone before she addressed the problem.

"I'm sorry, dear, but I was just so anxious to hear the news." She practically wriggled on the bedside chair. "You see, last evening when I was on my way to the Drake's, I heard the most remarkable report on the radio. It seems they might have discovered a body in the gazebo's foundation."

I felt the blood drain from my face. *"They've what?"*

"Well, you know how badly the park was damaged," she began slowly. "It seems that with the structure down, and the foundation in such poor condition, it was decided they should repair it before starting to rebuild. I'm not in construction, of course, but that seems very sound reasoning to me."

"Mother," I said patiently. "The point."

She seemed on the verge of a sulk, but the frown was quickly replaced by her excitement.

"I don't know all the details, but I assume they had a jackhammer or something breaking up the old concrete. Anyway, one of the workers found what he thought was a bone among the debris. The project shut down until the police and coroner's office arrived. Until they determine whether it's human or not, the city's at a standstill—at least as far as the gazebo is concerned." She reached for the remote which was affixed to the bed rail.

"Anyway, I imagine they want to get it all rebuilt before the Labor Day shindig. None of the other parks are big enough." She pressed in the number for the local station. "You mind?" She asked, her finger hovering over the volume button.

"Carefully." I warned. "I want to know what's going on as much as you do. What I don't want is a riot."

Mother grinned, her playful expression making her look much younger than her fifty odd years.

After adjusting the volume, her hand remained on the rail, and I picked it up, amazed at how small and fragile it seemed. Raising it to my lips, I kissed the back of her hand.

"Oh you silly!" She feigned embarrassment, but I could tell she was touched by the gesture.

"Since the storm five days ago, the citizens of Linden have been trying to pick up the pieces of their lives." The anchorwoman gazed seriously into the camera. "Despite the devastation in University Park, the city improvised with its Independence Day celebrations, bringing a bright spot and ray of hope to all those who have suffered."

"This sounds more like one of those tabloid shows than the news."

"Sh-sh!" Annie Tanner pulled her hand from mine and placed all her attention upon the TV.

"Now, the community is once again shattered by a grisly discovery in University Park. We're live with Brent Bradley reporting from the park."

"Thank you, Renee." Bradley's pretty-boy looks made his somber expression look like a parody. I wanted to comment about this to my mother, but she was too caught up in the tabloid sensationalism of the reporting style to even notice how melodramatic they were making the situation.

Not that I wasn't interested. The park, the gazebo, were my favorite spots in the city. I couldn't begin to count the number of times I'd painted the area, roamed its pathways, or sat dreaming in the gazebo. After all these years, the magic of the place still remained. Perhaps the wildness and untamed woods were gone, but it was, and would forever be, my special place of adventure.

"That's right, they began the excavation this morning at dawn, Renee," Bradley was saying. He appeared to be some distance from the foundation, the area directly behind him ringed with yellow tape and posted with uniformed officers.

"The painstaking work could be likened to that of an archeologist on a dig, from what I understand." The reporter continued. "The workers have to be careful not to disturb the remains—which, the authorities are now certain are human. There has been some speculation that the individual might be a victim of the Linden Stalker, the man—"

"Good heavens!" My mother's hand went to her mouth as she stole a look at me.

I could see the terror in her eyes and sensed what she was feeling more than she could ever realize.

"It's all right, Mom." I told her quietly. "I know all about it."

"K-know...about...how?"

"I'll tell you later, right now—"

"It appears as though something's happening. We have a lot of activity at the site of the dig. Some of the workers have moved away—they seem to be very upset. Perhaps we'll be able to have a word with one—uh, now the stretcher is being brought up, so they have evidently found what they were searching for. If you can hold on for a moment, Renee, we'll try to get the story from one of the men who were in on the dig."

While Bradley was off pursuing the workmen, the station went to a commercial break. The moment the ad came on, Mother turned to me.

"Tell me." Although she spoke the words calmly, I knew the emotion that lay behind them.

Without a great deal of preliminary details, I told her the story very simply.

"So you see, the Drakes were right in telling me when they did. If I'd heard the story from Hargrave—"

"That monster!" Mother said vehemently. "Always poking around where he didn't belong. I'll never forgive him for trying to interrogate you when you were so ill. He had some nerve, but after your father got through with him, well, I'm surprised he still works in law enforcement."

I didn't bother to tell her that I doubted that much intimidated the inimical detective. She was studying me closely, her face filled with fear and concern.

"It's just a story, Mom." I told her reassuringly. "A tale about what happened to a little boy a long time ago."

"But you're that little boy, Richard. And we-we never—"

I shoved down the side rail and slowly lowered my feet to the floor. She was in my arms before I'd left the bed.

"It's okay. I can accept what happened. I'm not separating into different personalities, that's not what I meant by referring to myself that way." I tenderly took her chin and raised her eyes to mine. "I was the boy, yes, but the man hasn't been adversely affected. Trust me."

She nodded tearfully, took the tissue I offered her, and hugged me tightly once more before releasing me.

"Ha-have you any questions?"

"We're back." The anchorwoman quickly summed up what had been going on in University Park then deferred to their remote operation.

I shook my head in response to my mother's inquiry and pointed toward the screen. She nodded with a barely audible sigh of relief.

"We're here with Miles Billings who just a few moments ago was assisting in the excavation of the body from the foundation of University Park's old gazebo. Mr. Billings, can you tell us what all the excitement was about?"

The man stared white-faced into the camera, not uttering a sound.

"Mr. Billings?" Reporter Bradley gave a hesitant smile before covering the mike and whispering to the workman who looked like he was in shock. Coming out of the off-mike caucus, Bradley's face had turned a rather unattractive shade of red.

"It seems Mr. Billings would rather not talk about his experience." Bradley and the cameraman moved away from the unfortunate workman in pursuit of another quarry. Even before the reporter got the other man to face the mini-cam, I recognized him.

Detective Jack Hargrave's steely grey eyes raked over Bradley in contempt. He lifted the yellow tape sealing off the area and gave the younger man a look of defiance, challenging him to follow.

Bradley was obviously smarter than he looked. Remaining outside the work zone, he prepared himself for a difficult interview.

"Detective, can you tell the citizens of Linden what is happening now? We know a body has been discovered, but can you fill us in on the details?"

Hargrave pulled a stick of gum from the pocket of his typically wrinkled suit coat and slowly unwrapped it, his eyes never leaving the reporter's face. Narrowing those icy grey orbs, he stared at the camera and popped the gum into his mouth.

"You seem to know about as much as I do, Bradley." He said stonily. "You've been on this beat enough, you tell me what's gonna happen now."

Bradley swallowed audibly, clearly regretting he'd stopped this particular police officer. Nonplussed, the younger man nearly dropped the microphone. But before things got completely out of hand, Hargrave decided to turn professional. He grabbed up the mike, kept his eyes glued to the camera, and flashed an apologetic smile.

"As I'm sure you understand, this discovery has come as quite a shock. I apologize for being so short a moment ago, Brent. Of course I'd be happy to answer your questions."

The reporter's recovery time was remarkable. Taking the microphone back from the detective, he tried not to show his relief in this sudden turnaround.

"We appreciate that, Detective. Are there any details you can share with us?"

Hargrave's arrogant stance and smug expression succeeded in diminishing the young reporter's confidence in himself. The detective leaned in toward the mike, the power of his physical presence causing both the cameraman and Bradley to take a step backward.

"What we have is the skeletal remains of a child or small woman. Until the coroner has the opportunity to examine the remains, we won't know for certain. We'll try to make a positive ID through dental x-rays. If that fails, we have a few pieces of jewelry that were discovered in the same area as the body."

"I see. Do you believe there is any validity to the rumor that this might be a victim of the Linden Stalker?"

Hargrave raised his expressive eyebrows, squared his meaty shoulders, and looked directly at the reporter.

"I wasn't aware there were any rumors, Brent. Something you guys started?" He asked, sarcastically. He turned back to the camera. "The pouring of the foundation and that rather unfortunate period of time in the city's history just happen to coincide. We will, of course, be checking our records for cases involving missing persons—"

"Good morning." Nicole Grant smiled brightly as she entered the room. "I see you've got on the local news. Isn't this remarkable?"

Today she was wearing a soft yellow sundress that swept just past her knees and she'd pulled her golden brown hair into a ponytail that hung in tiny curls to the top of her shoulders. She looked cool and as sunny as her smile—and also quite beautiful.

She gave me a kiss on the top of my head, giggling in response.

"Getting fuzzy up there. You'll be back to your old self in no time at all."

I pulled her down for a better kiss, temporarily forgetting my mother's presence and the drama going on at the park. Her lips were as soft and warm as I remembered them from when—five days ago?—it seemed like a lifetime. And yet, even in those few seconds when our lips met, I felt again that pull, the invisible tether that seemed to connect us.

"When you two come up for air, I'll give you the lowdown," Mother was saying. The amusement in her voice matched the approval on her face—something I'd never seen before in regard to one of my relationships.

"Excuse me, Annie, but your son can be rather forceful." Nicole blushed, pulling away from me and going to stand next to my mother's chair.

"Just like his father, I'm afraid." She agreed. "I'd begun to wonder if he had any of his father's good sense and am glad to see it was inherited after all. Just took its own sweet time coming out." She smiled at Nicole's bewildered expression and laughed at my threatening one. "You almost look fierce with that bald head, darling, but give it a rest. You and I both know I'm right."

It was her subtle way of telling me what she never had before; she hadn't liked any of my other girlfriends, but Nicole was a keeper. Unless Nicole mentioned it, Mother had no way of knowing how new our acquaintance was or how quickly we'd been drawn to one another. But Annie Tanner was not one to deal in trivialities. Once, a long time ago, she'd told me she would always know what was best for me at a glance. Today she'd reaffirmed that statement.

While they were discussing the details regarding the skeleton of University Park, I was wondering how Nicole and I would go on from here. The tie we both had to Jenny brought us together, and the diagnosis of the tumor created the means of making that bond even tighter. But now that the operation was over, my dependence on her at an end, would what we knew about one another be enough to form more than this tentative relationship we'd begun? After all, searching for Jenny was hardly the foundation on which to build a lasting relationship.

"So this discovery might have something to do with a twenty year old case? How fascinating!" Nicole set her purse on the stand, then turned back to my mother. "It's so incredible. Who'd have thought?"

Who'd have thought, indeed. It was almost eerie to think that some poor individual had been lying beneath the gazebo all these years, the sight of family and community activities. It was like dancing on someone's grave!

"Could be the body of a child or a small woman." My mind reran Hargrave's statement, the information suddenly very important.

As I was busily reaching at straws, an aide came in with a couple of balloons attached to a large jade plant. Before she set it on the stand along with the fresh flowers from my mother and the Drakes, she handed me the card.

"Give me a call when you're feeling better Rich." It wasn't signed, but it didn't have to be.

"Ooh, that's beautiful. Who's it from?" Mother got up to examine the plant.

"Chuck Stinnet."

"Really?" She said, surprised. "Must've had one of his lady friends pick it out." She looked over the plant, then said, "Now you've got someone to keep you company, I think I'll run and get some breakfast. I'd better call Janet while I'm at it. I wasn't the only one unable to sleep last night. She and Edmund were up past three in the morning. Probably the reason I had trouble sleeping in the first place." She came over and placed a kiss on my forehead. "I'll be back in a little while."

She'd no sooner walked out the door than in walked Dr. Jerome Astin. This was the first time I'd seen him since right before surgery, and I held out my hand to thank him.

"You're quite welcome, Richard." He said, setting aside his clipboard. "Now let's take a look at you."

Astin gently removed the bandages and probed my scalp with his fingers.

"You're coming along nicely. A few more weeks and your hair will cover the scar, and the whole thing will be but a memory." He stood back and regarded me thoughtfully. "The medicine keeping the discomfort down?"

"Yeah, it hasn't been too bad. Will the migraines return?"

He picked up my chart and flipped back through the pages.

"They're related to an incident twenty-one years ago, are they not?"

I nodded. "I understand you treated me then as well."

Astin drew the extra chair to the side of the bed, acknowledged

Nicole's presence, then sat down.

"Dr. Noland tells me you don't remember much about that summer," he said, peering at me over the top of his glasses. Removing them, he placed the glasses into a case in his breast pocket.

Doctor-patient confidentiality, huh? I made a mental note to question Joyce about it.

"No, I don't. But lately some of the memories have returned. As far as your taking care of me, I'm afraid I still draw a blank on that."

"Now here I thought I was an unforgettable character." Astin's face broke into the grin that was so reminiscent of the actor Raymond Burr. "However, after the trauma and the coma, I don't find it difficult to believe. I, on the other hand, remember it all quite clearly."

"Really?"

I watched as the doctor pressed the nurse's call button. After he'd ordered a replacement bandage which would be "a bit smaller than the old one," I geared myself toward the refusal of my next request.

"Would you mind sharing the information?" I asked, switching off the television to eliminate the chance of distraction.

Although Nicole knew nothing about the subject being discussed, she sat quietly by, not uttering a word. I figured explanations could come later, and rather than filling her in and possibly missing out on this opportunity, decided it would be better to seem a little rude at the moment than to lose a chance that might never come again.

Astin glanced at his watch. "I have a little time, so why not. What would you like to know?"

I gave him what I hoped was my friendliest grin.

"Anything you can tell me."

Dr. Astin nodded, his expression contemplative. "As you know, you were in pretty bad condition by the time you got to the emergency room. Besides the skull fracture, broken collar bone, and numerous contusions, you were suffering from shock and exposure. Shortly after your arrival, you began having seizures, and we nearly lost you."

"I almost died?" Inhaling had become difficult. Nicole noticed my distress and was at my side in an instant.

"Perhaps you shouldn't—" She began.

"I have to know." I answered calmly. "Please go on, Dr. Astin."

Though he appeared reluctant to continue, he did as I requested. "It happened twice. The first time was right after you were brought into the ER." He sighed deeply. "God only knows how long you'd lain out in the storm before Edmund Drake found you. He'd done his best to cover you until the ambulance arrived, but between the trauma of the head injury and the—er, let's just say you were one sick little boy. We tried our best to stabilize you, but you just started to slip away." He looked at me long and hard. "That time there was an entire emergency room staff to keep you alive. The next, well, I'd say that one was something of a miracle."

Dr. Astin rose to his feet, sighing heavily as he moved about the small room. He looked so much like the famous actor that, for just a moment, I felt as though I was watching some kind of production. The impression vanished when a nurse came in with a tray containing all the paraphernalia necessary to rebandage my head. The doctor took the tray, dismissed her with a slight smile, and returning to my side, set about preparing the gauze pads and tape.

"The second time," he said, picking up the story, "I believe was two or three days later. As you know, you remained comatose for nearly two weeks, and during those first few days, the prognosis was extremely poor. You didn't seem to respond to stimuli, and it was the general opinion that you would not recover." Noticing my expression, he smiled kindly. "I'm sorry, Richard. Perhaps Miss Grant is right, and we should postpone this discussion until you're stronger."

"No, no. I'm fine, really. Please, go on."

Was this the information I'd been missing all this time, the link that pulled it all together? If it was, I needed to know now. I didn't want him to stop his story just because I may have lost all the color in my face, and my hands had suddenly gone numb.

"If you're certain." He finished the bandaging, put the extra gauze and tape back on the tray, then stepped away from the bed. He appeared to be looking to Nicole for direction and, bless her, she just smiled and nodded.

"Yes, well, as I was saying, the next time occurred a few days later."

"Let me explain something first." He folded his hands in front of him. "Your parents or the Drakes were constantly at your side, refusing to leave you alone even for a moment. Now, the Drakes had gone home earlier that morning to get some sleep, but your parents refused to budge. I know that during those two days neither had more than a couple hours of sleep between them. They wouldn't eat, either, and combined with all their worrying about you, they were beginning to show major signs of fatigue.

"The entire staff had been working on them, trying to get them to eat, to get some rest. Finally, one of the nurses was able to convince them it would be in your best interest for them to take care of themselves. She offered to remain with you until either the Drakes returned, or they got back from the cafeteria."

The sun coming in through the blinds put zebra stripes across Astin's body, placing his eyes in shadows and making his expression not quite discernible. Still, it was clear from the tone of his voice the incident was something that had continued to haunt him through the years.

"She had good intentions, Richard, but we were shorthanded that day. She hadn't been with you for more than a couple of minutes when she was needed elsewhere. She didn't think it would hurt, figured she'd be gone and back in short duration." He raised his hands palms upward. "Afterward, she swore she was gone no more than five minutes, but that was, of course, enough time for you to go into arrest.

"I was in another wing, had just left a patient, when this young woman came up from behind me and told me that I was needed in your room immediately. I never thought to question her, why should I? I mean, it was obvious from her distress that it was an emergency, and for some reason I've never quite understood, it simply didn't occur to me that there was something out of the ordinary about the situation.

"I don't believe I've ever moved quite so fast. I was in your room in seconds, or so it seemed, ordering a crash cart. Just before the cart arrived, I turned to tell the young woman she'd have to leave. She was standing just inside the doorway, tears running down her cheeks. When our eyes met she said, "You have to save him"." Astin shook his head, a strange look of confusion on his face.

"For years afterward I've thought I imagined the rest—I was so concerned about you, had already turned from her and begun CPR." One of his fine-boned hands rubbed at his eyes. "Perhaps it was my imagination or the stress, but I could have sworn that she'd added "You have to save him so he can save me"."

The sudden gulp of air filled my lungs so quickly it left me choking and gasping for breath. While Nicole gently patted my back, Astin poured me a glass of water which he encouraged me to drink. My heart was hammering inside my chest; my mouth, despite the water, was dry as dust.

"The girl," I croaked. "Did you know her? Could you describe her?"

"I didn't know her, asked your parents and the staff if they'd seen her or knew of her. No one did. As for describing her, that's easy. She looked a great deal like your portrait on display in the Fine Arts gallery."

"Jenny." I whispered, stunned.

This time it was Nicole's turn to choke. As Astin and I tried to help her regain her composure, her lovely face flushed, blanched, then flushed again.

Nicole took in a deep breath, clenched her hands in front of her, and looked hopefully into my eyes.

"Not *your* Jenny," she cried, her deep sapphire eyes filling with tears. "Don't you see? It was my mother. My mother saved your life."

Chapter 21

Nicole's rather remarkable conclusion had broken ground for further discussion, something neither of us thought appropriate with Dr. Astin present. For his part, the doctor was obviously pleased to have the identity of my mysterious benefactor revealed after all these years. He had no reason to question why Jennifer Grant might have saved my life, or how we'd come to this deduction. There was, after all, his statement that the young woman had looked "a great deal" like my portrait of Jenny, so why question the hand of providence? But while my doctor might be satisfied with the discovery, the glances Nicole and I exchanged held many questions.

Jerome Astin cleared his throat, put on his doctor smile, and resumed his role as my physician. He was in the middle of telling me he'd ordered a CAT scan when my mother returned.

"Purely precautionary, I assure you, Mrs. Tanner." Astin said quickly, seeing her sudden look of panic. "We want to make certain everything is clear before sending your son home tomorrow."

It took some doing, but he was finally able to convince Mother that I was coming along very well. She seemed a little more agitated than usual and appeared to be having some difficulty concentrating on what the doctor told her. Several times she asked Astin to repeat what he'd said, then she'd nod and smile in a somewhat distracted manner. While she was concerned for my welfare, it was clear that something else was troubling her, and this change in her behavior had me worried. She was anxious to conclude this interview with my doctor, maybe even anxious to leave the hospital entirely.

"Perhaps you should go on back to the Drakes and try to get some sleep." I suggested after Astin had gone. "You look exhausted."

"I *am* tired," she admitted. "But I really hate to leave you, dear. I know how boring it can be in the hospital. Besides, Richard, I feel better being with you. It's horrible how the imagination works overtime when I'm not here."

I could tell she was deliberately avoiding what was really bothering her. Even Nicole was perceptive enough to see this.

"Look, I've an errand to run," Nicole said, with a sly wink at me that was intercepted by my mother.

"Oh dear, am I that transparent?" Mother put a hand on Nicole's arm to stop her from leaving. "You don't need to go."

"It's all right, really. If you want to speak with Richard alone, I understand."

I watched the little drama being played out before me with interest. Both women were so concerned about not offending the other that it was really quite touching. Nicole had just as quickly become a fan of my mother's as Mother and I had been taken by Nicole's unique charm and compassion.

"No, no." Mother protested. "You thought that was why—not at all, Nicole." Sinking onto the edge of the chair, she laughed a little nervously. "It's not that I didn't want to speak while you were here, dear, it's that I didn't want to say it at all."

I knew from the tone of the conversation and my mother's propensity to go off on tangents that it would be better to nip this in the bud. With a tolerant smile, I reached out for one of the hands she was wringing in her lap.

"Spill it, Mom. What's going on?"

"This is going to sound terrible, but here it is. It's Trifles and Treasures. That's my little gift shop," she told Nicole with a smile. "We started the place about ten years ago when things were just beginning to boom down in Branson. Since then it's built up quite a business. Anyway, when Rick died—Richard's father—I took on an assistant as well as a salesclerk, a nice young thing with stars in her eyes. Anymore that's the place for it, you know, with all those theaters going up. They're calling it the new Nashville, or something like that." She grimaced when

I started to roll my eyes. "Anyway, it seems that while I've been away, the little gal—the clerk—finally managed to get some work at one of the theaters, and Edna, my assistant, never bothered to replace her. On top of that, I just found out Edna closed up the shop a week ago and won't go back to work until I return. Talk about unreliable!" My mother shook her head. "I was certain when I hired Edna that she would be able to handle anything, whether I was there or not. Discovering now that she has a problem with a shop full of people, well, needless to say I'm not very pleased. Too bad Edna wasn't the one to run off to the theater. Even as young as she was, I think the girl could have managed Trifles better."

"So you need to get back home," I said solemnly. The pained look on her face was almost too much to bear. "It's okay, Mom. You heard Dr. Astin. I'm getting out of here tomorrow."

She nodded. "True. But you and I both know that it will be several weeks before you're truly up to par. In the meantime, who's going to look after you?"

It didn't take a genius to see where she was headed. Nicole gazed at me over the top of my mother's head, her face turning a lovely shade of pink.

"I mean, Edmund is still busy with the summer session, and Janet has so much catching up to do because of our trip that neither of them will be able to look in on you much. Chuck Stinnet is simply unreliable even in the best of times, and it would be far too much of an imposition to ask Nicole here. She has her grandfather to consider."

Now I was blushing.

"Mother, please. I'm perfectly capable of taking care of myself."

"Of course you are, dear. Under ordinary circumstances. But you've just undergone a very dangerous surgical procedure. No, no, it would be better for me to stay here." She rose, and coming over to the bed, began to readjust the blanket and pillows. "It will give me a chance to fuss over you a little. And when you've regained your strength..."

As much as I adored my mother I didn't want to spend the next couple of weeks cooped up with her in my apartment. We were bound to get on one another's nerves, and I had no desire to ruin what I'd always felt was a wonderful relationship.

"Annie, if I may?" Nicole touched her on the shoulder to get her attention. As my mother turned to her, Nicole gave me a hesitant smile. "My grandfather is scheduled for an out-of-town business meeting all next week. Besides, as I told you before, he has an assistant who is also his constant companion." She took my mother's hands within her own. "Checking in on Richard is no problem for me—"

"I couldn't ask you to give up your time—"

"You're not asking. I'm offering." Nicole lowered her eyes. "It should be obvious by now that I don't mind keeping your son company."

It was exactly what my mother wanted to hear. It not only got her off the hook without making her feel like she was deserting me, but she looked as though she'd made the coup of the century. While she went off to phone the unreliable assistant, Nicole and I laughed nervously at the less than subtle attempt at matchmaking.

"Maybe when she gets back we could go out on the sun porch." Nicole said, recovering with a grin. "It's a beautiful day and the fresh air is bound to do you some good."

"Along with the other patients and visitors who just might keep Annie Tanner from embarrassing us even more." I wiped a tear from my eye. "I'm afraid she's never been very good at hiding her motives. With one exception, she's always been pretty transparent."

Even while we laughed I wondered how Mother had managed to hide what she'd known about my accident all these years. Perhaps it had been the added strength and conviction of my father, or maybe it was as simple as the natural instinct of a mother to protect her child.

The thought made the need and desire to discuss these things even stronger. I was suddenly eager to share the story with Nicole and to get her thoughts and reactions, as well as talk about how and why her mother might have been able to save my life. But since it was something I'd rather not speak about in front of my mother, it didn't appear as though there would be much opportunity for the conversation in the near future.

The remainder of the morning was uneventful, the highlight about an hour spent on the sun porch. This proved an excellent diversion for all of us and succeeded in taking Mother's attention off my relationship with Nicole.

It was one of those rare July mornings with little to no humidity, the air fresh with a clarity and sky so blue it filled you with energy. As we sat soaking up the warmth of the sun we were entertained with more stories of my mother's vacation—until her interest waned as she was drawn by the discussions going on around us.

It seemed the entire hospital was abuzz with news of the discovery in University Park, and there was little doubt the body was yet another victim of the Linden Stalker. At first, the talk made my mother visibly uncomfortable; she kept stealing sidelong glances at me to see my reactions to what was being said. But, gradually, her fondness for intrigue got the better of her, until she finally moved her chair so she would be closer to the action.

"She's quite a lady." Nicole whispered, leaning in close to me.

"That she is." I grinned, taking a look at my mother's face as she listened avidly to the conversation at the next table. She no longer tried to hide her natural curiosity but allowed her interest in the topic to replace her worry and concern for my well-being. I saw this as not only beneficial, but a comfort, believing this show of interest meant she was letting go of the fears that had haunted her these last twenty-one years. Perhaps the professor was right after all. Maybe she did possess more strength than my father and I had given her credit for.

When I turned to Nicole, it was to find she had thrown her head back to the sun. Her eyes were closed, the hint of a smile on her full, sensuous lips.

I studied my companion from the high cheekbones down along the curvature of her jaw to the smooth line of her neck and across the stretch of her bare, lightly tanned shoulders. Against the sunflower color of her dress, the skin of her breastbone had a satiny sheen that was incredibly beautiful.

I took in a deep breath that felt ragged within my throat. The old romantic in me was rearing its head, making no room for denials. I may know very little about the girl next to me, but there was one thing I knew for certain: I was truly falling in love with Nicole Grant.

I may not be able to help the way I felt—not that I wanted to fight it—but there was a way to remedy our knowledge of one another. I cleared my throat to get her attention.

Nicole opened her eyes slowly as her hand sought mine where it rested on the arm of the wheelchair. As our fingers interlaced, she turned to me with the same frankness I'd seen in her face since our first meeting.

"So, what did you think about Astin's story?" I asked quietly.

"It was very intriguing." She readjusted her position, pulling one leg beneath her. Regarding me thoughtfully, she straightened her dress over her knees. "Please don't take this wrong, but I got the impression you might have been one of this Stalker's victims."

"That's what they tell me. My memory is sketchy at best. What I mean is, up until recently I could only recall bits and pieces of that summer. And absolutely nothing related to the incident itself."

"But now some of it is coming back?"

I nodded. "I think so. They come as dreams but are far more realistic. The trouble is figuring out when it's imagination and when it's an actual memory. It's not always easy to distinguish."

"So you don't remember my mother?"

The million dollar question.

In my mind's eye, I saw the professor's home office as it looked when I was a child. "Jenny" was standing nearby, concentrating on my alphabet drawings as she had in my dream. But was it a dream? Could that incident have any basis in reality, or was it simply another example of the past and present colliding within the dream realm?

"Richard?"

I offered her a smile in return for the concern in her voice.

"I don't know. I'm sorry, but that's the best I can do." I shook my head. "I'm trying to make sense of what I'm experiencing, but right now it seems so disjointed. Random thoughts and events with a sequence I'm not certain of."

She squeezed my fingers. "It will come to you. Don't fight it." She grinned, her dark eyes twinkling. "Right now you need to recover your strength. There will be plenty of time to piece things together later. But isn't it interesting to learn that we've yet another link between us?"

I had to admit it was. It also made me even more curious about Jennifer Grant and her possible relationship to my mysterious Jenny. I didn't have the resources available to try to find either of them to get the answers I wanted, but Nicole and her grandfather did. Where before the thought of helping Robert Grant had been abhorrent to me, I now accepted the idea wholeheartedly. I couldn't wait to get out of the hospital and back into shape. I wanted in on this. Maybe by helping them I'd be helping myself in the long run.

After a quiet lunch on the sun porch, we returned to my room to await my appointment for the CAT scan. Throughout the meal, the conversation remained fairly general, and in spite of my mother seeming more thoughtful than usual, we had a pleasant time. It wasn't until we were in my room that she revealed what was bothering her.

"Now they're saying the body's that of a child." She told us the latest gossip in hushed tones, shaking her head sadly over the rumors. "When I think about what happened to you, I just—just thank God that Edmund found you before it was too late." Her eyes brimmed with tears as she came into my arms. "This has brought it all back, the fears, the doubts and indecision. I should be ashamed of my fascination for the subject!"

"It's all right, Mom. I'm fine. You can't let this get to you." This was one occasion where my words could not soothe her.

"And how can I do that? We were lucky, Richard. Some other family wasn't." She pulled away from me and stroked my cheek. "But you're really okay, aren't you? You know what happened and are able to deal with it?"

"I'm not going to fall apart if that's what you're asking. You and Dad taught me a lot about keeping things in perspective, and that's exactly what I'm trying to do."

"And are you able to deal with it as well?" My mother asked, eying

Nicole speculatively.

"I, uh, I think so." Nicole peered at me uncertainly.

"We haven't had a lot of time to discuss it." I interjected. "Mom, you can't beat yourself up over what happened. You weren't even here."

"But we were later. And all those years afterward when we never spoke of it." The pain came straight from her heart. "We never wanted to hurt you, Richard."

All the years of silence, all the times I'd wondered what they were hiding, everything came to the surface revealing an Annie Tanner I'd never seen before. While my mother and I talked about the incident that had long been taboo, Nicole moved a chair near the window to give us some space. Now and again I would glance over to find her looking at us, her deep sapphire eyes glistening with tears. I thought how hard this must be on her. She'd come to me looking for help in finding a possible sister and had been thrust into the middle of a virtual stranger's life crisis instead.

It was surprising how quickly my mother and I were able to lay some of the ghosts from the last twenty-one years. I think I succeeded in relieving her of the fear and guilt she felt for trying to suppress my curiosity and any memories I might have of that summer—and she helped me understand that the rift I'd felt between my father and I had nothing to do with my art, and everything to do with his fear of my memory returning.

Not everything could be resolved in such a short space of time, but we knew we were on the right path. Mother accepted my ability to handle whatever truth I might uncover, while I reassured her that I did not hold the past against them. It offered a form of closure for both of us, something that had been long in coming.

As glad as I was that things were now out in the open, I was even happier when the Annie Tanner I knew and loved wiped away her tears and replaced them with a sunny smile. In no time, she was back to regaling us with her vacation adventures, beaming at Nicole and reeling us both in with every word.

During her story about Stonehenge the phone rang, startling all of us. Mother picked it up and handed it over to Nicole with a curious expression on her face.

Nicole barely uttered a word, but from the way she paled during the primarily one-sided conversation, it was obvious something was terribly wrong.

"I have to go," she said, her voice shaking almost as much as the hand that returned the phone to its cradle.

She grabbed at her purse where it lay on the corner of the stand, nearly knocking over both vases of fresh flowers. Mother was able to catch them before they spilled onto the floor.

"Are you all right?" We both asked her at once, even though it was perfectly clear she wasn't.

"Has something happened to your grandfather?" I started to get up from the bed, but my mother stopped me with a look.

Nicole just stood and stared at us for a moment, her dark blue eyes lost and confused. When she finally focused on me, she shook her head slightly, a single tear running down her cheek.

"I have to go," she said again, this time making good on the statement and heading for the door.

"You stay put." My mother looked at me sternly. "I know you're concerned, but we don't need you collapsing on us. I'll see to Nicole."

With that, she was quickly at Nicole's side, guiding the younger woman out the door.

I hated the feeling of helplessness that came over me as I watched them leave. I'd always felt in control, willing and able to come to the rescue...

The rescue. Would I ever stop thinking in those terms, expecting to be the hero of the day and carrying off the lovely lady into the sunset?

My laugh was self-deprecating, ringing in that tiny hospital room to bounce off the walls and mock me. Where did it come from, this vision I had of myself that I must be some larger than life individual?

"Capable of leaping tall buildings in a single bound." I muttered as I resituated myself on the bed.

Had it anything to do with those adventure games the professor used to organize? I remembered always trying to outsmart the others, trying to be the best, the hero who solved every clue. But surely that alone couldn't be responsible—

"Ready for another test, Mr. Tanner?"

I recognized the technician from radiology and smiled. Her arrival would force—or perhaps it was better to say allow—me to put off this self-analyzation for another time. Procrastinating was something I was becoming fairly good at.

When I returned to my room, I was surprised to find Janet Drake waiting for me. It was the first time I'd seen her since she and Mother returned from Europe, and I was amazed at how gaunt she looked. Instead of doing her good, it appeared as though their vacation had been extremely hard on her health.

"You're looking better, Richard." She gave me a vague kind of smile as she watched the aide help me into bed. "When I was here a few days ago you were still pretty out of it. It's nice to see you up and about."

Janet remained seated in the chair Nicole had taken near the window. The glare of the early afternoon sunlight made her complexion appear pasty.

Squinting, I motioned for her to come nearer which she seemed to do with reluctance.

"It's good to see you, too." I told her, opening my arms for our traditional hug. "Still feeling the jet lag?"

Janet patted my shoulder, took my chin in her hands, and studied my face.

"Can't say I like this new look, dear, but you'll do." This time the grin she gave me was genuine. "Why didn't you let us know what was going on—Oh, never mind. It's over now, and Annie has assured us you're doing wonderfully, that's all that counts. Speaking of your mother, where is she?"

"I imagine she's still with Nicole." I laughed. "Mother seems quite taken with her."

"So I've seen." Janet moved to the chair situated close to the bed. "Do you think that's wise, Richard, this relationship you've developed with Nicole Grant? After all, it was her grandfather who put you here in the first place."

"I've come to look at it as a kind of blessing." I told her. "I must admit it didn't seem that way to me at first, but circumstances and reason prevailed. Think about it. If Grant hadn't gone off the deep end and knocked me out, I may not have found out about the tumor until it was too late."

"That's rather magnanimous of you, Richard. But then, I'd expect nothing less." Lily Reston breezed into the room and over to the bed with barely a glance at Janet. She gave me a very platonic kiss on the cheek and a quick hug that left behind a hint of her musk cologne as she moved away.

"I see you got our gift." She plucked the card off the jade plant and frowned. "I should have known better than to allow Chuckles to handle this. Oh well, where were we?" Her blue eyes narrowed. "Robert Grant," she mused. "If memory serves me correctly, he was Linden's very own version of a mobster."

"I wouldn't exactly call him that," Janet said, eyeing Lily in disapproval. "He was a wheeler and dealer, yes, and was reputed to have quite a volatile temper. But as far as I know it was all perfectly legal."

When Lily shrugged her shoulders, the spaghetti straps of her gauzy sundress fell. As she tugged them back into place, careful not to disturb the precisely formed curls that hung over each perfectly tanned shoulder, she flashed Janet a frown.

"My parents always said he made his money fast and dirty. Not that it matters. What does, however, is how Richard's doing." She seemed to be placing far more emphasis on the words than was necessary, almost as though she was issuing a challenge.

"I'm fine, Lily, thanks. You look terrific. New hairstyle?"

"Not too young for me, is it?" She asked, toying with one of the curls.

"My point about Robert Grant, Richard, is that you must watch out for the man." Janet threw Lily a withering glance. "I realize he's getting up there, but I understand that he employs a bodyguard."

"I've already had the pleasure," I said, recalling muscle-bound Jim's meaty hands as they jerked my arms painfully behind my back.

"Precisely. If any of the rumors about the man have even an iota of truth, I should not want you to be in a position that might prove dange—"

"Janet. And Lily Reston, isn't it?" My mother smiled her greetings. "And here I was worried you might be alone and bored."

Alone and bored might have been better than feeling as though I'd stepped into the middle of a disagreement of some kind. Janet and Lily had been friends long before I'd met Lily; now they were regarding one another with thinly veiled hostility. I didn't understand it.

The memory flashed suddenly into my mind; the hysterical girl in Janet's office, the voice that had gone from raving and out of control to almost brutally calm. I remembered all of it: accusations, suspicion, and a kind of anger that sent a cold chill along the base of my spine.

Memory? Maybe I understood them more than I realized.

"How's Nicole?" I asked, trying to shake off that sudden, uncomfortable revelation.

"I'm not sure, poor thing. I insisted on driving her home since she was so upset. The child hardly spoke all the way there. I never did get anything out of her."

Knowing my mother as I did, I found that difficult to believe. And this, in turn, made me even more concerned about Nicole.

I started to reach for the phone.

"Give it a while, dear. I'm sure she'll call when she's able to collect herself." Mother shook her head sadly. "It's true what they say; when it rains, it pours. I mean, that poor kid was already on the verge of collapse when we left here, and I thought it couldn't get any worse. She'd started coming around in the elevator, not enough to tell me what was going on, but enough that she wasn't leaning on me so heavily." My mother grabbed the railing at the foot of the bed. "She was calming down, you know, and as we rounded the corner to the exit we heard this poor man ranting and raving at the top of his lungs. She said she didn't know him, so I suppose it was what he was yelling that did it."

Annie Tanner seemed totally oblivious to the fact that she had three people listening intently to what she was saying. My mother's eyes glazed over and were looking at some point far beyond this room. The knuckles on her hands turned white with the force of her grip.

"It was that workman they tried to interview this morning. They had him in restraints, and he was still fighting them off, screaming for someone to listen to him. We tried to hurry past, but it was hard not to hear what he was shouting. I mean, you would have to be deaf not to have heard."

"Mom?" I said, trying to call her back. "Mom, what happened? Why was Nicole so upset by this guy?"

She slowly came back into herself, shaking from head to toe as though re-entering her body.

"What he said, of course," she said logically.

"And what was that?" I persisted.

"That they uncovered a girl in the cement. A girl that turned to bones right before his eyes."

Chapter 22

There wasn't much that could follow such a story. Nor did anyone look as though they had any intention of trying to top or refute what Mother had heard. The silence that ensued was almost deafening, the emotional reactions on my companions' faces seeming to come from the very core of their being.

Imagination has been something that's always served me well. I'd reveled in its use as a child, indulged in it through the difficult years of growing up, and incorporated it into every drawing and painting I've ever done. It wasn't difficult for me to imagine the stress those workmen had been under since the discovery of that first bone. Anyone with knowledge of Linden's history and the timeframe when the gazebo was constructed would be able to deduce the obvious: the body was yet another victim of the famed Linden Stalker. Going from there wasn't difficult either.

As far as I knew, I was the only male victim of the madman. Ergo, it only made sense to conclude that the bones in the cement grave belonged to a woman, hence the claim of having seen a girl entombed within the cement. The line of thought seemed reasonable enough to me, the explanation perfectly logical.

But in watching the women, my mother, Janet, and Lily, and their slow process of coming around after the story was told, something kept me from sharing my brilliant conclusions.

I absorbed the reactions of each, the confusion and disbelief on my mother's face, her eyes holding a strange brightness I would only have associated with a high fever; Lily's paleness had increased her beauty, the peach of her blush and nearly turquoise contacts in her eyes the only color in her face. She'd taken in a quick, deep breath then clutched at her throat as her eyes glazed over in alarm; and Janet, with her unusual arched brows that gave her the perpetual look of surprise, stared at my mother, stunned and appalled, her forehead a mass of furrows. It was a story out of a nightmare or a Gothic thriller whose sole purpose was to shock and frighten—cheap theatrical tricks and special effects which were suggestive of much worse than you could ever imagine.

As thought-provoking as it was, I guess I wasn't as receptive as they were; Hargrave's tour of the morgue was likely responsible for that. So I watched and waited, wondering about the horrors each one might be picturing in their mind, and worried about what could be happening with Nicole.

Recovery varied from each woman, and by the time things were back to normal, they'd decided it was time to say good-bye. Little was said to me, even less to one another, but the hostility was gone. It had been an unusual visit, to say the least, but I wasn't complaining.

Because she'd gotten so little rest the night before, I was able to convince my mother to go with Janet. It had been a busy day, and I was tired enough to sleep through what was left of it. An all clear from Astin signaled the confirmation of my release the following morning, and I wanted to be rested and strong enough to handle the event.

If I was checked on throughout the night, which was a reasonable assumption, I couldn't say for certain. Even without the aid of medication, I quickly fell into a kind of drugged sleep, induced no doubt, by the day's activities. It was a deep, peaceful kind of sleep filled with normal dreams that flowed gently one to another to soothe and restore the body for yet another day.

The bed shook violently, startling me and yanking me rudely awake. I was still so dopey that nothing truly registered when I first opened my eyes, so I allowed them to close almost immediately. When the bed jerked again, I forced myself into a sitting position even before my eyes responded to the command to awaken.

"Come on, Tanner, the day's awastin'," said a gravelly voice nearby, the tone harsh and demanding.

The bed quaked again before I was able to focus.

"Okay, okay, I'm awake." I glared at the perpetrator of this vile game, not at all surprised to find Detective Jack Hargrave sitting in the bedside chair glaring back at me. "What the hell are you doing here? And what time is it, anyway?"

Hargrave pushed at the bed again.

"Would you cut that out!" I looked down to find his feet planted against the bed frame. Even in the dim morning light I could see the dirt and mud in the creases of his pants and on the sides of his shoes. There were dusty prints on the sheet where he'd planted his feet, but he made no effort to move them.

"What is it about you that makes people want to protect you so badly?" He shook his head, his narrow grey eyes mere slits in his craggy face.

"Perhaps it has something to do with the fact that I've just had major surgery." I answered dryly as I raised the back of the bed to a sitting position.

"Yeah, well, whatever." He dismissed what I'd said with a thrust of one foot against the bed. This time it barely moved but was still enough to be irritating. He saw my expression, smirked, then slowly removed his feet from the frame.

"Hey, don't get me wrong, Richard, I'm really glad you're on the road to recovery. Personally, it'll save me a lot of work. And believe me, right now I can do with all the help I can get. I haven't been to bed in the last," he consulted his watch. "We might as well call it fifty hours. With the exception of the catnap I took here, sleep and I just haven't been able to connect." He leaned forward, rubbing his face with the backs of his hands as he stifled a yawn. "I'm tired, overworked, underpaid, and not at all happy with the present state of affairs down at the station."

"I sympathize with you—"

"Yeah, I bet you do."

"But I hardly see what any of this has to do with me. If you're here about Tara—"

"That's a score we have yet to settle, Richard, old man. But try again."

"Or what I intend to do about Robert Grant—"

"Ah, we're getting warmer."

It didn't take long to lose your patience when dealing with someone like Hargrave. In my opinion, this was not only how he planned it, but the way he preferred it. The closer you came to becoming a loose cannon, the more he wanted to push and provoke you into going completely out of control. Then he would have you dead to rights. He was the one who held the cards, the man with the power, and if you were smart, that was something you didn't want to forget.

I knew I had an option. I could press the call button and have a nurse in here in a matter of minutes, but what good would it do? He may be forced to leave now, but he'd be back. And would keep coming back again and again until he got what he wanted. Relentless, that was Detective Jack Hargrave. Cool, imperturbable, cynical, and persistent were only some of the adjectives that came to mind. The others didn't bear repeating.

"Okay, so if you're not here to interrogate me about Tara or Grant, then just what, exactly, do I owe this dubious honor, Detective?" I stared him straight in the eyes, refusing to waver even when he gave me his most deadly glare.

He pushed his feet against the chair, tilting it back on two legs. This would have been no easy task. It wasn't one of those utilitarian items with a wood frame and uncomfortable vinyl seat. This chair was heavy duty, the hospital version of a comfortable, upholstered easy chair designed for visitors who might spend hours at a patient's bedside. Yet even as heavy as it was, and as awkward as it appeared to keep at that forty-five degree tilt, Hargrave managed it with ease.

"You'd have to be dead not to know what's been happening," he said with a sneer. "I've come to get your take on it."

"You come here at," I grabbed up my watch from the stand, "At six o'clock in the morn—"

"Three, actually."

"To ask me what I think about what? The body that's been found? Give me a break, Hargrave. Or is it you're so damned fixated on my being guilty of something that you've decided to charge me for this twenty-one year old crime?" I didn't even try to keep the sarcasm and contempt out of my voice. "Go ahead, Detective. Put on the cuffs and drag me down to the station to question me about a life of crime that began when I was ten years old." I held out my wrists in a mocking gesture that succeeded in eliciting a wry smile from the man.

"That's very good, Richard. I've got to hand it to you," he reached into the pocket of his wrinkled jacket and pulled out a stick of gum. "You've a helluva sense of humor. A little droll, perhaps, but who am I to talk?"

"Don't you ever change suits?" I wrinkled my nose in disgust, realizing that the stale odor I'd been smelling was coming from him.

He laughed, a dry, scratchy sound that should have made his throat hurt.

"A clean shirt yesterday afternoon was about all I had time for." He released the chair, and it slammed to the floor. I was surprised the noise didn't bring in the cavalry.

"It's strange that you should connect yourself with the skeleton we found. Don't you think?"

I shrugged, wearying of his game. "Twenty-one years ago the foundation to the gazebo was poured. The timeframe for that and my assault are about the same."

"Not about, *are* the same."

The sun had risen enough to lighten the room considerably. The rays filtered through the slats of the blind, striking Hargrave's eyes and turning them silver. He leaned forward, placed a hand on the bed rail, and gazed at me intently.

"They practically coincide, Richard. The workers finished up just before the storm struck that night. The night you were found."

I could feel the fine hairs on the back of my neck stand up as my spine tensed and goose bumps broke out on my arms.

"Let's play a little game, shall we?"

I didn't bother to retort that we already were. I sat perfectly still, watching his every movement, hanging on to his words.

"We find a body, a skeleton in cement that was poured July first twenty-one years ago." His voice was slow, deliberate, a cadence that was hypnotizing. "Identifying her wasn't hard. You go back twenty-one years, look at the Missing Person's reports, and for an area this size you have what, three maybe four to choose from. Sure, there's always the chance she was dumped here from somewhere else, but that wasn't the Stalker's style. So you go on the assumption that it's someone local, which narrows the possibilities considerably.

"Next you look at the physical descriptions. Not much help in a case like this unless there's something remarkable about the skeleton. In this instance there was. Female between four eleven and five two. Well folks, time to compare and contrast. We've got two missing adult males and two females. The guys we can eliminate right away, the women are another matter. Both of them were small, no taller than five two, so you dig a little deeper, and bingo, we have a winner." He pushed himself out of the chair and began to pace the room.

"Even without dental confirmation we know who we've got because only one of the girls went missing around the correct time. Not only does she meet the skeletal qualifications, but the jewelry reported found at the scene are also specified in the file as being on her person the last time she was seen. So we have a match, and I can confidently move the young lady from Missing Persons to Homicide, a likely victim of the Stalker bastard.

"But something about the case is still bothering me, so I dig even deeper in my memory. And you know what I come up with? You. Little Richie Tanner. You're the connection, the missing link." He eased back onto the chair and stared at me long and hard. I wasn't certain what kind of reaction he was expecting, but the sweat on my brow and upper lip must have been a satisfactory beginning. He actually smiled.

"What it boils down to, Tanner, is that I never forget a face. Sometimes it might take me a while to make the connection, as it did with you, but once I make it, the memories come back as clear as yesterday's news." He narrowed his steely grey eyes as his craggy face maintained its contorted semblance of a grin.

"Jennifer Grant's case had nothing to do with you—Ah, I see I've gotten your full attention now. That's right, Richard. Jennifer Diane Grant, beloved daughter of that nasty old geezer who popped you one the other night. At least now you know why he went off like that when he saw the painting. The old man might be a little senile, but he's still one tough customer.

"Damn," he coughed as he smacked the side of his leg. "I knew there was something about that portrait the moment I saw it, but like with you, I couldn't quite put a finger on it." He reached in his pocket, withdrew what looked like a photograph and tossed it to me.

"Meet the real Jennifer Grant, not some angelic, halo-toting version."

It was a three by five studio portrait of Jennifer with a very small Nicole standing at her side. The royal blue backdrop enhanced the violet of the mother's eyes while it made the daughter's appear almost black. Jennifer Grant's waist-length, chestnut hair hung in waves over one shoulder as Nicole was snuggled close against the other one. The smiles were sweet, the subjects more than simply attractive, yet without that special allure found in either Grant's painting of his daughter or my portrait of Jenny.

Beauty and innocence had been captured in this photograph, a memento of mother and daughter. Jennifer's face seemed to radiate happiness and pride, Nicole's pure contentment. It made me sad to think that none of it had lasted.

I glanced up at Hargrave to find he had put his head back and closed his eyes. His right hand pinched the base of his nose as the left scratched at the stubble of his beard.

So what was I supposed to say? To see? Sure, the resemblance between the women was unusually strong, it was something I'd already discovered. But I hadn't been painting Jennifer Grant—

"The subconscious is a weird thing, you know. There's no explaining how it works or the turns it may take. Two cases with no evident connections, both dead ends that stuck in my craw for years. Then something like this happens and wham! It hits me, and I can't believe it never occurred to me before." Hargrave seemed to be really looking at me for the first time. His mouth quirked up oddly on one side while he ran a hand through his thinning hair.

"You look weird after all that hair. Not at all like your old man."

For a moment I thought he was going to leave me hanging there as a cruel joke, a "choose your own ending" kind of thing. It turned out he'd just been distracted by the vast change in my appearance.

"Wouldn't you say it was a little strange to discover that the principle players in these unrelated cases turned out to be the same—especially if you factor in your current crowd of friends? That wasn't something I'd have been able to guess all those years ago, but maybe it explains my reaction to you a few weeks back. A kind of sixth sense, the way a cop remembers uncooperative or evasive witnesses. And I've got to tell you, Richard, that's all I had to deal with in both cases. Everyone turned deaf and dumb with a suddenness you'd have thought was catching.

"Bottom line. It looks as though both you and Jennifer Grant were in the park at about the same time that night twenty-one years ago. She met up with a murderer, you with a rapist. Which brings us to the really big question: was the perp one and the same?" The intensity of his gaze bore into me, creating ripples of shock that spread from the pit of my stomach as I, too, came to an unbelievable conclusion.

"What have you got hidden inside that brain of yours, Richard Tanner? What really happened to you that night? And more importantly, *what the hell did you see?*"

I swallowed heavily, a sound I was sure could be heard far beyond this tiny room.

"You think I might have witnessed—no," I shook my head in disbelief. "You're wrong. I would have remembered something like that."

He laughed, a cruel, grating sound that increased my discomfort. "After being beaten and raped? Hell, the shock of your own experience was too great for you to handle, Richard, so what makes you think you'd be able to separate the two incidents?"

The overhead light snapped on suddenly, and we both turned startled expressions toward the nurse entering the room.

"Good morning, Mr. Tanner, it's time—" She stopped abruptly, giving Hargrave a withering look. "I thought we'd agreed that you would wait for normal visiting hours, Detective."

"You agreed." Hargrave smirked. "By normal visiting hours I intend to be asleep."

"Something you no doubt robbed my patient of."

"Come on, Sheila." Hargrave coaxed. "This is important."

"So is Mr. Tanner's rest." She moved into the room like a commander overseeing his troops. "And the name is Shelly, not Sheila."

"Shelly" was a tall, statuesque redhead with a knock-em-dead figure. Her clear green eyes bore into the detective with a look that brooked no opposition. Hargrave may have finally met his match in this lovely young nurse.

"If you'll excuse me," I said getting up from the bed. "I'll only be a moment."

Still clutching the photograph of Nicole and her mother, I side-stepped Shelly and darted into the bathroom, glad my mother had thought to buy me a pair of pajamas for my hospital stay. I closed the door before turning on the light, believing it might muffle the discussion going on outside. But not even the flushing of the toilet could completely shut out the sound of their voices—Hargrave's insistent, bordering on anger; Shelly's cool and professional, yet still commanding respect—she expected to be obeyed.

I splashed some cold water on my face, catching sight of it in the mirror as I reached for a towel.

Hargrave was right, I did look weird. My dark eyes were in stark contrast to the paleness of my face with its day's growth of beard, and my head had an outgrowth of peach fuzz with an as yet indeterminate color, all of it adding to the strangeness of my appearance.

I dabbed at the water while churning the latest information over in my mind. It was impossible to believe Hargrave's scenario, that I might have seen or been a part of anything other than my own encounter with a madman. Besides, if I had been a witness to a murder, wouldn't the killer have made certain I was dead and not just hoped the beating he'd given me had accomplished that for him?

I took another look at the photo, drinking in all the details.

Suddenly I recalled the vision I'd had after hearing about the assault on Tara. There in the darkness, pummeled by wind and rain, I saw again that wide, flat board, heard the sickening sound as it smashed into flesh, and watched helplessly as a wavering figure collapsed into the mud at the base of the gazebo. I had taken the vision as something my imagination conjured up to go along with the news of Tara's attack, accepted it as fantasy. But what if it wasn't? What if Hargrave was on to something? Was it possible I'd witnessed a murder that resulted in my own assault?

I gripped the rim of the sink, bile rising into my throat.

We weren't talking about just any murder. This was about Jennifer Grant, Nicole's mother, possibly the mother of my Jenny.

Jennifer Grant, the woman Astin claimed saved my life…

My breathing became constricted, blood pounded loudly in my ears.

PORTRAIT OF JENNY

How was it that hearing about myself had seemed so impersonal, as if it happened to someone else, yet the moment another person was involved I suddenly felt the violation?

"Mr. Tanner? Richard? Are you all right in there?"

Shelly's concerned voice echoed oddly in my ears. I took a handful of water and forced myself to swallow it before I answered. I could hear the shush shush of her shoes as she moved away from the door, and taking a deep breath, went out to join her.

Hargrave was gone, something Shelly noted with a kind of smug satisfaction. She spoke very little as she took my vitals, mentioning only that it looked as though it would be a beautiful day. I congratulated her on her success with the detective, and could tell by the look in her eyes that she counted it as a major accomplishment.

"Well, everything looks fine." She smiled. "You'll be out of here by noon. You do have someone to see you home?"

I nodded, thanked her for all her help and kindness, then settled back against the pillows as she left the room. She was no sooner out the door than she popped her head back inside with a rueful smile.

"I forgot to tell you. The detective left you a note. I put it on the corner of the stand." She grimaced. "Sorry." After a less than cheery wave, she was gone for good.

I picked up the sheet of paper, braced myself, and read Hargrave's message.

"Too bad we were interrupted just as we were getting somewhere," it said, the detective's sardonic voice ringing within my head. "I may not trust you, Tanner, but I can't believe you don't want to get to the bottom of this. I expect to hear from you soon."

I wadded up the piece of notebook paper and tossed it toward the trash can. My luck must be changing; I actually made a basket.

Breakfast came and went, and there was still no word from my mother. I was getting antsy, anxious to be back in my own apartment. Within the comfortable, familiar surroundings it would be easier to face the memories that were suddenly rushing at me from all directions. Once home, armed with a notepad and pen, I would start a list of everything I could recall. From there I would try to decipher which were actual memories and which were products of my overactive imagination. Somehow, I had to find the answers—waiting for them to come in their own sweet time was a luxury I no longer had.

With all of this in mind, I thought about giving my mother a call but decided against it at the last moment—just as I'd done when considering a call to Nicole. After all, I was still a little unnerved, and that was something I'd as soon keep from both women. Mother was scheduled to leave for Branson first thing tomorrow morning, and I wanted to keep it that way. If she had any indication there was something going on or troubling me, she would cancel her plans and insist on staying with me until she felt I was well enough to handle things on my own—and knowing my mother, that might mean indefinitely.

As far as Nicole was concerned, finding out that her mother had been dead all these years could not have been easy for her, especially when she'd recently come to believe that the mysterious Jenny was her long lost sister. Having to deal with the possibility that her new love interest—and I sincerely believed I was that—might have witnessed her mother's murder was not an issue she needed to deal with at this time.

I was growing increasingly restless, which only made me aware of how tired I still was. Reason demanded action, but I opted instead to grab a little more sleep. But the moment I closed my eyes, Hargrave's words came back to me in a rush.

There was no escaping the thoughts he'd evoked. Nothing could shut out this sudden overwhelming need to know if what he suspected might be true. And if it was...

"And here I thought you'd be so excited about getting out of this joint that you'd be up and dressed."

My eyes flew open to find Joyce Noland a few feet from the bed.

"Sorry if I startled you," she grinned, sheepishly. "You feeling okay?"

She placed a cool hand on my forehead, and satisfied I wasn't running a fever, turned my head from side to side.

"A little peaked, perhaps, but the bruises are about gone. And what's this? Thinking about growing another beard, Richard? I'd hoped that was just a phase you were going through." Joyce's pale eyes danced merrily behind the thick lenses of her glasses.

I rubbed the bristle on my chin. "Thought I'd wait to shave until after you sprang me. My form of celebration."

She raised an expressive eyebrow. "Really? Well, I suppose in your current condition it would be a fairly safe activity." She handed me a paper off the clipboard she was holding. "These, my friend, are a list of do's and don'ts. There are a few restrictions, but nothing you can't live with, I'm sure. You've been scheduled for an appointment with Dr. Astin a week from Monday, and we'll go from there. If you take care of yourself and stay out of trouble, you'll be back to normal in about a month. Think you can handle that?"

"I'll do my best," I quipped. "Does that mean I'm free?"

Joyce nodded. "As of this moment you are officially released from Linden Community Hospital. Thanks for waiting this time." She laughed; I grimaced. "As soon as you've a ride home, let the nurses know and they'll see you to the door. I can't say I'm sorry to see you go," she smiled. "You had me pretty scared for awhile."

"You're not the only one."

The phone rang, and Joyce turned to go.

"Could you wait for a moment?" I asked, picking up the receiver. With her nod of confirmation, I lifted it to my ear.

"Richard, dear, I'm running a little behind this morning. I hope you haven't been worried." There was a touch of apprehension in my mother's voice. "We've something of a problem—nothing big—just a, er, little irritant is all. But the good news is that Nicole called and should be arriving there soon."

Before I had the chance to say anything, she rushed on.

"She'll see you get home all right and tight, and I'll be there shortly. Keep your chin up," she said, then abruptly hung up.

I sat looking at the phone, feeling as though I'd been caught up in a whirlwind. No, not a whirlwind, a hurricane. Hurricane Annie to be exact.

"Yes?" Joyce looked at me expectantly.

"I'd explain if I could figure it out myself," I told her.

"Your mother?"

I nodded. "Oh well, I'll find out soon enough. Do you have a couple of minutes?"

Joyce consulted her watch, then gave me the go-ahead. As briefly as possible, I filled her in on the details of my early morning visit with Detective Hargrave. She listened attentively, her eyes growing larger and more intent by the minute.

"I've a friend, a psychologist who specializes in hypnosis therapy. Her name's Katie Glasser, and I'd be happy to contact her if you'd like."

"Thanks. I'm not sure how far I'm ready to go at the moment, but it's beginning to look like hypnosis is the best alternative. Before I give you a definite answer, I'd like to see if I can get a little more information from Hargrave. I've the feeling he can shed considerably more light on the subject than he's done so far. If I've some connection to Jennifer Grant—"

"Oh God." Nicole was standing just inside the doorway, white as a sheet. She reached for the knob to steady herself, took a deep breath, then slowly advanced into the room.

"You know then?" She asked quietly. Her deep sapphire eyes were red-rimmed and swollen, her entire demeanor shaky. It was obvious she'd had a rough night, and I wondered why she'd dragged herself here this morning.

"Yeah. Hargrave was here with the news bright and early this morning." I swung my legs over the side of the bed and gave her an encouraging smile. "I'm sorry, Nicole. I know how much you were counting on—"

"No. Don't." She shook her head. "It's over, and we have to go on from here." She fussed nervously with the neck of her coral-colored tank, then brushed her palms against the matching culottes. "Are you ready to get out of here?" Her smile was less than enthusiastic but was a brave attempt nonetheless.

"I've just cut him loose, so he's all yours." Joyce patted Nicole's shoulder, the compassion she felt for the younger woman plainly reflected in her expression. "How's Robert taking it?"

"Surprisingly well. He's been at the police station and morgue most of the night." Nicole rallied a true smile. "This has brought him a form of closure after all these years of wondering. Now that he knows what he's up against he's ready to do what it takes to find the answers." She peered up at me. "And from what I heard when I was coming in just now, that might have something to do with you, right?"

"Hargrave seems to think so. And, much as I hate to admit it, I'm afraid he might be right."

She took in what I had to say, inclined her head, then looked away. I could tell that Joyce was becoming increasingly uncomfortable and was relieved when she moved toward the door.

"You let me know what you decide," Dr. Joyce Noland said at the door to my room, suddenly very business-like. "I can have Dr. Glasser here in twenty-four hours."

I thanked her, then turned my attention back to Nicole who'd gone to the closet and pulled out an overnight case.

"Annie packed a few things for you. Some jeans, I think, shirt, underwear." She pulled my robe off the hook and put it over her arm. "I can walk you down to the bath if you'd like." She held out my robe.

"Nicole." I went to her, put my hands on her shoulders and tried to get her to look up at me. I wanted so much to take her into my arms and comfort her, but something told me that right now would not be a good time. "Let me help you. If we can find Jenny—"

She shook her head. "What difference does that make now? None."

"I don't understand."

"Don't you see, it was just a coincidence after all. Some crazy, unexplainable twist of fate."

"But the resemblance, Nicole. You can't write it off so simply. Don't you see? She's got to be your sister. That's the only explanation."

Again she shook her head. "Nice try, but that's impossible. No,

Richard, please. I really don't want to discuss it right now. Let's just get you down to the bath so you can finish up and go home. I've left your number for my grandfather if anything should come up, and Annie is expecting us within the hour." Her dark eyes pleaded for my understanding. "We'll talk, work things out. Just not right now. Okay?"

I could feel her desperation, and as frustrated as it made me feel being unable to help her, for once in my life, I didn't even try. I felt like a heel, but figured she knew better what she could handle at the moment than I did. So I followed her the short distance down the hallway and set about getting myself cleaned up, so I could go home.

It came to me as I was toweling myself dry, a thought so fantastic that I had to hold onto the edge of the sink to keep my balance.

If Jennifer Grant was already dead by the time I got to the hospital, who had alerted Dr. Astin and led him to my room a few days after the assault? Not Jenny, she would have only been a child. Then who?

Astin said the woman looked remarkably like the portrait of Jenny. Two women who looked alike might be a coincidence, but what were the odds of three? Just what the hell was going on here!?

Nicole was waiting for me back in my room, gathering together the few items Mother had brought for my comfort. She gave me a sincere grin, revealing a single dimple in her right cheek, something I hadn't noticed before.

"I've already taken the plant and flowers out to the car," she said, her voice and attitude returned to normal. "I'll be done here in a moment."

She took the overnight case from me, commented that she was glad I'd shaved, then returned to her task. We were getting ready to call for a nurse when an aide walked into the room. She was very young, a little nervous, but had a bright, contagious smile.

"Oh good, you're still here," she told us both. "When they told me you'd been dismissed, I was afraid I wouldn't catch you."

"Is there anything wrong, Brenda?" I asked, spying her name tag.

The use of her name seemed to make her feel more at ease. With a deep sigh, her eyes lit up, and she shook her head.

"It's just that I didn't want you to leave before I could give you back your charm."

"Charm?" I asked, confused.

"Well, I thought that's what it was. It was dark, and I didn't get a good look at it."

She strode past us, pulled out the top drawer of the bed stand, and removed what appeared to be a Gideon's Bible.

"I was working graveyard the night before your surgery, so you won't remember me. Anyway, when I came in to check on you around three, your right arm was kind of flung off the bed and I noticed you had something in your hand. I knew you were scheduled for surgery in a couple hours, and I didn't think you'd want to chance it getting lost, so I put it away for safe keeping."

Nicole's gaze questioned me, but all I could do was shrug.

"I thought it must be a charm or maybe a crucifix or something. Whatever it is, I knew it was special to you because you were holding it so tightly. I thought I'd never get you to release it without waking you. But I did!" She said, triumphantly. "You didn't even come around, just rolled over onto your side and started snoring." She giggled.

With the flourish of a game show model, she held out the Bible and allowed it to fall open on the object nestled within its pages.

"I know it wasn't the smartest of hiding places, but I counted on the Bible to keep people honest." She looked down at the object that had already mesmerized Nicole and me. "Goodness, what's all this? I know it didn't look like this when I put it there. I mean, it was dark, yes, but I would have felt it if it had been so dirty." She moved toward the trash can and was just about to dump the contents when I was able to stop her.

"No, please, that's all right, Brenda. I'll take care of it." Did my voice sound as oddly as I felt? It must not have, for Brenda smiled even wider as she handed me the Bible.

"Thanks for putting it away for me," I told her, forcing a grin.

"Sure. Glad to help. You take care now."

"Wh-where did you get that?" Nicole asked when the girl had gone. It was a strangled sound that seemed to rip from her throat.

Carefully, my heart thudding against my rib cage, I lifted the pendant from between the pages of Psalms. The sun caught the silver and gold chain, and in spite of the dirt, it sparkled in the light. As the ankh came free from the pages, a tiny pebble that had been caught in the cross fell back onto the Bible. Placing the book on the stand, I inspected the pendant closely.

"Where?" Nicole asked again.

"Jenny. Sh-she gave it to me that night. I thought it was just a dream." I was still so stunned by what I was seeing that I couldn't look at her. "But I don't understand this. I mean, she was wearing it. She slipped it off, put it in my hand, and said something. What was it?"

"What does it say? On the back, the inscription, Richard, what does it say." Nicole had come to stand next to me. She reached out toward the pendant, then quickly drew her hand away.

"It shouldn't be so filthy. There shouldn't be all this crap on it." I worked at the imbedded dirt and tiny bits of rock with my fingers, refusing to believe what I saw.

"The back, Richard," Nicole said, breathlessly. "Is there an inscription?"

"Cement," I told her, amazed, as I turned over the ankh. "It looks like cement." I rubbed the back of the ankh against my pant leg, then lifted it to within a few inches of my face.

"Forever. It says 'Forever'."

Nicole cried out, blanched, then started to fall. I tossed the pendant toward the stand and caught her just before she hit the floor.

As I sat with Nicole's head cradled on my lap, I looked up to see what happened to the ankh.

It had landed neatly atop the Bible—Psalm 23.

Chapter 23

We remained at the hospital long enough for Nicole to get her bearings. And because of the overwhelming emotions we were both experiencing, had decided that, for the moment, it was safer not to speak. Once in her car, it was as though a veil had been lifted, and she turned to me, her hand held out before her.

"May I see it?" She asked, the corners of her mouth trembling slightly.

I removed the pendant from my shirt pocket and gently placed it in her hand.

"I've never seen another like it," Nicole spoke quietly. "It's so unusual. See how the chain is twisted, silver and gold, to match the ankh?"

"It's beautiful. Nicole—"

"Mother said that the original chain wore through, and grandfather replaced it with this more expensive one. He figured if she wouldn't give up wearing it, it might as well look more presentable." She laughed.

"Nicole, don't you see, it can't be the same—"

"My father gave it to her the day I was born. She vowed to never take it off."

"Nicole, please. Look at me. Talk to me."

Her rich blue eyes locked onto mine, her mouth, which I suddenly realized was so like her mother's, slowly formed into a smile.

"It was found in the debris, Richard. One of the first things the workers recorded. Then, somehow, it got misplaced on the way to the morgue. I thought it was gone for good. But it was only an illusion. You had it all the time."

I took her by the shoulders and shook her gently.

"Stop it, Nicole. You're talking crazy. You can't believe—"

"That my mother's a ghost?" She shook her head, her smile widening as her eyes filled with tears. "She saved your life, remember? Astin told us about it yesterday."

"He was mistaken," I said, failing to even convince myself.

Again she shook her head. "No. I don't think so. Look," she took a deep breath, then slowly released it. "I'm not cracking up, and neither are you. Something's going on here, something big. So big we can't get a real fix on it. But it's real, Richard, and we're going to have to accept that." She swallowed audibly as she pushed away the tears that started to track down her cheeks.

"The aide said she'd taken it from you early in the morning, just hours before your surgery. Three o'clock. That was around the time the tornado set down in University Park. Four full days before they broke through the cement and found her body." Nicole's eyes glistened in the sunlight.

Even with the windows down, the air in the car was stifling. Overnight the humidity had shot up, the wind had ceased to blow, and the sun beat down relentlessly—a typical July day in Missouri.

"Let's be reasonable." I held up my hand to keep her from interrupting. "I'm about as open-minded as they come, but this is beginning to sound like a Halloween segment of *Unsolved Mysteries*! I can see where you're going and can even understand why your explanation for what's happened might appeal to you. But for God's sake, Nicole, I spent three days with Jenny at my apartment. I touched her, like I'm touching you now. She was real, not just some figment of my imagination."

"Okay, she was real. You saw her and painted her portrait, a portrait that looks uncannily like the one of my mother painted twenty-two years ago."

"Coincidence."

Her jaw tightened as she continued to regard me steadily.

"You said that when Jenny gave you the pendant she spoke to you. What did she say?"

She was making this sound so sane, so reasonable that, for a second, I forgot what was being intimated.

"I don't know," I shook my head. "I can't remember. Hell, I was so groggy from the stuff they'd given me right before you left, that even that's a blur."

"Think, Richard. It might be important. It might tell us if we're on the wrong track."

"How can you—"

From out of the blue, I remembered the last thing Jenny said as she'd pressed the pendant into my hand. I gulped back a sob as I forced the words through lips that were suddenly parched.

"Colie." Nicole's eyes grew large. "She—Jenny said to give this to Colie. That's you, isn't it?" The sun coming in through the windshield surrounded her in a halo of light.

She nodded. "That was her pet name for me. Grandfather hated it because it reminded him of my father and how Mother had run away. I always thought it was her way to remember my dad." She took my hand, enclosing the ankh between our palms.

"People have reported seeing ghosts or spirits since the beginning of time. We thrive on the stories when we're kids, always trying to top our friends at parties with the scariest story of them all. It's said that for every myth, every legend, there's some basis in reality." She gazed at me thoughtfully, our hands still entwined.

"You ever hear about that ghost in...Chicago, I think it is? Resurrection Mary is what they call her. Anyway, the story goes that this young girl was killed in an accident coming home from a dance one night in the early thirties. She was buried in Resurrection Cemetery, but according to the legend that's not the end of the story.

"It's said that to this day people will pick up or drop off a mysterious girl in a party dress in the area of the cemetery. Sometimes she just disappears from their car, other times she's seen walking in the cemetery. If something like this can be possible, why couldn't my mother come back?"

"I'm sorry, but I can't believe this stuff. It doesn't make any sense."

"That's because we're logical beings who demand scientific proof before we can accept something is possible. But you believe in God, don't you? You rely on faith, right? You trust in what you can't see but feel in your heart to be real. Why is this any different?" The intensity of her eyes held me. "If someone had unfinished business, a strong will and purpose to survive, don't you think it could be projected onto their spirit after death? My mother was murdered, taken away from me against her will. She would have every reason to come back, to see justice was done."

I guess this was what you got when you became involved so quickly with someone you hardly knew. It was a shame, really. I'd believed I was falling in love with Nicole, and she with me, but I wasn't up to dealing with someone who was delusional.

I gently released her hand, leaned back against the passenger seat, closed my eyes, and counted to ten very slowly. I was nearly finished when a tinny sound drew my attention. Opening my eyes, I saw she'd hung the pendant on the rearview mirror.

"Hargrave thinks you might have seen my mother being murdered." It was a statement, spoken without looking at me. "That makes you connected to her in a special way. Or maybe it's as simple as your tumor. Perhaps it made you more receptive, or maybe just susceptible to hallucinations. Something. I don't know. I don't understand."

The thought slammed into me. Hallucinations? Was that possible? Did that explain the altered sketches and the charcoal, "A Study in Black."

"She was real, Nicole. We're not dealing with a ghost. A clever woman, perhaps, but not a ghost."

"No, not a ghost," her voice was almost a whisper. "An angel."

I nearly choked as she started the car and pulled out of the parking lot. I'd come successfully through brain surgery only to find myself in a car next to someone who was losing their mind. Try as I might to push this discussion off on her grief, the sudden discovery of her mother's murder, I continued to feel uncomfortable in her presence. Which made me feel guilty as hell.

An angel indeed! As if I was the kind of person who would be chosen for such a heavenly privilege; my own beautiful, enchanting, guardian angel sent to protect me. From what? My memories of the most traumatic time in my life? Well, if that had been her mission, she'd certainly failed. Since running into Jenny that rainy afternoon in the park, I'd remembered more about that summer than I'd ever thought possible. That wasn't protection, that was—

Thoughts jammed my brain, as something akin to an electrical charge caused me to jump in my seat.

"Richard?" Nicole pulled over to the side of the road. "Are you all right? You're very pale all of a sudden. Should we go back to the hospital?"

"No. No, I'm fine. Really," I croaked. "Go on. I'm anxious to get home, settled in."

I avoided her intense blue eyes, kept mine riveted to the passing scenery.

Jenny had been nervous, afraid to leave the loft because "they won't let me come back." What had she meant by that? I could never make heads or tails of it. And her story about her father and child, *her daughter*. She'd told me she would have gone to them if she could, but it was impossible.

Damn! Here I was trying to make a case for Nicole's delusions about her mother.

But Jenny had been so good. Too good. "If it seems too good to be true, it probably is." Did that apply to people as well?

Yes. But—

When the professor dropped off the miniature of Stonehenge, Jenny claimed she'd hidden in the bathroom. I'd accepted her explanation at face value, and like everything else, hadn't forced the issue. Like a lovesick school boy, I'd taken the little she'd given me, eager to lap it up and offer her up my heart on a silver platter. Silently, I'd asked for everything, verbally, nothing. I'd spent three wonderful yet maddening days in her company during which time I couldn't remember if she'd ever eaten or gone to the bathroom.

This was crazy!

Yeah, it had to be if I was thinking in those terms.

Nicole pulled into the narrow alley separating the Weisher's building and the one next door. She carefully maneuvered her car into the space beneath the stairway, shifted into park, and removed the keys from the ignition. She did it all with such deliberation that I knew she was struggling whether or not to say what was on her mind. Finally, she drew herself up and turned to me.

"I'm sorry. I don't know what's gotten into me. I mean, well, I do know, but—Oh dear God, Richard, since yesterday afternoon I've felt like I've been hit with a bulldozer or something. You were right when you said nothing makes any sense. I'm sure there's a logical explanation for all that's happened, and as much as I would like it to be possible, we can rule out all that supernatural mumbo-jumbo."

A sigh of relief? It was more like a complete exhalation of all the air in my entire body. I covered her right hand where it still gripped the steering wheel. She would be okay. She had to be.

Just as she'd promised, Mother was already waiting for me in the loft. When she heard us on the stairs, she came out onto the landing, waved, then called to someone inside the apartment. Chuck and Professor Drake quickly joined us, each taking an arm to help me up the remainder of the stairs. They both acted pleased to see me, though a little more solemn than I would've liked. And as we passed my mother in the doorway, I could tell they were all pondering how to tell me something.

The moment we reached the top of the stairs I could tell Mother had been in one of her cleaning frenzies. The smells of furniture polish, floor wax, and kitchen cleanser overpowered the more pleasant odors coming from the bakery below, assaulting my senses and insulting my attempts at housework.

Once inside, Chuck released my arm and the professor lightened his grip as we made our way to the sofa. I looked around, noticing the recently vacuumed rugs, the unusual shine on the coffee and end tables, neatly stacked magazines, newspapers, and mail, as well as the empty trash cans and recycle bins lined with convenient handle-tie bags. My mother had outdone herself.

I thanked everyone for their assistance, told Mother how great the place looked, and moved into a more comfortable position on the sofa—facing forward with my legs propped on a corner of the freshly polished coffee table.

"So, what's up?"

Both Chuck and Mother turned to the professor. It was obvious they didn't want any part of the explanation.

Edmund Drake cleared his throat, gave Nicole an apologetic glance, then drew his bushy grey eyebrows into a straight line across his forehead.

"Because of the stories that are bound to come out, it was decided that it would be in the best interests of both you and the university to withdraw the "Portrait of Jenny" and "A View From the Bluffs" from the exhibition. I know how upsetting this might be—"

"No," I said, shaking my head. "Under the circumstances it seems logical. I saw the news report when they found the body. That kind of sensationalist reporting style will succeed in bringing about more of the same. Something I'm not ready to handle at the moment, and the gallery shouldn't have to. What about the others with Jenny?"

"As Mr. Grant was so kind to point out to several members of the board, the remaining pieces in the collection depicting her aren't as obvious." He smiled, ruefully. "Even if he hadn't been so insistent, Richard, I would have made certain they were removed before the news broke about the connection between you and the gallery. I'm sorry it has to be this way but am glad you understand."

"Yeah, well, I'm feeling pretty congenial at the moment." I didn't bother to tell him that the second Grant's name was mentioned, I'd been ready and willing to defy anything the man wanted. It was a petty and childish way to react, but I couldn't help not liking the guy.

"Where did you put them?"

"Over there." Chuck pointed to the parson's table in my work area.

Both paintings had been turned inward, not viewable to apartment visitors.

"We can move them if you want, Rich. Just give the word."

Chuck started for the studio to show his willingness to help, but there was something about the tone of his voice that said he'd rather pick up a rattlesnake than be forced to handle those paintings again.

"It's all right. Leave them."

Just as I'd thought, Chuck was only too happy to comply. He came back into the living room, plopped down on a nearby easy chair, and flashed me one of his McCartneyesque grins. The others in the room remained standing, staring awkwardly at one another—and at me. Mother finally relieved Nicole of my overnight case and, sitting on the other end of the sofa, began to sort through the items inside. This signaled a memory for Nicole that the plant and flowers were still in her car, and before Chuck was able to get the words out, Professor Drake had already volunteered his assistance.

It was like I was in a B movie where the dialogue was as stiff as the actors' performances. Perhaps it was me or the strange, uncomfortable conversation Nicole and I had earlier that made everything take on a kind of surreal appearance. Whatever it was, I was tired of guessing games— with or without Hargrave at the helm.

"Oh!"

Mother's surprised tone brought me out of my reverie. I looked up to find her holding my pajama top in one hand while studying the photograph that Hargrave had given me of Jennifer and Nicole.

"A memento from Detective Hargrave." I told her, reaching out for the picture.

"When?"

"You mean when did I see him?" She nodded. "He helped me welcome in the new day." I took the photo from her, glanced at it briefly, then placed it on top of the stack of mail on the coffee table. I could tell she was itching to ask about Hargrave's visit, yet was reluctant to do so. This was a little out of character for my mother, but considering the subject matter, understandable.

"Before I forget, dear, Dr. Noland called about a couple of prescriptions she'd forgotten to give you this morning. They've already been filled and are in your medicine cabinet in the bathroom. She said the directions are on that paper she gave you." She threw Chuck a rather curious look that sent him from the chair.

"I'll go check on the stuff you ordered from Mrs. Weisher," he mumbled, then headed toward the inside door that led to the bakery's kitchen.

"We haven't much time before the others get back," Mother said in her most conspiratorial tone. "What did that detective want now?"

I shrugged. "Nothing, really. He told me they'd ID'd the skeleton and that there was a possibility that Jennifer Grant and I had been in the park at the same time. Theories. That's all."

"Janet and Edmund mentioned much the same thing last evening. About the incidents almost coinciding. I don't like the sound of this, Richard. That man's trying to connect you to that poor woman's murder. You were only a little boy, for Heaven's sake. What could you know about it?"

What, indeed? My mind seemed to taunt.

"He's stumped, Mom," I said, reaching out to pat her arm, a reassuring gesture that I hoped would do the trick. "He's got a twenty-one year old crime with little to no clues and a dragon breathing down his neck." Dragon. That was a pretty good description of old man Grant if I had to say so myself.

"Hargrave was hoping I'd remembered something that might give him a lead. That's all it was."

She nodded uncertainly, then got up to put away the various items from the suitcase.

Nicole and Professor Drake came back with the flowers and proceeded to place them in various spots throughout the living room. Finished, Nicole commented that she should be getting home.

"But I'll be back first thing in the morning. If you want me, that is."

"Of course he wants you, dear." Mother answered, coming into the room and giving Nicole a hug. "And as soon as you're both up to it, you'll come down to Branson for a few days. How does that sound?"

"Wonderful. Thank you, Annie." Nicole hugged my mother back, her eyes on mine, questioning.

"Maybe we can continue with our discussion, get to the bottom of things." I told her with a sly wink.

"At least give it a try?"

I nodded; rising from the couch and opening my arms, she came to me without hesitation.

"Do me a favor?" I whispered. "Call Hargrave and ask him to meet us here tomorrow afternoon."

She pulled out of my embrace, her dark eyes wide with curiosity.

Mother and Professor Drake had gone into the kitchen to give us a little privacy. Still, I kept my voice low while I maintained a vigil on their activities.

"Ask him to bring the files on your mother's case and mine, or at least some of the notes. Tell him that if he wants me to help him, he first has to help me. Maybe he has something that will unlock my memories once and for all."

Nicole quietly agreed to relay the message in spite of the doubt written across her face. She held my hand as I walked her to the door, her grip tightening as she opened the screen.

"Thank you for understanding, for not kicking me out of your life when I went off the deep end." She grimaced. "I suppose it runs in the family."

I kissed her on the forehead, then watched as she descended the stairs.

I turned to find both Mother and the professor regarding me with a mixture of affection and speculation—the latter reflected mostly by Uncle Edmund.

That brought me up short. It had been a long time since I'd referred to him that way—even in my thoughts. But, suddenly, I was back in his home office, sketch pad on my knees as he leaned over and talked to me about the drawing assignment he'd just given me.

"Isn't she a lovely girl, Edmund?" The sound of my mother's voice brought me sharply back to the present. They were both smiling at me in a sly, Cheshire-cat manner that was annoying. I met their smiles directly, refusing to be taken in or embarrassed by any assumptions made on their part.

"She's been a good friend." I said simply. Before either of them had time to make further comment, I rushed on. "Now that I've the two of you alone, you want to tell me what else is going on?"

Mother started to protest but could tell it was useless.

"Janet and Edmund have kindly offered to take me home this afternoon so I won't be forced to ride the bus." She lowered her lashes, her face flushing. "I feel so badly about all of this, dear, but I really don't see any alternative. It's nearly a six hour drive, you know, and it will be far more comfortable in a car than on the bus."

"Is that all that's bothering you?" I couldn't help being amused by her expression. "I wish you'd stop thinking you have to stick around and take care of me. They wouldn't have released me if they didn't think I could manage. I thought we'd settled this."

"It's all here; bread, donuts, and those little sugar cookies you asked for." Janet and Chuck burst in through the inside door, startling all of us. They put the food on the kitchen table, laughing and talking about some amusing story Mrs. Weisher told them as they were waiting.

Mother busied herself with putting the items away while Janet and the professor escorted me into the living room.

"She can't help herself, son. She feels guilty about leaving you when she might be needed."

"That's right," Janet readily agreed. "A woman's instinct is to protect the ones she loves, and that's especially true for mothers." She gave my arm a squeeze. "Just show her a little understanding to take the sting out of having to return home, Richard, and she'll get over it."

I thanked her for the sage advice and tried to make the hour before their departure as easy on my mother as possible. This meant going so far as agreeing to the suggestion that Chuck camp out on the sofa overnight so I wouldn't be alone my first evening home. Chuck actually seemed more enthusiastic with the idea than I did—he must be between girlfriends once again.

I was ready for some pain medication and a nap by the time they'd gone. Chuck assured me he could amuse himself, switched on the TV, and eased into the most comfortable of the overstuffed chairs. Satisfied my "babysitter" was set for a couple of hours, I trooped down the hallway into the bathroom to grab the medicine.

I was practically blinded by the sparkle of chrome and porcelain. Clean towels and washcloths had been set out by the tub, the bathmat was practically unrecognizable as mine—I never particularly excelled at housework and laundry, but it was times like this when I realized I'd never fully heeded my mother's directions regarding such things.

The medicine chest had been cleaned and organized as well, every label facing neatly to the front to make it easier to distinguish between old and new. Capsules in hand, I reached for the glass I always kept by the sink and wasn't a bit surprised to find it gone. Back in the kitchen, I caught sight of Chuck on the sofa, his head bent forward as he studied something in front of him.

He hadn't heard my approach, had remained hunched over the object before him. At first I was going to forgo my curiosity and ignore him; the last few hours had taken a lot out of me, and I really wanted a nap. But the nearly imperceptible shake of his shoulders made that impossible. Keeping my eyes on him, I moved quietly into the room.

Nestled within his large hands was the photograph of Jennifer and Nicole Grant. Chuck's light brown eyes were bright with unshed tears, his face a study of torture.

"Want to talk about it?" I sat nearby, watching as he attempted to recover himself.

He placed the photograph back on the pile of mail, briskly rubbed his eyes, and stared up at me, a wistful expression on his face.

"I don't suppose you remember asking me that question once a long time ago." It was a rhetorical statement; as well as he knew the history of my memory loss, it seemed to him a moot point. "I met you that summer,

Rich. I never told you that, did I?"

I sat quietly, waiting while he ruminated over past events until he felt comfortable putting them into words.

"You seemed like a great kid," he said finally. "Smart and witty—that hasn't changed much, which is probably why we've become such good friends." He flashed his sardonic grin, but I had the impression it was more for his benefit than for mine.

"I never mentioned the incident," he continued, "Because it didn't really matter. It was a one-shot thing; Janet was busy with another student, and I followed you into the professor's office to wait. You know my big mouth. Well, it was twice as big at the time, and before too long I'd spilled my guts."

A notation for my memory notebook when I had the chance. Meeting "Charlie" hadn't been a dream after all.

"Charlie?"

"Yes, well, my mother considered the nickname "Chuck" inappropriate. Said it sounded like a cut of beef. When I finished my masters, I was ready for a change. I thought "Chuck" sounded more macho." He laughed at this, a sound full of self-contempt. "So you do have some memory of the incident?"

"A little," I confessed. "Something to do with being engaged to one girl while actually wanting another one. Seems completely in character for you."

"Touché. Now it would be the norm; back then it was a first. *The* first." He shook his head sadly. "I'd thought this was all behind me. Over, if not forgotten. Now they've found her body there'll be fingers pointing and accusations flying the way it was twenty-one years ago. I suppose there's some kind of sweet justice in that. The irony of ironies."

"So, the other woman in the triangle was Jennifer Grant?" His confirmation put another item in the memory column: the discussion I'd recalled between Lily and Janet. "She was the reason you broke off your engagement to Lily?"

Chuck appeared fascinated by the palms of his hands. He was concentrating on them so hard, I began to wonder if he'd even heard my question. But suddenly he was on his feet, taking long strides toward the west bank of windows, as though anxious to put as much distance between us as possible.

"She was the most exquisite woman I've ever known. When I saw that painting of yours, my heart was literally in my throat. You remember how I acted? Hell, Richard, you could've knocked me over with a feather! I thought she'd come back. Then it hit me that it couldn't be her because she hadn't aged a day in the last twenty-one years."

"We think Jenny must be a relative of some kind," I explained. But Chuck wasn't listening. He was lost somewhere within his own inner torment, a hell he was trying to exorcise by talking to me.

"I'd met her old man at some function or other at the university. We'd hit it off right away—one letch to another, maybe. I don't know what he saw in me, and I didn't ask. We talked about my background, the degree I was after, and my plans for the future. By the end of the night, I felt like he was ready to adopt me. Anyway, when he invited me to dinner, I jumped on it. I had no idea what he had in mind, and when I found out what it was, I was already head over heels for the girl.

"And it wasn't just her beauty, Rich. She had this charm that radiated from her without visible effort; it was just there. And Nicky, she was the icing on the cake. To this day, I can hardly stand my sister's brats, but Nicky was different. Like her mother."

"So Grant set the two of you up?"

"Yeah." He released a deep breath. "Jennifer never led me on; she was up front from the beginning. She was in love with some guy she knew her father wouldn't approve of. She offered her friendship, which I gladly accepted, while I continued to hope for more."

He remained with his back to me, his face to the windows. Some of the tension had gone from his shoulders, but the way his hands were bunched at his sides was a clear indication it hadn't completely departed.

"When Lily found out, she confronted me in the Snack Shack." He turned then, a wry smile on his face. "It's said history repeats itself, and in a sense I suppose it did. But the incident involving you and Tara was mild in comparison to the one I had with Lily. She not only threatened to kill Jennifer, but added that if she ever caught me with her again, that she'd castrate me. Let me tell you, I believed every word."

No wonder they'd both been so upset by the news Hargrave was in charge of Tara's assault case! As close friends of mine, the possibility of being questioned by the detective must have made them apprehensive about the past being revived.

And then there was Lily's reaction to Jenny's painting. If she'd hated Jennifer Grant as much as Chuck intimated, it explained why the sight of it made her ill.

"And when Jennifer disappeared?"

"We were among the first to be questioned. It didn't help that shortly after the fight in the restaurant I was seen grabbing Jennifer by the arms and forcing her in my car. When she'd jumped right back out, I shouted for her to stop, and she took off running." He returned to the couch, sat down heavily, and put his head into his hands. "I wouldn't have hurt her for the world, Rich. You've got to believe that. I was in love with the girl. Really in love. But after twenty odd years of love-em-and-leave-em, seducing girls in my classes, and all the rest of my promiscuous lifestyle, I doubt very much anyone is going to believe me." He looked up, his light brown eyes staring intently into mine. "I don't know what happened that night twenty-one years ago, but if you saw anything, Richard, if you start remembering, I hope you'll come to me first."

He cleared his throat, and as he stood up abruptly, there was a kind of gleam in his eyes that I couldn't define. He strode into the kitchen for a glass of water with me staring after him, wondering if I'd just been issued a challenge or a warning.

And exactly how much my friendship really meant to him.

Chapter 24

I awoke the next morning to the smell of bacon frying. It took a few minutes to acclimate myself, with thoughts of my mother and the hospital still uppermost in my mind. Recognizing my own room in the loft erased any leftover confusion, and climbing out of bed, I readied myself to face my long-time friend, Chuck Stinnet.

It had been an awkward evening. Thank God for VCRs and movies on video cassette! Even before Chuck had been talked into staying with me, he'd rented several newly released movies for my entertainment. This turned out an excellent diversion after his story of involvement with Jennifer Grant—especially true since the movies were all comedies.

So we made it through the evening, barely speaking unless to comment on one of the films, and sacking out early to keep from actually having to carry on a conversation. It wasn't because I wanted it that way; I didn't. I had a million questions I'd like to ask, but it was obvious Chuck had said all he was going to about the subject.

I pulled on a pair of jeans, chose a shirt from the closet, and moved on to the bathroom for a shower. The bacon smelled even more enticing in the hallway, causing my stomach to growl—a sign Chuck must be feeling better this morning.

Lathering up, razor in hand, I stared hard at my reflection. Did I really think the man I'd known the last nine years was capable of murder? If we'd been talking about the seduction of the most chaste woman, the answer would be an unequivocal yes; Chuck would've been able to charm a chastity belt from releasing its prized possession. But murder? My instinct was to say no, to stand beside my friend and proclaim him incapable of such a thing. Yet something gnawed at my insides. Something, some instinct or internal warning system told me not to be so hasty in making a decision. It was always possible he was holding back some information which might prove vital in the long haul.

And then there was his "request" to be the first to know if I should happen to remember anything about that night. Why? If he was innocent, what was he afraid of?

It wasn't an easy thing to suspect a friend of wrongdoing—and murder...

After I'd finished cleaning up, I returned to my bedroom to pick up the notepad listing my confirmed and possible memories. I'd started it last night after the final movie, carting it back to the bedroom with me after saying goodnight to Chuck.

I'd been itching to get it started since the idea first occurred to me but had been reluctant to do so in his presence. I'd spent about an hour jotting things down before I became too sleepy to continue. Now, I glanced over the list, surprised to find it so short, and closing the cover, headed for the kitchen and breakfast.

Nicole was before the stove with her back toward me, standing on tiptoes to reach into the cupboard above. She was barefoot, her lightly tanned legs were also bare from the bottom of a pair of shorts that ended with a row of fringe. She was wearing a mint colored halter top that appeared to tie in the front and revealed the smooth skin of her flat, narrow midriff. Her golden brown hair was straight and loose, a shining, glorious mass that fell to just below shoulders that were strong and well-formed.

She might believe in ghosts, but we could get around that, get her some psychological help. It was nothing to be ashamed of, and after growing up with her grandfather, if that was the worst of her traits, I could learn to live with it.

"What are you looking for?"

She dropped down on the balls of her feet and spun around with a startled "Oh!" as she grabbed her chest.

"Sorry. I didn't mean—" We were both laughing so hard that we were soon in one another's arms.

Kissing her was the most natural thing I'd ever done. It was an extension of myself: my lips, hers; her arms about my neck, mine encircling her waist; our bodies touching, hungrily seeking, demanding all the other could give. Natural, the other half to make one whole. All this, and only knowing her a week!

"Good morning." She pulled gently from my arms. "The bacon. Don't want it to burn."

I reluctantly let her go, asking again what she'd been looking for.

"Salt. You're out." She lifted the strips of bacon from the pan one by one and laid them across a paper towel to soak up the grease. As she moved to one side to start the eggs in another skillet, I got the salt down from the cupboard and set it on the counter.

"I talked to Hargrave. Scrambled or fried?" She asked, an egg poised in her hand ready to crack.

"Over easy, please. So what did he say?"

"That he'll be here at two. As far as the files," she wiped her hands on a dish towel and turned to me. "He said there was no way in hell you were getting your hands on them. That's almost verbatim, I'm afraid," she winced at the memory. "He's not the most likable guy, is he?"

"No, he isn't." I agreed. "So he's not willing to share any more information than the sketchy crap he fed me yesterday morning. How does he expect me to remember if he's not willing to help jog my memory? So why's he coming over then, to try and grill the memories from me?"

"Well, he didn't exactly say he wouldn't cooperate," she turned back to the stove and carefully flipped the eggs. "He said he would review what he had and give you a brief run-down. Enough to "set you on your ear," was the way he put it. He also had some crazy notion that in talking to me he might be able to find out something new. I guess my grandfather refused to allow the police to question me after he'd filed the Missing Person's report."

"That shouldn't come as a surprise. I mean, what were you, five, six?"

"Six. And although I wouldn't have been able to shed any light on the matter then, I might be able to now. Remember what I told you about my mother's diaries? I brought the last one with me. The one that mentions her involvement with the artist."

She dished up the food and carried the plates over to the table that was already set with orange juice and coffee, including a single rose in a bud vase at the center of the table. It looked nice, homey. I could easily learn to live like this.

We turned to neutral subjects during breakfast, talked about the weather and how the humidity continued to rise over night. Right now the loft was cool, but if the predicted high came true, by mid-afternoon, the place would be like an oven. The apartment contained two window units placed at opposite ends of the building. We decided to turn them on after breakfast. Riveting conversation, no, but at least it didn't promote heartburn.

My offer to help with the dishes was firmly refused, so I took my notepad and wandered off into the living room. Looking out over the open living area, I still couldn't believe how clean and orderly my mother had managed to make it and resolved to try to keep it that way.

"Oh, Richard, I moved those paintings away from the table where they'd set them yesterday," Nicole called out over the running water. "I was afraid they might get knocked over, or that maybe something from the table might spill and ruin them. So I put them against the wall with some others. That okay?"

"Great. Thanks."

The stacks of canvases against the walls in the workroom made it impossible to guess which were the ones of Jenny without physically looking through each one. For the time being, that was fine. But eventually, I might just hang them for my own viewing enjoyment.

I settled myself comfortably on the sofa, legs bent with feet propped against the edge of the coffee table. Noticing the photo of Jennifer and Nicole, I tucked it beneath the stack of still unopened mail. She was acting sane again this morning, and I didn't want to chance something setting her off.

I flipped open the cover of the notepad, licked the end of my pencil, and closing my eyes, tried to concentrate.

I'd already listed my conversation with "Charlie," the discussion I'd eavesdropped on between Janet and Lily, how the park looked in the days before I was assaulted, and how upset I'd been because I wasn't allowed to go to my treehouse. I added my boredom and frustration because Frank Murray had gotten sick and Mary Rogers suddenly developed an intense dislike for boys. Janet and Edmund Drake had been too busy with students and classes to pay much attention to me—something that never happened before. And, finally, I listed how strained their relationship had been that summer. As a child, I'd felt something was wrong, yet had been unable to pinpoint exactly what it could be. Now, looking back on that summer, I recognized the signs of a marriage in crisis. They'd both tried to ignore it, tried to conduct business as usual, but I'd known them too well to be fooled.

I flipped to a new page, contemplating the addition of the dream/memory of "Jenny" visiting me in the professor's den. I still wasn't clear under which category this belonged, but I started writing down all I could recall, from her dancing eyes to Janet Drake's icy stare when she found the girl with me.

The more I wrote, the faster my heart seemed to beat. I heard the blood rush into my ears, felt the thud of it in every pulse point, growing stronger and stronger until I finally set down my pencil and placed my head between my knees. My head might hurt, but it wasn't anything like the migraines I'd grown used to.

Back to Jenny.

I still had no explanation for the way Janet treated her, and it was the lack of clear knowledge which made me hesitant in declaring it an actual memory.

What about Tara?

Okay. It was true Janet had a deep-seated aversion to Tara almost from the beginning. But it didn't help matters that Tara seemed to sense this and feed off it for the sole purpose of further irritating Janet Drake. That was Tara, and Tara could in no way be compared to either the Jenny I'd painted, or the girl I'd met in the professor's den.

So where did that bring me?

"What's that?" Nicole asked, leaning over the back of the couch to peek at what was on my pad.

"It's the list I told you I was going to start. Sure memories versus possible dreams."

"No, that." She pointed to the lower half of the tablet where I'd unconsciously begun to doodle.

Well, doodle was hardly the word. I stared in amazement at the tiny drawings: apes, bears, cats, dogs, and elephants; I'd always started that way.

"I was drawing the alphabet."

"May I?" I handed her the notepad, and she laughed. "This is wonderful, Richard. The kids at school would get such a kick out of this."

"It was one of the professor's favorite assignments. Whenever he thought I wasn't taking my lessons seriously enough, he'd have me draw the alphabet. Usually he requested animals, which wasn't so bad, but sometimes he would insist on food or strictly birds. The birds were tough ones. I would have to sit with a dictionary or encyclopedia on my lap to try to come up with them. But my favorite was this." I flipped over to the next page to demonstrate.

"You see," I told her as I drew, "Only one letter besides the "M" really conforms to the shape of a bird. It's the one time you can truly get into the art form, from the gentle curvature of the neck right down to the last tail feather." I continued to sketch, a growing excitement building within me. "The professor used to hang these all over his office. When students or friends came over he'd point to them and talk about how clever I was—Oh my God."

"It's a swan," Nicole said close to my ear, a touch of nervousness barely audible. "It's just like—"

"The signature on your mother's portrait," I finished for both of us. I gazed down at the creation in my lap, remembering that day in Nicole's house and how the memories had slammed into me from out of the blue. I'd gone to check out the name of the artist and had found myself confronting a piece of my past.

"Swann." I gulped in a breath that caused me to cough spasmodically. When I'd finally recovered, I pulled Nicole around the sofa to sit next to me. Holding her hand tightly within my own, I looked away, closed my eyes, then brought them to rest on hers.

"When Jenny showed up that night six weeks or so ago, I'd just finished "A View From the Bluffs." There was a nasty storm. Thunder, lightning, wind, and hail. I was surprised when the knock sounded at the door. Even more surprised to find her standing on the porch soaked to the skin." I swallowed a little more carefully this time. "She didn't seem to see me at first. I don't know, maybe her eyes hadn't adjusted to the light. But as I reached out to bring her inside, she said the word "swan"."

"Oh!"

"Yeah. Wild, isn't it? Anyway, she kind of fainted then, and afterward, well, all I thought about was her." I searched Nicole's face for an answer to a question I already knew neither of us had. "What's it all about, Nicole?"

We sat there for a long time, looking at one another, holding hands and thinking our own private thoughts. I didn't blame her for not mentioning her theory again; I'd done a pretty good job shooting holes in it—and her—yesterday.

Did it mean I was ready to believe in ghosts? In some strange kind of divine intervention that allowed murder victims one last chance for justice? To be truthful, I didn't know what I believed. Reason, for sanity's sake, suggested a logical explanation. But there were too many times life had proven logic didn't always work—my apologies to Mr. Spock and all the other Vulcans.

"If Professor Drake is Swann," Nicole was saying, "then that means he and my mother—"

"Were having an affair." As unbelievable as it sounded, I didn't dismiss it as a possibility.

"She was in love with him," she continued, a wistful note in her voice. "It's not just what you see in her portrait, Richard, which literally radiates off the canvas, but it's all through her diary. I mean, his name is never mentioned, but it didn't have to be. She referred to him as her artist, the one man who knew how to interpret dreams and visions into reality."

I raised my eyebrow at her curiously. "That almost sounds like something you said to me."

"So I plagiarized," she pouted. "It was for a good cause. Look, I know the Drakes drove Annie home yesterday afternoon. Did they happen to mention when they expected to return to Linden?"

I shook my head. "No. But it's a pretty long haul. Are you thinking what I am?"

"We have to talk to him, Richard. We have to get him to open up, see if what we suspect is true. If he was in love with my mother, he might have some idea what she was doing in the park that night."

"Yet another piece to the puzzle." I sighed, hating to involve him, to virtually accuse him of having an affair over twenty years ago. But what choice did I have? I couldn't tell Hargrave what we suspected. I couldn't do that to the man who'd been a second father to me, my mentor as well as my friend.

We agreed to call later that night and try to arrange a meeting for the following morning. He usually wasn't as busy during the second summer session, so there was a good chance we could have our answers before noon on Monday. That led me to another item that as yet needed a decision; should I have Joyce Noland contact her hypnotist friend Dr. Glasser? I was still uncertain about the idea of handing my subconscious over to hypnosis. It wasn't that I was afraid of the procedure, more that I was leery of what it might uncover.

We spent the remainder of the morning getting better acquainted. She listened attentively to the story the professor and Janet told me about my "accident," a word I deliberately used to emphasize how hard my parents and the Drakes tried to keep the truth from me. She told me how it was to grow up with her grandfather, never knowing what had become of her mother. We shared childhood memories, adolescent dreams, and adult realities, cementing the bond between us in such a way that I knew would take more than a little innocent ranting to break apart what we had. After all these years of searching, it seemed the romantic in me might finally be satisfied.

Nicole actually let me help with the lunch dishes, perhaps because there weren't very many. When we were finished, she insisted I try to take a nap. I watched her go down the hallway to the bathroom, then stretched out on the couch with my eyes closed. I wasn't there two minutes when the front door flew open, and from the on-rush of cologne blasting through with the heat behind it, I immediately knew who'd come in.

"Wanna shut the door, Lily? You're letting out the little cool air we have." I sat up, watching as Lillian Reston left the main door open but firmly shut the screen before she braced herself to face me.

Funny, but I was no longer concerned with her trials and tribulations regarding Matthew Marzetti. There were much bigger fish to fry at the moment. But knowing Lily the way I did, and watching as she squared her wide, sexy shoulders, I knew I wouldn't be able to avoid whatever she had on her mind.

She was wearing a pair of cut-off jean shorts that were so tight it left little to the imagination. She had on a cerulean blue tank top that nearly matched today's contact lens of choice, and her blond hair had been pulled into a neat ponytail that hung in a series of ringlets down her back. She tossed me the clear plastic bag that contained the local Sunday paper, put her hands on her hips, and stared down her perfect nose at me.

Despite her cool attire, she looked hot. Perspiration dotted her brow and upper lip and was just beginning to show under her arms. This was not the calm, cool sophisticate and patron of the arts she usually portrayed. This was a woman who was afraid of something, or perhaps someone.

"Are you going to come and sit down or would you prefer to stand?" I laid the paper on the coffee table, got off the couch, and encouraged her to take a seat in a nearby over-stuffed chair.

"I can see you haven't read that yet, so let me give you a brief run-down. Some very quick-minded individual has already made the connection between Jennifer Grant," she spat out the name with distaste, "And your portrait of that girl. There's a rather lurid story on the Stalker, including the rumor that his last presumed victim was a young male, an attack which corresponds to the pouring of the gazebo foundation. They've even gone so far as to contact some of the workmen who'd been on the site, spreading another rumor about how the cement hadn't been mixed properly, too thin or something, but since it was so late in the day with a storm coming, they'd decided to spread a tarp over the mess and deal with it the following day.

"The damned paper's full of all the old stories from misappropriation of funds, the fits and starts connected with the park redesign, and every scandal regarding that period the creeps could dig up."

Lily finally took a breath, wiped a hand across her brow, and paced from the living room to the studio and back again.

"Personally, I don't give a crap about who whacked the bitch," she gave me a pointed stare, defying me to protest. "If you're expecting some heart-wrenching confession on how much I hated what she did to Chuckles and me, you can forget it. My main concern right this moment is how all this publicity is going to affect me and Art Magic. And believe me, Richard Tanner, once they get hold of your name, everything will tumble down to me and mine. And I refuse to have anything adversely affect us." Her blue eyes were like twin pieces of ice as they stared through me.

"Good afternoon to you, too," I said dryly. "You're welcome to take a seat, or stand if you prefer. Myself, I think I'll sit this one out." I perched on the corner of the sofa, allowed myself to relax against the high back that jutted out slightly, and kept my eyes on Lily the entire time.

"You're very cool when you consider this latest discovery. Aren't you concerned about what it could do to your career?"

"Hey," I spread my hands wide, "I haven't much I can say about the matter, remember? My memories of that time are virtually nil. As far as the media getting hold of my name after all these years, I guess I'll deal with that when or if it happens." I narrowed my eyes trying to pin her down. "Why are you so worried, Lily. Perhaps they'll drag my name into it, so what? Surely the publicity and curiosity it would create would tend to enhance and increase my popularity as an artist. Besides, my show at Art Magic is still more than six months away. So what's really bugging you?"

I caught sight of Nicole coming down the hallway from the bathroom, threw her a quick look to back off, then returned my gaze to Lily. Although she'd stopped her erratic pacing, she was still rocking back and forth on her heels as she wrung her hands in front of her. Realizing what she was doing, she crossed her arms and tucked her hands beneath them.

"It's not exactly the kind of publicity any of us need." She pursed her lips. "I'm sure you're already aware I was questioned when Jennifer disappeared twenty-one years ago. Some jerk had to tell the cops that I'd threatened to kill her when I discovered Chuckles was two-timing me. It was a stupid remark that didn't mean diddly but was blown all out of proportion. Your friend Hargrave was just starting out, trying to make some points with old man Grant or something, so he was on all our cases. I was never happier when nothing turned up, and they decided the fruit had run away just as she had when she was a kid."

From the corner of my eye I could see Nicole fighting to hold herself back. Thankfully, she remained where she was, covered by the shadows just beyond the kitchen entrance. Another quick glance in her direction, and her nod of agreement, assured me she'd stay put for the time being.

"As a compassionate human being, I'm sorry she's dead, but on a personal level, I wouldn't care at all if it didn't involve me." She inched forward, placed her hands on the back of the over-stuffed chair, and leaned toward me. "I've got a little money put away, Richard, and am willing to use it to help you find your model. What do you say? Would you like to find this Jenny of yours?"

Her ice blue eyes were too intense, her tone too anxious.

"Why? What's in it for you?"

"In it? Nothing." She flicked her hand as though dismissing the idea as ridiculous. "I simply feel that if we can locate your model there will be a lot less speculation about why you chose to paint that picture." She lowered her eyes, refusing to meet my gaze. "You're making too much of this offer, Richard. It's strictly business, a way to play up the resemblance of the two women and the coincidence of the entire thing. Take some heat off all of us." She shook her head, her long blond ringlets flipping over her shoulders. This was the Lily I knew well, the seductress who was not above using her feminine wiles and sexuality to get what she wanted.

"What about avoiding all the publicity?" Again I tried to probe past the surface, beyond what Lily was willing to outwardly show.

"If we have your model on hand, no one will be able to say she was something you've dredged up from your past—some buried memory from your subconscious that's come back to haunt you. For God's sake, Richard! Hargrave's already contacted my parents. He knows I'm in Linden and is trying to get hold of me for questioning. Questioning! More like an inquisition. How the hell am I supposed to accurately recall what happened over twenty freaking years ago!?" She shoved off the chair and resumed her manic pacing.

"I imagine he just wants to go over your former statement. It's reasonable, under the circumstances."

"How can you sit there so calm, act so circumspect about it all?" She stopped just a few feet in front of me, her beautiful face as hard as if it had been carved from a block of granite. "What is it, Richard? What are you hiding?"

"I'm not hiding a thing." Our eyes met and locked.

"H-have you remembered something? Do you know something about Jennifer Grant's murder?"

"Only what I read in the papers," I told her lightly. "Which isn't much at the moment. Aside from that, Hargrave was good enough to mention it to me before I left the hospital yesterday, but that's all it was. A brief comment, something he hoped would spur my memory."

I could tell Lily wasn't buying it. This time when she crossed her arms, her long nails bit into her soft flesh, scoring the tender skin.

"Jennifer Grant was nothing but a whore who went after other women's men."

I coughed loudly, a warning I hoped Nicole would heed. I didn't want to chance Lily spotting her and clamming up. But I needn't have worried. Lillian Reston was on a roll, spewing out the venom she'd kept inside all these years.

"She thought she was above the rest of us because her old man was some kind of small time crook who'd managed to get his hooks into local government," Lily continued. "Bet you didn't know it was one of his companies doing the park renovations. Ironic, isn't it, that it might have been his bungling employees that caused his daughter's death."

"Just provided the murderer a place to put the body." Detective Jack Hargrave said as he let himself into the loft. "Don't you realize how much cool air you're losing by keeping the door open like this?" He shut the main door then turned back to Lily, visibly gratified by her startled expression.

"Startled" didn't quite cover it. Lily not only jumped at the sound of someone else's voice but actually looked as though she might pass out when she saw who the intruder was. She didn't have the chance to recover from that when Nicole moved into the kitchen, her deep blue eyes and penetrating gaze letting Lily know she'd heard everything.

Lily extended her condescending expression to both Nicole and Hargrave, her eyes flitting over the daughter of her former rival. She flashed me a look that said she felt betrayed, then set her attention on the detective.

"Detective Hargrave." She held out a slim, tapered hand which Hargrave took with a smirk. "My parents mentioned you'd called. I was on my way to see you after I'd finished up checking on Richard."

"I'll bet you were," Hargrave commented, sarcasm oozing from his voice. "You want to make an appointment now, Ms. Reston, or should I call you?"

"Whatever's convenient for you, of course." Lily batted her fake lashes coyly. Perhaps she felt that emphasizing her feminine appeal would be a better way to handle him than the contempt she'd started with. As far as the detective was concerned, he looked amused but hardly taken in.

"Then I'll see you at nine tomorrow morning," he told her as his steely grey eyes raked over her body. "And you might want to inform your boss that he's next on the list."

While Lily sputtered, I sat up and took notice. What did Matthew Marzetti have to do with Jennifer Grant?

"If you're referring to Mr. Marzetti, he's not associated with Art Magic anymore, Detective. So if you have something to tell him, you'll have to pass along the message yourself. Now, if you'll excuse me?" She threw another look of distaste in Nicole's direction before she came over to where I was sitting on the arm of the sofa.

"Things aren't always the way they appear," she whispered as she gave me a kiss on the cheek. When she pulled back her eyes were a little watery, as though she was on the verge of tears. "Don't overdo, Richard." She cleared her throat to make the tone more conversational, but her expression held a warning. "We wouldn't want to see you back in the hospital."

Lily's departure was something to behold, almost as dramatic as Hargrave made his entrances.

"How long had you been on the porch?" I asked, not believing for a minute that his timing hadn't been planned to the second.

Hargrave spread his hands, shaking his head. "Hey, I'd no idea what she might say. Sure, I was listening for a while, like your friend there. Didn't want to interrupt the lady if she felt compelled to give a confession. I couldn't believe she walked into it so smoothly. It was a true work of art, if I do say so myself." He gave his sardonic laugh. "You're quick, Tanner, I'll give you that."

"Thanks." The attempt at a compliment hardly overwhelmed me.

I left the sofa arm and went to Nicole who was still just inside the kitchen entrance.

"You okay?" She nodded, her face flushed in anger and indignation. I took her by the hand and led her over to the sofa, indicating at the same time for Hargrave to take a seat. Before I sat down myself, I closed and locked the main door.

"Smart move." Hargrave nodded approvingly. "Miss Grant said you wanted some information. What did you have in mind?"

I sat on the sofa next to Nicole, pulled my notepad onto my lap and studied the man opposite me.

He was an arrogant bastard to be sure, cocky and so full of himself that you had to fight against trying to put him in his place. Not that anything short of physical violence might succeed in doing so, and I even had my doubts that would work. He knew his strengths, recognized your limitations, and quickly made it clear that if you wanted anything from him, you'd be forced to play by his rules. As I was not completely sure what those were, it was bound to be rough going.

I took in his slicked-back hair, noted how it was thinning near the front, and was surprised to realize he was wearing a clean shirt—although with a garish print—and a pair of Levi's that looked fairly new.

It was nice to know he wasn't always a slob.

"So?" He asked impatiently.

"Richard and I were discussing the fact that neither of us knows anything about either investigation," Nicole jumped in. "I was only six when my mother disappeared, and Richard, of course, suffered a major loss of memory as a result of his assault. Neither of our families has ever talked about the incidents, so we're basically in the dark. Perhaps you could enlighten us, Detective Hargrave, tell us a little of the background. We both want to help, but how can we if you keep our hands tied?"

Nicole's sweet smile and honest words did more to impress Hargrave than Lily could have in a million years. He gave her one of those odd smiles of his where his face did its contortionist impression, while his silver eyes actually crinkled in a show of warmth.

"You've got a point, Miss Grant—Nicole, but it would be against policy to turn over the files you asked for." Before either of us had an opportunity to protest, he held up a hand to stop us. "But I don't see what it would hurt to give you a run-down on possible suspects." He eyed me in contemplation. "Under the circumstances, it may be a good idea. If any of these bozos get the idea your memory's returning, and what I suspect is true, they might just decide to come and finish the job they started twenty-one years ago."

"That's a comforting thought." Even though it already occurred to me, I hadn't wanted to voice it, especially in front of Nicole.

"You will help us then?"

Hargrave nodded to Nicole, then turned to me. "Under the condition you keep me informed of anything, and I do mean *anything,* you might suddenly remember. I'm not screwing around here, Richard. That crap between you and your old girlfriend still makes me want to puke, but if she chooses to turn a blind eye and lie about what happened, what can I do without evidence? I still think you're guilty as sin, and she's playing a dumb act to save your hide, but that has nothing to do with what happened twenty-one years ago. We're talking murder now. Murder and the attack on an innocent little boy, and that's the way I'm going to handle it. I won't let what I feel about you now interfere with what happened then. If you play by the book, everything will be kosher. If you try to hold back evidence, I'll kick your ass in the slammer so fast you'll be picking leather out of your crack for weeks to come. We got a deal?"

"We've got a deal." I held out my hand to seal the bargain. Hargrave took it with a malicious grin, squeezing it hard enough to make me want to wince. Instead, I put all my effort into my own grip, returning pressure for pressure until he laughed and finally released my hand.

"It's always nice to start out with an understanding we both can live with. Now let's get to work." He pulled his small notebook from his pocket, flipped open the cover, and consulted what was inside.

Raising his eyes, he looked Nicole over from head to toe, obviously attempting to size her up. She may not be the beauty Lily was, but in her shorts and halter top, Nicole was every bit as sexy while maintaining a kind of wholesomeness that Lillian Reston never possessed. Nicole's rich sapphire eyes held a clarity and charm which bespoke of honesty and integrity, while the hands that lay tightly within mine revealed how nervous she was. Still holding her own without arrogance or defiance, she gazed back at the detective with a steady expression of curiosity.

Hargrave must have liked what he'd seen, for he smiled at her once again, making the perpetual sneer on his cruel lips disappear, allowing him to seem more human than usual.

"How much do you know about your grandfather's business dealings?" He asked, further surprising me with a show of kindness toward Nicole.

"Very little, actually. I know that he has invested pretty heavily in real estate, has played the stock market in the past, but that's about it. Why?"

Hargrave didn't answer. He gave a slight shrug, slid further back in the chair, and continued to consult his notes. After a moment, he cleared his throat.

"Nothing has ever been proven one way or the other, but there had been some past allegations of dirty dealing, scams and such. This is a little FYI, a kind of background to start laying the bricks on the foundation—no pun intended. What it does, however, is bring us to suspect and motive one: Matthew Marzetti, one time hood who turned to bigger and better things."

"You mentioned him to Lily," I said. "What has Marzetti got to do with this?"

"He worked for Grant. Doing exactly what is anyone's guess. What we know is that Grant arranged for Marzetti to keep an eye on his daughter—I guess she wasn't quite toeing daddy-o's line, so he had her followed. Turns out Marzetti didn't like to watch and not touch, and touching was a big no-no. After five years of devoted service, Grant booted him out, and Marzetti swore he'd get even with both father and daughter. He was rather verbal about this, too, bragging in the local bars about how he was going to get them both and have his sweet revenge. No woman was going to lead him on, tell him no, then squeal to papa."

"She knew," Nicole said suddenly, looking from Hargrave to me. "Remember what I told you, Richard, about the chauffeur or whatever he was?"

I vaguely recalled the conversation and nodded.

"So you knew about Marzetti?" Hargrave couldn't keep the surprise out of his voice.

"Yes and no." Nicole got up from the sofa and went to the small table near the door where she'd set her purse. "My mother kept a form of diary."

Hargrave moved in the chair to keep his eyes on Nicole. "Your grandfather know about this?" He asked, the anger resurfacing in his voice.

Nicole shook her head. "I doubt it." She told him about having found the books in her toy box years before, and realizing what they were, decided to keep her mother's secrets.

"Anyway," she continued. "It's not exactly the most revealing of things, mind you, nor is it very complete. But she knew she was being tailed, and her solution to be rid of the man was to get him to make a play for her. I can't say I agree with her methods, and it wasn't very nice, but she accomplished what she'd set out to do." She removed the book from her purse and handed it to Hargrave. "I've always kind of admired her for getting around the two of them."

Hargrave flipped through the pages of the diary.

"Yeah, well, she would have done better to leave things the way they were."

"Because of what happened, you mean?"

Hargrave's steely grey eyes stared thoughtfully at Nicole.

"Let's just say that Marzetti had already proven himself a tough customer long before your grandfather fired him. We'd had him down to the station a couple of times in connection with the Stalker case. Nothing panned out; there wasn't any hard evidence against him but enough circumstantial that if the prosecutor had any balls, he'd have indicted the man."

"You thought Marzetti was the Stalker?" This gave a whole new meaning to why the man was against my exhibition at Art Magic. If he were guilty of my assault, he wouldn't want to risk my recognizing him in a sudden memory flash right in the middle of the opening ceremonies before all his rich friends.

"He was a suspect. He could be tied to at least two of the victims, had motive and opportunity. Unfortunately, he also had an alibi for the others. Flimsy, but it held. Still, Marzetti was a pretty strong contender, and when Grant reported his daughter missing, he was only too happy to point a finger at his former employee.

"Marzetti was still in Linden, but since we couldn't pinpoint an exact time of disappearance, we had nothing to compare his alibi to. If we'd known then what we do now..." He let the sentence hang.

During the brief silence that followed, I jotted down this new information. Though none of it rang the proverbial bell as I'd hoped, there was always the chance that eventually I would make enough of a connection to something I was told that it would bring an onslaught of memories with it.

While I was writing, Nicole squirmed next to me, her dark eyes watching Hargrave as he concentrated on me.

"I'd like to know how it happened," she said slowly. "How and when Grandfather reported Mother missing."

Without diverting his attention from me, he spoke in the kind of monotone that said he had the information memorized.

"He came in July third, two days after he'd last seen her. He gave us a complete description, several photographs, told us about her penchant for walking in the rain—especially during storms."

As Nicole cringed beside me, I flashed to Jenny watching the rain drip onto her hand.

"I like the rain," she'd said with a smile. "I like the way it feels as it runs between my fingers."

I heard the soft melody of her voice just as it had been that first day in the park. She'd held her hand beneath the gutter, so the water could slide down her palm and trickle through her outstretched fingers. The vision was so powerful that I found myself starting in surprise as I came back into myself and found Hargrave opposite me, still describing the initial Missing Person's report.

"He knew enough about procedure," the detective was saying, "That he'd waited to make the report until after the forty-eight hour waiting period. After an exhaustive investigation with nothing conclusive to go on, we were forced to place the case on the back burner—something your grandfather never forgave the department for doing. Despite everything we managed to uncover, we had no proof, nothing to suggest foul play or to indicate this was a planned disappearance. As time passed and nothing more came up, with Jennifer's prior history of running away, it was assumed she'd done so once again." He lifted his shoulders in a slight shrug, his accompanying expression probably as close to compassion as Hargrave could come.

Nicole said a quiet thank you, reached over and squeezed my hand, and thanked me for my patience.

"Keeping notes, chief?" The familiar smirk and sarcasm was firmly in place. "That's good, Richard. Real good. You never know when a little information like this will come in handy. And, of course, you'll be wanting to share your brilliant deductions with me when this is all over."

He raised his expressive eyebrows contemptuously. "Now, are we ready to continue with our list?"

Nicole nodded while I regarded the man with the same caution I had from our first encounter. He'd undermined me once in the morgue; I wasn't about to let it happen again. With the same kind of flourish he'd demonstrated then, he set about to impress us with his next disclosure.

"Next in line are lovebirds Lillian Reston and Charles Stinnet. Lovers, that is, until one lovely, rich young lady makes it a threesome." Temporarily forgetting he was referring to Nicole's mother, Hargrave gave a dirty laugh that was more than a little suggestive. Catching Nicole's look of alarm, he stopped abruptly, but neither the leer nor the gleam of amusement in his eyes changed.

"Did your friends ever tell you about their little spat in the Snack Shack, Richard?" He taunted.

"I've heard a little something about it, yes."

He snickered. "Really? Then I would've thought you'd have learned from their mistake about airing your dirty laundry in public. Ah well, at least there's something for the record books. Anyway, there they are right in the middle of this knock-down-drag-out, and in comes the lady of the hour. In a wink, Miss Lily was standing over Jennifer Grant threatening to kill the girl if she didn't keep her hands off Charlie-baby. According to witnesses, Jennifer handled the situation as cool as you please. Smiled at Lily and told her she had no idea what she was talking about." He laughed again.

"By this time, Stinnet was between the women, trying to hold back his fiancé while Jennifer Grant made her escape." Hargrave regarded me speculatively. "They told you that, did they?" My failure to respond and steady gaze was enough for him to decide. "No, huh? Well, don't feel too badly about it, Richard. But I'll tell you something, if you liked that, then, you're just going to love this next part."

I guess I'd never understand how someone could gain so much satisfaction by causing another person pain or discomfort of any kind, but it was obvious Hargrave was enjoying himself immensely. He was in his element, and as long as he maintained the smug satisfaction that came from trying to shock and surprise us, he was bound to continue talking. And the more he talked, the better my chance of discovering something that might finally pull all the pieces of my past together.

"About an hour later," Hargrave continued, "Jennifer Grant was seen leaving Lambert Hall. Stinnet had managed to track her down and was waiting for her by the front door. According to eyewitnesses, she tried to avoid him but didn't succeed; he grabbed her and started pushing her toward his car. When she cried out, one of the guys on the scene attempted to help her and was slugged in the gut for his effort. It gave Jennifer the chance to make a break for it, but Stinnet was on her in a flash. He hauled her back to the car and shoved her inside, apparently unaffected by her cries for help.

"In the meantime, some friends of the kid who'd gotten hit ran into Lambert to report what was happening. They were able to enlist the aid of one of the instructors, but by that time, Jennifer managed to get out of the car and was running hell bent for leather across the campus with Stinnet yelling after her.

"A girl who was nearby gave us an affidavit that your friend Chuck Stinnet informed Jennifer Grant that he'd "rather see her dead than with anyone else." That sort of puts things into a different perspective now, doesn't it?"

Chuck's words rang in my ears as I tried hard to concentrate on what the detective was saying. "If you start to remember anything, Richard, I hope you will come to me first."

Had the air in the loft suddenly gotten heavier, or was I the only one who was finding it difficult to breathe?

I could see Lily threatening someone to protect what she believed was hers. It was easy to picture her looming over a small individual such as Jennifer Grant, their very difference in stature making her words appear far worse than actually intended. But for Chuck to go after any woman using force and manhandling her in the way Hargrave described simply didn't correlate—not with the Charles "Chuck" Stinnet I knew, anyway.

"Cat got your tongue, Richard? Find it hard to believe that lover boy Stinnet was such a hardass? Yeah, well, he tried to blame it all on the pressure he was under. You know, the trials and tribulations of school and the insane jealousy of his former fiancé. He'd claimed that all he wanted was a chance to talk to the girl." This elicited one of Hargrave's famous laughs filled with biting sarcasm. "Guess he'd never heard of the phone. Anyway, Stinnet wasn't as pure as he wanted everyone to believe. After what we learned of his encounters with Jennifer Grant, we decided to take another look-see into Mr. Charles Stinnet. Turned out that he knew both Missy Gordon and Hilary Brockton, the first and latest Stalker victims. We questioned him and checked his alibis, but other than the fact that Hilary and Lillian Reston were cousins and Missy had been in one of his classes at the university, there was nothing to link him to the actual assaults."

"Another dead end," I concluded.

"True, but those first few days of looking into Jennifer's disappearance things looked promising." Hargrave pulled a stick of gum from his shirt pocket and popped it into his mouth. Standing up, he stretched his muscles in a way that suggested he'd been sitting too long.

"So, from the beginning, you'd considered the possibility that my mother might have been one of this Stalker's victims?"

"Not exactly. We knew Grant had accrued a lot of enemies, and as I've already stated, there was her history as a runaway to consider as well. The connections were purely coincidental, the result of normal investigation into the last few days before her disappearance. When the same names popped up in her case, it was worth looking back over our information on the Stalker. You couldn't rule out anything." Hargrave fixed me with a pointed stare. "And if we'd been given half a chance to talk to you, *Richie*, or have you examined, maybe we wouldn't be forced to do this twenty-one years later."

"Anything else?" I kept my voice steady.

"Always save the best for last, kid. It keeps them riveted to their seats." He walked as far as the west bank of windows, stood for a moment before them, stretching his arms and back, then returned to the over-stuffed chair. As he sat down, he asked Nicole for a glass of water, following her every move as she went quickly to fulfill his request.

"You're a fast worker, Richard. Gotta admire a man for that." I didn't hear much admiration in his voice. As usual, I figured he'd chosen his words carefully, always looking for that double edge, the barb that could sink another dig. "Yeah, pretty quick on the uptake. Tara Morgan's out of the picture, with a little assist from whom, Richard? Huh? No answer? Too bad. Then along comes this Jenny that you claim you just happened to meet in the park one day. You're attracted to the girl enough to sketch and paint her portrait, but you don't know her name or where she comes from. Strange what seems to be enough for some people. But then, you're different, right? An artist, a sensitive." After a quick glance in the direction of the kitchen, Hargrave moved to the edge of his seat and leaned toward me.

"Smooth, Tanner, as smooth as they come." He said, lowering his voice. "But tell me, exactly how much did this little girlie really resemble Jennifer Grant, and how much are you relying on those so-called lost memories?" His grey eyes had the appearance of liquid mercury as they raked over me.

I met his stare with an equanimity that seemed to be eroding the longer our eyes were locked—and the more I considered what he'd said. Nicole broke the effect when she re-entered the room, setting a tray of cookies, ice-filled glasses, and a pitcher of lemonade on the coffee table between us. She appeared totally unaware of what had gone on between Hargrave and me, her usual good humor firmly in place despite the tone and topic of our discussions. Without asking first, she poured three glass of lemonade and handed the glasses, along with a napkin containing a couple of the Weisher's excellent sugar cookies, to both of us. We accepted them with a smile and a thank you, the detective's almost too sincere to be believable.

"So, in spite of your eventual conclusion that my mother must have run away, you actually had a considerable list of suspects with a motive to do her harm." Nicole eased back onto the sofa. She was so close I could feel the heat of her body radiate outward along the entire length of my left side, helping to further distract my attention from Hargrave.

The faucet in the kitchen dripped onto some unknown surface causing a tiny plinking sound. Faraway, a horn sounded, traffic rushed by on the street below, and I could hear the gentle crunch of the cookies as Hargrave chewed contentedly. It was peaceful, quiet, the hum of the air conditioner creating a false sense of tranquility as the sun streamed into the west bank of windows, filtered slightly by the occasional tree branch.

Hargrave gulped down half a glass of lemonade, set the glass on the tray, and wiped his mouth with the paper napkin. His eyes narrowed as his thin, cruel lips formed into the habitual sneer, fixing me in his sights.

"Guess the reason you didn't ask what Jennifer Grant was doing at Lambert Hall when she wasn't a student means you already know the answer." He flashed his contortionist's form of a grin. "Tell me Richard Tanner, was Edmund Drake having an affair with the girl, or were they just the friends he claimed they were?"

He didn't attempt to justify his accusation. Indeed, it appeared as though he'd spoken out of spite rather than from any real information or suspicions he actually had. Yet, even recognizing what was behind the statement, there are moments in your life when no matter how prepared you think you are, something can still come along and take you totally by surprise. That's what his question did to me.

I had to concentrate to keep my glass of lemonade from spilling as I set it back on the tray along with my uneaten cookies. The veneer of calm and composure I'd sworn to maintain had cracked, reminding me of the fissures in the base of the gazebo in University Park the last time I'd seen it. This train of thought led to the grisly discovery buried deep within the cement, the remains of a small, beautiful girl who had long ago been the center of so much controversy, Jennifer Diane Grant, whose life had touched so many of the people I knew and loved. Jennifer Grant, the mother of the lovely young woman sitting next to me.

"I've no idea what you're talking about," I croaked, finally recovering my voice.

I felt the movement next to me, Nicole's eyes upon the side of my face, but I refused to respond. Hargrave's expression told me he was simply guessing about a relationship between Jennifer and Drake; I wasn't about to add fuel to the fire. If he knew what Nicole and I discovered earlier that day—that the artist who'd called himself Swann was very likely a pseudonym for Edmund Drake—he'd be all over the professor in a second. So let him fish. He'd get nothing from me, and I was pretty sure Nicole would follow my lead. As I'd told her before, I owed the professor the courtesy of speaking to him first. I wasn't about to spill my guts over a hunch and set this barracuda loose on someone I cared about as much as I did Edmund Drake.

Hargrave regarded me with more than his usual amount of disbelief but for some reason, didn't call me on it. He brushed his hands together, ridding them of any leftover crumbs, then slowly tucked his notebook into his shirt pocket.

"We traced Jennifer over to the Drake's where Mrs. Drake informed the girl, in no uncertain terms, that she and her husband refused to become further involved in the situation between her, Stinnet, and Ms. Reston. From there, Jennifer returned home until around seven when the storm hit. She arranged with the housekeeper to put Nicole to bed, told her father and the housekeeper she was going out to walk in the rain and that she would be back when she'd had enough of the storm. That was the last time anyone saw her alive—with the exception of her murderer, that is. She disappeared into a stormy night to remain "missing" for the next twenty-one years." A vague look of apology was in his eyes when he gazed at Nicole.

"Why the Drakes?" I asked, curiosity getting the better of me.

"Excuse me?" Hargrave almost acted confused by my question.

"Why would she go to Lambert Hall? Why the Drakes?"

The detective considered my question for a moment, the look of confusion remaining on his hard features.

"Stinnet was close to both of them, had probably mentioned that he'd been discussing the issue with them. Janet and Edmund Drake were known for their compassion for the students." He shrugged. "Always seemed a little too good to be true, in my opinion. Opening their hearts and home for a bunch of kids to traipse in and out of their lives, with very little thought for the people they were imposing upon."

"I don't suppose you find that kind of selflessness possible?"

"You're right, Richard, I don't. At least not to that degree, and not unless they were getting something out of it as well." He laughed cruelly. "I may be a cynical bastard, but I do know a little something about human nature, and I never quite trusted that holier-than-thou-type of attitude. Those two had their fingers on the pulse of not only the university community, but of the city of Linden as a whole. Hell, when the Stalker first made his appearance, it was a delegation from the university led by the Drakes that got the city moving toward rezoning the park." He shook his head, his eyes glazing slightly at the memories.

"When the mayor and his family were suffering from their daughter's attack, the Drakes were there, spearheading a campaign to enlist the aid of both populations—the town and university alike. Later, they helped the mayor and city council with the park's proposal, convincing the city to vote for the renovations no matter what the cost. They remained active in the commission until the spring when Hilary Brockton was assaulted. They'd known most of the girls in one way or another, but this girl they knew well. Rather than increasing their resolve, it seemed to take the wind from their sails. They both withdrew from the mayor's commission and returned to their university activities. Why? I asked both of them that question when we were investigating the Brockton case and again when I was trying to discover their connection to Jennifer Grant. I didn't get satisfactory answers then, but you can damn well believe I will now." Hargrave stood, regarding both Nicole and me steadily.

"They put me off when I wanted more information about you, Richard, succeeded in turning your parents against the department as well. Whenever I approached them with questions, there was always an excuse; they were in shock, they couldn't understand how such a thing could happen, they just didn't know what to say. Popular people, the Drakes, upstanding citizens of the city and the university."

I expected him to continue, but he didn't. He just stared off into space for a moment, a reaction so completely out of character for him that it literally gave me goose bumps.

"So, what've you got for me?" His voice seemed as faraway and detached as he'd suddenly appeared. He'd always managed to make me uncomfortable, but this change of attitude increased the feeling considerably. Still, I did my best to cover what I felt and quickly went over my list of memories with him.

I related the incidents of meeting "Charlie," eavesdropping on Lily and Janet's conversation, and the frustration of being refused access to the park and my treehouse. I deliberately omitted any reference to Jenny's visit to the professor's home office as well as her possible connection to Drake himself. Hargrave listened in an off-handed manner, distracted by whatever thoughts had pulled him away during his speech about the Drakes.

"So where do we go from here?" Nicole asked, eyeing Hargrave with concern. When he didn't respond, she turned to me, cocking her head curiously in his direction, a silent inquiry for my opinion of the situation.

There was nothing I could say to explain the detective's odd reaction. Something in the conversation had obviously caught his attention, and now he appeared to be carefully weighing that information. At least, that was my interpretation of what was going on. For all I knew, Hargrave finally tipped the scales and had gone off the deep end into some kind of netherworld from which there was no return. But maybe that was just wishful thinking.

I cleared my throat rather loudly, startling Nicole, who gave me a tremulous grin in response. Hargrave finally turned his grey eyes to where we sat on the sofa. He seemed to have difficulty focusing on us, like he'd been looking at something far away and been pulled too sharply back.

"I've been thinking about being hypnotized," I told the detective as he continued to look at me with an almost vague expression upon his craggy face. "I've spoken to Dr. Joyce Noland, and she has an associate she believes might be helpful."

"Really?" Hargrave seemed to come back into himself as suddenly as he'd vacated our reality. "You surprise me, Richard. From your attitude, I didn't think you had any desire to come face to face with your past. What's brought about this change of heart?"

I had a retort already formed in my mind and nearly to my lips when I decided it wasn't worth the effort. Instead, I briefly outlined my discussion with Joyce and her mention of Dr. Glasser. Hargrave listened with interest, though it was obvious he was still preoccupied with whatever captured his attention earlier.

At his suggestion, I called Joyce and asked her to arrange a meeting with Glasser at her earliest convenience. Minutes later, Joyce called back to say I was in luck: Dr. Glasser was flying up from Springfield the following evening and would be happy to see me then. The meeting was scheduled for eight o'clock with the understanding that Hargrave was to be present from start to finish to record whatever memories the session might uncover. Although Joyce sounded somewhat reluctant to agree to this without first consulting Glasser, she finally consented to relay the terms and to give the psychologist what Hargrave referred to as "the bare necessities" of the case. The detective went so far as to grab the phone from my hand and spell out exactly what Joyce was allowed to tell Glasser about me.

"Don't want the doc to start out with any preconceived notions," he told my physician almost sharply. "I've had some experience with hypnotists before and know how they can lead their subjects into making certain remarks. We don't want any of that in this case. Richard's to be regressed to that day twenty-one years ago, period. What he remembers from that point on will come from him, not from some damned questions leading him down a garden path."

Once everything was arranged to his satisfaction, he hung up the phone and regarded us in silence for a few minutes. I think by this time, Nicole was completely in awe of the detective, not quite certain what to believe or make of him. For myself, I wondered what was going on inside that head of his. Something was up. Something had him so distracted that he'd cast his usual sarcasm and taunting aside. Not that he offered me any more consideration than usual; he was simply not going out of his way to antagonize me.

Finally, with a pointed remark that I keep on my toes, he strode to the door to let himself out.

"Oh, and Richard," his grey eyes narrowed as a beam of sunlight from the west windows flashed across his face. "Keep in mind that memories can be a dangerous thing. Especially in your case. You've not only the distant past to recall, but something a lot closer to home. Maybe while you're under, you'll slip and give us a nice confession of how you brutalized your ex-girlfriend." His eyes raked over Nicole, the leer on his face saying more than words ever could. "You two have a nice day now."

Chapter 25

Hargrave's final remarks resulted in an avalanche of questions from Nicole—and justifiably so. There were no counter accusations, no signs of distrust; she remained seated beside me, listening calmly as I attempted to explain my difficult relationship with Tara. With as much detail as possible, I related the many ups and downs right through the final, explosive confrontation that afternoon in the Snack Shack.

"I left the restaurant in the middle of a storm without the least idea of where I was going. I ended up in University Park and met the mysterious Jenny minutes later."

I went on to describe the encounter, how Jenny strangely disappeared when Chuck arrived, and how her image remained with me from that moment forward, an obsession, the like of which I'd never had before. I described how things snowballed that day, Tara's effort to damage my reputation with her fit in Lambert Hall followed by her hysterical visit to the Drakes, the scene she'd created when the Weishers refused to let her into the loft, and finally the nasty, demanding note she'd left on my door.

"That was it; I'd had enough. I was suffering from a migraine, and between the pain and the anger, I was in pretty rough shape, almost manic. I went through the apartment methodically seeking out anything that could remotely be called hers and proceeded to stuff it all into a large trash bag. When I was sure I'd eradicated her possessions and every last sign of her from the loft, I tied up the sack, put her name on it, and tossed it onto the porch." I grimaced at the thought. "At that moment, I might have been capable of just about anything—verbally. Physically, I was wiped out. I swear to God, Nicole, I never laid a hand on her."

Nicole's patience remained steadfast as I related how I'd taken some medicine then crashed on the couch until the nightmare awakened me early the following morning.

"When Hargrave came a little while later and told me what happened, virtually accusing me of the assault, I was stunned. There I was, my jacket torn to shreds because of the nightmare, and he confronts me with evidence that I wasn't always in complete control of my actions."

When I told her about the changes to the sketches, she released a startled "Oh!" but continued to sit quietly at my side as I went on with my story. I tried not to leave anything out. As painful as it was at times, I told Nicole everything I could think of, all the details of those harrying days before Tara declared my innocence which led to our eventual reconciliation. The more I talked, the more she urged me to continue, to tell her about the stormy night Jenny arrived on my doorstep—and the three days I'd spent in her company.

It was amazing how easily the words came, how cathartic it felt sharing these events with someone who was willing to listen without being judgmental. Talking to Nicole about the changes in the sketches and the charcoal produced without conscious knowledge wasn't nearly as difficult as my confession to Joyce Noland. Nicole's avid interest and bright eyes carried me through, her hand in mine encouraging when things got rough.

She finally had the whole story; she knew everything Chuck, Lily, Janet, and Edmund had told me about the Stalker and my own assault, Detective Hargrave's interpretation of the incident, and the bits and pieces I'd recently begun to remember. Added to this was the newest information provided today by the detective—random pieces to a puzzle with her mother appearing to be the one connecting them all.

"I think Hargrave's right," Nicole spoke slowly, deliberately. She got off the sofa and moved freely about the room. "His investigation pertained to my mother's disappearance, but it kept leading him back to the Stalker case. If what he suspects is true, further investigation of your assault could lead in the same direction—to my mother's murder."

She had a captivating fluidity to her movements. Her legs were long and slender, beautifully shaped, her body lithe and sensual. I could hear her speaking, understood the words, but I was lost in watching her.

"Richard? Do you agree?"

I tore my eyes from her, blinked, then looked back with more control.

"Of course." I nodded. "When Hargrave visited me in the hospital yesterday, he said about the same thing. Beyond that rough exterior, he seems to be pretty intuitive, except where Tara's assault is concerned."

Nicole dismissed that with a wave of her hand. "I believe you're right about his holding a grudge. He was thwarted on the investigation when you were a child, and whether it's logical or not, he's taking that frustration out on you now. Deep down he knows you're not guilty, but he's getting too much satisfaction in taunting you. He hasn't any evidence; Tara's not been overly cooperative in his eyes, so he's chosen you as a target." She shrugged. "He's got Tara's background as a troublemaker, so if he looks into it long enough, he's bound to come up with the answer. In the meantime, I'd suggest you not worry about what he said just now. I've every faith in you, Richard, and in Dr. Noland's diagnosis about the blackouts." She firmed her chin and snatched up my tablet from where it lay on the coffee table.

"Wait," I said as she turned to the page where I'd noted the dream/memory of Jenny's visit to the professor's home office. "That's not—"

Her deep sapphire eyes held a look of surprise when they met mine.

"You met her when you were a child?"

For a moment, I thought she might faint. I was on my feet in a flash, my arms going around her to steady her. She jerked away, backed up a step, and gazed at me in confusion.

"I don't know. I didn't say anything because I can't explain it, don't even know if it's a memory or just a dream." It was my turn to seek release in pacing. I was tired, my head throbbing, and so caught up in my own confusion how could I ever be expected to solve hers?

"Talk to me, Richard. Tell me what you remember, or think you do. It must have some significance or you wouldn't have written it down."

She'd listened to everything I'd told her, believed in me in the face of Hargrave's indictment, yet when confronted with words from a possible memory, a story that might involve her mother, she felt betrayed.

"You see the heading? Dream-slash-memory? I've already told you about being unable to distinguish between the two. Those other encounters on the first page, it wasn't till yesterday I discovered they were fact and not just the product of my imagination. And now there's this thing with Jenny, not Jennifer, Jenny. How do I know I'm not superimposing the girl I painted onto some past encounter? I mean, both Jenny and the past have been dominant forces in my mind, so it would only make sense for it to combine the two in a dream of some kind."

Nicole nodded, but I could see a lack of conviction on her face.

"It's possible, I guess. But Hargrave said Mother had been to the Drake's that afternoon."

"Um," I sighed. "His revelation..." I raised my hands in a form of surrender. "At that moment I felt myself seeking out the memory or dream, or whatever the hell it is. I tried to make it seem more real, flesh it out, but—" I turned toward the west bank of windows helplessly. The sun had begun its slow descent behind the oaks on University Way, the bell tower struck the half hour, and somewhere nearby was the wail of an ambulance as it rushed toward an emergency. Peace and tranquility reflected back to me as the siren made a mockery of what I saw.

It was how I felt inside.

"I've never been this open with anyone in my life. You know more of my history than my own mother!"

"I'm not doubting your honesty, or your integrity." Her voice caught in her throat, and I looked up to find tears rolling down her cheeks. "I admire you, admire the way you've been able to hold up through all this adversity. Look at what you've been through! On top of everything you've just told me, I can imagine what you must have thought when some crazy old man started badgering you about that beautiful portrait on display in the Fine Arts gallery! Then he knocks you out, and you're confronted with the discovery of a brain tumor!" She released a heavy sigh. "How could I act this way, feel wronged because you left out this minor detail? I'm sorry. I—" She turned away from me, hiding her face in her hands as the sobs shook her shoulders.

I went to her, took her into my arms, and held her tightly. I'd had more than my share of traumas in the last several months, there was no denying it, but I also knew where she was coming from. Jennifer Grant might have disappeared twenty-one years ago, but for her daughter, she'd only been dead a couple of days. All these years she'd been hoping, praying, that one day her mother would come back to her. In the space of a few hours, all that hope had been taken away. As well-adjusted as Nicole was, this sudden discovery was taking its toll. And her involvement with me and my problems couldn't be helping the situation.

Nicole gently withdrew from my embrace, a tremulous smile shining through the tears. One hand reached to brush at the tracks on her cheeks while the other went to the neck of her halter top. She lifted the ankh pendant from beneath her shirt, clutching it tightly within her hand.

"When I talked to Hargrave yesterday, he was pretty upset because they'd been unable to locate my mother's pendant. Before Grandfather left on his business trip, he'd gone over the department's head to the mayor, and I guess someone had been breathing down Hargrave's neck about the sloppy work they'd done." She lifted the pendant and fixed her gaze on the ankh. "I could have told them I had it, made up some kind of an excuse about how I'd gone to the park and found it lying in the grass or something, but I couldn't do it. I couldn't bring myself to take away what I thought of as a special gift." She raised her deep, sapphire eyes to mine. "Whether the girl who gave this to you was the spirit of my mother, or this anonymous person you painted, this pendant is, or was, Jennifer Diane Grant's. My mother's."

I'd no idea where she was headed or what she might say next but was prepared to extend her the same courtesy she'd given me.

"I guess what I'm trying to say is I don't care if it's just a dream, if it's possible you could be remembering my mother in any context, please tell me. Give me something else to hold on to. Because what you see in your mind is like yesterday for you, the memories so vivid and alive it's not like you're relating something that happened in the past. In that way, you'd be giving me a piece of my mother—I know how crazy that must sound, but it's how I feel. Can you understand? Can you try?"

Taking her back into my arms, I agreed to tell her anything I recalled—whether fantasy or reality. As for understanding, that was easy. Her comparison of my newly remembered past to more recent events was an uncanny perception on her part; I did, indeed, feel as though they'd only just happened to me. For Nicole, myself, even for the enigmatic Jenny, I promised to pay closer attention to the slightest hint of familiarity or nuance in both my waking and sleeping moments.

Later that evening, I phoned the professor's, surprised when neither Edmund nor Janet answered. I left a message on their machine for the professor to give me a call, simply telling him that I'd like to see him Monday morning if he had the time.

I'd managed to wear myself out pretty thoroughly. By eight, I could hardly keep my eyes open. Despite my protests, Nicole helped me to bed, insisting she would be nearby if I needed her. Sometime in the middle of the night, I rolled over and encountered her sleeping form, and she turned naturally into my arms. We remained that way the rest of the night, awaking together as the first hint of morning seeped between the blinds. There was a moment of awkwardness, but only a moment. We'd already gone through so much together, it seemed impossible to believe we'd only known one another for a short period of time. After that initial reaction of surprise, we passed the morning as though we'd been a couple for years, with a routine that was as familiar as it was easy.

My mother called before noon to let me know she'd gotten home all right and that she was in the process of getting her shop back in order. Rather than taking my word that I was doing fine, she insisted on speaking to Nicole to get to the "truth." They spent quite a while on the phone, Nicole giving me an occasional sly smile that let me know Mother was telling stories about me as a kid. I didn't let it bother me; I'd already confessed that Nicole knew more about me than anyone else; this made it even more official.

The morning went by without a call from the professor, and when I phoned his home again and still got no answer, I was beginning to get concerned. I put a call through to his office in Lambert Hall, and when that elicited no response, dialed his secretary. He wasn't expected in until one, she told me, suggesting that I could either leave a message or try Janet at her university office. Since I didn't want to risk alarming them, I decided to let it go; they'd have the message I'd left the night before, so surely that would be sufficient. If I hadn't heard from either of them by evening, then I would have a reason to be worried.

What started out as a bright, sunny day gradually grew to be increasingly overcast. By early afternoon, the last of the blue sky had been obliterated behind thunderheads that continued to threaten release of their contents on the city. As the afternoon prematurely darkened, the wind picked up velocity, leaking in through the cracks and crevices of the loft and whining eerily. Safe and snug next to me on the sofa, Nicole stole frequent glances out the windows and through the skylight, watching the progression of the approaching storm with an apparent dread. We listened carefully to the local weather forecast, wondering if Dr. Glasser would make it to Linden before the fury of the storm let loose.

Trying to take Nicole's mind off the weather, I suggested some music and a game of rummy. She agreed on the condition that she got to choose the music, and I was surprised that after fifteen minutes of looking through my tapes and CDs she happened to choose Dan Fogelberg's "Greatest Hits"—the CD Jenny had liked so much. To my further surprise, she commented that *Make Love Stay* was one of her all time favorites.

When Chuck called around three, Nicole and I had been napping, trying to get in a little rest before tonight's session with the hypnotist. Chuck was his usual gregarious, happy-go-lucky self, making lewd remarks about my latest conquest and his most recent involvement.

"So, aside from the sex, what's she like?" I asked, winking at Nicole who rolled her eyes then went down the hallway to the bathroom.

"That, Rich, is something I'd rather talk to you about in person—and I'm not referring to our sexual exploits here, my friend. That's between the lady and myself."

"Really. This is a first. But I have to say I'm glad to hear it. It's about time you found someone you would like to spend some time with out of the sack."

He laughed heartily. "Forever the romantic, eh? Well, perhaps you're right. I'm not getting any younger. But back to the reason I called," he hesitated for a moment, and I could hear him draw in a deep breath. "I was wondering if you might be up for a visit later on this evening. I have a couple of late classes, but I thought about dropping by around eight."

"I hate to put you off, but I'm afraid I have to." There was another deep intake of breath on the other end of the line, and I felt a sudden tension come between us.

"I've an appointment with a hypnotist this evening, and I've no idea how long it might last," I explained quickly, not wanting to put more of a wedge between us than my refusal already seemed to do.

"Are you sure that's wise, Richard?" He said, an earnestness in his voice I'd never heard before. "I mean, aren't you afraid what something like that might unleash after all this time?"

"Thanks for being concerned. But at this point, I feel it's a necessity. Joyce has arranged everything with a friend of hers, and Hargrave will be present as well. I've got to admit to being a little nervous, but the idea of getting things out in the open once and for all is also a relief."

My words were met with a silence that further widened the gap between us. Nicole came back into the living room, looked at me curiously, and I shrugged my shoulders. Just as I was about to say his name, Chuck finally spoke.

"You know, Lily had an appointment with Hargrave this morning, and it upset the hell out of her. She came out to my office in tears, called Marzetti from here. It wasn't a pretty sight, let me tell you."

"I'm sorry to hear that," I said, totally at a loss for anything better to say.

"Yeah, well, this news is bound to send her over the edge." There was no sarcasm or teasing in his tone now. "You sure you want to go through with this? That it's for the best?"

Was he asking me or telling me that I might want to reconsider?

"It's all set, Chuck. The wheels are in motion, for better or worse."

"Then Heaven help us all." He'd spoken so quietly I wasn't certain I'd heard him correctly. As I was about to ask him to repeat what he'd said, I heard the click of the phone on the other end. He'd hung up.

Relating the conversation to Nicole, I felt an icy finger trace the length of my spine, realizing too late that I'd made a mistake in confiding in my old friend. She tried to reassure me, but I knew she was thinking the same thing I was: three of the suspects in the murder of her mother would now be aware of the upcoming session with Dr. Glasser. If the guilty party was among them, they'd been forewarned of a possible threat to their continued freedom. And since they had killed before, what was to stop them from trying to do so again?

I'd never felt unsafe in the loft, rarely locked the door except at bedtime, but after Chuck's call, I knew that neither of us would feel comfortable until the door was secured. Afterward, in an effort to return to normalcy, we continued our card game, trying hard to regain a little of our earlier good humor.

It was around four o'clock when the lights in the apartment blinked on and off in quick succession. Within seconds, a rumble of thunder shook every window in the place. Hail began pelting the sides of the building and skylights, making Nicole cringe and then apologize for being so upset. About a half hour into the storm, matters were made even worse when Joyce called with a request that added to Nicole's apprehension of the storm.

"I've been asked to assist in an emergency surgery, Richard, was on my way out the door when Katie Glasser called. Because of the weather, her plane had to set down in St. Joe, so unless Nicole or Hargrave goes to pick her up, we'll have to cancel tonight. Look," Joyce was almost panting she was in such a hurry. "I haven't time to discuss this, they're just about finished prepping the patient. Katie's meeting some friends at the Holiday Inn downtown and will be in the restaurant waiting to find out what to do. Whatever the decision, you're to stay put, Richard Tanner, you understand?"

"Joyce—"

"No arguments. Let my service know what's going on," she said, and was gone.

Reluctantly, I gave Nicole the news, watching her pale slightly as she absorbed the information. While the present storm seemed to be abating, the National Weather Service had issued a warning for most of the night. I could tell Nicole was uneasy with the idea of driving down to St. Joseph alone, so I tried to get in touch with Hargrave as an alternative. The station said the detective was unavailable, then asked if I would like to speak with someone else. I started to leave a message for Hargrave to call back, but Nicole stopped me, shaking her head and telling me to forget it.

"I don't want to go, but neither do I want you to be forced into rescheduling." She squeezed my hand as a gentle reassurance. "Don't worry, I've driven in storms before. I might not be crazy about it, but I know how to handle myself."

Like everything else, Nicole Grant managed the situation well, taking control with an ease that was amazing to watch. She phoned Joyce's service to let her know what was going on, then called the St. Joseph Holiday Inn to tell Dr. Glasser she was on her way. They spoke for a few minutes, Nicole's answers not leaving me much to go on.

"The doctor wants to stop by the park if it's not raining too hard when we get back—she didn't explain why. Anyway," she grabbed an umbrella off the coat rack near the door. "Given the driving time down and back, the weather, and the trip to the park, I should be back in about two hours, give or take a few minutes."

I followed her to the door, opened it, and looked at her anxiously, uncertain whether I should allow her to leave.

"Don't worry," she smiled. "I'll be fine. And to make certain you are as well, keep the door locked."

"Yes, Mother." I gave her a mock salute, grinning like an idiot.

"I mean it, Richard. And it would probably be a good idea not to let anyone in, either. I doubt very much that Hargrave or Dr. Noland will be here until around seven-thirty, and by that time, I should be back. Till then, why don't you lie down for a while. The rest would do you good."

"My thoughts exactly. But before I do, I think I'll try giving the professor another call."

Her brow furrowed slightly. "Are you sure that's wise. I mean—"

It was my turn to insist she not worry. I'm not sure if I convinced her, but she finally went out onto the porch, quickly raising her umbrella against what had reduced to a drizzle. I was just about to close the door when she rushed back inside.

"Here." She lifted the ankh pendant over her head and carefully placed it around my neck. "For luck." Her expression was so serious that I leaned over to give her a kiss to break the stare.

I watched as she descended the stairs, saying a quick prayer that she'd be safe, then closed and locked the door.

Back in the living room, I dialed the Drake's number only to be disappointed once again. As I plopped down onto the sofa, I spied the stack of still unopened mail, considered ignoring it, but ended up picking it up anyway.

Most of it was the usual junk that seems to come in truckloads. There were a few bills I knew I could put off a while longer, a postcard Mother had sent from Scotland, and a long envelope with no return address but in a familiar hand.

It didn't surprise me Tara had written; I knew that would be the eventual turn of our relationship, a note or card now and then to finally dwindle away to nothing. I felt a little thrill of pleasure as I unfolded the perfume-scented stationery.

"*Dear Richard:*

My mother and I are off to L.A. with her newest boyfriend. But before we left, I wanted to drop you a note. I have no idea if this is important, so I'll leave it for you to decide what's best to do.

The night of my assault, I made a couple of stops before heading to the loft—and my run-in with my biggest fan. I hadn't bothered to tell Akiro, he was already upset as it was about my wanting to see you without him tagging along. Anyway, my first stop was Chuck Stinnet's. We'd had an, er, arrangement that he'd failed to hold up on his end— don't get shook, Richard, it wasn't one of my usual arrangements. Chuck owed me a favor for introducing one of my friends to him. Every time I asked for a return, he'd put me off, but I figured he'd give in on this one. I wanted him to help me get my stuff from you. No biggie as they go, but you never know. But he was so totally ticked at the way I'd acted earlier that day in Lambert that he practically threw me out of his joint—by the way, when did he and that Lily Reston start seeing one another?"

Chuck and Lily together again? Surely she was mistaken.

"My next stop was the Drake's," the letter continued. *"The professor wasn't there, and your friend Janet had a field day at my expense—well deserved, I'm sure, but still quite distressing.*

"Well, that's the lot of it. If you think Hargrave should have the information, please feel free to pass this letter along. I'm listing the phone number we'll be at, but I'm not going to sit around and hold my breath.

"Oh, and Richard, would you please ask the professor to send my painting C.O.D. to my mother's house in Chicago. I'm really anxious to see it. Take care, mon ami. Tara."

I reread the letter twice, trying to make heads or tails of the information. There was one thing, however, that was terrifyingly clear: Tara had managed to upset two of Hargrave's suspects in the Grant murder case—and at this point, it was easy to see how either of them might have stalked her, followed her on the shortcut through the park, and then attacked her. As clear as that picture was, I was lacking a motive. I couldn't imagine Chuck or Lily having enough of a grudge against Tara to try to kill her.

I turned my attention to the final paragraph, my curiosity increasing by the second. Had the professor seen something in Tara that urged him to pick up the brush again for a portrait, or could she be referring to some other kind of painting? Heaven knew he had enough of them.

The phone rang, startling me, and picking it up, I hoped it would be the professor so my questions and curiosity might be answered.

"Richard, dear," Janet's voice was light and happy, a complete contrast to my dark thoughts of a moment before. "Would you put Edmund on, please. We've a minor crisis with one of his advisees. You know how it is."

"I'm sorry, but he's not here."

"Oh? But I'm sure that's where he was headed." She sounded confused. "He left here about half an hour ago, as soon as he'd gotten your message. We'd stayed over in Springfield last night," she went on to explain, "And didn't get back home until right before our first class this morning. We hadn't even stopped by the house, so we didn't know you'd called until just a little while ago. Are you all right, dear? Do you need me to come over?"

I told her I was fine, and before I'd realized what I was doing, had broken the news about the session with the hypnotist. She acted excited, encouraging me to go ahead with the plans in spite of any doubts I might have.

"It's time to get this thing settled once and for all," she said firmly. "We've had that cloud over our heads far too long, dear. Far too long. I'm sure Edmund would agree wholeheartedly."

I was pleased to have her approval. It helped put me more at ease about having opened my big mouth once again.

"Do me a favor, though, and don't tell Mother. There'll be time for that when it's over and Hargrave is off my back for good."

We spoke a while longer with Janet offering me encouragement for the session to come. She signed off with a request for the professor to call her as soon as he arrived and a repeat of Nicole's admonition about receiving visitors.

The conversation helped firm my resolve to go ahead with the hypnosis, and boosted by her encouragement, I decided to take what little time there might be before Edmund Drake's arrival to rest. I laid back against the pillows in the corner of the sofa, closed my eyes, and listened to the gentle thrumming of the rain against the windows. Drifting in the pleasant space between sleep and reality, I thought about Tara, Jenny, and Nicole and how different they were from one another.

And as I floated closer to sleep, my thoughts turned to the past.

~

Munching on a Pop Tart, Richie sat amid the pile of books he'd used to decode Jenny's curious note. He'd carefully rewritten the passages on a separate sheet of paper before starting the process, and now, nearly an hour later, was fairly certain he'd uncovered the meaning to the cryptic message.

After spending several minutes looking up flowering trees and bushes in one of the gardening books, he'd realized he'd been making it harder than it was intended to be. The realization came suddenly with a memory of how he'd once referred to the patch of violets that grew around the large tree where they'd built his treehouse as "tree flowers." He'd been pretty little and didn't know the name of the flowers, but it had amused Aunt Janet and Uncle Edmund to such an extent that long after he'd quit saying it, they would still refer to it with a smile. It would be just like his uncle to bring it up now in one of his secret messages. Richie laughed, thinking about how Uncle Edmund was always testing his memory for different things.

The last part of that line, "The swan sings," had only one interpretation, Richie thought smugly. A swan was a bird, and long ago he had learned that a drake was the name used for a male duck. Since both were water birds, and he knew that Uncle Edmund would not refer to himself directly, it only stood to reason that in this game, the professor would be the swan.

For the next phrase he'd used the **Names and Origins** *book to look up "Jennifer." Though he'd quickly discovered that it meant "white lady," he was still uncertain about the meaning of the second half of that line. The only thing he'd been able to come up with to explain the "cries no more" section was thinking about how unhappy he'd been lately, especially when it came to being forbidden to go to his treehouse.*

"Darkness nears at eight o'clock" had to be the time he was supposed to meet his contact to receive the next set of instructions in the game. With this in mind, "Pluck a rose from off the stalk" certainly had to mean that the meeting place would be near the area they were staking out for the gazebo, a job Frank Murray's father was in charge of. There were some wild rose bushes not too far away that hadn't been dug up yet—at least they were still there the last time Richie had actually been in the park, so he knew about where he was supposed to be.

As he began gathering the books to return them to their places on the shelves, he looked down at his efforts and wondered about the final line of the message.

"And head for the distant shore."

Since the city had drained the pond in University Park before Richie's arrival in Linden that June, there was nothing to grab on to, not one place he could think of that could be referred to as having a shore. He didn't even have a guess for this clue, and that bothered him a little.

Still, he was satisfied with the rest of his translation.

He shrugged his shoulders, lifted the books into his arms, and striding over to the bookcases behind Uncle Edmund's desk, started to put them away. He was down to the last book when Aunt Janet came into the room. She still had that pinched look about her eyes that made her expression grim and more than a little foreboding. Richie jumped at the sound of her voice, nearly dropping the book on flowers that he was struggling to replace on a shelf slightly above his head.

"I just called Edmund, and he's going to be later than he'd originally expected. I told him we'd wait to have supper until he got home. That all right with you?"

Richie nodded. "I just had a Pop Tart, so I'm fine." He finally got the book in place, and turning around to face his aunt, he smiled, hoping that it might lift her spirits a little.

Janet Drake's long mouth only raised slightly at the corners. Her dark, almost black eyes drifted over him absently before they once again seemed shuttered and distant.

"Try not to snack too much, Richie," she said with very little inflection. "I've got pork chops and baked potatoes for later."

She didn't wait for a response, just went out of the den as quietly as she had entered. Richie was tempted to go after her, see if he might be able to distract her from her thoughts and get her to play checkers or continue with their chess lessons, but he decided against it at the last moment. If he got involved in playing a game now, he'd never be able to meet his contact in the park come eight o'clock.

Thunder cracked overhead, quickly followed by bolts of lightning that split the sky. He ran over to the window seat, parted the curtains, and stared out at the rain as it sluiced down the pane of glass in front of him. It was a little after seven, but because of the storm that rolled in late that afternoon it was already dark outside. It was going to be a nasty night for sure if it continued like this. But the thought didn't scare him, nor did it make him any less certain about going out in a half hour to see if he'd decoded the message successfully. He knew how tricky Uncle Edmund could be, and with this in mind, decided the current game might be the best yet.

The time seemed to pass slowly as it always did when you were waiting for something special to happen. Richie kept his focus on **Tom Sawyer** for as long as he could, but the roar of the thunder, the lightning streaking across the darkened sky, and the rain pelting the windows and sides of the house continually distracted him. The wind was blowing so hard it sounded as though someone kept slamming the back door, and he idly wondered why his aunt hadn't gone to latch it. The thought was a *fleeting one; he was too worked up and excited about the upcoming adventure to be concerned about the noise of a silly old door.*

Around seven-thirty, he ran upstairs to change. He didn't want to risk his aunt reprimanding him for ruining his good shoes or soaking one of his better shirts, so he put on an old t-shirt and the rattiest pair of sneakers he had. When he was dressed, he tip-toed down the stairs, crept stealthily along the hallway to Aunt Janet's office, and listened for a few minutes outside the door. Satisfied, he carefully maneuvered back down the hallway, quietly opened the front door, and stole out into the stormy night.

Free from the house, Richie happily kicked up the water that was flowing swiftly down the street toward the storm drains. It was raining so hard, the drains couldn't keep up with the deluge, and it was already ankle deep. He threw his head back, and his face was mercilessly pelted by the rain. Laughing, he took off running down the street, heedless of any danger the storm might pose. But by the time he got to the outer edge of University Park, his skin was stinging from the force of a sudden onslaught of hail. And nearly blinded by the rain and hail, Richie wondered for the first time if he might have made a mistake by coming.

He stumbled a couple of times in the ruts and strings that had been set out to designate eventual sidewalks. He fell hard, skinning his bare knees and palms of his hands, and splashing himself with muddy water that burned his eyes even more.

Richie couldn't believe how dark it was. He'd been to the park thousands of times—not so much lately, but even so, he knew his way around with his eyes closed. But tonight, even with his eyes open, he was having difficulty with direction. There were no street lights nearby, nothing to spell the darkness but the quick flashes of lightning that disappeared too quickly to make much difference. The wind, rain mixed with hail, and the blackness of the clouds overhead completed the eerie scene before him, making it seem like he was in some strange and foreign landscape with looming shapes and monster images slowly closing in.

He tried to shake off his fear, scolded himself for allowing his imagination to get so carried away. The danger he felt was because of the strangeness of this summer storm, the construction that had been going on in the park, and his anticipation for the adventure the professor had devised just for him.

In a sudden pyrotechnic display of nature, lightning illuminated the park with a weird black-light effect. As it flashed on and off and then on again, Richie was not only able to tell where he was, but had also spotted someone just a few yards in front of him. Grinning with relief, he called out, then began running toward the tall figure.

Once again he found himself face down in a puddle, his feet tangled up in debris of some kind. As he worked to get himself free, the sky lit up again, and he watched as a series of flashes revealed a bizarre play.

Was that the wind or a human scream? Richie was unable to distinguish. What he knew for certain was that there were two people standing near the ghostly cement forms that would one day be the foundation of the gazebo. As another bolt of lightning lit the scene, he recognized Jenny struggling with an unidentified person in a dark raincoat.

"Jenny!" Richie cried out as the girl fell to her knees.

He pushed at the branches caught in his shoelaces, and when he was unable to free himself, kicked off his sodden shoes. Standing, he started forward only to stop a moment later when the black-light effect of lightning revealed the progression of the battle scene in front of him.

Jenny was on her feet, pushing at the individual who was threatening her. They both fell, but before Jenny had the chance to regain her feet, the person in the raincoat was not only standing, but was swinging some long, flat object in Jenny's direction.

*Richie called out again, thinking that his voice might have been lost in the sudden crash of thunder. But maybe she **did** hear him. She seemed to dodge the blow, scrambled to her feet, and started to run.*

"Help! Richie, help me!" The girl cried, the eerie sound of her voice reverberating in the wind.

They were just a few feet apart when he heard a sound that stopped him in his tracks. It was kind of a dull thud followed by a horrible cracking like a hundred eggs being broken at one time. When the lightning once again lit the area, he saw the person in the raincoat swing a long, flat board toward Jenny's head as she knelt in the mud before him. He was so close he thought he could feel the disbursement of the air as the board smacked the back of the girl's head, and heard as her breath flew out of her.

This couldn't be real. It had to be an elaborate ruse, a part of the adventure game Uncle Edmund had created for his entertainment. That was the answer. That's what was going on.

*In spite of this explanation, Richie felt sick to his stomach; he was so terrified. But as scared as he was, he knew he had to get to her, try to help her. **To save her.***

"Uncle Edmund?" He called out, searching the darkness for the person who had wielded the board. "Jenny?"

He crawled on his hands and knees, feeling the ground in front of him, seeking where Jenny had fallen. When he had nearly convinced himself that he was right, that it had all been a part of the game, he found her. And in a flash of lightning, he saw that which nightmares are made of.

The girl's head lay at an unusual angle, and if that were not enough to tell him she was dead, the depression in her skull would have. He gulped back another cry, too terrified to release it. Shaking, he stood up, thrust his hands out in front of him, and started to run.

In nightmares you often find your feet too heavy to move, or that the more you run, the further your objective becomes. Either way, you know you are doomed. Richie Tanner realized in that instant that he had entered a nightmare from which there was no chance of awakening.

Yet even when he rammed into the solid mass, he refused to accept what he knew on some primitive level of his brain. His hands felt the cold, clammy raincoat beneath his fingers, but instead of encountering a human being, he was suddenly certain this was the skin of a monster. That certainty and fear gave him the courage to back away and try to retreat from the creature, hoping that it hadn't seen or felt him. But as he began to turn, to run away, he was grabbed from behind, and the thing was drawing him back, clutching him against its chest in a horrible embrace.

He tried to scream, but the sound never left his throat. He pushed out at the creature with his hands, kicked and kicked until his bare feet felt bruised and battered. There was pain, horrible, shooting pains throughout his body, and then nothing...

~

Perspiring heavily and shaking from head to toe, I was awakened by the sound of the doorbell. A nightmare, founded in reality, had left me as weak as a kitten with tears rolling down my cheeks and an emptiness in my heart that felt like it might never go away.

I stumbled to my feet as the bell rang again and, in spite of the other lights on in the apartment, switched on every lamp between the sofa and the front door. Turning on the porch light, I looked through the peephole but couldn't distinguish a thing. I knew the professor was on his way over, realized that Hargrave, or any number of others I knew could stop by, so it was more than curiosity that led me to action.

I'd only just pulled back the bolt lock when the door was shoved inward, nearly knocking me down. I stared at the figure in the doorway, my heart in my throat as I recognized the vision from my nightmare.

Chapter 26

What do you say when suddenly confronted by a nightmare? "Hi, how are you? How the hell did you manage to manifest yourself into reality?" The corny lines ran briefly in and out of my head, fostered by a fear I never knew I could possess.

I stared at the creature—for creature it seemed as it stood just within the doorway, backlit by the dim porch light and the darkness beyond. It was tall, of indeterminate build beneath the slick, dark plastic raincoat, its head hidden under the wide cowl hood of the coat. Not even its hands gave it away, for they were covered by long sleeves that seemed to go on forever. It pushed the door shut with its elbow—assuming at that moment that it possessed one—without a backward glance. A hand shot out from beneath a sleeve, felt for the lock of the door, and slid the bolt in place with an expertise that seemed amazing as it continued to stand facing me.

There was something familiar about that hand, about the slight odor of cologne that I could now smell. As alarmed as I was to be face to face with my worst nightmare, my brain was still working, processing the information and coming up with conclusions. But when it gave me its interpretation of the facts, my heart refused to accept them.

"I can see from your expression that you remember. Funny it should happen on the very day you were supposed to consult a hypnotherapist." Janet Drake pushed back the hood of the coat with a hand encased in a thin surgical-type glove. Tonight, I didn't find her arched eyebrows with their perpetual look of surprise amusing. Instead they took on a more demonic kind of appearance, her dark, nearly black eyes glowing beneath them like coals.

"When did you remember, Richard? When did the memories of that night return?" She took a step forward, her right hand still hidden as the left began to undo the raincoat's large buttons.

For every step she took forward, I moved back two, keeping my eyes glued to the woman who had been like a second mother to me.

"You didn't remember anything a half hour ago when I called or you wouldn't have been so eager to tell me so much. So what happened, Richard? What sudden revelation made the dam burst and set hell free?"

By this time, the sofa was between us—a simple piece of furniture that in truth represented a chasm of such magnitude and depth that it defied all reason.

"A dream." My voice came out stiffly, torn from a throat as dry as the ground of Death Valley.

She nodded as she removed the raincoat and tossed it onto the corner of the sofa. Her right hand, now uncovered, revealed the once deadly object she'd kept hidden beneath the coat. She saw where I was looking, gave me a broad, even friendly smile, then raised the broken end of the baseball bat.

"It's not much use anymore," she said, gazing at the item with a kind of affection. "It's served its purpose admirably, wouldn't you say?"

Was she asking for agreement? Approval?

How could this be happening?! This was Janet Drake, Aunt Janet, for Heaven's sake. This woman had taught me the joys to be found in literature, sat patiently teaching me chess, played countless games of checkers, monopoly, and other board games during those long summer days when there was no one else around to amuse me. She'd been there for me during my college years when I had become uncertain about my future and the choices that lay ahead of me. She'd comforted and encouraged me through failures in my relationships, buoyed my spirits and helped build back up my self-confidence while bestowing her warmth, love, and charm on me as though I was her own flesh and blood. There'd never been a time when I couldn't go to her and count on her to listen, to advise without lecturing, to care without demanding anything in return. How then was I supposed to associate that woman I knew so well with the one now standing before me—the monster that I'd seen take another woman's life and who had then tried to take mine as well?

"How?" I croaked, still refusing to accept, to believe.

Janet laughed lightly. "The correct question, dear, would be why, not how. You see, the how is obvious." She swung the bat with deadly force, making it sing through the air in front of her. She watched my expression of horror with glee, another laugh punctuating the swing of the bat.

"Ash is a hard wood, difficult to break. That's why they use it for baseball bats. I must have hit the grain wrong, as a ball sometimes does when it snaps a bat." She shrugged. "It doesn't matter. This old thing has been sitting in the back of a closet for years. It was yours, you know. You and Edmund used to take it to the diamond at the university every summer. You'd stay out there for hours and hours, hitting the ball back and forth between you. He'd always wanted a son, and when I couldn't give him one, he took his best friend's and made him his own." She gazed at me fondly, with a dichotomy of personalities I didn't find comforting at the moment.

"Then why?" I asked, hoping to keep her talking, stall for time. I glanced at my wrist and was disappointed not to find my watch in place. It was still on the coffee table where I'd put it before lying down.

"Don't worry about the time, dear," she said in her most comforting voice. "We've all the time in the world." Janet grinned then, tossed the broken half of the bat on top of her raincoat, and studied me intently. "Edmund's quite preoccupied at the moment. Perhaps tied up, in a manner of speaking." This time her laugh held a touch of the maniacal. "You see, yours wasn't the only message on the machine—though I have to admit it's the only one I didn't allow him to hear. Detective Hargrave left quite an insistent one, demanding Edmund's presence at the station. I thought it rather presumptive of the man, but dear Edmund responded with alacrity. Always the perfect citizen. At least on the outside."

Janet surprised me when she took a seat on the edge of the overstuffed chair. She smoothed out the legs of her brown cotton slacks, sat with her back straight, her head erect, her black eyes concentrating on my face.

"How are you feeling, Richard? Any pain from the surgery? Are those nasty migraines keeping you from sleeping—no, no, that's not right," she said calmly. "You just told me you'd been dreaming, ergo, sleeping. That's good. Very good."

"I'm fine, Janet. Doing very well, as a matter of fact." Keep your balance, I told myself. Stay cool and don't take your eyes off her for a second.

"I'm so happy. You know how worried Annie was when Edmund called us in Scotland? She was beside herself, couldn't believe she might lose you. I think she prayed all the way back home and didn't stop until your doctors told her you were going to be all right." Janet shook her head sadly. "But she's a strong woman, dear. Very strong. She'll get over it and go on with her life."

"Get over—" Now I was being stupid. Just because Janet was sitting there calmly, speaking in the most conversational manner, didn't mean she hadn't come here without an ulterior motive. She was taking her time, feeling me out, trying, as she always did, to put me at ease. She might be a cold-blooded killer, but she was also considerate and polite.

My mind reached out, grasping onto what she'd told me about the professor.

"Why was Hargrave so adamant about seeing Edmund?" I asked, my hands kneading the back of the sofa.

"I think we both know the answer to that one, dear. But if you want to play games, I suppose I can go along this last time." Again her hands brushed at the fabric of her slacks. "It's the same old story, I'm afraid. The detective just wasn't persistent enough to get it the last time, but I think time's changed him. Edmund won't be walking out of the station with his head held quite as high as it was going in. And that's a shame, but necessary. Hargrave still won't have anything to hold him on, and that, of course, is where you come in."

She could see that her words had confused me, and after a deep sigh and expression of irritation, she squared her shoulders, tightened her jaw, and fixed me with a pointed stare.

"Ever wonder why Chuck Stinnet gets away with so much blatant philandering, Richard? Why the university seems to close its eyes to his immorality? Why shouldn't they when he's got such a staunch supporter like my husband? Edmund Drake speaks, and the powers that be listen. He's built up quite a reputation for himself, and most of it is deserved. But the saying that "what they don't know won't hurt you" always helps." She moved restlessly in the chair, crossing and uncrossing her legs and finally jumping up and moving back toward the front door.

"I am not the most attractive or sexual woman in the world; it's something I've come to accept over the years. I've intelligence, a pleasing disposition, personality, and compassion. Edmund fell in love with those traits, but how could I expect to hold him when he was continually tempted by the young women that inspired him to paint?"

It was a rhetorical question, one that she neither expected nor cared to have answered. I watched as her pace quickened, her abundant energy and frustration radiating from within, increasing force with every step she took.

"At first, he only brought them up here to paint," she stopped for a moment, scrutinizing my face for a reaction. "You didn't realize this was once his studio, did you? Well, for that matter," she flipped a hand in the air. "I wasn't supposed to know, either. He'd purchased the property through an agent, had the remodeling done under the name of Swann, his pseudonym, and set up shop. He didn't want me to know he was pursuing his art career, something we'd agreed long before would be foolish. "Those who can't…",'" she said with another wave of her hand. "I suppose he felt too stifled, so he made some contacts and began painting to sell. Why he believed I would never discover what was going on, I've no idea, but that's of no consequence at this late date. Later, when I confronted him with my knowledge, he said that he'd wanted to wait and tell me after he'd made his mark. His mark!" Her laugh was filled with derision. "The only thing he made was the means for his own destruction and my humiliation."

Our eyes locked, Janet's so cold they could produce a frost in Hades.

"It was pure coincidence that Missy Gordon and Hilary Brockton were two of his models. What happened to them had nothing to do with whatever work Edmund used them for—and that's all it was with them, work. Had either of them ever mentioned modeling for Edmund, can you imagine what the consequences might have been?" She shook her head slightly. "But they were just pretty faces to place on the canvas, a few hours' diversion for a dreamer. Then he met that whore."

Her fierce expression and sudden change of demeanor made me prepare myself for action. Her coal black eyes widened, her hands clenched at her sides, and her voice contained enough poison to blacken her tongue.

"Oh, she was beautiful. I'll give her that. Those violet eyes and long chestnut-colored hair. She had a way about her that drew men to her in droves. She was so small and delicate-looking with enough honeyed charm to lure them in before she chose to break their hearts. Infatuation," she spat. "Edmund was entranced because of the potential he could see in producing her likeness. She took advantage of his romanticism, his weakness for loving beautiful things, and convinced him they were in love. Pah! It was as much a smokescreen as her relationship with Chuck Stinnet. He and Lily were perfectly happy with one another before Jennifer Grant came between them. Then they both went off the deep end. Lily was alternately threatening to kill herself, Chuck, and Jennifer, and Chuck was moping about saying if he couldn't have the Grant slut, neither would anyone else. No one could see what was going on. No one! Except me."

Janet Drake strode over to the opposite end of the sofa, and imitating my stance, placed her hands on the back and leaned forward.

"They were all so confused, so lost. Lily crying and begging me to find a way to help her, Chuck pleading with me to ask Edmund—*Edmund*—to help discover who the other man in Jennifer's life was. I almost laughed myself sick. Then the witch had the audacity to show up at my home, come in without being invited, and sit there talking with you as though you two were the best of pals! And that note she left for Edmund! Good God, she must have thought I was a total idiot." Janet flashed a deadly smile as she began to inch closer to me along the back of the sofa.

"You read it too, didn't you, Richie? You thought it was one of Edmund's game messages and set about figuring it out. That's why you went to the park, isn't it?"

I backed around my desk and was standing between it and the west windows. When Janet halted in the space separating the desk and the sofa, I stopped as well.

"It was to be his "swan song," did you know that? Did you realize that the note was to be his clue that she was now ready to run away with him?"

"And head for the distant shore," the phrase I had been unable to translate as a child.

"I see you understand what I'm saying, dear. I'm glad. I really am. I know how much this has been troubling you all these years."

"So you met her there," I said stonily, watching her like a hawk, trying to anticipate her next move.

"Of course. I arrived just before she did. There was nothing malevolent about it. I simply wanted to talk to her, explain there could be nothing between her and my husband." Janet's gaze lowered to the desk, sweeping over the contents until they spied what she was searching for.

I drew in a deep breath and moved down the landing separating the living room and workroom as she stared thoughtfully at the shiny metal of the letter opener. She turned it about in her hands, stroking the pointed tip in a bizarre kind of caress.

"What happened, Janet?" I asked, hoping to divert her fascination from the potentially dangerous weapon. "What made you change your mind?"

She glanced up at me, frowning. "She did, of course. She was quite proud to announce that she was pregnant with Edmund's child. She'd gotten the news that afternoon—right before Chuck accosted her in front of Lambert," she said this last part with a touch of wonder.

Janet stared toward the west bank of windows where darkness had set in early because of the storm. The sodium vapor street lights could barely be seen through the rain and fog, but I didn't believe that's what she was looking at. Janet Drake had gone inside her mind, back twenty-one years to the day when her way of life had been threatened—to a time when she saw no other choice but to murder her husband's lover.

She shook herself, coughed, then quickly turned to find me where I'd moved behind the parson's table in the studio.

"The moment she mentioned the child, I knew what I had to do. Edmund would have left me in the blink of an eye to have his own child. It wasn't vanity. It was life, the perpetuation of his lineage, the pride and show of manhood. Richie was enough to satisfy that urge, but only for a short time. He wanted his own son, and for that reason, Jennifer Grant could not be allowed to live."

Her movements toward me now were deliberate. She was coming to the close of her story, and once it was completed, so would my life end as she had intended those many years ago.

"Once you distracted her, dear, it was so easy. That very smallness that so attracted the male animal to her also made her very simple to kill. In a million years, I could never have planned anything so well. From you showing up to divert her attention, to the fact those workers had screwed up with the cement mixture, leaving it just a half hour before the storm struck with a vengeance. It was perfect. Perfect in every way."

"Except I survived," I said dryly.

She cocked her head to one side. "There was that, and I was worried about it for the duration of your coma. But when you came out of it, and had no idea what happened, you cannot know how elated I was. I'd never wanted to harm you, Richie, you just made it necessary."

Now I remembered what even my dream hadn't revealed to me. I saw the flash of lightning that showed me the identity of the person who tried to hold me and keep me from fighting to get away. I saw the black eyes staring down at me in horror, the hands that clenched at my throat and pushed me down into the ditch of water where Edmund Drake later found me.

An involuntary shiver ran the length of my spine as I continued my vigil. Perhaps under different circumstances I would have stood my ground, attempted to overpower and contain her until help could arrive, but I recognized the weakness of my body from the surgery and was reluctant to try anything so bold. If I could keep her talking, maybe there was still a chance to reason with her, make her realize that killing me would not be the solution to her problems.

Her next words quickly told me how wrong I was.

"Jennifer Grant was dead at my hands, and I had a witness. There was no other choice but to eliminate you as well. I started to drown you in the ditch but then was struck with the most brilliant idea. Once I managed to knock you unconscious, I stripped off your clothing and tossed it aside. That was the easy part; beating you was much harder." She grimaced slightly, the first sign of remorse she'd shown for her actions.

"I pretended you were the Grant slut, which made it much easier. I'd no idea you would survive, especially after I'd made certain you were laid in the ditch. The way the water was rising, I was sure—but you know what happened.

"I knew it was getting late, so I had to hurry. I grabbed up your clothes and took them over to the foundation. The cement was thick, but not as thick as it should have been after sitting all that time. I tossed the clothing in, then got the body. It took a while, but I was finally able to push everything beneath the surface. I kept working at it until I was sure no one would be suspicious. Then I pulled the tarp back across the area and weighted it down with boards, just as the workmen had left it. When I got back to the house, I took a quick shower then started calling around to your friend's houses asking if they'd seen you." The faraway look vanished from her eyes, and she locked me once again in her deadly stare.

"You set it up to make it look as though I was a victim of the Stalker. You used the guy's M.O., and when I survived, counted on my parents refusing to allow me to be tested. What would you have done if I'd suddenly remembered what happened?"

"I worried for a while, then I stopped. No one was going to prompt you to recall the incident and risk traumatizing you further. You had a few nightmares, some migraines as a result of the blows to your head, and I hoped those were an indication that the part of your brain which held those particular memories had been destroyed. Still, I continued to watch you for a long time. I'd no idea the attack on Tara Morgan would trip you into recalling anything."

"And you didn't take Hargrave into consideration, either."

"No, I have to admit that he didn't cross my mind." She was on the move again, slowly making her way around the parson's table, dodging the desk chair with amazing agility as she started to close the gap between us.

"What about Tara, Janet? Why did you assault her?"

"The little witch was constantly at Edmund about you, about everything that didn't suit her to a T. I knew he found her attractive, in a purely sexual way. I saw that look come back after all the years of lying dormant. I followed him, watched as he started painting her—in the nude, no less, right there in his office! So I watched, and I waited for my chance. I'd no idea it would come as it did, allowing me to get revenge not only for myself, but also for all the misery she'd been putting you through these last couple of years.

"Do you find that difficult to believe, Richard? That in spite of everything, I've loved you as much as I would my own child?"

At the moment, I didn't think anything she said would surprise me, but I wasn't about to tell her that.

Unexpectedly, Janet snatched up the pan of cleaning solvent which still contained several brushes, and threw it at me. I managed to dodge out of the way, ran up the step into the living room, and made for the door. To slow Janet down, I shoved the small table in the entryway into her path and pushed it over, sending the lamp and other items atop it flying in her direction. I flung back the bolt but hesitated as my hand latched onto the doorknob.

What was the chance that either of us could make it down the steep, rain-slicked stairs without getting hurt?

The question became a moot point because that slight hesitation had allowed Janet to catch up to me. As I whirled around to face her, I watched as she parried the letter opener as though it were a sword and she an expert fencer.

"It doesn't have to be this way," I said, trying to appeal to the reason that I knew still lay behind this facade of madness.

"It's the only possible way it can be," she said with an apologetic smile. "Don't get me wrong, Richard, I don't regret your survival or the friendship we've shared these last twenty-one years. What I regret is giving into the anger that sent me after Tara Morgan. It's my fault those memories of yours were resurrected; I realized that the moment I saw *her* portrait in the Fine Arts exhibit." Janet's thin lips were tightly pursed and her brows angled sharply as her forehead furrowed. "I was always taught to clean up after myself. That if I was responsible for a mess, then I was responsible to set things back in order. Don't you see, dear, that's exactly what I'm trying to do now."

How can insanity lie dormant, festering beneath the surface of an individual's personality so that it reveals no trace of the madness lurking within? Quite easily, it seemed—at least in the case of Janet Drake.

As I moved away from the door, Janet lunged at me, striking a glancing blow at my left shoulder with the blade of the letter opener. The cotton t-shirt ripped, and my arm was streaked with blood as I grasped onto her wrist and forced her arm slightly back. We struggled, doing a strange dance back and forth, past the upturned table in the entryway, stepping over a phone book, slipping on papers. She kicked out at me, tried to scratch my face and distract me with one hand while the one holding the weapon attempted to inch its way toward my throat.

I should have realized that we were coming back to the step down into the work area, but I was too busy concentrating on the blade of the letter opener as it glistened in the lights. We were holding so tightly to one another that when I stumbled and fell backward, I brought a startled Janet with me, giving her a new advantage. Perched above me, her eyes danced in triumph as she shoved a knee into my groin and then prepared to finish the job.

"Mrs. Drake!"

The downward descent of the opener was halted by the alarmed voice. I felt my heart skip a beat, saw Janet blanch as she turned with a look of horror on her face.

Still racked by the pain in my groin, I made use of the distraction, dragging myself out from under Janet's legs, and staggering to the other side of the work area. It wasn't until I'd put enough distance between us to feel safe that I looked to see who'd come into the loft.

I'd been expecting to see Jenny, certain it was her voice I'd heard moments before. Instead, Nicole stood in the entryway, a strange shadow encasing her as her deep, sapphire eyes glared at Janet with a ferocity I'd never thought to see in them. But what I saw, and what Janet saw, somehow wasn't the same.

"Y-you should be dead. Buried!" My long time friend cried out in shock.

"I am," Nicole answered solemnly, the timber of her voice so uncannily like Jenny's that as she advanced slowly toward Janet, I thought my eyes were playing a trick on me. "You saw to it."

Janet nodded, her right hand still poised in readiness to strike, to kill.

"But you came back. Came back to haunt me, to force me into taking the life of a child I love. How could you do that? How could such evil survive?"

"Is it evil to want justice?" The voice demanded calmly. "To save Richard and have my own child know that I did not abandon her?"

It was Nicole speaking, I saw that with my own eyes. But, no matter how impossible it seemed, I was forced to accept that what I heard was not Nicole Grant's voice; it was, without a doubt, Jenny's.

And in my heart, I knew that meant Jenny was Nicole's mother.

Janet sprang toward Nicole with an unexpected nimbleness. Nicole lost her balance, reeled under the impact of the other woman's body, her hands grasping at Janet's wrists.

Without conscious thought, knowing only that I needed to save Nicole from a madwoman, I plucked up the nearest canvas from where it stood propped against the wall and flew to Nicole's rescue.

The canvas was heavy and awkward as I raised it above my head and brought it down with all my might on Janet's head.

The specially treated fabric, stretched taut on its wooden backings and covered with layers of paint, split first as it struck the upraised blade of the letter opener, then was rent apart as it crashed over Janet Drake's head. From the corner of my eye, I saw Nicole stumble backward at the same instant Janet crumpled to her knees, then fell slightly forward. But it was Janet's scream of abject terror that captured my attention, her fixed stare at the tattered remnants of the face that gazed up at her from the ruined canvas. Her black eyes were wide with fear, her face contorted in horror as the scream died on her lips, and she collapsed in a faint atop the shreds of Jenny's beautiful face.

I grabbed the letter opener from Janet's hand and flung it across the room before checking to make certain she was indeed unconscious. Satisfied, I made my way over to where Nicole had fallen when the edge of the painting struck her. I knelt before her, gently lifted her chin to raise her head, and carefully pushed her hair aside to check the left side of her forehead. There was a slightly raised mark where the corner of the portrait had grazed her, a tiny bead of blood already clotting in its center. Our eyes met as I cupped her face tenderly, grateful tears stinging the corners of my eyes.

"Richard, your arm!" The interlude was broken by her cry, and she examined my shoulder, her fingers gentle as they probed the area of the cut. She gave a sigh of relief when she discovered it wasn't much more than a scratch.

"What happened just now?" I asked as I gazed deeply into her beautiful eyes, studying the woman before me for any sign of change or supernatural possession, or whatever I'd witnessed moments before. But it was Nicole I held in my arms, her body, her voice, her tenderness and compassion not that of a... A what?

"I'm not su—"

"Holy hell!"

Hargrave made his usual dramatic entrance followed closely by two uniformed officers. He looked about him, scrutinizing the area carefully before directing his colleagues to proceed. Going over to where Janet still lay unconscious, Jenny's ruined portrait gazing up at her from around her shoulders, there was a genuine smile upon the detective's face.

"I see you made good use of that," he said with a touch of irony. "Shame to ruin such a beautiful thing, but under the circumstances, appropriate."

As he lifted the tattered painting over Janet's head, she came to with a start. Seeing the officer across the room, she prepared to bolt, but when she spotted the professor entering the loft, she sank back onto her knees with a little cry.

Edmund Drake stood in my entryway, his hooded eyes sweeping across the loft. They lit momentarily on Nicole and me, his distress and expression of despair almost breaking my heart. Shaking his head sadly, he watched as his wife of nearly thirty years was handcuffed and led away by a uniformed police officer. With a last apologetic look in our direction, he squared his wide shoulders, threw back his head, and followed the two out of the apartment.

"I got Glasser's call on the way over here. Sounded like a lot of mumbo-jumbo to me, but after the day I've had, I was ready to believe about anything." Hargrave scratched his head as he scanned the apartment, a look of acknowledgement on his face when he spotted the broken bat atop Janet's raincoat. "Looks like your old friend threw you a party."

"One I wish I hadn't been invited to," I answered.

Nicole and I helped one another up, our arms clinging to the other for support and reassurance.

"Yeah, well, it happens." His steely grey eyes locked onto mine. "I take it you remembered just a little too much for Janet Drake's comfort."

As briefly as possible, I related what happened, refusing to give in to the weakness and exhaustion I felt. I was sure such activity hadn't been on my doctors' lists of do's and don'ts when they sent me home from the hospital.

Nicole tried to convince me to sit while Hargrave offered to call an ambulance. I refused both, knowing it wouldn't be long before Joyce arrived. I'd get all the medical attention I needed at that time, and I was sure it would be more than I even wanted. I continued to stand, my arm draped about Nicole's shoulders, hers about my waist.

"But something tripped your memory yesterday, didn't it?" I asked Hargrave, once I'd finished my own story.

"Yeah," he nodded in agreement, a look of surprise, even approval, upon his craggy features. "It was weird, but as I was telling you about the Drakes, I remembered how in the middle of all that Stalker business, I'd decided I needed a way to relax and unwind. We were burning ourselves out, and that was a danger. So I turned to an old love, art, and enrolled in one of Drake's adult classes.

"Hell, I haven't thought about it in years, but there it was, clear as day. And what do I remember the most? The models. And it hit me like a bolt of lightning. Hilary Brockton was one of the models who had posed for the class. When she was assaulted, I saw it as a coincidence. There was no way to connect the upstanding, righteous professor to the case, so

I let it go. But suddenly, right in the middle of telling you two about the investigation, I made the connection: Missy Gordon had been one of Drake's art students, you were his protégé, and Jennifer Grant's painting was hanging on the Wall of Honor in the Fine Arts building. Bingo!" He shook his head. "You can't believe how stupid I felt, or maybe you can." He laughed at the irony of his words.

"So you called the professor to the station." I prompted.

"Sure. Had a hell of a time getting through to him, but when I did, he seemed real cooperative. Almost too cooperative, if you know what I mean. You see, I'd already had my run-ins with your other pals, Reston and Stinnet, and they were so tight-lipped I was ready to throw the book at both of them. But after my talk with the professor, I discovered that his wife had been working on them. Did a pretty good job, too. Seems neither of them had ever gotten over their relationship, here they were at a crossroads, prepared to give it another try, and all this business about Jennifer Grant pops up. Janet Drake managed to convince each of them that the other was guilty of the murder, and they were so blinded with trust in her and their feelings for one another, they believed her—looked to you as their enemy."

That explained the warnings, the veiled threats. Funny that those were easier to accept than the picture of Lily and Chuck as a couple.

"The professor knew?" I asked, alarmed by the sudden thought.

"Not a clue. It was this creepy feeling I got during the interview that made me head over here. Then they transferred Glasser's call, and what she had to say scared the crap out of me. That's a weird one, your Dr. Glasser. Says she's a sensitive or some such mumbo-jumbo." He laughed heartily. "But what she said...You wouldn't believe."

Right now, I'd believe about anything.

"Well, two in one shot, Detective. Why don't you celebrate, and have your suit cleaned on me?"

Hargrave opened his suit jacket, looked down at his dirty, wrinkled trousers, and grinned.

"What this? Why it's still got a couple day's wear left," he proclaimed with another good-natured laugh that sounded eerie coming from him. "And not just two, good buddy. If that psychologist, sensitive—*whatever,* is able to deliver, and can convince the department she's got the goods, we might nail our Stalker yet." His smile faded suddenly, his eyes narrowed, and he reached out and grabbed the ankh where it lay on the outside of my t-shirt.

"Where the devil did you get this?" He was no longer the strange, amicable human being from a moment before; his irascible personality had returned with a vengeance, and his voice was sharp with anger as his eyes bore into me.

I squeezed Nicole's shoulders and smiled as I stared directly into the detective's steely grey eyes.

"A beautiful girl gave it to me for luck," I said steadily as I removed the ankh from his grasp. "And to remember."

The End

Continue reading for the first chapter of An American Gothic.

Quotation: "Beauty too rich for use, for Earth too dear," William Shakespeare, *Romeo and Juliet*

Sign up for Forget Me Not Romances newsletter and receive a cookbook compiled from Forget Me Not Authors!

ABOUT THE AUTHOR

Romantic mystery/suspense *Portrait of Jenny* is the newest book of 2010 ACFW Carol Award winning author, Alice K. Arenz. A member of American Christian Fiction Writers, her first three novels were honored by two finals and one win in ACFW's Carol Award: cozy mysteries *The Case of the Bouncing Grandma* (a 2009 finalist), *The Case of the Mystified M.D.*, (2010 winner), and mystery/suspense *Mirrored Image* (a 2011 finalist), all re-released by Forget Me Not Romances, a division of Winged Publications. Last August, *An American Gothic*, also a romantic mystery/suspense, was released by Forget Me Not Romances.

Visit her at her website www.akawriter.com

Books By Alice K. Arenz

An American Gothic

Mirrored Image

The Case of the Bouncing Grandma-Book 1 of The Bouncing Grandma Mysteries

The Case of the Mystified M.D.-Book 2 of The Bouncing Grandma Mysteries

AN AMERICAN GOTHIC

Alice K. Arenz

PROLOGUE — February 20, 1998

"What's your response to the allegations that you're responsible for Amy Webster's death?"

"No comment." I shoved at the microphone and averted my face as another journalist snapped a photo. They followed me from the steps outside the apartment building all the way to my car, bombarding me with the same questions they'd asked over the last two weeks. Tears burned my eyes as I tossed a canvas tote onto the passenger seat, aware that every move I made, every expression, or lack thereof, was fodder for these bottom feeders.

A barrage of questions and accusations were hurled at me, multiple voices converging into an impossible melee of noise.

As I climbed into the driver's seat, one of the sharks grabbed the car door.

"How did it feel to supply the little girl with the drugs that killed her?"

Heaven help me.

After a slight tug-of-war, and more than a few dirty looks, I slammed the door in their faces.

I took my time getting to my grandmother's house, going out of the way in the hope of leaving the entourage behind. It was useless, of course; they already knew everything there was to know about me.

The smell wafting out of the house took me back to memories of a childhood that hadn't always been easy. Grandmother had done her best, I knew that deep in my heart, but it didn't soften the hurt and rejection I'd often felt. I'd loved her in spite of it all and eventually learned to cope with the deaths of my parents even while she continued to grieve. Now, she was gone, and it was up to me to close the final chapter of her life.

After depositing the tote in my old bedroom, I walked through the five-room house in a daze. Where to begin?

I unloaded boxes from my car and carted them into the house, relieved not to see any reporters outside. With luck, they were off on a new assignment.

The rest of the morning was spent making stacks—things to save, things to throw, and things to donate to her church's rummage sale. Searching through my grandmother's belongings was a painstaking ordeal best done on autopilot, the emotion attached to most items almost too much to bear.

When my stomach growled, a look in the fridge was enough to make me lose my appetite. The food was in such advanced state of decay it was hard to recognize items through the mold and fuzz that clung to everything.

I slammed the door, reached for my bottle of cool water, and tried to silence the grumbling in my gut. Another half hour went by, the protests continued accompanied by some lightheadedness, convincing me of the need to eat before my blood sugar dropped any lower. Would it be possible to get to McDonalds and back without anyone hounding me?

I'd just grabbed my purse to make a run for it when there was a knock on the back door. Part of me said to ignore it, while my forever curious side decided to check it out.

"It's me, Lyssie," came the muffled voice.

I opened the door to my boss and mentor, Dr. Angela Hadley, director of Langston Children's Center.

"It appears your retinue is gone," she reported, scooting into the kitchen. "Mine, however, were hot on my trail. I'd no idea this city had so many reporters!" She held up two bags with the McDonalds logo. "Had a feeling I'd find you here, so I took the initiative and brought you some food."

I tried to clear some space on the table so we could use it for lunch. A copy of *Time* on top of a stack of newspapers fell to the floor, revealing an envelope with my name scrawled across it. Taken aback, I returned the papers to the table and sank onto a nearby chair, staring at the envelope.

Dr. Hadley placed a salad and packets of dressing in front of me. "Water?"

I nodded toward the counter where I'd set a cooler filled with bottles. Not wanting to do so, but feeling compelled at the same time, I lifted the envelope off the stack. Beneath it, the headlines on the top newspaper screamed—*LOCAL INTERVENTION WORKER ACCUSED IN CHILD'S DEATH*. A picture of me being led away by a police officer accompanied the article.

I hurled the paper across the room, barely missing Dr. Hadley as she returned with our water bottles. Without a word, she set them down and tried to appear nonchalant as she folded the next newspaper and placed it beneath the table. She hadn't been quick enough—*LYSETTE DANIELS IMPLICATED IN CHILD'S DEATH* burned into my retinas.

"Lyssie?" Angela Hadley held out her hands, her compassionate expression making it difficult not to respond.

I put my hands in hers, bowing my head as her clear voice rang out in the stillness of the house.

I shouldn't have, but I tuned out her prayer. When she was finished, I withdrew from her grasp, my attention returning to the envelope. After a deep breath, I pulled open the flap. I read the enclosed note then gazed up at my boss in amazement.

"What?" she asked, holding her hand out for the small slip of paper. "*I will turn darkness into light before them, and make crooked ways straight*," she read aloud. "Um, that's Isaiah, I think."

I removed my fork from the plastic wrap and opened the lid on the salad.

"This is going to be over before you know it and you'll be back at work—"

"I'm not going back."

"The kids miss—"

"I'll never work with children again. I'm going to take a long vacation, stay at Tan-Tar-A down at Lake of the Ozarks. My inheritance will allow me to do that." I poked at the salad, wondering if I'd actually be able to eat it without getting sick.

"A sabbatical will help get your head together." Taking a bite of her own salad, Dr. Hadley watched me with concern. "So, you got the house sold. Is it a thirty-day escrow?"

I nodded but refused to depart from the original topic. "I won't return to Langston."

"Lyssie—"

Tears burned in the corners of my eyes. "It's always been my dream to write. A mystery, suspense, maybe an old fashioned gothic. Give me a mystery filled with clues to solve and I'm happy. It's a lot better than being the headliner in real life."

"Elizabeth Webster is throwing up a diversion—"

"I'll sit in the sun at Ha Ha Tonka and write, then sleep and dream without being afraid. Maybe even fall in love at first sight and live happily ever after!"

"You always were a romantic," Dr. Hadley came over and took me into her arms. "You'll get through this. We all will."

While I cleaned up after lunch, Dr. Hadley shuffled through the stacks of newspapers remaining on the table.

"Isn't this the family of the girl you roomed with in college?"

I looked at the headline she indicated—*FOXXE/COURTNEY FAMILIES SUFFER ANOTHER TRAGEDY.*

"Must be another report on the death of Pier's father last month. There's been talk it wasn't an accident." I dried my hands on a towel. "I've been meaning to send her a card."

Later, after Dr. Hadley had gone, I returned to the kitchen and picked up the newspaper with the story on the Foxxe family. As I read the article, a strange tingling sensation etched its way up my spine.

"Edward Foxxe, CEO of Foxxe Industries, died just two weeks ago when the car he was driving missed the Mull's Hill turn south of Bristol and plummeted into the valley below. Ryan Foxxe, his son, was gravely injured in what is now being considered a possible deliberate act by a person or persons unknown.

"On the heels of this tragedy, Dylan Courtney, model and inspiration of FoxCo Toys' Dylan Doll *series, has been reported missing by family members. Miss Courtney was last seen leaving the corporate offices of Foxxe Industries approximately two weeks ago, just days before the mysterious traffic accident that killed her stepfather, Edward Foxxe. Miss Courtney is also a "person of interest" in regard to the arson of Garrett Law Offices, attorneys for Foxxe Industries. While there is no apparent connection linking the two incidents, police indicated that they will be looking into Miss Courtney's activities prior to her disappearance..."*

PORTRAIT OF JENNY

Printed in the USA
CPSIA information can be obtained
at www.ICGtesting.com
LVHW080245041223
765614LV00013B/1064

9 781944 203337